DIFFICULT GIRLS

DIFFICULT GIRLS

VERONICA BANE

DELACORTE PRESS

Delacorte Press
An imprint of Random House Children's Books
A division of Penguin Random House LLC
1745 Broadway, New York, NY 10019
penguinrandomhouse.com
GetUnderlined.com

Text copyright © 2025 by Veronica Bane
Polaroids © by Tetra Images/Getty Images (top) and Westend61/Getty Images (bottom);
Blond © by Irina Bg/Shutterstock.com; Brunette © by Javier Díez/Stocksy;
Blood © by Melnikov Dmitriy/Shutterstock.com and Evgeni ShouldRa/Shutterstock.com;
Texture © by DGIM studio/Shutterstock.com and Nuchaba/Shutterstock.com
Author photo by Jessie Felix Photography

Penguin Random House values and supports copyright. Copyright fuels creativity, encourages diverse voices, promotes free speech, and creates a vibrant culture. Thank you for buying an authorized edition of this book and for complying with copyright laws by not reproducing, scanning, or distributing any part of it in any form without permission. You are supporting writers and allowing Penguin Random House to continue to publish books for every reader. Please note that no part of this book may be used or reproduced in any manner for the purpose of training artificial intelligence technologies or systems.

Delacorte Press is a registered trademark and the colophon is a trademark of Penguin Random House LLC.

Library of Congress Cataloging-in-Publication Data is available upon request.
ISBN 978-0-593-90398-8 (trade) — ISBN 978-0-593-90399-5 (lib. bdg.) —
ISBN 978-0-593-90400-8 (ebook)

The text of this book is set in 12-point Mundo Serif.

Manufactured in the United States of America
10 9 8 7 6 5 4 3 2 1

The authorized representative in the EU for product safety and compliance is Penguin Random House Ireland, Morrison Chambers, 32 Nassau Street, Dublin D02 YH68, Ireland, https://eu-contact.penguin.ie.

Random House Children's Books supports the First Amendment and celebrates the right to read.

To my mom. Thank you for teaching me the power
of being a difficult girl with a dream.

And to every girl who has ever been told that they're too much,
too loud, too sensitive, too difficult. You are everything you
need to be. Don't let anyone tell you otherwise.

CHAPTER ONE

SATURDAY, JUNE 14
10:23 P.M.

TONIGHT, I'M GOING to make out with Grey Larsen.

If everything goes according to my plan, his hands will run across my bare shoulders. He'll tell me that the color black is perfect for me and that the eyeliner I redid three times is flawlessly balanced on both sides. He'll tell me how good it is to see me out of my work polo shirt, how he knew immediately that we were meant for each other, how he only hopes I'm into him, too. He'll say he doesn't care that I'm an usher and he's a performer—what he feels for me can't be contained.

I first met Grey Larsen exactly thirty-four hours ago. Well, not *exactly* thirty-four. I don't know what the minutes are. If I did, that would probably be cause for concern. But no, I only know the hours, which is totally reasonable given who Grey Larsen is. What he looks like. What he stands for.

Also, I guess that "met" might be a bit of a stretch. I should say that Grey Larsen first breezed into my life yesterday a little bit after twelve-thirty p.m. I had spent the morning training at Rocket Theater—the "4D" theater at Hyper Kid Magic Land, where I am now employed—before heading with my fellow usher to the patio tables outside the Caf.

That's when I saw him.

He was part of a group of people who approached from the road, people who walked with ease and confidence. They were dressed in street clothes, not polos like the rest of Hyper Kid's employees. Sweatpants. T-shirts. Plain but cool sneakers. As they came closer, I saw that their faces were overly done in comparison with what they wore, each one dusted and painted to give them perfect complexions, their eyes framed by liner and false lashes.

Performers, I realized. And in the middle of them, there was a laugh, something like a bark, a wild howl tearing through the air, finding its way to me.

It makes sense then that, tonight, he's dressed like a wolf with ears he probably constructed himself and a tail pinned to his black spandex shorts. It's not strictly a costume party, but I've been told that everyone in the Entertainment department sees any and all parties as opportunities to break out costumes. It's part of their theatrical nature, or so people say.

But Grey. Grey is beyond. Can I describe him? He's tall. Tonight he's in a sleeveless black tank that makes his pale skin seem milky in the kitchen light. His hair is a mane of long golden strands that graze his cheek when he talks. There's a mole beneath his chin and a tattoo of a snake on his bicep, plus others that I can't quite make out on the underside of his arm. His nose is pointed, his lips are smooth, his eyes are blue, blue like the river that runs between our hearts.

He doesn't know it yet, but he's exactly what I need tonight.

I thought that the Hyper Kid Magic Land job alone was the answer, the fix that I needed to adjust the path of my life, but I was wrong. That was only a stepping stone. Being with Grey would erase everything that's gone wrong in my life. After all, rebranding myself after what happened is the first step of my plan, and what better way to rebrand than as the girlfriend of a soon-to-be star? According to Google, if I'm to move on from the "incident," as Assistant Principal Taggert called it, I need a clean slate. I need to prove that the mistake I made was just that—a mistake, a deviation, an outlier to be ignored based on the rest of my sixteen-year-old life.

This party is also a gift. It's the Beginning of Summer Party, an annual tradition that I lucked into by getting hired three days ago. It's a sign of how well I'm already fitting in that someone invited me tonight. People can clearly see that I am dedicated and trustworthy, so much so that my fellow usher Ivy asked me at the end of my shift yesterday, "So are you coming to the Beginning of Summer Party?"

And now I'm here. Here and ready to win Grey's heart. True, the night has had a few . . . bumps, but they're nothing I can't overcome. After last year, I'm determined to obliterate any and all obstacles. I refuse to be kept down again. I will not focus on the negative. Not tonight. Not after everything I've fought past to get here.

It would be easier if I weren't alone. Technically, I know a handful of people here, but not well enough to just walk up and join their conversations. For a moment, I wish Caroline were here, until I remember why, exactly, she's not. Caroline was my best friend, the person who knew all my secrets . . . the person who knew me better than anyone.

Until she didn't.

Now I have to manage by myself. I focus on the room, on the people swirling by in their costumes as the blasting house music echoes off the walls. It's a strange mix, this party, of people my age and adults who also work at the park. The alcohol and costumes seem to be at war with the fruit and cheese platters spread throughout the different rooms, but maybe that's what all parties look like. It's my first one, so I can't really say. Either way, the location is my favorite part. The house we're at is tucked away in the forests and hiking trails that make up San Joaquin Hills, the perfect place for secret rendezvous and new beginnings.

I've waited for the right moment with Grey, and the time has come to make my move. He lingers in the kitchen, a red cup in hand as he surveys the food. I've followed him from the living room and am now ready to appear casual and approachable, cool and intriguing.

Breathe, Greta, I tell myself. You'll never get another moment like this. You just have to pick the right words.

"I'm partial to Gouda," I say to him. "It's the nicest cheese. Much better than cheddar."

He jumps—maybe I should've made my presence clearer before speaking. His blue eyes sweep over me, quietly appraising.

"I'm Greta," I tell him, fluttering my precariously loose false eyelashes. "I'm an usher."

"Oh yeah, that's cool," he says, and then looks away toward the window just behind us, above the sink, the one that's cracked open and is allowing the night breeze to infiltrate the smoke and dust and cologne of the party. I know I probably shouldn't have led with cheese, but I didn't want to get too personal. Now I can feel opportunity slipping away, and panic starts to set in.

Touch me, I want to scream at him. Touch me and kiss me so we can start and never stop. *Please* kiss me.

"So," I say instead. "What's your favorite cheese?"

He looks at the floor, and I don't blame him. I'm actually talking to him about dairy. I'm inwardly cursing myself, desperate to right this conversation, when I hear someone screaming.

"It's time! Oh my god, everyone! It's time!"

I turn at the sound of the loud, slightly piercing voice, finding its source standing in the living room, bouncing up and down. It's a girl, unfairly beautiful, with dark red hair that she's dusted with gold glitter. I think she must be dressed up as some kind of mermaid, because she's wearing a sort of shell bra and tight blue shorts over her pale, freckled skin.

"What's going on?" I ask Grey, watching as the crowd coalesces in the direction of the girl. His eyes have locked on her as well, an easy smile cracking on his face. I'm not even sure he heard my question.

"Have a good night, Greta," he says, then chugs his drink and places the empty cup on the counter. "Enjoy the cheese."

"But—"

He's gone before I can finish the sentence, moving toward the crowd. For a moment, I watch him, unsure if I should follow, after my spectacular failure.

But of course, the girl did ask for *everyone* to go. And I'm part of everyone. Besides, I want to see what's going on. So I edge around the corner until I find where the crowd has ended up, everyone pressing against each other, facing a large TV mounted on the wall above a fireplace. The girl is there, too, standing off to the side, waving at everyone with hands tipped with long, sparkly pink nails.

"All right, everybody," she says, voice carrying over the noise. "I know this is what you've all been waiting for."

There's a sharp sort of glint in her eyes, and I wish I knew who she was. I look around for someone to ask, someone who I know, but I only recognize these people in a fuzzy sort of way. I wish I could find Ivy. Since she invited me, she'd be my safest bet. A social launching pad who could introduce me to other people. But I don't spot her anywhere. I don't even see Grey anymore, though he must be here somewhere since I just saw him. I try to look for him, but I'm blocked on all sides.

"Technically," the girl says, drawing my eyes back up to the front, "this won't air until tomorrow. But James himself sent me a copy just for tonight so that we can make the party extra special."

She picks up a remote, waving it in the air like a wand. "Are we ready?"

Someone shouts, "Get on with it, Lauren!" while other people wolf whistle. I watch the girl's—Lauren's—smile grow as she clicks the remote, making the empty screen flare to life.

Immediately, I recognize the anchors from *Rancho Paloma Morning News*, both of them beaming brightly. Mom watches this show while I get ready for school—or she used to, when I was still going—and she's always been a big fan. At the sight of them on the screen, the entire crowd seems to swell just a little closer to the front.

"Good morning! I'm Jade Burns, and this is Kenneth Diego, my cohost," says Jade Burns. "We're excited today to take you into the newest attraction at Rancho Paloma's iconic theme park, Hyper Kid Magic Land."

This earns a few whoops from the crowd, and several people hold their cups up in salute.

"This new show is being brought to us by Rancho Paloma local legend James K. Murphy," Kenneth Diego continues. "We're being promised a musical adventure full of twists, turns, and magical talismans, and lucky for you, we've got the inside scoop. Here's Joe Lynskey with more."

The news desk is quickly replaced by a sweeping aerial shot of the nearby Rancho Paloma coastline that turns and dives over Hyper Kid Magic Land itself, showing us the famous gondolas overhead before picking up with footage of face characters, close-ups of rides, and a glimpse of one of the theater marquees. Everything's primary colors and smiling faces before we settle on a new shot that makes my heart flip.

Because there's Grey, right at the center, hands on his hips and beaming. He's no longer wearing sweatpants or a wolf tail. Instead, he's on the screen in head-to-toe khaki and a wide-brimmed hat that he tips toward the news anchor interviewing him. There's a girl next to him, also in khaki, with her blond hair peeking out from her own adventurer hat in two long braids. She's wearing bright red lipstick and a bold smile, one hand on her hip as she grins into the camera. More whoops sweep the room at the sight of Grey and the girl.

"All right, parents, try to hold on to your kids," Joe Lynskey says with a toothy smile. "I'm here with Hyper Kid himself, along with his trusty pal Ranger Quickdash. And in their new show, Jungle Jam, you'll see them get into an adventure like never before."

I gasp. When I did my tour of the park, we stopped to watch each of the shows. Jungle Jam was by far my favorite. And it wasn't just because I could watch Grey's rippling muscles, though that was certainly a highlight. No, something about Jungle just . . . moved me when I was there. Sure, Mega Boost has the stunts, the gymnastics and flips through the air, the comedy. But Jungle has emotional resonance.

"Emotional resonance?" Ivy snorted when I told her that on the tour. She was accompanying me so she could point out the "entertainment-specific nuances," but mostly she used the time to criticize my tour guide and my accompanying excitement. "Be so fucking for real."

I winced at my own lack of cool, but she said it with a laugh, so I didn't take the comment too hard. But even if it *is* slightly uncool, I can't help that Jungle calls to me. There's something about it that's, well, magical. It's the heart. It's the swell of the musical numbers and the energy of the audience. And yes, I admit it.

It's the performers. Each of them commanded the stage, fulfilling their different roles with a mesmerizing confidence. Grey was Hyper Kid, an adventurer with a heart of gold. Then there was Ranger Quickdash, a beacon of feminine bravado and charisma. For comic relief, there was Dingle, Hyper Kid's loyal dalmatian, and the sinister but comically flawed villain, Grimson Gangles.

But if I'm honest, while they were all great, there was one performer who stood out above the rest—even beyond Grey. For as spellbinding as he was, she was beyond. She was magic unbottled on the stage.

Mercy Goodwin.

She plays Perky the Red Panda, the character on which the entire show spins. She's the one hidden in the jungle, the one with access to the elusive Golden Panda. She's the one who, somehow, made a twenty-minute theme park show seem like full-on theater. The one who, beyond a red panda suit and accompanying face paint, stood out from the rest.

They're panning to her now, actually, showing shots from the show itself, lingering on Perky the Panda as she bursts out of the jungle set, eyes wide and sparkling as she races around Hyper Kid and Ranger. It must be Mercy, I think. Who else could make a hush fall over the entire room?

"Because, parents, there's something in this show for you as well," Joe Lynskey is saying now, no longer at the front of the park but walking through Adventure Theater itself. "James K. Murphy himself has told us that he suspects some of these fine performers might even find their way to Broadway one day, like Mr. Murphy himself once did. Just take a listen to this snippet of Jungle Jam star Mercy Goodwin."

The screen returns to the shots of the show, with Mercy's Perky standing center stage belting out her song that touches on heartbreak and friendship and new beginnings. Because I was right. No one commands a stage like Mercy. Even now, after she finishes her note and the camera pans back to Joe Lynskey, his eyes are shining with literal tears.

"I'm sure I'm not the only one with goose bumps," he says. "But for now, I want to tell all of Rancho Paloma not to miss out on this fantastic show."

And then, we're back to the front of the park. Grey and Ranger are there again in khaki. Perky's next to them now—which must mean Mercy's in there—and Grimson, tall and lanky and menacing. And off to the side, cut off so that only the arm and the edge of a floppy dog ear are visible, is the fluffy black-and-white costume that belongs to Dingle. This is the image the screen freezes on as the room erupts with cheers and applause.

"Where's Grey?" someone's saying. "Someone get him a beer!"

"Allie, your lipstick looked incredible."

"How about that song? *Hello*, high notes."

I look around, trying to follow the congratulations being tossed around the room. The excitement's infected every person, doubled possibly by the general inebriated state. With the video over, the music picks back up, pulsing once more through the house, causing the group to disperse and separate. I stay in the living room, hoping to find Grey and use this as my conversational springboard for a second round.

But instead of Grey, I spot Lauren, still standing near the front, her eyes pinned on the screen. Gone is her upbeat expression from before, her waving hands. Now her fingers stiffen around a red cup in a vise grip so tight that the plastic is dented under her grasp.

A girl next to her is saying something, her hand on Lauren's shoulder. This other girl must be another performer, as she's also beautiful, with deep brown skin and long braids falling over her shoulders. She's wearing a glittery emerald minidress, each sequin catching the light and flinging it back out into the now nearly empty room. Neither girl seems aware of me, and my skin prickles, knowing I should leave. But there's something about Lauren and the nearly crushed cup in her hand that makes me stay, curious. I edge around the corner slightly so they can't see me, even if they turn their heads, and then I lean back, listening.

"I don't care, Kara," Lauren's saying. "Didn't you see her tonight? She's such a fucking whore."

At the words, it's like I'm thirteen years old again, on the night I accidentally stepped into a puddle of icy water outside Caroline's house, the shame and the sting of the freezing cold zipping through me at the same time. Back then, the shame came from knowing that Caroline would be furious that I'd "ruined" the jeans she had let me borrow.

But now . . . the shame comes from someplace much worse. Because they must be talking about *me*, harsh words bouncing between them like the foosball on the table in the next room. Their voices curl around each word with venom that I recognize from months of being on the other end of this. Months of having similar sentences flung at me in person and in my DMs until, finally, I gave up and deleted the apps from my phone.

How is this possible? How do the people here already know about me? It was bad enough that I ruined things with Grey with the cheese, but I thought I had time before everything got out. How—

"I'm sure they got more B-roll of you," the other girl—Kara—says. "They always do that for TV spots and reuse it later. It's really not that big of a deal, Lauren. Don't let it ruin your night."

I'm still frozen, but something inside me shifts, allowing me to breathe again. Because of course they're not talking about me. This is about the video. Or, more specifically, *someone* in the video.

I glance around the corner so that I can see them, Lauren still staring daggers at the screen before she punches the remote and the TV goes dark. Her other hand crumples the red cup completely and lets it drop to the ground. She huffs, tossing her red hair over her shoulder, stomping the cup with her foot. I duck back, just in case she decides to move out of the room.

"I knew it," she snarls, apparently staying put for now. "I knew they'd focus on that *bitch*. Why am I even surprised?"

"Lauren—"

"Little Miss Mercy is going to steal every fucking role," Lauren grinds out. "If I don't do something, she'll get every TV spot, every commercial. James said they're trying to do something with that reality show he was telling us about, some date with the lead guy and his kid, and he's totally going to give it to her. He's going to give *everything* to her."

"You don't know that," Kara says, sounding tired. "Hell, at least you got to be in this thing at all. I'm supposed to be lead Dingle, remember? You're lucky he asked you to step in when I got sick."

Lauren spits out a laugh. "My *arm* was in it, Kara. That's it. But things are going to change. She's not getting another goddamn thing. I'll make sure of it."

"Lower your voice," Kara urges. "She's probably here somewhere."

"I hope she is here," Lauren snaps. "I'll tell her to her face. In fact, let me find that bitch right now."

I realize at the sound of stamping footsteps that Lauren's leaving the living room, headed straight for me. Just before she rounds the corner, I manage to duck against the wall, but she doesn't seem to notice me or anyone else in the house as she careens down the hall, Kara following close. As they fly past, I dare to look up, catching sight of the fire in Lauren's eyes for just a moment until both she and Kara are gone.

It makes me shiver, that blaze of anger. Because I know that look, the disdain, the disgust that burns there . . . it's exactly like the look Caroline gave me over a month ago. The last look before everything changed for good.

It jolts me, that realization. Because I'm being reckless. I can't afford to mess up tonight, can't afford to have someone catch me eavesdropping. My reputation can't take any more hits, the kind that could come if someone thinks I'm some loser hunting for gossip. I need to be trusted here. I need to be welcomed. After all, Grey Larsen smiled at me tonight. I can't afford to throw that away.

Because this is the start of my new journey, and I can't allow any distractions. I need to stay focused on winning people over, not listening to obviously private conversations. I need to redirect my energy and find other people at this party to befriend, to charm. And I will. I must.

Tonight is the beginning of the rest of my life, and I refuse to let anything else get in the way of it. I tuck that thought into my mind, straighten my shoulders, and head in the opposite direction Lauren and Kara went, determination thrumming in my veins.

CHAPTER TWO

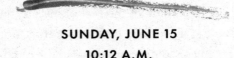

SUNDAY, JUNE 15
10:12 A.M.

"WHEN IN DOUBT, you must assume that the fluid in front of you is blood."

The man saying this to me is at least a hundred years old. He has the kind of wrinkles that you could hide quarters in, and they tighten now as he frowns at me.

Gene is my trainer today at Rocket 4D Theater, and he takes his job as seriously as handling the nuclear codes. I can tell he's not sure about me, no matter how hard I try to show him that I've already memorized the employee handbook. For the past two days that we've worked together, I've accepted every one of Gene's suggestions: hold the broom with exactly this many inches between your hands when you sweep, stand outside at precisely fifteen minutes before showtime and not a minute after, ensure that your belt buckle is centered under the buttons of your red polo shirt.

I do it all because I respect Gene and, more importantly, because I must keep this job. Each day since my interview, I've woken up terrified that someone will take this away from me.

And I can't afford to lose anything else.

"Never touch any kind of fluid without first taking the proper safety precautions," Gene warns me, holding up a shaky finger in front of my face. "Doing so puts you at risk of serious infection—and even death."

At the final word, he turns his cloudy gray eyes back to the puddle between our feet, and I follow his gaze. It's dark red, splattered wide across the concrete. Both Gene and I wear the same shiny black leather shoes, the kind I generally associate with lunch ladies. On me, they look large, and the calf-high red socks that I am required to wear with them don't help. Gene's red socks are covered by his blue slacks. Regardless, I know he's still wearing them under there because it's a rule, and Gene follows every single one.

"When approaching a possible contamination," Gene says in a heavy voice, "it's important to—"

There's a snort of laughter to our left that cuts Gene off. I turn to see Ivy, our other usher, shaking her head as she watches us. She's sitting on a bench, an erotic novel called *Under the Evertree* propped up in her lap.

"Gene, you've gotta chill," she says, shutting the book as she hops up from the bench. "You and I both know that isn't blood."

Gene's eyes narrow, his furry gray eyebrows knitting together.

"Ivy," Gene begins. "You know the protocol. All fluids must—"

"That's not a *fluid*," Ivy insists. "That's literally a Popsicle. You can see the stick."

She points down, and I'm momentarily distracted by the lines of a tattoo peeking out of the sweatband she has to wear on her wrist to cover it up. Raw power emanates from every inch of Ivy, from her black-brown curly hair to her perfect cat eye to her dark emerald nail polish that's the ideal shade for her deep tan skin. This is technically against dress code, but no one says anything to her about it. Not even Gene.

I wish Ivy was my trainer today. She's nineteen and already training other ushers, a clear example of her excellence, even if she and Gene occasionally—often—disagree. But today, since she's not my trainer and is just the other usher stationed here at Rocket, she's spent most of the day lounging on the blue benches reading. Apparently, though, this was something she just couldn't let slide.

I'm grateful. Because as much as I want to abide by every one of Gene's rules, there's no denying that what is slowly widening in puddle form on the ground is, indeed, a red Popsicle. The stick that Ivy pointed out is buried somewhat by a small mound of red ice, and there's nothing bloodlike about it once you really look. I peer up at Gene, finding his eyes still narrowed, some fight happening internally.

"I'm trying to get Greta to understand protocol," he says. "And if—"

But Gene's distracted. Outside the open doors, a large crow caws and lands on the ground. Gene's face takes on a different expression, the kind I've only ever seen in war movies.

Birds are Gene's natural enemy, specifically this crow. A white line snakes across its beak, some kind of scar from tormenting other long-suffering theme-park employees. Gene abandons the Popsicle to move slowly toward the bird. He cups his hands over his mouth and caws at it, but it doesn't move. So he grabs the nearest broom, hoisting it up near his side like a sword.

Ivy smirks. "Well, that takes care of that."

I blink from her to Gene. "Should I . . . help him?"

"Yeah," Ivy says, rolling her eyes. "You should go get rags and some cleaner for this fucking bloodbath."

She grins at me, and something inside me swells. I force myself to not rush to the back for the rags and cleaner, instead attempting to look casual and nonchalant as I go, the way Ivy is now as she checks her nails in the dusty light of the empty theater.

When I come back with a bucket full of rags and cleaner, she directs me on how best to deal with the Popsicle, then takes some of the rags to start cleaning the benches. The rags themselves are almost paper-thin, made from the worn-down shirts of former employees, so you need at least five to really make any progress. It also doesn't help that the way Ivy chooses to clean the benches is by putting a spray bottle in one hand and a rag in another, followed by sprinting down the aisles between the benches, spraying and wiping in one motion before switching to get the other side. This is definitely not Gene's approved method, but one glance outside shows me he's still in a standoff with his bird, so I let it go and focus on attacking my own mess.

It's as sticky as I imagined, the sugar practically glued to the concrete. There's a syrupy scent that mixes with the ammonia from the cleaner, and I momentarily wish I'd grabbed the gloves that I know Gene would have insisted I wear. But it's too late, so I go in the way Ivy showed me, spraying and wiping with the rags.

I wonder what it would look like to have to clean up actual blood. Would it wipe away this easily? Would it pool the same way?

The thought makes me pause. At some point, I probably will have to clean up actual blood. Someone might break their nose after running too fast on the benches. They might slice themselves on one of the sharp metal edges of our old fences. They might fall and crack their knees on the concrete walkway outside the theater.

Or something worse might happen.

Someone could die.

That's happened here at Hyper Kid, after all.

It came up in my research, though I already obviously knew the basics. Everybody who's grown up here in North County knows what happened when the park opened, about the girl who died. It's the kind of story so bloody and gruesome that it gets passed around at slumber parties and during breaks in class. There was never any resolution, so the story's only gotten more twisted as time goes on. But the basics have always stayed the same.

It was twenty years ago, and Hyper Kid Magic Land was about to open to the public. The park was hosting a staff-only preview party with a few rides open for the employees to try before the public got the chance. Not everything was done yet—there were still a couple of weeks to go—but mostly, everything was ready. The people interviewed about that night said that it all smelled like fresh paint and construction. They talked about the ample food and drinks. It was a celebration, the kind of night when nothing should go wrong . . . and yet everything does.

She was a performer. Beautiful. Well liked. "Sweet," according to one article. They also said she had a "bright future" ahead of her, the way doomed girls always seem to.

It's funny, I guess. Assistant Principal Taggert used to tell me I had a "bright future" ahead of me, too, back when I was a freshman.

Before I destroyed everything. Everything that I am determined to rebuild in a way that that girl from twenty years ago will never be able to. She'll always be frozen in time, frozen in a moment when her choices—good or bad, no one actually knows—caught up to her.

There's one picture of her that everyone seems to love, her senior photo, taken on the beach with her dark brown hair flying over her shoulder.

There's another photo, too, from later, that they always liked to put next to the senior photo. One that was leaked. One of the crime scene. Her hand, bloodied and slashed, flung out of the tarp that covered the rest of her body.

This is where the details start to get fuzzy. No one knows when she died that night—though there are countless true-crime theories—and the firsthand accounts of her friends all stop around seven p.m., when the girl left their group. The only confirmed detail after that is that her body was found the next morning in one of the gondolas that swing above the park. It was a janitor who found her, casually sweeping in the shadow of the ride. He felt a drop on his cheek and assumed it was rain.

It wasn't.

"God, working Rocket is the worst," Ivy says, jolting me out of my thoughts as she comes up beside me. She looks down at where I've managed to scrub the Popsicle away, leaving nothing but a wet ring behind.

I stare at it. For some reason, I think of that janitor twenty years ago. Did he have to clean up the blood? Probably not, right? It would've been a crime scene. They would've brought in professionals.

"This is, what, day two of your Rocket training, right?" Ivy asks me, cracking her neck. "Hopefully the old guy will sign off on you after today. You can't live like this, Greta. It's too much."

It breaks me out of my thoughts, the way Ivy uses my name, appeals to my plight. I nod more than I should, soaking up her energy, her disdain, her everything. I relax my shoulders as she relaxes hers. She sighs, and I bite my lip, resisting the urge to sigh, too. I want Gene to respect me, to be awed by my work ethic and attention to detail, but I *need* Ivy to like me. I need her acceptance more than I think I need air. And I know it's pathetic, but I can't help it.

"Right," I say, holding the damp rags in my hand. "And how—"

There's a crash from backstage, the sound loud and carrying, like something heavy and metal has tumbled down and struck the floor. It brings Gene running back in, breathing hard, his gnarled hands clinging to his broom.

"What'd you do?" Gene asks, eyes narrowing at Ivy.

She huffs. "Clearly, nothing, as I'm standing out here."

Gene growls the way my neighbor's Pomeranian does whenever anyone tries to approach it. He continues wielding the broom as he walks up and onto the stage, then crosses behind the giant screen. Ivy and I look at each other before hurrying after him, my breath catching slightly as we go. I think back to the training that I received on my first day, about how it's my job to secure the theater safely. I wonder if some rogue child wandered backstage, or perhaps it's a Hyper Kid superfan trying to get back into the employee-only areas.

I follow Ivy behind the screen. All the lights are on, so it's easy to see the heavy equipment back here, dust swirling in the light. If we keep walking, there's a door that leads to the tiny supply closet that operates as a break area for the Rocket ushers. At this show, we run everything with the press of a button, so the room only needs to be big enough for the two ushers who are stationed here each day. But even for two people, it's stretching it. There's one bathroom, a few chairs, the rolling baskets we keep for the used glasses from the show, and walls of lockers that are full of old park maps, flyers... just generally anything that someone decided needed to be stored rather than thrown away. Ivy told me on my first day that this is sort of the Hyper Kid way.

"Everything might look perfect on the surface," she said as we walked by a broken-down ride. "But look too close, and you'll see the shit buried just beneath the paint job."

Beyond our tiny room is where we find Gene. It's another small space, but this one houses more technical equipment needed to run the Rocket show, plus more storage. I've never been in there because we're not allowed, but Gene is standing in the open door now, giving me the chance to peek over his shoulder.

"Neil?" Gene gripes. "What in God's name are you doing back here?"

Now my breath really catches. Because Neil is my boss.

At Hyper Kid, the hierarchy is fairly straightforward. Each department has its standard employees, like me, separated out into categories: For us in Entertainment, that means ushers, technicians, and performers. Then, for each category, there is an assigned lead, designated by a different-colored polo shirt and tasked with jobs like scheduling and payroll. This lead reports to the supervisor, and the supervisor reports to higher-ups in the park. In Entertainment, we have two supervisors: James K. Murphy for performers and ushers and Michael Haggerty for technicians.

Neil is the usher lead, and it's obvious that power is new to him. He is the one who interviewed me, and the experience was a short but illuminating one. With all my preparation and practiced answers, I made Neil nervous. Not that I can take much credit for that. Human beings in general seem to make him nervous, especially at this particular moment.

It's now abundantly clear that he was the crash we heard. He's standing up now, but there's dust all over his pants that's clearly from a pile of cables that he tripped over. His blue polo is slightly askew, as are the glasses on his face. The gel that he's used to subdue his dark blond hair is now making it stick up in a weird way, and his eyes have the look that a rabbit's do when you shine a car's headlights on it while the sun's still coming up.

Neil doesn't answer Gene. Not directly. He looks around at the floor, mumbling, and as I get closer, I can see that the floor is littered with the same old maps from our break room. Neil starts picking them up, muttering something about "keeping records." I try to inch even closer, but Ivy takes my sleeve and nudges me back.

"Neil," Gene barks. "I'm going to need to insist that you exit this area. Only technicians are supposed to be back here."

Neil's eyes dart to Gene, narrowing in a way I haven't seen before. He puffs up his chest, though said chest is bordering on concave. He edges forward, half his face cast in the shadow of the room, the other flashing in the light.

"Now, Gene, maybe I need to remind *you* that I'm the lead here," Neil says, his voice somewhere between a whine and a squeak. "I've got full permission—"

"You should go get the glasses," Ivy whispers to me. "This is about to turn into the world's most boring pissing contest."

I look from Ivy to Gene and Neil. She's right. Gene's edged closer into the room, and they're standing inches from each other, arguing about the maps. Maps I'd actually like to see, frankly. They have that vintage vibe, old, classic Hyper Kid, but at the look of disgust in Ivy's eyes, I decide not to push my luck. In fact, I never want to do anything to get on her bad side, anything that would make her look at me the way she's looking at Neil and Gene.

So I turn around, grabbing the basket from the break room that's close to bursting with dirty 3D glasses. I push it out the door and into the clean summer air, leaving Neil and Gene's argument behind me.

Even though I've studied everything I can about Hyper Kid, I've had to accept that some things cannot be learned online. Not everything has been posted about in a Reddit forum or in a YouTube deep dive. Some things, like the politics of my department, need to be learned through my own careful study and observation.

I don't mind. I like these quiet moments, pushing the glasses cart up the hill and back toward Wardrobe. It shakes beneath my hand on the uneven concrete, the smell of cigarettes from the nearby employee smoking area wafting over. I wrinkle my nose at it, rolling the cart faster to avoid the stench.

Ushers are only allowed to enter the Wardrobe area if they have glasses in hand and only through the back door. We are to deposit the dirty glasses as quickly as possible, disrupting the Wardrobe employees as little as we can. On my first day training at Rocket, Gene stressed this point at least sixteen times. I am to be "invisible," according to him. Which is fine. There's not much happening in Wardrobe other than the constant hum of their washing and drying machines, except when they have to help an employee at the front with a new replacement polo. The job looks, frankly, depressing, and I'm eager to get out of here and back to Ivy.

I dump the glasses into the designated container, emptying

the sack and watching the plastic clatter from one receptacle to another. Then I replace the now-empty bag and load my cart with trays of clean 3D glasses. A pair catches on the metal edge, and I'm wrenching the arm free when I come face to face with them.

Eyes. Staring right at me.

I can't help it. I jump, gasping at the sight. The costume's been propped up and leans forward, large, bulging eyes leering down at me. It's the red panda costume from Jungle Jam, all red and brown and white fur, the cartoonishly large smile suddenly a seriously creepy smirk. It takes me a full second to force myself to breathe at the sight of it, especially since I don't remember seeing it when I walked in.

And then there's its arm. It's handless, or maybe I should say pawless, as the paws are worn like gloves by the performer. But beyond its missing digits, there's something about the right arm that's clearly . . . wrong. It's been cut, straight down the side, the rip jagged and frayed. Not to mention that where it's cut is not the usual white of the fur, but rather there are dark brown splotches. Dark brown and . . .

Red.

When in doubt, you must assume that the fluid in front of you is blood.

"You need something or what?"

I jolt at the voice, whipping around to see a girl with heavy black eyeliner and thick bangs staring at me. She glances from me to the panda, an almost accusing glint to her eyes. As if *I* did that to the costume.

"I was just bringing the glasses," I say. "I'm going now."

She snorts. I grab my cart, anxious to leave, but she steps in front of me, peering closer.

"Hang on," she says. "I know you."

Oh, god. I know this look. It's not a friendly sort of familiarity. This girl doesn't know me, but she knows *of* me. It's the same terror from last night when I mistakenly thought the girls might be talking about me, except this time, I'm right to fear what this girl knows. I'm right to need to get away.

"I'm running late for my next show," I say, trying to nudge the cart around her, but she stands firm.

"No, I totally know you," she says, squinting in the direction of my name badge. I watch her lips move as she sounds out my name, see the moment full recognition hits her gaze.

"Of course," she whispers. "You're the girl who—"

I push forward on the cart, striking her hard in the toe. She yelps midsentence, jumping aside. I can hear her cursing at me, and shame and anger burn inside me. No doubt she'll use this moment against me. I turn around, mumbling an apology, spewing more excuses. But I can tell from her eyes that she doesn't believe me.

But it doesn't matter. She's just a random Wardrobe employee, right? No one else has to know what I did. I shut my eyes against the sun as I exit Wardrobe and hit the outside sidewalk at a fast walk.

I can't think about it, about what that girl could do or about what I did. That is a trap I can't afford to fall into.

This is going to be a good day, I remind myself. Nothing bad is going to happen.

And yet, even under the blazing sun, the girl's disgust follows me outside, coating me in dread.

CHAPTER THREE

SUNDAY, JUNE 15
10:58 A.M.

BY THE TIME I get back to Rocket with the glasses, Neil is gone and Gene has returned to his battle with the bird. Ivy has resumed reading her book, and the usual dust swirls in the dim light of the theater. To get the glasses up to the top of the theater, I take the winding way outside where the guests usually line up, feeling the warmth on my skin.

I've decided that there's only one way to put the girl and her mention of my past out of my mind. I need to replace that bad memory with other ones, smother the mention of what I did with thoughts about what I'm going to do here at Hyper Kid. I need to exchange my past for possibility, and to do that, I need to make a list of all the things I'm looking forward to.

I go through it in my mind, focusing on today alone. If Ivy's right, I might soon be signed off on here at Rocket, and then I'll be able to work at the other shows in the park. Shows like Jungle Jam. And if I'm at Jungle, that means being with Grey. Grey and . . .

Mercy Goodwin.

My mind drifts back to the party, seeing her on the TV screen, hearing what Lauren said about her. After I overheard the other girls gossiping, I'd decided to go splash some water onto my face to get myself recentered. That's what they always did in the movies, right? I searched through the house, finding nearly every room locked and with obvious noises of occupation coming from inside. That is, until I found one room down a long hallway, its door propped open slightly, a lone person inside.

A person who jumped away from the door when I walked in, bright hazel eyes wide with fear as she flung her arms in front of her, as if she meant to force me back out of the room. For a moment, her lips parted, and I thought she might scream.

But then, as her gaze took me in completely, her entire face softened and her arms fell to her sides. Her breathing steadied as she brought her hand to heart, a relieved smile spreading over her face.

"Greta," she said.

I froze, hand still on the open door, turning to face her. I'd recognized her, even without the black eye paint and red panda suit, because Mercy Goodwin is the kind of person you don't forget. But I hadn't expected her to remember, let alone recognize, me. I stared at her in disbelief, taking her in. Even in the dull light of the bedroom, she looked radiant, wispy platinum waves falling artfully around her face, just skimming the tops of her shoulders. Her white denim jacket was covered in patches and draped over a black dress, her pale legs tucked into high black boots. The kind of outfit that looked effortless on her but that I would've never been able to pull off.

"How'd you know my name?" I practically squeaked.

"You're the new usher," she said in a soft, raspy voice. "You watched the show today. I'm Mercy, by the way. I play Perky."

She said it as if I wouldn't know, and suddenly, words stumbled out of me, as awkward and frenzied as I felt.

"Of course!" I said, voice and pulse racing simultaneously as I tripped forward to take her hand and shake it. "Oh my god, yes, of course. I mean, you were amazing, you were incredible, and then your song was featured on the news, or, I guess, it's going to be featured on the news—"

A sound cracked behind us, making Mercy jump backward and yank her hand away. I looked over my shoulder at the still-open door where a couple had crashed into the wall, pawing at each other with frenzied anticipation. Then more people thundered down the hall, breaking them up, leaving us in silence again. I glanced from the open door to Mercy, who was back to wringing her hands.

Suddenly, I thought of the news video, to Lauren's rage and the crushed red cup in her perfectly manicured hand. Had Mercy heard the awful things Lauren said about her?

"Are you . . . are you okay?" I asked.

Her gaze flitted from the open door to me, reminding me of a pigeon I'd once had to wrestle from my dog Jasper's jaws. The way it had stayed very still on the ground, eyes wide, wings slumped, waiting for the crash of teeth to return.

Mercy smiled, though it seemed forced, especially for such a talented actress. And when she spoke, her voice was strained.

"Can we close the door?" she asked, adding quickly, "It's just so loud. I'm . . . I don't do well at parties. I shouldn't have come here tonight. It was a mistake."

I blinked at her, my gaze jumping from her and back into the hallway for a millisecond before I pushed the door closed. "A mistake? Why?"

It struck me that maybe I was asking too many questions, questions I was definitely not entitled to ask. I didn't know Mercy, not even a little bit. I waited for her to give me a huffy response or flat-out ignore me, but she didn't do either. She just sighed and leaned back onto the edge of a desk, fidgeting with a necklace chain that hung over her dress.

"It doesn't matter," she said. "I thought maybe I could talk to the right people. But that's never going to happen. I just need to leave."

She began to pace the room, eyes snapping to the door with every sound. She was so unlike how she'd been when I saw her in Jungle. Even after the show was over, when she'd come down for meet and greets with the families, there'd been a calmness and a quietness to her demeanor. Now she was edgy and wary—though of what, I had no idea.

Ivy had warned me during training that performers were like this. As I'd stared at them with awe, she'd elbowed me and shaken her head.

"They're all overly dramatic assholes," she'd said. "Don't feed their egos. They might literally explode if you do."

Which was fine for Ivy to say. Ivy has probably never had a problem finding a friend or making connections. Ivy isn't coming back from the brink of reputation hell. Ivy is apparently immune to the charm of people like Grey and Mercy. I am not, nor do I want to be.

But still, as I watched Mercy pace, I wondered if that was what

I was seeing. An exceedingly dramatic reaction. Lauren had been over-the-top, right? Maybe this was the same thing, just in a different font.

She stopped suddenly, head jerking to a small window in the corner of the room. She went to it, throwing open the curtains, looking out. Over her shoulder, I could see the winding trails behind the house that she was staring at. Was she waiting for something—or someone?

"Funerals are quiet, but deaths—not always," she murmured, staring out into the dark. "Of course."

"Excuse me?" I asked, and when she didn't seem to react, I moved closer. "Mercy, seriously, are you okay? Do you . . . Can I help you with something?"

She whipped around, looking at me as if seeing me for the first time. She bolted to me, taking my hands in her cold ones. Her hazel eyes burned into mine, bright and shimmering.

"You're working tomorrow?" she asked, voice no longer strained but urgent instead.

I nodded, even though I was confused.

"Could you meet me tomorrow?" she asked, and when I nodded again, she softened like she had when I first came into the room. "Of course you will. There's something about you, Greta. I can just tell."

Her words were a balm, sliding over every one of my insecurities. I felt like I was glowing from them. And, I admit, I was struck by her intensity. Because even though she wasn't on a stage, even though she was there in that dark room, lit only by the moonlight sneaking in through the small window on the opposite wall, there was no denying that Mercy was magnetic. Her questions felt like lines a character would say, delivered effortlessly, and I was desperate to hear what came next.

"There's something I need to show you," she said, glancing again at the door as she dropped my hands. "Would twelve-forty-five work? I'm not sure if that lines up with your lunch, but hopefully, it does. Because this is important, Greta."

"What is it?" I asked, breathless. Because this was what I had been waiting for. Something *important*. Something for me.

But she shook her head. "I can't tell you here. You'll need to see. But tomorrow, all right? We can meet by the employee break area near the Bionic Coaster. I'll give you my number."

My heart had hammered as I told her my number and she sent a text to me. I saved her contact so that the text thread now blared *Mercy Goodwin* at the top.

"Our lunch starts at around twelve-twenty-five, I think," I said. "I can confirm, but I'm ninety-nine percent sure that's right."

She laughed, and I smiled. I'd meant it as an honest confession and apology, but it didn't matter that she hadn't taken it that way. Or maybe she had. Regardless, her voice was soft and gentle.

"I'll trust you on that," she said. "And in the meantime, I think I'm going to get some air."

She glanced again at the window, then brushed off her jacket and walked to the door, placing her hand on the handle before turning to face me. Her eyes seemed to sparkle in the light, and that was the moment I understood what people meant when they said "star power."

Mercy Goodwin wasn't just beautiful. The other performers were beautiful. But Mercy was starlight crystallized into a single person, and it radiated off her with every move.

"Thank you, Greta," she said at the door. "See you tomorrow."

Thinking about the moment now, though, makes me pause. The rest of the night was a blur, ending sooner than I'd hoped thanks to Mom's curfew. I didn't see Mercy again or talk to anyone else, really. I went home, went to bed, and woke up early for my shift. I tried to focus on Gene and his rules and making sure I impressed both him and Ivy. But now . . .

I check my watch. Two more shows to go until Ivy, Gene, and I will take our lunch. Two more shows until I find out what exactly Mercy has to show me. Does it have something to do with what the other performers were talking about? Or something else entirely? Or maybe it's what Ivy said, and Mercy was just being weird and dramatic.

Possibilities. So many more possibilities to focus on other than the traps that I walked into in Wardrobe. All I need to do is keep moving forward.

Nothing can go wrong as long as I do just that.

CHAPTER FOUR

SUNDAY, JUNE 15
12:16 P.M.

THE NEXT SHOWS pass without incident, other than Ivy not being "sufficiently present," according to Gene, who seems more agitated after another lost battle with the crows.

"It's your body language," he tells her once the guests have left. "They can read your lack of enthusiasm through your posture. You know what I always say. Back straight, arms in—"

"Gene, for the nine hundredth time, you aren't training me, all right?" Ivy says, not exactly snapping but also keeping her tone clipped in that way that ends discussion. "You're training Greta, and it's time for lunch."

"Hmph," Gene says, checking his ancient watch. "Lunch doesn't start for another four minutes. I think we should do a deep clean of the benches. It's important to take pride in our work."

"Absolutely not," Ivy says. "If you want to do free work during your break, that's on you, but you can't teach Greta to work through lunch. You know that's against company policy."

Gene's watery eyes narrow, and I can tell he wants to fight Ivy on this. But in the end, he just grunts and returns to his sweeping.

"Thank god," Ivy says, lowering her voice. "Come on. Let's grab our stuff."

We head to the back of the theater, grabbing our bags from the lockers. I half expect Neil to be back there, poking around like before, but it's empty. As I'm hooking my bag over my shoulder, I pull out one of the park maps that I've been keeping in my pocket, looking for the best way to get to Mercy's meeting spot.

"You know, you don't actually have to have the map memorized," Ivy says, glancing over. "You'll learn it over time. And if Gene told you otherwise, he's just being an ass. He's been here so long that he basically thinks he owns the place. You saw how he was to Neil."

I smile. "Oh, no, I was just double-checking where the Bionic Coaster is. I told someone I'd meet them there during lunch."

"Oh, gotcha," Ivy says. "I can show you. It's on the way to the Caf."

"That would be great," I say, folding the map into my pocket.

The Caf is all the way on the other side of the park. We can walk around, taking the service road that connects all the back areas, or we can go straight through the middle by cutting through the various lands. On my first day, I learned that there are pros and cons to each path: the employees-only path takes longer, but the direct path makes you a prime target for guest questions. Since I'm meeting Mercy in Techno Terrace, we take the way through the park. It's technically faster since it's a fairly straight shot, but we're almost immediately bombarded by lost guests reading maps upside down. I half expect Ivy to ignore the guests, but when a small child approaches her and asks her a question in Spanish, a smile instantly blooms on her face and she kneels to answer them.

"El mejor ride?" Ivy asks, bending closer to the child to look at their map. "Sería El Dragón."

She makes a growling noise that makes the child giggle. Next to them, I stand with my arms crossed and a bright smile on my face, plastered there per the guidelines in the Hyper Kid employee handbook. I wish I could add to the conversation, offer some meaningful tidbit about the park, but I don't know even a fraction of the tips that Ivy knows.

I tried, on my first day, to memorize as many details as I could during my tour of the park. As we wound our way through the different lands, I did my best to mentally note the important details that the employee leading us through would mention: where a bathroom was, the popularity of a certain ride, and—most pertinently for me—where the various shows were. I attempted to write things down in my notebook, but with all the walking, it wasn't an effective way to capture the details. Then I tried to ask the guide to repeat himself a few times so I could commit the details to memory, but I was told that I was "asking too many questions" and ignored the rest of the day.

Thankfully, I was able to fall back on my own studying of the park's map and website, plus the laps I do each morning before my shift officially starts. I'm now used to the different lands and their booming sound effects and thematically dressed Hyper Kid, Ranger, and Dingle so they can match wherever they are, be it the black-and-blue-themed Space Land or the rugged terrain of Desert Valley.

"No te pierdas nuestro espectáculo Mega Boost," Ivy tells the wide-eyed child, pointing at the map. "Es nuestro espectáculo de acrobacias. ¡Saltan de los edificios!"

I recognize the name of one of the other shows, Mega Boost, the stunt show. As Ivy describes it, the kid gets more and more excited, bouncing up and down and looking eagerly back at their mom. I catch her looking at Ivy gratefully, and it's easy to see why. Ivy's perfect at everything.

After Ivy points the family in the right direction, we resume our walk to Techno Terrace. Techno Terrace is themed after Hyper Kid's forays into the tech world, a slightly dated land focused primarily on cars, wires, and general machinery. There are roller coasters and other rides that shoot guests straight up into the air, meaning there's never a shortage of screams echoing at any given time.

Ivy walks me over to the right of the Bionic Coaster, pointing to a nondescript door that employees are slipping in and out of.

"Break area's back there," she says. "If you finish early, you remember how to get to the Caf?"

I nod, even though I doubt I'll be finishing early. Clearly, what Mercy needed to show me was of the utmost importance.

"Thank you," I tell her, and she gives me a wave before turning on her heel.

I wind my way toward the entrance, ducking through the door. It swings open to the back area of the park, which is immediately one thousand times grayer than the main park. It's a little bit jarring to go from all the color of Hyper Kid to plain concrete and a couple of rubber-coated tables. The chairs are taken by a handful of employees scrolling on their phones. I don't see

Mercy, so I take a seat at one of the tables. I get out my own phone and send her a text letting her know that I'm here, and then I wait.

It would be easier to sit here if I had my own social media to scroll through. Near me, I see one of the restaurant workers swiping from video to video, laughing as they go. But for me, social media is a minefield that I can't dare to go back to. Not after everything that happened. I shudder to think of the DMs that would be waiting for me, the comments. . . .

I shake off the memory, focusing instead on my surroundings. Even back here, I can hear the screams of the park. Happy screams, mostly, the kind of screeching that comes when one of the roller coasters does a loop or speeds up along its track. But occasionally, there's the scream that I associate with terror, the high-pitched, keening sound of someone deeply regretting their decision to step on board that particular ride. It makes me glad that my path led me to Entertainment rather than Rides. I don't think I could've dealt with the sheer endlessness of it all.

I get out my lunch, absently popping a cheese stick and some trail mix into my mouth while my foot jiggles beneath the table. I wish Mercy would hurry. I check my phone. Even though I technically only have thirty minutes for lunch, my next show doesn't start for over an hour. Still, I want to make sure we have enough time to fully go over everything that she wants to show me. Especially given how freaked out she seemed. I think of her wide eyes, the way she kept having to calm herself down. How she was looking out that window, watching the woods.

Mom watches too much Lifetime and *Dateline,* which means I watch too much Lifetime and *Dateline*. And I can't help but think that the way Mercy was acting . . . it was like she thought she was in danger. Like when I burst into the room, she was expecting someone else. Someone terrible.

But who? Or what? Or—

Or maybe she just doesn't want to talk to you.

Caroline's words might be only in my head—words that she never even actually said—but it doesn't make them any less potent. They stick to me like all real Caroline memories do, shame roiling inside me. I force myself to push it all aside. Mercy's kind. She's different from Caroline, different from all of them. And I promised her I'd be here to help.

I finish off my bag of trail mix. I eat my peanut butter and jelly sandwich, too, the peanut butter sticking in my mouth. Finally, after fifteen minutes pass, I consider texting Mercy again, asking if she's running late. But then I start to wonder if I'm committing another sin that Caroline was always on me about and overblowing this whole thing. Maybe this isn't any kind of catastrophe and I just messed this up and got the day wrong. Was it today that we were supposed to meet, or was it tomorrow? I could've sworn she said it was today, but maybe I had that wrong. I should've confirmed with her via text, just to make myself feel better, to make sure. Now, though, I'm stuck. What do I do? Wait around? Message her? Will that look desperate?

It doesn't help that I swear the boy at the next table keeps glancing at me, then blinking back at his phone. He looks older than me, old enough that some high school drama should be years behind him. But if he does recognize me . . .

I decide I'll go to the Caf. If Mercy does message me, then I can just walk back here and tell her I thought I had the date mixed up.

Yes. That's the right plan.

I grab my stuff and head straight for the Caf.

The Caf's hidden around the corner in Mega Town, so even from the access road, I can hear the looping sound effects of smashing and grunting and a narrator telling me that "this is where Hyper Kid comes to face off against his toughest opponents." Carts and cars rumble along the access road, and the space near it is dotted with polo-clad employees from all over the park. Rides, Food and Beverage, Security, even the upper-level management in their plain dress clothes... everyone comes to the same watering hole. I walk in, finding it's not too crowded at the moment. Still, the Caf's pretty small on the inside, just a place to order, a vending machine, two inside tables, and a door that leads to the slightly larger patio. I can see right away that Ivy's not in here, so I peer past the glass doors that lead out to the patio. And there, seated at one of the large blue tables, is Ivy, surrounded by other Entertainment people I met yesterday.

There's Keenan Miller, a tall, gangly kid with explosive blond curls and sunburned skin who talks with a twitchy sort of excitement. He's sitting with Jackie Pacquing, whose long, shiny black hair and double ear piercings immediately stir my jealousy. Silvia, another one of the ushers, sits at the end of the table. She's older, with brown skin and chin-length black hair that puffs out slightly beneath her navy bucket hat.

"I still say you should've told Gene to come," Silvia's telling Ivy as I walk up. "It's not good for him to work through lunch."

Ivy shrugs. "You know Gene. Thinks he knows best. Hell, he

was even trying to tell Neil what to do this morning. You should've seen— Hey, Greta! You came after all!"

She grins right up at me, making me blush with pride. She slaps a spot next to her, and I practically fall into it.

"Your meeting must've been pretty quick," Ivy says. "Get everything figured out?"

I nod, the shame of the lie filling me. But it's better than admitting that I started to go full *Dateline* conspiracy theory when left by myself.

"We were just talking about Gene," Ivy says. "How he's gotten even worse in his old age."

"Hey, be careful who you call old," Silvia clucks, even though she must be at least twenty years younger than Gene. "But it's true. Gene does like things his way."

"He needs to chill," Ivy says. "I don't care if he wants to arrange the sponges in the bathroom, but he's not making me or Greta do it. No way."

Silvia sighs, nodding along. "All this stress. I told him it's bad for his health. Pero como no quiere, no."

I stop listening as she and Ivy continue to talk about Gene because a group of people is approaching from the road. A group that walks confidently.

The performers.

At once, I scan the group, looking for the two people who I've been aching to see all day—albeit for very different reasons. I find Grey right away, walking with ease at the front of the group, his head tossed back as he lets out his signature barking laugh. My eyes long to stay on him, but I can't help but also search for Mercy in the group. I look for her platinum hair, her birdlike frame . . . but she's not here. Instead, the other three girls are in a cluster, the one closest to Grey talking animatedly to him as she slaps his arm playfully. I jolt as I recognize the red hair spilling out of her messy bun.

"Lauren," I murmur, insides cooling when I see how she keeps finding different excuses to touch Grey's muscles.

"I see Lauren's reputation's already gotten out." Keenan smirks, following my gaze. "She's the worst Perky. Hasn't hit *any* of the notes so far today."

"Keenan," Jackie warns, lowering her voice. "Don't be a dick."

"She's playing Perky today?" I ask, forcing myself to tug my gaze away from the pair of them. "But I thought Mercy played Perky."

Ivy raises an eyebrow. "How do you know Mercy?"

I blush. I can't exactly tell her about my conversation with Mercy at the party, so I say, "Oh, I, um. I saw her during my tour. And in the TV spot last night."

Ivy considers this, then takes a bite of her salad. "Right. The roles rotate. No one could do this show seven days a week."

"So Lauren was supposed to work?" I ask, trying to eliminate one of my theories. "Not Mercy?"

Ivy shrugs. "Don't ask me. I don't have their schedules memorized."

"I wish it was Mercy," Keenan says. "*She* doesn't sound like she's strangling a cat."

"Don't let Lauren hear you say that," Jackie warns, glancing past him to Lauren, who's still giggling against Grey as they move ever closer. "She's had it in for Mercy since rehearsals."

The thought makes me pause, remembering the conversation I overheard at the party. Lauren's obvious jealousy. Her anger.

Little Miss Mercy is going to steal every fucking role.

"But why?" I ask. "What happened—"

But Jackie shushes me as the performers get within earshot and approach the Caf, which is a good thing because Grey's proximity knocks the air out of my lungs anyway. I swallow, heart thudding, as he nears the table. Will he remember me from last night? But instead of stopping he passes and disappears inside with Lauren. The other two girls sit down at the table next to us and pull out bagged lunches. Without Grey to examine, I watch the girls instead, realizing I recognize them, too. The girl from the party now has her black braids twisted up into a claw clip on her head, while the other girl's long blond hair swishes in a ponytail. And while I didn't see her at the party, I do recognize her from my tour.

"Allie plays Ranger," Jackie offers next to me, following my gaze. "And Kara's Dingle. God, they're so pretty. I wish I knew Kara's skin-care routine. She's a *goddess*. And you know Allie's parents are, like, super famous surfers, right? She's definitely going to go pro or model or something."

"Allie's so fine," Keenan says, which makes Jackie slap his shoulder.

"What, you can say it but I can't?" Keenan mumbles, massaging the place where she smacked him.

"I'm shocked Allie's letting Lauren hang all over Grey," Jackie says, ignoring Keenan and changing the subject. "That girl is brazen."

"Uh-huh," I say, not really listening now because I can see Grey again through the glass windows of the Caf. He's waiting for his food inside, and Lauren's no longer attached to his hip. He's by himself, I realize, and now might be the perfect moment to approach him.

Because I have to approach him. There's no question. For English class last semester, Ms. Grundy assigned me Herman Melville's *Moby Dick* to read and reflect on as my independent reading assignment. In *Moby Dick*, the narrator relentlessly chases after his target—his white whale. And now, sitting on the threshold of the cafeteria, I realize that I have found mine, that the moment last night at the party was just a hiccup on the way to our future love affair. Because of course the first meeting wouldn't work out. You don't catch a white whale on the first attempt. There must be some sort of chase.

"I'll be right back," I say absently, standing up and moving toward the Caf as quickly as my feet will carry me. I nearly bump into some Retail employees as I edge around the tables, but I avoid them at the last moment. I burst into the Caf, nose immediately filled with the competing smells of the different food available: greasy burgers, reheated fries, pozole. I walk around the crowd toward him, holding my breath as I close the distance between us. Ten steps. Five steps. Four.

He turns just as I step up next to him.

"Oh," I say, startled by the intensity of his gaze on me, so close. I swallow, taking in the soft curl of his hair over his blue eyes that he pushes back with his hand. The white of his shirt, sleeves pushed up slightly so I can see his bicep muscles and the edge of his curving tattoos.

"You're the girl from the party, aren't you?" he asks, breaking me from the brief moment when my soul left my body. "Ginger?"

"Greta," I breathe, heat filling my cheeks.

"Right," he says. "Nice to see you again, Greta."

This is the moment when I need to say something. This cannot be another cheese incident. I need to be witty, charming, magnetic. He's waiting for me to say *something*. And—

They call his name for his food, and he turns to grab a hot dog in a red plastic basket. He blinks at me a few times, giving me another opportunity, but my mouth has gone dry.

"Well," he says. "Guess I'll see you around."

And then he leaves, heading out to the patio.

Because, once again, I absolutely fumbled this opportunity.

Is this really my fault, though? I forgot just how magnificent he really is, the intensity of the physical specimen before me. Clearly, I need to be prepared next time. Because there will be a next time, and I will have to be ready.

I buy a bottle of water from the vending machine so that I don't return empty-handed, then shuffle back to the table, avoiding looking too closely at the performer table. My shame would be too evident.

"Oh, good," Ivy says as I sit down. "You're back. I wanted you to hear Jackie's story about the stunt performers at Mega Boost."

I settle in, trying to listen, but I've been distracted again.

This time, though, it's not Grey who's drawn my attention. It's a different boy. A boy sitting across from us, whose brown eyes are wide as he looks at me. No, not just at me. He looks from me to his phone to me again, as if he's trying to place me.

No.

Not *if*.

He's looking at me as if he already has . . . as if I'm here, standing in front of him, but I'm also there on the screen.

My insides instantly constrict, panic setting in like a fire in my heart. I see nothing, as if all the color has been sapped out of my vision and I'm seeing only black and white. I'm not thinking as my hand lurches forward and I slam my palm over his phone.

CHAPTER FIVE

SUNDAY, JUNE 15
12:52 P.M.

"WHAT THE FUCK?" Keenan exclaims as the table shakes between us. Jackie, Silvia, Ivy . . . all of them stop talking and stare at me with wide, horrified eyes.

It takes a minute for me to process what I've done, even after I look down at the table where I've pinned the boy's hand and phone beneath my palm. Nothing seems to compute as I sit there, frozen, breath catching in my chest. I don't really see the boy in front of me. It's like he's blurry, and even though I vaguely understand that his lips are moving and he's talking, all I hear is a muffled roar. Everything slips and slides in my mind, dangerous jelly that I can't begin to decipher.

I'm not here, not really. I'm in Assistant Principal Taggert's office, and he's turning a different phone over and pushing it in front of me. The floor is dropping out from under me as I see what's on the phone. As I see myself. As I see that—

"Greta?" Ivy's voice says, breaking through my panic. Her hand is on my shoulder. I can feel the soft pressure of it. The boy's face finally coalesces in front of me, and he's looking back at me with soft brown eyes. Black hair that's fluffy and falling in front of his face. Full lips that are slightly open as I look down at his hand, the one I'm still essentially holding. And as much as I want to stop holding it, I can't. Because I can't let him move his hand. I can't let him reveal what's on his screen.

"Damn, Dealer," Ivy says, looking from me to the boy. "What the hell were you looking at?"

Her tone is playful, but my insides have turned to stone. I know what I look like. I know these are not the actions of a normal, "well-adjusted person"; clearly, Assistant Principal Taggert's description of me from May still applies.

"Hey," the boy says, speaking in a quiet voice, the kind I imagine people use when approaching a horse that is ten seconds away from bolting. "Greta, right? Do you . . . do you have something against *Tetris*?"

I blink at him. He's smiling as he nods down at the table, and I follow his gaze as I attempt to breathe. His deeply tan hand and arm are covered in black smudges, and as I watch, he gingerly flips his phone so that the screen is facing up underneath our palms. The visibility is splintered by our hands, but I can already tell that the green and purple and yellow boxes filling up the screen are not what I expected to see.

My breathing comes out choked now as I understand that the worst part of me, of my history, isn't about to be revealed.

But then another realization hits, and I continue to stare as the screen fills fully, a *Game Over* flashing between my index and middle fingers.

I am holding a strange boy's hand, a hand that I slammed

down in my frenzied attempt to conceal the truth. I have been holding said hand for at least a minute now, possibly more, and everyone is watching. Well, at least Ivy is watching, and so are the other ushers. Is Grey watching? No, Grey is chatting with the other performers. But the people surrounding me now . . . they're looking at me like I'm insane.

And I must be insane, or maybe I'm just frozen, because I don't move. I stay there, willing myself to be able to teleport back in time to the moment before I lost my mind.

"Greta?" Ivy asks, her voice softer than before, her hand still on my shoulder. "Everything okay?"

I swallow, pull my hand away from the warmth of the boy's. He's still watching me, a little half smile playing on his face as if this is funny. As if my pain, my anxiety, are both a big joke. I decide to hate him as I turn my blushing face away from him and focus on Ivy, deliberately avoiding Keenan's arched eyebrow and Jackie's open mouth. Silvia is pointedly ignoring this conversation, pretending to be very absorbed in her phone.

"Sorry," I manage. "I, um, thought I saw a mosquito. West Nile can be deadly, you know."

I wait for the axe to fall. Wait for them to make excuses to leave the table or to tell me that I should go. Wait for it to all come crashing down.

"You're good," Ivy says, stealing a fry from the boy's plate. "Your instincts are spot on, you know. Dealer really can't be trusted. Who knows what sort of nefarious shit he's got on his phone."

I blink, not understanding. She gives me a wink, then wags the fry near the boy's face as laughter bubbles up from the table. Laughter that, I realize slowly, is *not* at my expense.

"Ah, man, don't call me that," the boy says, still smiling his half smile as he leans back in his chair. He casts his brown eyes in my direction, but I drop my gaze before he can connect.

"You can't escape the past, Dealer," Ivy says ominously, right before popping another fry into her mouth. "And just so you know? Greta might be the best usher we've ever had, so you better keep your dealing habits on the low if you want to avoid her finding out."

"Relax," he says, running a hand through his fluffy hair before he finally meets my eyes. "You're gonna freak her out."

"Dealer or not, you can trust Liam," Keenan says. "My man's the best technician in the whole park."

"God, I wish you were at Mega Boost," Jackie says to Liam. "Literally all the cues today have been like a minute off."

A technician? Something in me brightens. I haven't met any technicians yet. We don't need them at Rocket, where all we have to do to run the show is press the Start button. And now, as I realize that I'm not about to be persecuted for my strangeness, I understand that the boy in front of me may just be a worthy person to know.

"Hello," I say to him, throwing out my hand. "I'm Greta Riley Green, the new usher."

"So I've heard," he says with that infuriating half smile. "Liam Danilo Miramontes."

He takes my hand, and I realize too late that this is the second time in several minutes that I have made this boy touch me. Or that I have touched this boy. My cheeks heat again, and I snatch my hand back. He continues to watch me, clearly amused.

"Also known as Dealer," Ivy says with a smirk, reaching over to ruffle his hair, making the fluff even fluffier.

Right. Not just a technician, apparently, but also a dealer. I've never met one in real life. At school, of course, I've heard of them. I've seen and smelled their product, but they've always remained cloaked in mystery. He doesn't check many of the stereotypical boxes for a dealer, though. He looks too soft, too, well . . . dorky. But I've learned the hard way that appearances can be deceiving.

"Anyway, back to what I was saying," Liam says in a "we're done with that" voice, batting Ivy's hand away. "Hard-shell tacos—"

"Oh my god," Ivy groans. "Don't tell me you're still on this. A hard-shell taco is not a taco. Seriously, we're going to have to pull your Mexican card."

"What's wrong with hard-shell tacos?" Keenan asks. "My mom makes them in the microwave. Tastes just like Taco Bell."

"Do you see the problem here, Liam?" Ivy asks. "*Keenan*, the whitest of white boys, likes them. That should tell you everything you need to know."

"Look, I'm not denying that a real taco is a soft taco," Liam starts, but Jackie cuts him off.

"Next thing you know, you'll be calling lumpia an egg roll," she says. "And I'll have to take your Filipino card, too."

"Fine, fine," he concedes. "A hard-shell taco is not a real taco. And I know lumpia's not an egg roll, obviously. Can I have my cards back, please?"

"As long as you accept the truth," Ivy says. "Anyway, how's Jungle going?"

Liam shrugs. "Just the usual. We did have a kid try to jump on Allie, though. That was exciting. But Silvia here got to them before they could stick the landing."

He pats Silvia on the shoulder, and she smiles at him, pride streaming off her.

"Gracias, mijo," she says.

"Where was Keenan?" Jackie asks, elbowing Keenan in his side. "Too busy daydreaming to notice?"

"I wasn't daydreaming," Keenan grumbles. "I was just—"

Jackie cuts him off by flicking a piece of food at him, and Keenan's grumpiness is swiftly replaced by a grin. Silvia edges away to avoid any friendly fire, holding up her hands in surrender.

"Aw, Silvia, lemme make it up to you," Keenan says. "Lemme go get you a Twix from the vending machine, on me. Call it a peace offering."

Silvia initially resists before finally acquiescing, telling him to make it a 3 Musketeers instead. Keenan leaves us to get the chocolate, and the table settles back into its easy rhythm as everyone picks at their food.

"You know, Silvia's been here since the park opened," Ivy says. "Just like Gene."

Silvia nods and smiles. "So much has changed."

"Wasn't the first show here something space-themed?" I ask, remembering my research. "Something like what we have at Rocket now, except it was live action. And it was at Adventure Theater. I think it played for two years?"

"Cosmic Conundrum," Silvia says with a laugh. "It really rolled off the tongue."

"Damn, I didn't realize I had a Hyper Kid historian on hand," Ivy says, nudging my shoulder with a grin. "I bet you've memorized all kinds of trivia, haven't you?"

I blush. Again, I'm not sure at first if she's making fun of me. But there's a softness to her expression, and when I glance at Liam, he's looking at me in a similar way. Maybe a little bit of fun at my expense, but mostly, I'm part of the joke rather than the butt of it. I take a drink from my bottle of water before continuing.

"I like learning about things like this," I say. "It makes me feel . . . I don't know. Prepared."

Liam nods. "I get that. So what other obscure facts do you know?"

I bite the inside of my cheek, thinking.

"Mostly Entertainment facts," I say. "Stuff about the shows. Like, Mega Boost came out a year after the park opened, and it's been here ever since. It uses twenty-seven different stunts in eighteen minutes. There are a few famous people who got their start here at Hyper Kid. Peter Menendez, Vanessa Thompson, Ingrid—"

"And Hailey, obviously," Jackie says, almost making me jump. I'd nearly forgotten she was still here, since she's been so quiet for the past couple of minutes. I look over at her, where she's scrolling through her phone. She looks up and meets my gaze.

"You know, Hailey Portman?" Jackie asks. "That girl who died on the gondola when the park opened."

I nod. Of course I know about her. I was just thinking about her this morning.

"I mean, I don't know if it counts as 'getting her start' here," Ivy says. "She's famous because she was straight-up murdered. Not exactly the same kind of 'famous' as the people Greta was talking about."

"She was going to be an actress," Jackie argues. "She would've been famous, but some asshole cut her life short. She counts."

"Then you also have to count the Gondola Killer," Liam reasons. "Since he was also made famous. Not that I'm saying he *should* be famous—"

"Can you call someone the Gondola Killer if they only ever killed one person on a gondola?" Jackie asks. "Seems like a bit of a misnomer. And no, he doesn't count."

"Plus, we don't know she died on the gondola," Ivy says, twirling her fork with her fingers. "There're all those rumors. Most people actually think she died in Adventure Theater."

Jackie waves her hand. "No way. The gondola is for sure. Her and that deadbeat boyfriend of hers went up there to screw around. She told him she was cheating on him, and he stabbed her right there."

I blink. I know this theory. Apparently, Hailey was dating her high school theater teacher, some guy in his late thirties who was super popular and well liked in the community. The theory goes that she was leaving him because she'd found someone her age, and he confronted her about it the night she died—to clearly violent and horrific results. Though there's always been a hole in that theory.

"But he wasn't an employee," Liam says, seemingly reading my mind. "And it was an employees-only party."

Jackie rolls her eyes. "Oh, and the security that night was so top-notch, right? Then why were the cameras down all over the park?"

"They weren't officially open yet," Liam argues. "Some things were still in flux—"

"Which is why that sleazeball could've easily snuck in," Jackie says. "Now, if you ask me, the real question is the murder weapon. I mean, she was stabbed, what, thirty times? And they say—"

"Actually, I don't think we should be talking about this," Ivy says smoothly, her voice like a knife through butter. She glances from Jackie to Silvia, whose eyes have narrowed.

"Oh, I'm sorry, Silvia," Jackie says, cheeks flushing. "Did you . . . did you know her?"

There's something heavy about the silence that follows Jackie's question. Each of us seems to have frozen in response as realization hits everyone. Or at least, it hits me. Silvia was here when the park opened; she worked in Entertainment. Of course she knew Hailey. I continue drinking from my bottle as we all wait for her answer.

"Why you kids are always asking about this, I will never know,"

Silvia says, but she doesn't sound mad. More . . . tired. But there's also a slight glint in her eye when she speaks next.

"I didn't know her well," Silvia says, leaning forward. "We trained on ushering the show during rehearsals, obviously, since the park wasn't open. So we were familiar with each other. And I did get to watch her perform. She was . . . special."

She takes a breath and adjusts her glasses before continuing.

"We spoke that night, actually," Silvia says. "She told me about a play she'd just wrapped up. A classic at the Civic. She was very confident. Big dreams."

Silvia sniffs, leaning back.

"It just goes to show," she says simply, "that you never know what's around the corner. Live your life in a way that you're proud of. Tomorrow isn't guaranteed."

"Wow," Jackie says, eyes wide. "So you talked to her that night . . . and then later, some asshole just—"

She's cut off by Keenan returning with the chocolate bar, which Silvia accepts with a smile. I can't tell if she's glad to be done talking about Hailey or not, but she looks relieved for the interruption.

"Are there any people working now who you think are going to be famous?" Jackie asks, offering up a slight subject change.

"Definitely not Lauren," Keenan grumbles. "Maybe Allie. God, she's so—"

"Technically, someone famous already works here," I say, noticing the steam starting to pour out of Jackie's ears. My distraction works, and everyone's heads swivel to me.

"James K. Murphy?" I offer. "The director of Jungle?"

Keenan arches an eyebrow. "The Entertainment supervisor? Are you kidding?"

I shake my head, remembering how the *Rancho Paloma Morning News* team talked about him. I did even more research after that and found out that he's been referred to as "Rancho Paloma theater royalty."

"He's been on Broadway," I say. "The articles I read said that he decided to move here so his family could have a quieter life. He started working as a supervisor, and then last year, he wrote Jungle Jam. Apparently, it's a really big deal that he did that. That's why Jungle was on the news."

"Oh yes," Silvia says, nodding. "We were very lucky to get him. We're getting lots of publicity because of that."

"I dunno, man," Keenan says. "I think you guys have the wrong dude. That man looks like a dad. There's no way he's famous."

"Enough of this," Silvia says, rolling her eyes and stretching. "Time to get back to work."

"Ugh," Keenan says. "How is it time already? We just got here. And we've got like forty minutes until the next show."

"Keenan, don't you dare complain," Jackie snaps. "Not when you have AC to go back to. Some of us are suffering in ninety-degree weather, remember?"

"Yeah, whatever," he says. "But your show is better. Don't tell James, but if I have to hear that fucking panda song one more time..."

He mimes slicing his neck with his thumb. Most of the table laughs, but Silvia's mouth sets into a thin line.

"You can't be mad at me," Keenan says, pointing at the chocolate bar. "Not now!"

But he does give in and follows her as she heads down the road. The performers are also gathering their things, as is Liam. Ivy says we might as well get going, too, so we all get up, ready to splinter in opposite directions.

I'm throwing away my empty water bottle when I'm aware of a presence at my side. I look over, expecting Ivy, but it's Liam, hair flopping in front of his face.

"You know, if you're interested in Hyper Kid trivia, I know all the good places," he says. "Like the castle turret. Have you been there yet?"

His smile is easy and disarming and distracting. I avoid looking at him directly, reminding myself that this boy is dangerous. No doubt this is a line that he uses on all potential new drug customers, sussing them out, telling them to meet him at specific spots for sales to "go down." But he's picked the wrong girl. I have a new path, a new focus, and I will not be pulled from it.

"I'm good," I tell him, expecting him to look hurt by my chilly rejection. But he just grins wider, running a hand through his hair.

"All right," he says. "Well, Greta, if you change your mind, you know where to find me."

A shiver passes through me, even though the heat is threatening to plaster my polo directly to my skin. I stare at Liam as he gives me an extremely corny salute. He joins Ivy as she walks down the road, leaving me to follow in their wake.

As they go, the reality hits me that, for roughly thirty minutes, I was a part of their group. I was part of their conversation, their dialogue, their reality. They swirled around me, the cosmic pieces in my new Hyper Kid solar system.

It takes everything I have not to try to fling myself into their orbit.

CHAPTER SIX

SUNDAY, JUNE 15
1:04 P.M.

WALKING PAST JUNGLE is like walking past the Garden of Eden. There, in that room, all dreams come true. There, on that stage, Grey plays the part of Hyper Kid, filling the space with his talent and raw magnetism. Magic happens in that building. Yes, I've only seen the show once, but those eighteen minutes were life-changing. It was like being on the ground floor of one of those fancy high-rises that they have in the movies, knowing that this is just the beginning.

One day, at least one of the people in that theater will be famous. Someone other than James, and even people like Keenan will recognize their talent. Sure, I suspect it will be Grey. Or Mercy. Even though I'm annoyed at her for ignoring my text, there's no denying that she, too, is talented. Maybe even more talented than Grey, but right now, I'm not willing to give that to her.

Even the theater itself is famous. After all, Jungle Jam takes place in Adventure Theater, the oldest theater in the park, technically. Mega Boost was brought in after about three months of the park being open, making it the oldest running show, but Adventure Theater had a show that opening day. And of course, that show was Cosmic Conundrum, as Silvia said.

And Hailey Portman was supposed to be the star.

Literally. She was playing a star that somehow gets knocked out of orbit and needs to find her way back. I think her character's name was Carina, but as far as the news article took it, that role was Hailey's and *she* was the star in the show, only instead of getting thrown from orbit, she disintegrated, disappeared, exploded.

She burned out before anyone could know what she truly was.

Ivy pauses to talk to Liam outside the theater. We took the road that cuts through the park so I could see more of it, and now, we're standing underneath the marquee of Adventure Theater. But I drift slightly because there, a few paces ahead, is the gated-off entrance to the gondolas themselves. It's strange seeing it for the first time in person, especially since it looks so ordinary compared with the pictures people post of it online. Ever since the park opened, the gondolas have been closed. People argue online all the time about why they were left up: Some say the price of their removal was too high, especially after the park paid out Hailey's family, while others say the park secretly welcomed the added traffic of true crime fanatics who wanted a look at the gondolas themselves. Regardless, the ride's entrance exists as if frozen in time. There's the blue-and-yellow sign above the attraction with a smiling Dingle and Ranger that declares this RANGER AND DINGLE'S AIR GONDOLA ADVENTURE, the space to wait in line, the sign posted with the rules of riding the gondolas. But no one, outside of testers and people who rode the gondolas during that first party, has ever ridden this ride. No one has needed to wait in line.

People do, however, take pictures at the entrance to the ride's line, and they post those pictures online with captions like *I can't believe this is where it happened* or *A piece of history, whether we like it or not* or, less sensitively, *Do you think there's still blood up there?*

With that last question in mind, I tilt my head to look up at the gondolas, unable to keep from wondering the same thing. I round the corner to the place where the line for the ride was meant to snake around. There's a mural painted to the side of it, closing in the line, of cartoon Ranger and Dingle careening into the sky on their own gondola. A few years ago, there was a fake news article going around that said some teens had gotten in and vandalized the mural and made it so everything was red like the sky was bleeding, Dingle's eyes were blacked out, and Hailey's body was dead on the ground. But it was just Photoshop. Really, really good Photoshop.

A shiver snakes along my spine. It's strange to be standing here, feet away from where a person died. Even though I guess, if I really think about it, I stand where people have died all the time. I just don't know it. On the walk to school, there's a memorial for a kid who was hit by a drunk driver. Someone might've had a heart attack in the grocery store we go to, and someone's definitely died at my doctor's office. Death's been everywhere, but it's only in places like this—places where we know it's happened—that we pay attention.

I glance back up at the gondolas again, and I can't help it. I really do wonder if there's still blood up there. Maybe in the crevices where they just didn't scrub hard enough—

"Jesus fucking Christ, Allie, I told you I took care of it."

"I don't believe you. Not after you spent all night making a scene."

I whip my head around. I recognize those voices coming

around the corner. One of them is definitely Lauren, and the other sounds like one of the other performers from lunch. Not Kara this time. Allie.

"You're not my boss, okay?" Lauren snaps. "And why do you even care? I told you, she's fucking your boyfriend—"

There's a grunt, followed by a hissing intake of breath. Did one of them grab the other? Then there's the shuffle of feet, and my heart kicks up as I realize those feet are now coming straight toward me. I search the area, realizing there isn't really a good way for me to exit since I'm essentially trapped here by the line. If I left, I'd have to walk past them. And I should. That would be the simple thing to do. But then they would know I was back here, and that I heard them. They might even think I was trying to listen to them, and after Lauren nearly spotting me at the party, I definitely can't handle that. They'll for sure think I'm some sort of weirdo stalker loser.

I make a gut decision and dip under the metal chain that closes in the line, duck around the edge of the mural, and hide behind it where the line continues to curve.

I've just disappeared from view when Allie's and Lauren's voices burst out behind me, their footsteps stopping just a short distance away. They must also be hiding here, in the shade of the gondolas, tucked away from the guests.

"Stop saying shit you don't know anything about," Allie says. "We need to focus. Did you clean up the blood or not?"

Blood? What blood? Whose blood are they talking about?

"Yes, obviously," Lauren says. "I did exactly what you told me to. I—"

A scream rips through the air, making me jump, and I drop my phone. I curse inwardly as it clatters to the ground. It was just some kid screeching nearby. I hold my breath as I grab my phone, hoping Lauren and Allie didn't hear me, and I wait for them to appear around the corner, but they don't. I take a breath, leaning closer, catching the tail end of whatever Lauren's been saying.

"—am telling you that none of this matters," she says. "Little Miss Mercy finally got what she deserved. No one cares about her, anyway."

Now my heart doesn't just kick up. It surges into overdrive, hammering against my rib cage. Mercy? Was I possibly right to think that maybe something happened to her? Was Lauren not supposed to be here today after all? Because it's not just *what* Lauren's saying that's ringing a thousand alarm bells right now. It's the pure, unadulterated hatred in every syllable.

Allie tries to say something. Maybe it's Lauren's name. But it's clear the conversation's over. There's the sound of someone stomping away, and then a sigh followed by the shuffling of other feet. My mind's spinning.

Mercy was supposed to work today, and she didn't show up. And last night, Mercy looked terrified. And now . . . now, I overhear Lauren and Allie talking about something she "deserved."

Something that involved blood.

I turn over my phone, which is dirty but not cracked, and brush it off, then pull up my text thread with Mercy. Well, my one-sided text thread. I start to type out a text to her, checking in, even as my pulse thuds in my ears.

I yelp when my phone vibrates in my hand, blaring an alarm at me that's tagged *Five minutes*. Oh, god. My warning for the next Rocket show. Where did the time go? As much as I need to process whatever I just heard, I can't risk being late.

I burst out of the gondola line and bolt around the corner, looking for Ivy and Liam, but the area's empty. Ivy must have thought I ditched her and took off. I hurry as fast as I can in the direction of Rocket, my heart pounding in my chest.

Mercy Goodwin might not have blown me off after all. In fact, something else might've happened to her. Something that might even be keeping her from work.

Something that Lauren—and Allie—might have caused.

CHAPTER SEVEN

SUNDAY, JUNE 15
1:13 P.M.

I MAKE IT back to Rocket with barely two minutes left before the preshow routine begins, and I get an earful from Gene as a result.

"We cannot afford to be a minute off," he tells me. "People are depending on us, Greta."

"I know," I say, pushing the door open backward as I pull the glasses cart outside. "I'm really, really sorry. I just got... distracted."

"Distractions cost lives," Gene says, pointing a gnarled finger in my direction as he follows me. "In our world, we must be constantly prepared for the unknown."

"Oh, lay off, Gene," Ivy says, popping up next to him. "She wasn't even late."

He opens his mouth to argue, but guests have started to wander over at the sight of me and the glasses cart, so he zips up whatever further lecture he had for me. I'm sure I'll hear the rest of it, though, and I'll deserve it.

What was I thinking? This is only my second day of training, and here I am, ready to throw it all away. Even if what I overheard is still burning through me. What would Ivy say if I told her? My whole body still feels electric, and my phone feels heavy in my pocket. I want to text Mercy, just to check in again, but I don't want to risk getting yelled at by Gene.

"Don't listen to him," Ivy says, reading the worry on my face. "You know how intense he gets."

I nod, but I can feel tears of shame burning behind my eyes. I've always hated how easily I cry in moments like this, and I'm sure I look pathetic to Ivy. She's perpetually unbothered, and I wish I had even an ounce of her confidence. Maybe I will talk to her about what I heard after the show. I'm sure she'd tell me it's nothing, but it would help put me at ease.

"Seriously," she says, putting her hand on my shoulder. "Don't worry."

I nod again, pasting on a smile for the guests as I begin to pass out the plastic 3D glasses. It's not a big crowd, just a handful of families who follow the lines behind me to wait next to the closed doors.

"Not that it's any of my business," Ivy says, "and, again, it's not a big deal . . . but where were you? Liam and I were talking, and then I looked over and you were gone. Did something happen?"

"Oh," I say, blushing a little. "I just sort of wandered over to the gondola ride. I think the conversation at lunch made me curious, you know?"

Ivy considers this, twirling a curl around her finger. "That makes sense. It's sort of weird to think that that happened here, huh?"

"Yeah," I say, handing another person a pair of glasses. I wait until they're out of earshot to keep talking.

"It's surreal," I say. "And I can't believe Silvia knew her."

A realization hits me, and I glance over Ivy's shoulder to the theater, where Gene's standing at the bottom level.

"Wait, if Silvia knew her, did Gene?"

Ivy laughs. "Who knows? He'd probably say it's unprofessional to talk about it if anyone asked."

I chew the inside of my cheek, trying to imagine Gene talking to Hailey. It's hard to picture, which means he probably kept his distance the way he does now.

"Ah, shit," Ivy says, glancing behind me. "One of those brats is trying to climb through the bushes. Hang on."

She darts behind me, heading down to the lower level, where some kid is indeed trying to launch himself through the hedges. I laugh a little, then turn back to the park as I wait for more guests. My heart feels lighter, thanks to Ivy's reassurance, and the plastic glasses in my hand are oddly comforting.

That is, until I see them.

It's four boys, moving like a multilimbed amoeba of chaos, chucking popcorn in arches at one another as they stomp across the concrete walkway, straight in my direction.

The breath's knocked out of me. Obviously, I knew that, logically, it would be impossible *not* to see anyone I knew. It's a huge theme park. Sure, it's only been two days, but it's just basic math when you really think about it. The park employs over five hundred people and has a capacity for thirteen thousand guests. Even if we're at half capacity, that means that, just at a mathematical level, someone I know will be here, working or attending.

Plus, it could be worse. It could be the unthinkable. It could be him.

But logic doesn't help me now. Now, my first instinct is to run at the sight of them.

Logan Murphy. Jared Zissi. Tayden Vosse. Gunner Gibson.

Each of them has a variation of the same floppy, semi-wavy hair, except for Jared. Jared's falls in a long, stringy, oily curtain in front of his eyes. His voice carries the loudest as he launches a handful of popcorn at Logan. Because who cares if someone has to clean it up? Who cares when you are varsity-lacrosse royalty?

I tense. If the four of them are here, it means that . . . well, it means that while it could be worse, there's no telling that it won't get worse.

My breath hitches. My eyes might even water as the boys zigzag in my direction, oblivious that I'm here, watching them, my feet rooted to the spot.

"Miss?"

I'm jerked back to reality by a woman materializing on my left, forced to stay in place to assist her. I paste on a smile, hoping I'm not shaking.

"Yes?" I ask. "How can I help you?"

I try not to look behind her, try not to track the boy amoeba that still flails nearby, inching ever closer. Because they won't come here, right? It's a kids' show. There are roller coasters to go on and costume characters to torment. This can't be their destination.

"These glasses are broken," the woman huffs, holding up the pair of glasses I handed her minutes ago. "See how they're all warped? And nothing's in 3D, let alone 4D."

"They won't work until the show starts, ma'am," I tell her, but she ignores me and grabs another pair from my cart. She throws them on, using them to look up at the already three-dimensional sky.

65

"You should have just given me these ones," she gripes, then heads off into the theater.

I don't argue. Gene would. Gene would tell her that the glasses are 3D but the show has special 4D effects to dazzle the guests during its brief run time. But I don't have any extra breath to use, because now that she's gone, I can see the boys. All of them. They're squirting each other with their Gatorade water bottles, the ones they would always leave behind in class, the ones I know they never, ever clean. Tayden opens his mouth to catch some of the water, choking when it hits the back of his throat.

Maybe he'll choke to death, I think wildly.

"Greta?"

I whip around to where Ivy stands beside me, her eyebrow arched as I clutch my chest.

"Uh, you okay?" Ivy asks, and I nod. I try to focus on her Creamsicle-colored eyeliner, not on the boys behind me. But I'm useless, unable to resist peeking back over my shoulder. They're still there. Still close enough. But the show must be starting soon, and then I can lock them out, can keep them all far, far away.

"You know them or something?" Ivy asks, following my gaze. I appreciate that her eyes instantly narrow at the sight of them.

"No," I say, too quickly. "I mean, yes. They go to my school—or, I mean, we went to school together. They were in some of my classes."

The words are coming out like pinballs at random, out of my control and unpredictable and unlikely to hit any semblance of a target. I need to shut up. If I talk too much, I might tell Ivy about why these boys hate me, about what they did to me, and what I did to them in return.

"I know the type," Ivy says, her voice practically a growl. "They think they're better than everyone. Think they know everything. Think that gives them a right to hurt people, to stomp on anyone in their path."

I blink at her, momentarily caught off guard. "Yes. Exactly. How'd you know?"

Her eyes flick to me before cutting back to the boys.

"Like I said," she says softly. "I know the type. Absolute dick-heads."

I turn and follow her gaze. Gunner and Logan have taken off their shirts and are whipping each other with them. An older maintenance employee stops and waves at them, no doubt asking them to put their clothes back on. They laugh at her, laugh so loud that it carries like an arrow. I force myself to look away because I've heard those laughs. I was walking to class, and they had their phones, and when I got around the corner and saw the screen—

"Hey, Hyper Pals!" Hyper Kid's voice booms out of the speaker. "Get behind those blue lines and strap on your adventure caps, because we're about to get Hyper up in here!"

Relief floods me. I can go inside. I need to go inside. But then I look at Ivy and see that she's still watching the same spot.

Because the boys aren't just closer. They're walking toward us, eyes locked on us.

No. Not us.

Me.

"Greta?" Logan asks, smirking as he walks up, the rest of them giggling behind him. "Jesus. Almost didn't recognize you."

His eyes sweep up and down, from my lunch-lady shoes to my polo, and linger on my name tag. No. Not my name tag. On my chest.

I want to die, right here. It's like earlier, when I was talking to

Grey and couldn't find the words. Except now, it isn't awkwardness that's drying up my sentences. It's fear and hatred and shame and everything in between.

"Hey, asshole," Ivy snaps, jolting me. "We have a show to get to. Are you coming in or not?"

Logan's eyes narrow, beady and sharp. "Did you just call me an asshole? I'll have you fired."

"Go ahead and try," she says. "Now, like I said, are you coming in or not?"

I've never seen Logan cowed, not even a little bit. But right now, as he glares at Ivy, he's momentarily silent. It lulls me into a false sense of relief that's instantly shattered when he speaks again.

"Seems like you found a friend," he says, gaze swinging to me before moving back to Ivy. "But that's a mistake."

Ivy shakes her head. "Come on, Greta. We need to get inside."

She tugs on my sleeve, but I'm frozen. Logan's still glaring, but his lips have curled into a cruel smile. A *satisfied* smile.

"Come on," Ivy repeats, and now I do move. I grab the chain that we use to close off the waiting area between shows, stretching it from one end to the other. I wait for Logan to move as I do, but he doesn't, so I have to snap it on with him inches away from the chain. I swallow a breath, avoiding his eyes as I turn around.

"You know she's actually psychotic, don't you?" Logan snaps, his voice a whipcrack in the silence. "But it's your funeral, I guess. I just wouldn't trust her if I were you."

It's like he's dunked a bucket of ice water over me, the cold burning through me instantly. I'm back in the locker room, and I'm standing there in the dark. There are sirens in the distance. Everything's crashing down—

I lift my eyes to Ivy's, waiting for her judgment, her questions.

"Luckily, I know better than to trust a prick like you," Ivy says, and then she sets her chin and waves me in after her.

I duck inside the theater before anything else can happen. I whip my finger in the air for Gene to close the doors, fighting back the tears that pool at the corners of my eyes. My polo's suddenly itchy, the starchiness of the fabric sticking to my skin.

There's the rumble of a rocket, and the audience gasps as the show begins. I try to focus on it, but through the blurry images, Assistant Principal Taggert's voice echoes in my memory.

Greta, these just aren't the things that honor-roll students do, he chides. *Perhaps it would be better if you did the rest of the semester . . . remotely. These things, we can try to contain them, but with only a month to go . . .*

I blink both him and my tears away. I shake my head, scanning the audience, looking for something to steal my attention, something that isn't a land mine from my past.

It isn't too packed, maybe sixty or so people, everyone focused on the screen and the 4D effects. Soon, the theater is doused in fake "snow." I watch the tiny flakes, fighting for air in the dark, pushing my barbed memories down further and further. . . .

Until I notice someone in the dark.

It's not Logan or Tayden or any of the boys, but it *is* someone I recognize. My boss, Neil, stands on the other end of the theater, a clipboard in hand that he's scribbling on. His glasses flash as the screen lights up, and even though he's across the room and covered in shadow, I swear his eyes sweep across me.

I gulp. Gene told me that Neil sometimes does pop-ins to check on the ushers as "quality control." As the lead, it's his job to make sure we're all following the rules. Gene even warned me that if Neil catches me doing something "uncouth," I could be fired.

Did he see me come in almost late? When did he get here? He must've come into the theater through the greenroom's back entrance, so neither Ivy nor I saw him. Or maybe she did. . . .

I look for her in the crowd, finding her seated on one of the benches in the back, behind all the guests. Her foot bounces, and she twirls her hair absently around her fingers. My chest tightens. We're never supposed to sit during shows. It's one of Gene's many rules, yes, but it's also clearly spelled out in the Entertainment handbook. Has Neil seen her? He must have.

I try to think of a way to signal to her that he's here, but I can't figure out anything that won't be obvious to Neil. I can't text her. Texting's also against the rules, and in this dark, it'll light up instantly. I can't wave or walk over to her. I'm frozen, stuck trying to communicate telepathically.

Stand up. Please, please, please stand up.

But she doesn't. The rest of the show finishes as it always does, and Ivy doesn't get up until the guests have already started to leave. I grab my broom, eyes darting from Ivy to Neil. She doesn't seem to have noticed him yet, or maybe she's pretending not to.

But he's noticed her.

He strides over to her, his footsteps echoing in the nearly empty theater. There are still a few stragglers gathering their things, so Neil keeps his voice down as he gestures angrily at Ivy. I've never seen him look so red, and even from where I'm standing at the top of the theater, I swear I can see a vein pulsing in his temple.

I nearly jump when Gene steps up next to me, clucking his tongue as he leans on his broom.

"I warned you," he tells me. "Neil's a patient boss, but even he has his limits. All people do. And it's about time Ivy got told off for not following the rules, especially with her being a trainer. Maybe now she'll finally see."

I don't know what to say to that, so I just keep sweeping, trying not to look too obvious as I sneak glances at Ivy and Neil. At one point, I swear she points her finger and its sharp, talon-like nail is so close to his eye that I worry she'll cut right through it, and he responds with something so full of barely contained venom that his hand—directed at Ivy—shakes. I creep closer, pretending my target is a smattering of popcorn under one of the lower benches.

"—going to find out about this," Neil's saying, his voice a low hiss. "This can't be covered up for much longer."

"Maybe you should have thought about that before," Ivy snaps back, but then her brown eyes catch me and zero in. I swallow, slamming my own gaze to the ground, but it's too late. She crosses her arm and tosses her curls over her shoulder.

"Is that all?" she asks Neil, her unaffected tone back in her voice, sounding so bored it's like the past several minutes never even happened. I can't believe she's talking so dismissively to him, especially after he clearly chastised her and threatened her job.

Neil's face burns, but he straightens up. He seems to be digging around for the words to launch at Ivy, but he must not find what he's looking for. In the end, his already thin mouth settles into a thinner line before he finally speaks.

"This needs to be a tight ship," he says, wiping his glasses on his shirt. "All of you need to be better. No more mistakes."

Gene, who's still sweeping to the left of us, looks up. Initially, he looks pleased, but then the "all of you" settles into understanding, and his mouth drops open. But before he can argue, Neil pops his glasses back on and turns on his heel, stalking out across the stage.

"What an asshole," Ivy says, her own eyes narrowing. "I'm sorry, Greta. Sorry, Gene. You guys didn't deserve that."

"It's okay," I say. "I mean, I was almost late. . . ."

"Almost," Gene huffs, to my surprise. "But not actually. Why, that little . . . First he makes a mess in the tech-only area, and now he's trying to tell me how to do my job? Why, I . . ."

He grumbles, white-knuckling his broom as he swish-swishes in the other direction. Ivy and I watch him before turning to each other, and I can tell she's trying to keep from laughing.

"Let's hope you get moved to Jungle soon," she says. "It's such a better gig. Farther from the main office, for one. Too far for Neil to walk to with that stick up his ass."

I snort out a laugh, then cover it, wondering if Neil's hiding on the other side of the screen, listening in.

"Oh, I don't know," I say. "I did just start here yesterday. I probably won't get moved for a while, right?"

Ivy shakes her head. "Not necessarily. Neil usually likes to get the new ushers trained on all the shows right away so they're more flexible to schedule. If he has multiple places to put you, that makes his life easier."

"Oh," I say, hope ballooning in my chest. "So you think I have a shot?"

Ivy nods. "Yep. And he will. Even if he still thinks you need to memorize his handbook. Especially after . . . well, you saw."

And I did see the way Neil and Gene looked at each other. For Gene, it was a slap in the face, especially after his continuous efforts. And after he'd spoken . . . well, not exactly highly of Neil. But somewhat.

Neil's a patient boss, but even he has his limits.

I glance back at Gene now, tracking him as he moves across the upper benches, his body arched over, the top of his spine visible through his polo. He glances down, past Ivy and me, to the black curtain that Neil disappeared behind.

Gene's right. Everyone has limits. Everyone has a tipping point.

Mercy's terrified face at the party appears in my mind, Lauren's cold voice echoing in my head over the image, each syllable sharp with jealousy as she crushed that cup. And then today, Allie and Lauren talking about blood. Did something happen last night, just after Mercy and I talked? Something that Allie and Lauren know about, or maybe had a hand in?

The thoughts spin as I move to get the glasses, but that trips another memory. A memory of Wardrobe and a certain ripped costume.

Everyone has limits.

What happens when someone's pushed right over the edge?

CHAPTER EIGHT

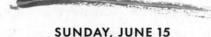

SUNDAY, JUNE 15
6:56 P.M.

MOM'S IN THE middle of dyeing her hair when I get home from what was a truly exhausting day. She pops her head out of the bathroom the second I walk in the door, her brown eyes framed by delicate creases, her hair plastered to her head, wet and sticky from the dye. As an event planner, she's always worried about being "presentable" for clients, never allowing a single gray hair to make an appearance. Jasper, our black-and-white cocker spaniel mix, is next to her at the door, barking and whining to be petted as soon as I edge my way in.

Mom holds her hands out in front of her. "Well? Still everything you wanted and more?"

I grin, bending down to pet Jasper as I do. "Gene told me I 'exceeded all expectations.' He said he's going to recommend me to be cleared for work without a trainer."

Mom squeals, then rushes forward to hug me and Jasper. In

the process, she gets a little bit of dye on my cheek, but neither of us cares. It's only semipermanent.

"I told you," she says. "You're shining, hon."

My heart swells at her encouragement. It's always been her and me against the world, especially since things fell apart with her and Dad. They're technically still together, but only legally. One day, they'll finalize the papers, but until then, he's a ghost that floats in occasionally and wrecks things when he does.

"All you needed was a little course correction," she says, giving me a final squeeze before heading back to finish up her dye.

Her words make my heart stutter, just a tiny bit. Course correction. Because of what happened. Because of my mistakes.

Suddenly, I'm back at the lunch table, panicking because of what I think Liam is going to reveal to the group. But I can't let myself get caught up in a shame spiral. I have to push through. I can't dwell on what came before.

If only it were that easy. If only there weren't all this weirdness with Mercy and Lauren and Allie making my mind spin to the worst possible scenario. It makes me pause at the stairs, looking at Mom.

"Mom?" I ask. "When . . . when do people start looking for a missing person?"

She glances at me as she dabs some dye on, smiling a little.

"More Lifetime? Or have you branched off into true-crime podcasts?" she asks with a chuckle. "Oh, I dunno. I think things really hit the fan after a day or so. Why?"

I nod. "Nothing. Just . . . you know. Like you said. A podcast. I was just curious."

"Let me know if you like it," she says. "I'm always looking for something to relax to after my events, you know."

I nod and then head upstairs to my room with Jasper at my heels. As soon as we enter my room, I sink down onto my bed and watch him dig around for one of the many toys he's hidden here while I ruminate on Mercy. Mom's probably right. If anything actually has happened to Mercy, I'll know by tomorrow, right? But shouldn't I say something? What if Mercy's really hurt? After all, that panda costume . . . that looked like blood, didn't it? Which is exactly what Allie and Lauren were talking about—

But then I remind myself that the panda costume was in Wardrobe. Surely if someone brought that to Wardrobe, there would've been questions. And Allie and Lauren . . . well, I didn't hear the whole conversation. It's cryptic, no doubt about it. And if there really is bad news about Mercy, I can come forward. Right? But now . . . now I really, really don't want to be the kind of person who Ivy rolls her eyes at, who everyone thinks makes things up for attention.

Right?

After all, I did great today, even with everything that happened. After Gene had time to cool off from Neil, he seemed more focused than ever on clearing me, and now, thanks to that, I'm completely trained on Rocket 4D Theater. Maybe now it'll be just like Ivy said and I'll get the opportunity to train at Mega Boost or—I inhale a sharp, hopeful breath—Jungle Jam with Grey.

It could happen. A new path could be carved.

No.

A new path *will* be carved.

Just as long as certain things don't surface.

I glance over at Jasper, who is joyfully disemboweling his stuffed toy, and my eyes fall on last year's yearbook on my bookshelf. I realize that the positive thoughts will not be able to win out right now. Which means that my only option is to give in to the negative thoughts, to let them fuel me. To let them remind me of why this job is so monumental, so vital to my survival.

I grab the yearbook and flip through it until I find the page. *His* page.

Half the page is taken up by a photo of the varsity boys' lacrosse team. I run my finger over the boys kneeling in the first row, skipping over Logan and the others, until I find Brad in the middle, his chest thrown out, the only one smiling with his teeth.

Next to Brad, there's a purple Post-it with my notes written on it. At the top, I wrote his name: Brad Kensington. Below it, I wrote things like *thinks he'd be a good fit for reality TV* and *works at the doughnut shop*. I probably also wrote something about how he asked me to tutor him in precalc, how he told me he liked smart girls, how he smiled at one of my knock-knock jokes, the one about the sloth. Now those words are gone, hidden under vicious cross-outs and ink smudges. Now there's only one word left.

Asshole.

When I first met Brad, every moment felt like confetti. Focusing in class was impossible, not when I had texts from Brad vibrating in my pocket. Little messages that kept the dreams in my head spinning, dreams about meeting in empty locker rooms after he finished lacrosse practice or about accidentally on purpose running into each other in the school library. Each message was an invitation for conversation and possibility and more.

The messages weren't long. They were concise because Brad, like our tenth-grade English teacher, valued "economy of language." His messages of "u up?" and "ok" were little poems for me to decipher, more to analyze in what was left out than what was left in.

I played coy, obviously. I'd studied enough videos to know that this part of the courtship was vital. According to the experts, I needed to remain aloof and mysterious so that he'd want to know more, so that he'd ask me questions beyond the parameters of precalculus.

Still, coy did not—and does not—come naturally to me. Every moment, I hungered to write back to him. When he asked, "u up?" I initially drafted him something about my plan to do both a face and a hair mask. But then, on reflection, I deleted it all, set a timer for six minutes later, and then, when the alarm went off, replied: "Yeah."

This was our romance. It was unexpected. Brad and I were both sophomores, but it was anticipated that he'd make lacrosse team captain in his junior year. He had the muscles on his arms and legs to prove it, and once, I'd seen him take off his hoodie in AP World History, revealing the hard planes of his stomach. I wanted to let my fingertips skate across them.

It was a Sunday night when it happened, the moment when I thought everything was going to change between Brad and me. Abs-skating was clearly imminent.

Brad: u up?
Me: Yeah.
Brad: ive been thinkin about you
Me: Really?
Me: I've been thinking about you, too.
Brad: i bet uve got a killer body

It was then that everything inside me melted. A "killer" body. Me? I'd looked down at my stomach, at that moment hidden beneath a thick Hanes sweatshirt and sweatpants, and considered his statement. My stomach was on the softer side, not like the permanently toned stomachs the lacrosse girls loved to flaunt during practice. My softness did mean that I was relatively busty, a feature I was always eager to play up.

But a "killer" body? I guess I liked my legs. I was short, but they were on the longer side. My arms weren't weirdly short or long. My butt wasn't going to win any awards, but it also wasn't what my mom called a "pancake butt."

I bit my lip, trying to figure out how to respond, when another message popped up.

send a pic

He added three winking emojis, which I knew meant he was seriously invested. Brad never used emojis. Of course, looking back, this should've been my first red flag.

Instead, the dreams exploded in my mind. Was he asking me what I thought he was asking me? I typed out a response.

I'm wearing pajamas. Not very cute. Ha ha.

His reply was instant.

take them off

At school, I'd heard of people sending nudes, but I'd never seen one. They were something that older kids did, something mysterious and wild to be done when someone entered the field of dating. Was this that moment for me?

I had glanced at my closed door. Mom and Dad were attending their two-hundredth round of doomed couples' therapy. Caroline, my then best friend, was still heading home from that weekend's Junior State of America convention. I was home alone on a Sunday night.

Slowly, I peeled off my Hanes sweatshirt. Then my gray T-shirt. I looked at myself in the mirror on the back of my door. Freckles dotted the pale skin of my neck and collarbone. A plain black bra covered my breasts. I pulled back a bit of the fabric to look at what was hidden underneath, but then I put it back.

I couldn't do it.

Could I?

I pulled up Google on my phone, starting with *Should I send a nude?* but ending up on a boudoir photographer's video series about how to take the sexiest pictures of your chest. In a moment, I had unhooked my bra and let it fall to the floor. From there, I hoisted my phone up in front of my mirror, snapping pictures as I angled and twisted my body. I was careful to make sure my lips looked pouty and my green eyes glazed in that hot-girl way I'd seen so many other girls at school effortlessly wield. I had mixed success in the sixty or so pictures I took, partly because my round face and freckles tend more toward cute than hot. I tried putting my wavy, chin-length light brown hair up rather than down, then brushed it down again, then tucked it behind my ears, then pulled it back up again. I took more photos, then examined each one for imperfections. Most of them I deleted. But there was one. One where I looked . . . was it pretty?

I'd kept my sweats on in the photos, but my breasts were bare. My free hand was on the front of my hip, my thumb suggestively hooked on the waistband of my sweats in a pose I'd seen other girls use. I might not have looked full "hot girl," but it was the hottest I'd ever looked.

My fingers hovered over the keyboard, and then, I hit Send.

Brad replied just once. A fire emoji.

But it fueled me.

I considered sending more, but I forced myself to hold back. One was enough for now, especially knowing that, tomorrow, I'd see Brad. This was the ultimate coy move. He'd have to ask me for another, and then, I'd be ready.

In the morning, I was in a giddy haze when Mom dropped me off, practically buzzing with possibility. In my first period, I answered every question the teacher asked, on a high no one else could meet.

Then they pulled me out of class.

Assistant Principal Taggert sighed as I walked in. I sat down, confused, worried about SAT classes being canceled or some other travesty. I looked at Assistant Principal Taggert, terror zipping through my every limb as his eyes settled on mine. It would be the first time I'd been in his office, but it unfortunately wouldn't be the last.

"Greta," he'd said. "Are you aware that it's illegal to produce and send child pornography?"

At the sting of the memory, I slam the yearbook shut. This is why I need a new start. This is why I need Hyper Kid Magic Land more than I need air. I need to erase everything that happened from the moment I sent that picture. I need to be someone new, a Greta so powerful that no one cares what she did when she was a sophomore.

But what if they find out? I think back on that moment with Liam, the way he looked from me to his phone and up again. And that's just the picture. What if he knew about—

You were wrong, I tell myself fiercely. He was playing *Tetris*. No one cares about that picture anymore or anything that came after. No one is going to find out. They even seem to maybe like me. Right?

Mercy did, at least. Her words from the party roll through my mind.

There's something about you, Greta. I can just tell.

I pull out my phone, turning it over in my hand. Maybe what I need to do is just . . . close the loop. I stop spinning my phone and open the text thread with Mercy. Before I can think about it, I type out a quick message.

> Hey. Were we supposed to meet today? I wasn't sure if I got the days wrong. Hope everything's okay. I can meet tomorrow instead if that works. Or not, if you don't want to anymore. No worries either way.

And then I fire it off, resisting the urge to edit or revise a single word. I throw my phone onto the bed and collapse next to Jasper, letting the day's events wash away from me, focused only on the future.

Hyper Kid will be a place for new beginnings, and I won't let anything stand in my way.

I don't put the yearbook back onto the shelf. I open a long plastic bin under my bed, the one full of "memories" that Mom insists I keep, memories like faded PE clothes from middle school and beaded necklaces from summer camp. I put the yearbook inside a sweatshirt and close the lid of the bin.

I am potential. I am possibility.

And I will not be held back any longer.

CHAPTER NINE

MONDAY, JUNE 16
8:29 A.M.

AFTER A NIGHT of strange nightmares involving Mercy running through the trails in San Joaquin Hills, I wake up on edge. Images of her screaming at me about "the blood" coupled with red dripping down her cheeks linger even after I splash water onto my face. I check my phone to see if she's responded, but there's nothing there. Dread pools inside me, and I pull on my polo with shaky hands.

When I get downstairs, I half expect the *Rancho Paloma Morning News* to be covering a found body or a missing person, but instead, Jade Burns cheerfully dissects the new summer trend involving homemade glitter slime and inflatable backyard pools. I force myself to breathe. Clearly, if something were wrong, it would be all over the news. Our tiny coastal town is like that, fixating on every last morsel of information. Especially Hyper Kid–related news. After all, the entire town spins around the park. So I exhale. Surely, if something had happened to Mercy, Jade Burns would be covering it.

The universe sends me another positive sign as soon as I walk into the Wardrobe lobby, where we all swipe our cards to clock in. Because there, standing in front of the water fountain, checking his teeth in a mirror that hangs on the wall, is Grey.

He's wearing turquoise leggings and a thin yellow tank top, one with the fabric of the arms scooped out so that I can see the side profile of his bare chest. It's the least amount of clothing I've seen him in since the party, and the cut of the tank top reveals several tattoos I haven't seen before: a skeleton riding a skateboard just under his right nipple, a tic-tac-toe board to the left of that, and what looks like the start of a dragon tail underneath that. He's turned away from me, facing the mirror, so his expression is hidden as he collects his golden mane of hair into a ponytail that he then twists into a bun. It sits lopsided on top of his head, messy and free, just like Grey himself.

I pause in front of the clock-in machine, frozen at the sight of him. My last two attempts with him were so awkward, so substandard, but I refuse to make the same mistake again. Now I will be confident. After all, my vision for myself does not include mewling cowardice. I am going to be all power and decisiveness.

"Good morning," I say, keeping my tone casual but bright as I slide my ID card through the machine. I keep my eyes down, avoiding looking directly at Grey. I am a person of mystery, of intrigue. I demand attention rather than pursue it.

Unfortunately, Grey must not hear me, or maybe he thinks I'm speaking to the lone Wardrobe employee who's currently folding shirts. Thankfully, it's not the same girl as before. This girl looks older and extremely unbothered by the world at large. In fact, as I pocket my card and stride across the lobby, she doesn't even look up.

"Going to be a hot day," I say, stopping at the fountain behind Grey to fill up my water bottle. "Good thing we have air-conditioning."

From this angle, I can see his reflection in the mirror, and he can see me at the fountain. Through the glass, his eyes catch mine, and I swallow. No turning back now.

"Greta?" he asks, glancing over his shoulder.

I nod. I can't tell what tone he was using to say my name, but the point is, today, he got my name right. I'm not Ginger. I'm *Greta*.

"Hello," I say. "I was just saying that it's, um. Going to be hot today."

I try for a casual smile, but I realize too late that I've left my water bottle under the refill spigot for too long and it's now overflowing. The water spills out over my hand, so I jerk the bottle back, cursing as I dump out the excess. I glance at Grey, who's still looking at me over his shoulder, his expression unreadable. My cheeks burn. A third failed attempt to talk to Grey, and this time, I didn't even get past the first sentence.

But then, to my surprise, Grey turns around fully and takes a few steps toward me. He leans against the wall and crosses one leg over the other, then folds his arms in front of his chest so that his biceps stretch and pop as he looks down at me.

God, those eyes. I could sink into them. Drown in them.

"Happens to me all the time," Grey says, smiling so that he reveals a flash of white teeth. "It sneaks up on you."

"It really does," I say, breathless. Because oh my god, oh my god, oh my god. He's talking to me. He's actually talking to me.

"Are you working my show today?" Grey asks.

"Not yet," I admit, but hope is pooling in my stomach. "I mean, I'd like to. It's just up to Neil if—"

"Your stuff's done," a voice behind us snaps, jolting me out of my conversation with Grey. It's the girl who was folding the shirts, and she's holding up a hamper and nodding in Grey's direction.

"Thank you," Grey says, smiling at the girl before glancing back at me. "Duty calls. But hopefully I'll see you soon. It's been . . . well. It's been sublime."

"Sublime." The word seems to melt in the air between us. I hang there for a second, hand still wet from my water bottle, as I watch Grey stride over and grab the hamper with one arm. The action lifts his shirt, exposing his lower abdomen. I think seeing this much of his skin might permanently alter my brain chemistry.

"Later," he says, winking before he disappears through the door.

It's his wink that does it, sending me over the edge and filling me with confidence and purpose. I need to talk to Neil, obviously. I need to advocate for myself and insist on working at Jungle. Yes, I've only worked at Rocket for two days, but like Ivy said, Neil will want to diversify my training so that I am the Swiss Army knife of ushers who he can put anywhere. Now I just need to convince him that that next place is Jungle.

I need to be near Grey, who has shoved all other thoughts out of my brain as I now walk toward the Entertainment office. I get to the door that leads inside and throw it open, mustering up every ounce of courage I can before stepping into the cool air of the building.

The Entertainment office is fairly small, just a small cluster of cubicles grouped together around a whiteboard, where this week's schedule is pinned up with a clip. Most of the desks here are empty right now; they belong to supervisors or other leads who are presumably off doing very important work around the park. Or they're able to come in late, a perk of having achieved so much. Either option could be correct.

But one desk is occupied. Neil's turned away from me, facing his ancient PC. The computer itself is surrounded by a collection of Pop! figurines, Hyper Kid memorabilia, and a few pictures of himself throughout the park. There's also a small army of decorated name tags, many of which are clearly seasonal and exclusive, that he's arranged like a frame around his monitor. Anyone looking at Neil's desk would deduce instantly that he cares deeply about the park, which means I need to convince him that I harbor a similar passion. I step carefully toward him, taking in a breath as I ready myself.

"Good morning," I say, my voice high and bright and, I admit it, squeaky. Nerves have strangled it, and unfortunately, the pitch makes Neil jump in his chair.

"Sorry!" I say. "I didn't mean to scare you."

Neil lets out a breath and bends down to hunt for his glasses, which toppled off his face, revealing his computer screen. A picture of Hyper Kid Magic Land sits front and center, an old one that must be from when the park opened, with a headline below it blaring A BEAUTIFUL YOUNG ACTRESS WAS MURDERED—BUT WHO GOT AWAY WITH THE CRIME?

Neil pops up before I can read any more, shakily adjusting his glasses. He closes the window he had open, and next week's work schedule fills the screen.

"Greta," Neil says, out of breath. "You—"

"I wanted to talk to you," I say quickly, before he can shut me down, "about why I should be trained at Jungle."

Neil and the zit between his eyebrows stare at me.

"As I'm sure you're aware," I say, stretching my smile as wide as it goes, "Gene cleared me at Rocket yesterday, which means I am now a prime candidate for training at other shows."

"Oh," Neil says, a cough turning into a slight choke before he recovers. "Well, yes. Eventually, we'll want you trained on Mega Boost and Jungle—"

"I believe Jungle should take precedent," I say. "You see, I've always been incredibly adaptable, and Jungle stood out to me on my tour. I believe I would be a prime candidate for ushering there. My reasoning is trifold—"

A loud bang cuts me off as the door to the office slams open. There's a flash of blond hair, and then Allie steps decisively into view. She's striking even without any makeup, wearing a tight white tank top that seems even whiter because of her suntanned skin. Her blue eyes don't even blink in my direction, but instead, fix themselves on Neil, who visibly squirms under her gaze as she stomps forward.

I can't blame him. Allie is the kind of beautiful that seems unreal, like she was plucked from the cover of a surfing magazine, right down to her still slightly damp blond hair, which has been tucked back in twin braids that graze her shoulders.

"We need a Perky," Allie says by way of greeting. "Mercy's out again."

Instantly, my insides turn to ice. Mercy's out *again*. Which means she *was* supposed to be here yesterday. Which means she hasn't been at work since . . .

Since the day of the party. Has anyone even seen her since that night? Or . . . or was the last time she was seen . . . when I saw her?

Lauren's words from yesterday float back to me.

Little Miss Mercy finally got what she deserved.

I blink from Allie and back to Neil, examining their expressions. Allie just looks annoyed at this inconvenience, while Neil looks like he's frozen, the only movement his mouth as it opens slightly wider, panic flashing across his eyes. Do I tell him now about the blood? I open my mouth, starting to sort through the words—

"She called out again?" Neil hiccups after a moment, finally gathering words. "Is she . . . is she still sick?"

I blink, mouth still open. Mercy called out? Meaning . . . she's not decapitated in a ditch somewhere like she was last night in my dream?

"I guess so," Allie huffs. "She told Grey, not me."

"Well, he's the performer lead, so she should be communicating with him since James isn't here," Neil says, clearly relieved that this isn't his responsibility. "And Grey's taking care of it?"

"Obviously," Allie says, rolling her eyes. "He's calling people now to try get someone in for Mercy, but we might have to cancel the first show if they can't get in here in time."

"Oh no," Neil says, going even paler than I thought was humanly possible. "That can't happen. Absolutely not."

"But what about Mercy?" I ask, suddenly unable to contain myself. "What's wrong with her?"

Allie, who hasn't spared me a glance, suddenly *does* look at me, her gaze . . . judging. And not in a good way.

"And who are you?" Allie asks, eyes sliding up and down as she clucks her tongue.

Oh no. Why, why did I have to blurt that? Why can't I control myself and keep every little thought from tumbling out? Because I can't admit I heard them talking, and Allie's right. I *don't* know Mercy. One conversation at a party doesn't count. But still . . .

There's something I need to show you.

"I've just... I've just heard that she's very, um, dedicated," I say. "And if something's happened to her..."

As I trail off, Allie's gaze turns withering, her eyes narrowed at me.

And oh no. I know this look. This is the way Caroline looked at me when she saw me as past the point of redemption.

"Yeah, well, even 'dedicated' people get sick," Allie says coldly. "She told Grey she's been throwing up all morning. Not that it's any of your business."

Now I'm the one who goes pale. Allie's words are like an ice pick, stabbing me clean through. Mercy's just sick. She texted Grey. Which means...

She responded to him, but she didn't respond to me.

"Right," Neil says, shifting in his seat. "I should help Grey attend to this, er, performer emergency. You'll have to, um, excuse me, Greta."

No, I think, horror lancing through me. I hadn't even gotten to my key evidence. Now all he'll be taking with him is the anxiety of this moment, and I'll never get scheduled at Jungle. I stand up, starting to say something to him, but he doesn't even look at me as he turns and leaves with Allie through the office doors. I hate that tears sting in my eyes.

I've failed. Again. I went too hard. I was too annoying, as always, too much, always too much.

"You push people away," Caroline told me once. I swore to put that Greta behind me, but here I am, doing it again. Ruining my chances for something better.

I slink out after Neil's voice has faded away.

When I first interviewed with Hyper Kid, it was Neil who was my interviewer. He wore the blue polo, the one that signified his leadership role. I so desperately wanted to impress him, to make him see me as worthy of my own name tag, and I'd succeeded. I even thought I might convince him to put my entire name on it: Greta Riley Green. He had said he thought it was too many characters but that maybe they'd figure something out down the line, which turned out to be a blessing, now that I think about it.

The point is, he believed in me. Until now. Until this moment when I did just what Caroline said I would and pushed him away.

My phone buzzes, reminding me that it's time to head to Rocket. I can't afford to be late, not after my disastrous conversation with Neil. I need to be a model usher. And yet I can't get my mind straight with everything that's just happened.

I don't realize there's a person standing behind me until I turn around, running right into their hard form. Someone who smells like coffee and is taller than me by several inches. Eyes blinking at the impact, I try to place who it is that I've collided with.

"I'm sorry!" I sputter, just as my eyes jump up and connect with warm brown ones. The same eyes from yesterday that widened at the sight of me, just as they do now.

"Hey," Liam—the *dealer*—says, his voice soft but heavy at the same time. It seems to tumble out of the corner of his mouth as he flashes another half smile.

"Hello," I say, stepping back so that I can dust off my navy pants. Not like anything happened to them, but I need something to do with my hands. I can't explain why Liam's brown eyes unnerve me, but they do. Possibly because I know that he traffics in illicit activity.

He moves around me to get to the wall of folders, plucking out a green one. He sifts through it and pulls out an envelope. I idle there, watching him, not sure what to say. He's a dealer, yes, but he's also a technician, and I need as many allies as I can get.

"Where're you working today?" I ask.

He pockets the envelope. "Jungle. You still stuck at Rocket?"

"For now," I say, cheeks burning. "I was trying to talk to Neil about training at Jungle soon, but our discussion was interrupted."

Liam considers this, nodding a few times as he grabs a walkie-talkie and clips it to his belt. I wait for him to say something more, but he doesn't, instead allowing the quiet to settle between us. After a while, I can't stand it, so I say something else.

"I know I haven't been here that long," I say, taking his silence as the obvious judgment that it is, "but I think I would be excellent at Jungle. I was just about to describe my collaborative spirit and—well, the point is, it was trifold."

That gets that damned half smile out of him. "Do you mean threefold?"

He's making fun of me. I glare at him.

"You know what," I say. "I need to go to Rocket."

I barrel past him, heading for the door, but before I can reach for the knob, it swings open. I manage to step back just in time as Ivy appears in front of me.

"What the hell, Greta," Ivy says, holding a hand to her chest. "You scared the shit out of me."

I start to answer, but she catches sight of Liam behind me and waves at him. I mumble an apology but also take the opportunity to duck under her arm and slip out the door, needing to get away from the Entertainment office as quickly as possible before I say or do something else ridiculous.

It's Liam's fault, I tell myself. He's the common thread in my awkward encounters. Well, I guess I can't exactly blame him for what happened with Neil. No, that was someone else's fault.

That was Mercy's fault.

I swallow as my legs carry me toward Rocket. Somehow, the words "Mercy" and "fault" don't coincide well together, making my mind slippery.

I should be done with her, since she's clearly ignoring me, especially since we only talked at the party. But then I remember her haunted expression and how she sounded when she told me about whatever she needed to show me. She sounded urgent, practically trembling with fear. And now she's gone again. Sick, according to Allie. And Grey, technically. Which means it must be the truth, right? Unless there's more to it. Could Lauren and Allie have done something to *make* Mercy sick? Is that where the blood comes in?

I decide to send Mercy another text, even if it seems desperate.

Hey. Heard that you're sick today. Hope everything's okay. 🖤

Is the heart too much? I don't know, but I force myself to hit Send. Now I just have to wait.

I prep for the first show in a haze. When Ivy shows up, she grumbles about needing coffee and asks if I can pass out glasses. Gene's here, too, since the three of us were already scheduled before Gene signed off on me, so we'll just alternate among the three of us working each show. Gene's making the most of this, apparently, and is in Wardrobe because he thinks one of our carts of glasses wasn't sufficiently cleaned. So when it's officially time for preshow,

I proceed to the top with the cart alone. But the entire time, my mind can't unstick from everything that happened this morning. Starting from the moment I walked up to Neil's desk—I walked up to his computer, and he was reading about . . .

A BEAUTIFUL YOUNG ACTRESS WAS MURDERED—BUT WHO GOT AWAY WITH THE CRIME?

Neil was reading about Hailey Portman and the Gondola Killer.

I wonder if Silvia told Neil we were bothering her with questions, or maybe Neil was just going down a rabbit hole of his own. But either way, now I'm also thinking about the killer. About the gondolas, swinging above the theater at this very moment, collecting dust inside.

Ivy and Jackie talked about not being sure where Hailey was actually attacked. Was it in Adventure Theater, like Ivy said, or in the gondola itself, like Jackie believed? Or was it somewhere else entirely?

And *when* did she die? Was she still alive for at least a few minutes in that gondola? Did she scream, but get drowned out by the noise of the party? Did she try to rock the gondola to attract help, but no one was paying attention?

I look up now, just as my timer goes off to tell me to go inside. The gondolas are there, overhead, the one above me a bright, bold yellow, just like the 3D glasses in my cart. A shiver goes down my spine, and I turn away, wheeling the cart inside and giving Ivy the signal to close the doors. They shut, and in moments, the show bursts to life on the screen. I watch from my place at the top, but I'm not really paying attention. My mind is swinging back and forth, just like the gondolas above.

Was her death like being rocked to sleep, or was it excruciatingly painful through to the end?

Did she hope her friends would find her as she closed her eyes? Did she curse her killer with her last breath?

Did she—

There's a sharp squeal as the projector and lights pop out in one fell swoop, blanketing the theater in darkness. I've barely registered my loss of sight when someone screams.

CHAPTER TEN

MONDAY, JUNE 16
10:48 A.M.

BECAUSE THE UNIVERSE hates me, Liam is the one who arrives to fix the malfunction that caused the power outage at Rocket. Earlier with Grey was a fluke, a false omen of good, because this day has just been one problem after another. After the power went out, Ivy and I had to find a way to manually open the doors so we could let out the howling children and their angry parents, though Gene thankfully rushed out to deal with the majority of their ire. It helped because not many people want to be mad at someone as ancient as Gene. As soon as they saw his watery eyes and white hair, they seemed to lose their edge. But that was a brief moment of bliss because now we're stuck with Liam.

While he examines the giant screen, Ivy and I sit on the stage, legs dangling over the edge. I try not to look too often at Liam, but I can't help it. He's lying down on his back so that he can get under something on the side, and as he moves his hands, the sleeves of his button-down shirt slide back. The muscles there pop slightly as he works, making me bite my lip and turn away.

This, of course, is my problem in a nutshell. I cannot read clear red flags. Liam has been nothing but obnoxious and mocking, and yet, my body betrays me when I look at him. It's exactly what happened with Brad. I ignored the red flags. But that won't happen again. I will stay focused on Grey, the safe and mature choice.

Up above, there's the sound of a distinct caw—a bird caw, followed by a human caw. Gene.

"Are you sure Gene doesn't need help?" I ask Ivy.

Gene insisted on going upstairs to stand beside the yellow A-frame sign that features a grinning cartoon Dingle the Dalmatian, a thought bubble above her head reading WUH-OH! SHOW CLOSED FOR NOW. COME BACK SOON!

"It's a waste of time," Ivy's saying, picking at her cuticles. "Either they read the sign or they don't. But if Gene wants to do it, that's his prerogative."

"So what's the diagnosis?" Ivy asks over her shoulder. I can hear Liam tapping something, hidden behind the giant screen.

"Not sure yet," he calls back. "Could be that the projector overheated. Or the SDI dual video board failed. Not sure what happened with the lights yet. But you'll be down for at least the next hour."

"Thank god," Ivy says, stretching her arms. "I love getting paid to do nothing."

"Ahem."

At the sound of Neil's voice, I turn my head to find that he's appeared on the other side of the stage. Since I last saw him at the office, his skin has gone from white to whiter to now a pale pink.

Even his ears look red as he pulls off his glasses and begins to haphazardly clean them on the edge of his polo.

"Oh, hello, Neil," Ivy says, lying down farther on the stage. Clearly, she isn't taking the scolding he gave her yesterday very seriously. I, however, can't afford such a laissez-faire attitude and shoot up and onto my feet.

"Neil," I say. "We were just waiting for Liam to finish."

But Neil doesn't seem to be hearing what I've just said. His eyes are on Liam as Liam continues to fiddle behind the screen.

"I've called Mike, and he's on his way," Neil says. "He'll know what to do."

"You called Mike?" Liam asks, his head appearing around the edge of the screen. "But I thought he was checking on the Mega Boost system today."

"This is a bigger priority," Neil says, rubbing his hands together. "And he's the supervisor, so he'll know better how to, well. How to handle this. Anyway, I'll wait for him here. You all . . ."

He fumbles the words, eyes darting from me to Ivy to Liam and back to me again. I swear the zit pulses in my direction as a bead of sweat runs down his temple.

"You should leave," he says at last. "Go to, um. Go to Jungle in the meantime."

I freeze. Did Neil just say what I think he said?

Ivy seems to think the same thing. "Are you kidding?"

Neil shakes his head. "I am not. You are being paid to be here, as you said, and you might as well go make yourself useful. Besides, Greta . . . weren't you saying you wanted to be trained there?"

So I didn't mishear him. He really did say that. My clumsy request actually worked. This day isn't ruined. On the contrary, my first assessment that today would be a perfect day was correct.

"Neil, I never thought I'd say this, but that's a great idea," Ivy says, smiling. "Should we tell Gene? He's waiting upstairs with the A-frame."

"No," Neil says, hiccupping slightly on the syllable. "He should stay out there. Out of the theater. With the guests."

Ivy arches an eyebrow but shrugs.

"You got it, *boss*," she says, saluting him.

Liam walks over to us, his hair somehow even fluffier than it was moments ago.

"We should get going," he says, checking his watch. "Preshow starts soon."

He grabs his remaining tools, then reclips his radio to his belt. We follow him, leaving Neil behind us. I glance over my shoulder to see his eyes trained on me, but he looks away quickly. And there's something about his look. . . .

"Is Neil okay?" I ask Ivy quietly as we reach the top of the stairs and head out into the sunshine.

She laughs. "No. He's a nervous wreck. I wouldn't be surprised if there's a pool of his sweat on the stage when we get back."

"It's weird that he called Mike," Liam says as we head out into the park. "This seems like a fairly straightforward fix."

"I guess he's having a stressful day," I say. "First Mercy called in, now this."

"He should be grateful we didn't have to cancel the first show," Liam says. "Lauren barely made it."

"Lauren," I say, seizing on the opportunity to ask more about her. "She's the one Keenan said was sort of, um, jealous of Mercy?"

Ivy snorts. "That's putting it mildly."

"She's just not as good as Mercy," Liam says diplomatically. "But who is? I mean, Mercy's incredible. It'll be cool to say I know someone who makes it to Broadway."

"Let's calm down a little, Dealer," Ivy says with a laugh. "We're still talking about Hyper Kid, you know? None of the performers are *that* good."

I blink at her. Not that good? Sure, I've only seen the show once, but Mercy was clearly exceptional. And Grey, too. Even the news anchors said something along those lines. I start to say as much, but Ivy cuts me off.

"Listen, Greta, I thought we covered this during training," she says. "Whatever you think you know about the performers, trust me, you don't. Holier-than-thou, backstabbing assholes who think they're God's gift to humanity because they can carry a tune. And some of them can't even do that."

I stare at her, my mind racing. Because even though Allie said Mercy called in, I can't drop my fear. Not yet. But maybe if I press for just a little more information . . .

"Sure," I say, hoping I sound more casual than I feel. "But I bet lots of performers get a little jealous, especially if they share a role. It's normal how Lauren's acting, right?"

Liam snorts. "I don't know about normal. I'm pretty sure she'd find a way to push Mercy off the stage if she could figure out a way to make it look like an accident. Certain actors can be pretty cutthroat."

I trip over a discarded pacifier, managing to right myself only at the last second thanks to Ivy catching me by the arm.

"You think she hates her enough to . . . to murder her?" I say, eyes widening.

100

"He's just being dramatic, Greta," Ivy says. "Don't worry. Lauren's a lot of things—flighty, always talking shit, untalented—but she's about as violent as that rock over there."

I blink. "But murderers use rocks to kill people all the time."

And, I want to add, you didn't see her at the party. Because now that I think back, all I can focus on is how she seemed like a snake ready to strike at the first person who moved.

"Okay, so it was a bad metaphor," Ivy says with a shrug. "The point is, don't worry about the performers. All they do is bring drama and bullshit. Liam, back me up here."

I look from Ivy to Liam, waiting for more, but Liam's gone unexpectedly quiet as his eyes find the ground. It makes me think of Allie and Lauren's argument, about the mysterious blood, and I wonder if Liam knows what they were talking about. What did they do to Mercy, and is whatever they did the reason behind her absence?

"Sure, but Mercy's different," Liam says. "You of all people know that, Ivy. Even if—"

"Oh, look!" Ivy says, cutting him off. "We're here already."

I don't miss the look in Ivy's eyes, even as she tries to point me and my gaze to Adventure Theater's marquee looming in the distance. Liam was saying something about Mercy, something that Ivy knows "of all people." But why didn't she want to talk about it? Have I just not earned her trust? I try to read Liam's expression, but he's already pressed ahead, standing under the marquee as he flings his arms wide. The cartoon characters that look over the top of it are cast in shadow from the gondolas overhead, making the whole thing look more ominous than I expected.

"You ready?" Ivy asks, squeezing my shoulder. "No turning back now."

101

She's joking, obviously. To Ivy, this is just another show. Maybe a show with some perks, but still just another show at a job she tolerates. But for me this is a step in the right direction. A step toward Grey. A step toward my new beginning.

And yet, something's been soured. Mercy's absence looms just like the gondolas, and I can't shake the feeling that something's off—even if she did call in sick. It's making me overanalyze everything. Like Ivy. A moment ago, I swore, she looked like she was hiding something, but now, she's smiling easily at me. I *need* to shake this off because I can't afford distractions, not now.

We walk under the marquee toward the blue doors of Adventure Theater. There's upbeat music, triumphant and orchestral, suggesting the promise of intrigue and, well. Adventure.

Everything today seems to have been purposeful, like the hand of fate guiding my path. From talking to Grey in Wardrobe to the show going down at Rocket. But what if it's more than just helping me get to Jungle? What if there are answers here for me? Because if I can unravel whatever it is that Allie and Lauren were talking about, then maybe I can put my mind at ease about Mercy. I just need to keep my eyes and ears open for opportunities.

"I'm ready," I say, following Ivy into the theater.

Adventure Theater is smaller than Rocket, but it sports the same concrete floors and stadium-style blue benches. As soon as we walk in, Liam and Ivy both exhale at the air-conditioning that's keeping the place at least twenty degrees cooler than outside.

"You better be on your game, Dealer," Ivy says, turning to Liam with a wry smile. "It's Greta's first time."

As much as I love Ivy, I wish that she would've chosen literally any other words. I blush all the way down to my lunch-lady shoes, and my only saving grace is that Liam doesn't seem to hear her—or maybe he's pretending not to—as he heads up to his tech booth. Still, that doesn't save me from Ivy's eyebrows as they wag up and down.

"I mean, it's not technically my first time," I try to explain, glancing in Liam's direction. "I saw the show before. I just haven't, um, ushered—"

"Greta! Ivy!" Silvia calls, mercifully saving me from my ramble. She walks over to us with a wide smile, Keenan following behind her.

"What're you doing here?"

"Rocket's down," Ivy says. "Neil told us to come here to help you out. Didn't want us to be 'doing nothing' while we're getting paid."

Silvia sniffs. "Well, I suppose I can understand that. Not that we need much help."

"You're just in time," Keenan says, crossing his arms over his chest. "I was telling Silvia about how I saved someone's life last weekend."

My eyes widen. "You saved someone's life?"

Keenan's grin broadens, though I notice a muscle ticking in Silvia's forehead that warns me that this story might not be as impressive as Keenan's making it out to be. When I glance over at Ivy, she rolls her eyes.

"I was on the beach," he says dramatically, holding his hand above his eyebrows like a sea captain. "Just watching the waves, seeing what there was to be seen. Someone like me, I'm always alert. Always on guard."

Silvia sighs and rubs her temple, but Keenan's undeterred.

"I see this kid in the water, and then I see how the water's moving," Keenan says. "Little guy doesn't even notice that he's in a riptide. But I'm always aware, like I said. So I didn't hesitate. Dove right in."

Ivy snorts. "*That's* how you saved someone's life? You pulled them out of a riptide?"

"Hey, close to one hundred people lose their lives to riptides every year," Keenan snaps, immediately miffed. "It's nothing to joke about."

I look at Silvia. Her mouth has thinned into a line, but she doesn't say anything.

"Sure, but you made it sound like you jumped in front of a car or something," Ivy says. "Aren't you, like, a lifeguard in training? Isn't it your job to pull people out of riptides?"

"The point is," Keenan says, glaring at her, "who knows what might've happened if I wasn't there? In fact, I think the universe made sure I *was* there. Like every moment in my life added up to that moment so I could save that kid."

"Or," Ivy says, "you did the bare minimum of human decency by doing the right thing? Because—"

Silvia waves her hand. "It was very brave, Keenan. We're all very brave. But Ivy was going to tell us why she's here. Ivy?"

"Well, we're basically using this as training time for Greta," Ivy says, seizing the opportunity to change the subject. "Think you could help?"

Silvia brightens. "Ah, of course! I'll give you the tour, Greta."

Keenan stays behind to regale Liam with the story, even though Liam could clearly hear from the tech booth. I let Silvia lead me around the theater, Ivy tagging along as both of them chime in to tell me different details about everything. There are two sets of four doors that lead into the theater from the park side, one set that closes off the theater to the outside world, and others that close off to a hallway that stretches behind the theater and leads to the greenroom.

Silvia tells me that this makes it slightly more complicated for us because we have to make sure that the guests don't sneak around the back and run into a half-naked Dingle the Dalmatian in the greenroom.

The way Silvia talks about the greenroom is as if it's a mystical place. Ushers aren't allowed to go in, and the technician will only enter if there's a problem.

"The show moves too quickly for the cast to use it during the performance, of course," Silvia explains. "They wait in this hall and behind the stage when we're live. But once it's over, the greenroom is their sanctuary."

"You're making it sound way gnarlier than it is," Keenan says with a laugh, appearing from around the corner. "What do you think they have in there, Silvia? Dead bodies? Are they conducting sacrifices? Because I'm pretty sure it's just lockers and a shit ton of body spray, thanks to Grey."

Silvia shakes her head, exuding the kind of energy I associate with trail guides and dog trainers that need to control a situation.

"It's a private place, that's all," Silvia says. "I just want Greta to understand. Are you ready to go? We open in two minutes."

"Relax, relax," Keenan says. "Of course I am."

"Did you forget, Silvia?" Ivy asks innocently. "Keenan's always ready to jump into action."

Keenan starts to say something back, but Silvia gives him a small yet effective push toward the doors. As they go, Ivy shakes her head. She turns to me, smiling broadly.

"Well, time to shine. I know you watched on the first day, but why don't you stay here with Liam and watch from the booth?" Ivy says, pointing up to where Liam's sitting, at the top of the benches. "Try to pay attention to what we do during the show so you can get a sense of the moves. Sound good?"

I nod, even though my immediate urge is to follow Ivy. But Ivy doesn't want a stage-four clinger. She wants a friend who can socialize with anyone, even dealer-technicians with unassuming fluffy hair. So I nod confidently, assuring her that I can handle this.

Liam's tech booth is at the center of the upstairs benches, blocked off slightly by black mini-walls that sit just a little taller than the benches themselves. Liam lets me inside the booth, and I sit down next to him on the blue bench behind the control board. The board itself is marked up with tape and permanent marker and a few sticky notes saying things like *Keep the booth clean* and *Check mics before start*. There's also a showtimes list that's been cut out from the park map and pinned to the side of the booth.

"This is where the magic happens," Liam says, proudly gesturing to the board.

I notice that Liam's button-down shirt is slightly askew. He must have missed the first button or something. I think about telling him, but it seems too intimate. As I'm considering this, a voice from Liam's radio buzzes up, something about a protein spill at Mega Town. Liam turns the knob to the off position.

"No updates about Rocket yet," he says. "I guess they're still working on it. Might be the fuses. That system's a lot fussier than this one."

I nod, watching Keenan move through the audience that's streaming in now. He guides people to their seats, encouraging them to sit near the front. I also notice he's collecting blue and purple passes from some of the guests.

"Those are the volunteers," Liam says, clearly watching me watch the other ushers. "They wave the jaguar puppets around during Hyper Kid's song in the jungle. They hand out passes in the morning to get them here. It was James's idea. It keeps the show fresh and 'unpredictable.' Can be a little bit of a nightmare if a kid goes rogue, like the other day when one of the kids tried to bolt backstage, but it's usually not too bad."

He chuckles a little to himself. "One time, Ivy had to physically catch a kid who tried to launch himself off the stage. It was pretty badass."

I glance at him, realizing as I do that we've somehow gotten closer. He looks up and must realize it, too, because he shifts slightly just as I shift slightly, making our knees briefly touch, though he pulls his back quickly.

"Sorry," he says. "Booth's kind of small."

I know I must be flushing furiously, so I grab the nearest conversation topic I can think of.

"So, have you known Ivy long? She seemed pretty intense about the performers earlier."

I wince almost immediately. This seems almost like gossip, and I don't want Liam to think I'm that kind of person. But thankfully, he just sort of shrugs.

"We've known each other since middle school when I moved into her neighborhood," he says. "She was always a grade above me, but I'd see her walking to and from school. We took a class together in ninth grade, and we just sort of became . . . well, I guess friends."

I smile, arching an eyebrow. "*Just* friends?"

He laughs. "Oh, definitely just friends. I mean, she's awesome, don't get me wrong, but we've always had a brother-sister kind of vibe. Plus, the people she dated were always sort of . . ."

He fumbles on how to describe it, glancing at me sort of sheepishly before finally saying, "Assholes."

I blink.

"Maybe that's not fair," he says. "They weren't all assholes. But I dunno. Ivy always seemed to fall superhard, and the people she went out with just . . . didn't always seem to be as into her as she was into them. Which I always thought was weird, but whatever."

I nudge him with my shoulder. "Are you sure you didn't have a crush on her?"

I don't know why I'm asking, or why my heart seems to flutter as I wait for his answer. I don't care, obviously. I like Grey.

He laughs again, eyes dipping down before rising to mine. In the light of the theater, his brown eyes spark with light as they blink at me, his lashes impossibly long. The kind of lashes that one hundred coats of mascara would never get me anywhere close to.

"Definitely not," he says quietly. "When I know I like someone, it's always pretty obvious."

I stare at him, at the intensity in his eyes, then look away as my heart thuds in my chest. I keep my eyes ahead, focused on Keenan as he chats with some of the guests. It's safe to watch Keenan.

"So," Liam says, drawing me back to him. "Did you wanna tell me what you really thought I was looking at on my phone yesterday?"

Instantly, it's like everything stops moving again, like I'm back underwater at the table. It's like I'm watching the boy amoeba get closer and closer, hearing Logan warn Ivy about me. I'm melting under the weight of the Wardrobe girl's eyes. My secret, dangling closer and closer to the edge.

"I mean, you don't have to," Liam says quickly, because apparently he can read on my face that he's hit a nerve. "I just . . . shit, sorry. I shouldn't have said anything."

I glance at him. He looks actually apologetic, which, I guess, if I think about it, makes a little bit of sense. Of course he doesn't understand why I would freak out on him. He's a dealer, a dangerous guy, perhaps, but in this moment, he doesn't seem like he's trying to be a dick. He seems like he knows he's stepped in it and is stumbling to recover.

"I just wanted you to know that you can tell me, you know, if I'm doing something that bugs you," he says. "Like, it's cool. I won't do it again. But, you know, I just didn't know what I . . . you know what, never mind."

I blink at him. I recognize the look of alarm and "What the hell did I just say?" flashing across his face because I've been there. And maybe this is me ignoring an obvious red flag, but I can't help it. I have to throw him something to pull himself out of this hole.

"I've only met one other Liam before," I say, steering this conversation firmly into safe territory. "He was one of a set of twins. His brother was Noah, and they were British. But you don't seem British."

He jumps on the lifeline, smiling. "I dunno, I guess? My dad picked it because it's Irish, and he's mostly Irish. My mom didn't like it at first. She said I didn't look like a Liam, especially as a baby."

As he says it, I imagine a smaller, rounder version of Liam, though with the same amount of fluffy black hair.

"What did she want to name you?"

"Javier," he says. "After my grandpa."

"Interesting," I say.

"She got the other two names," Liam continues. "Danilo and Miramontes. Danilo's my grandpa's middle name on her dad's side, and then Miramontes is my mom's last name."

"Guessing they're not Irish?"

Liam laughs. "No, definitely not. My mom's half Filipino and half Mexican."

I nod, remembering the taco and lumpia conversation from before.

"Well," I say. "I'm not exactly sure what I am. I thought about doing that spit DNA test, but my mom saw some documentary about how they track you with it, so we just guessed."

When I finish, Liam's brown eyes are a little wider, but he doesn't say anything.

"So do all the shows besides Rocket need technicians for every show?" I ask, keeping the conversation going. This new, safe conversation that doesn't make my heart beat faster than necessary.

Liam nods. "Right now, we just have Jungle and Mega Boost. They both need sound cues, and this one needs sound and light cues. With Mega, only one character is mic'd up, so you have to time all the dialogue with the rest of the performers' mouths, you know, since it's a stunt show. We do a little of that here, but not a lot. Mostly, it's all live dialogue."

He picks up a set of black headphones, holding up one side to his ear. Then he smiles at me. "Wanna listen? It's just them getting ready."

I stare at the headphones. The performers. Mic'd up. Grey's words waiting for me to hear them. I barely contain the urge to rip the headphones from Liam's hand, forcing myself instead to gingerly take them from him before putting them on.

"—hiding something from me." My whole body stills. It's Allie. "Don't bullshit me."

I shouldn't be hearing this. Liam clearly didn't expect this crackling anger on the other end of these headphones. My eyes dart to him, waiting for him to take them away, but then he flashes me a thumbs-up instead, reminding me I'm the only one who's hearing this. And as much as I know I should stop listening, I can't. Especially when I hear the next voice, one that makes my heart tumble.

"No one's hiding anything," Grey says, his voice deep and rhythmic. My toes tingle at the sound of it.

"Lauren told me what she saw at the party," Allie continues. "I can't believe you'd do that, and—"

"You're believing Lauren now?" Grey asks. "After everything? What about what *you're* hiding, Allie? What about—"

Suddenly, another voice washes over Grey's, a high-pitched female voice that drowns out his and Allie's conversation completely.

"Test, test, test, test—oh, shit, where's my mask?"

Then lots of scratching sounds, and suddenly, Liam's hand is brushing against mine so that I almost fall off the bench.

"Sorry," he says, gently taking the headphones back from me. "It's time."

Right. Time for the show. I catch my breath and turn toward the stage as, out of the corner of my eyes, I see Liam press several buttons. Grey and Allie's conversation sticks in my mind, like honey trapped on your fingertips that you can't quite get off.

What about what you're *hiding, Allie?*

I knew Allie wasn't trustworthy, and here's my proof. And yes, Allie also accused Grey, but clearly, she can't be trusted. She's flinging things at Grey to hide her own dubious intentions. And Lauren. Both of them are involved in this—I just need to figure out how.

I pull out my phone, hiding it under the corner of the booth and turning the brightness down. I check my text thread with Mercy, just in case a message has come through. But there's still nothing.

Allie did something. Lauren *definitely* did something. She cleaned up the blood, after all. But how can I figure out what? I tuck my phone back into my pocket, trying to focus. The lights go down in the audience and flare up on the stage so that we can see that we're in some kind of museum, based on the portraits and paintings hung on the white walls. There's a pause, and then a guitar riff streaks through the theater and Dingle's characteristic bark sounds from backstage.

Immediately, the crowd screams with applause. I'm caught up in their rumble, their anticipation as Dingle's dog-bark sound effect travels as though Dingle is running right next to us, then behind us, then next to us again. Then two masked people covered head to toe in black appear on the stage.

"Get that dog!"

"Dogs aren't allowed in a museum!"

Next to me, I see Liam clicking the buttons that start these sound effects and, I realize, the dialogue. The two figures on the stage aren't actually projecting these bits of dialogue—Liam is.

Liam sees me looking and smiles, whispering, "Those are actually the performers who play Perky the Panda and Grimson, the bad guy. They double as the security guards."

More barking. The men run after the sound, and then we hear

the skittering of dog paws and an explosion of gold confetti over the stage as—bam!

A trapdoor is thrown open, and from it, the unmistakable form of Dingle the Dalmatian emerges. It's obviously not really a dalmatian. This is clearly a person in a dalmatian suit, a person whose hands are covered by paw-gloves and whose face is painted white to blend in with the rest of the costume.

"There's Kara," Liam whispers again, unaware of my racing mind. "She's the best Dingle."

"Run, Dingle!"

Just then, Allie bursts onto the scene, decked out in head-to-toe khaki. From looking at her now, long hair pulled back in two braids, beaming as she strikes a pose for the audience, you'd never know she's done anything wrong in her life.

The mic'd conversation circles back to me at the sight of her. It hits me that Allie's also clearly trying to deflect this onto Grey, trying to pin him with something he has no idea about. She accused him, didn't she, of hiding something? But she's the one with secrets, and I'm not going to let her get away with it. In fact, I'm starting to think she lied about Mercy calling in, too. Maybe she put words in Grey's mouth. I don't know. But I intend to figure it out, especially since I can't help but feel like I'm *meant* to figure it out.

Something inside me prickles, Keenan's words from earlier echoing.

I think the universe made sure I was there. Like every moment in my life added up to that moment so I could save that kid.

What if Mercy's been pulled into her own deadly riptide?

What if I'm the one who's supposed to pull her out?

With that thought in mind, I glance to the hall that leads to the greenroom.

What do you think they have in there, Silvia? Dead bodies?

I know Keenan was exaggerating when he said that. But what if that's where my answers are?

"I'll be right back," I tell Liam, sliding out of the booth. "I just need to check something really quick."

Before he can say anything, I've snaked my way through the crowd and out the back doors, the ones that lead to the path behind the theater that pops you out right next to the greenroom. I think Ivy catches me leaving, but I move quickly, both to avoid disrupting the show and to slip away from her eyes.

The door's unlocked, so I open it and step inside. It's empty, filled with the smell of paint and apple air freshener. There're three couches, a row of lockers, and a bulletin board with showtimes, the week's schedule, and various objects that must represent inside jokes. The walls are covered in black-and-white photographs of shows past. There're a few color printouts, too, some headshots, and some framed clippings from magazines. And in the middle of it all, there's one framed headshot and a small plaque with a pair of photos next to it.

I move toward the headshot, even though I can already guess who it is. Long dark hair. Deep brown eyes. Full, pouty lips smiling in a way that suggests she knows you've already hired her.

Hailey Anne Portman, it says.

November 2, 1986–June 20, 2005

I turn from Hailey's face to the plaque and the pictures. One of the pictures looks like it must be from the original Hyper Kid show because I recognize the Adventure Theater stage, plus the cosmic-themed costumes. Hailey's in the middle, beaming in a silver dress. The photo next to it is of another show, maybe local theater, and Hailey's also in the middle, though this time, the whole cast is in 1950s-style costumes, with Hailey in a formfitting white dress. I focus next on the plaque, reading the short tribute.

This greenroom is dedicated to Hailey, who sang every note like it was her last. May her talent be a light to all of us.

For a moment, I just stare at the words and at Hailey, looking back at her in the photos. Whether in her headshot or the group photos, there's no denying where your eye goes. Her smile is an anchor, yanking you forward. I focus on the non–Hyper Kid cast photo, reaching out to touch it through the frame. She looks younger here, but also entirely grown-up in a way I don't think I'll ever look. Worldly in the way the seniors at school always are, like they've learned secrets about life that we'll never dream of.

I force myself to pull away from Hailey, remembering that I came in here for answers, and I don't have much time. The show's only twenty minutes, after all, and it's already partway done.

I don't even know what I'm looking for. I decide I'll look through the lockers. Maybe Grey's. As a lead, he might have some kind of report about what happened. Not that he'd probably keep that in his locker . . . but still. I need to check. I can't explain why, only that I feel like if I don't, I'll lose out on something important. Like a call you have to answer, even if you don't know who's on the other end of the line.

But instead of Grey's, I open Allie's locker first. It's decorated with Polaroids of her at the beach, posing next to a surfboard. She looks so gorgeous that my stomach hurts. But other than that, there's nothing but spare makeup, deodorant, and a cream-colored crochet-weave bag that her phone's sticking out of. It's in a thick, gauzy pink case, and at the sight of it, my fingers itch to grab it.

But no. I can't go through Allie's bag, let alone her phone. God, what am I doing here? What am I even looking for? Instantly, my breath quickens. Once again, I've found myself in a precarious position.

You don't think things through, Greta. You never have.

It's my dad's voice now, flitting through my mind. His disappointed tone from that last meeting, the one when my entire life imploded.

I slam Allie's locker shut. This was a bad idea. A very, very bad idea. I need to get out of here. Fast. I move away from Allie's locker like it's a spider poised to jump, forcing my feet toward the door—

But then, I stop.

There's a locker at the very end of the row, door wide open. It's full of small, clear bags of makeup and toiletries that are so organized I wonder if they've ever been used. But it's the name on one of the bags that makes me stop.

Mercy.

I move like someone possessed toward Mercy's locker, as if it's calling me forward. Unlike Allie's locker, there isn't a bag or a purse in this one. Of course there isn't. Because Mercy isn't here.

But there is something else.

It's a playbill for a show, and I pull it out to get a closer look. The paper feels glossy under my fingertips, and I trace the show's title at the top where it's written in blocky handwriting: *A Streetcar Named Desire*. Underneath the title, there's a sketch of an old-timey house, and I run my fingertip along that as well. As I do, something inside the playbill slips, and two pieces of paper flutter to the floor. I pick them up, expecting the announcements they sometimes tuck into a playbill when the cast has a last-minute change. But instead, both slips are handwritten, though that's where the similarities end. One looks like it was scribbled on scratch paper in large, swirling letters, while the other is on lined paper and folded up so I can't see what's written at a glance. I look at the first one, scanning the page.

> LITTLE MISS MERCY. LITTLE MISS PERFECT.
> I'M WARNING YOU, BITCH.
> DON'T EVER DO THAT SHIT AGAIN. DON'T FORGET WHAT I CAN DO TO YOU ON THAT STAGE <u>AND</u> OFF IT. AND IF YOU CROSS ME AGAIN, I SWEAR TO GOD I'LL BREAK YOUR PRETTY LITTLE NECK.

I stare at it, horrified. There's no name signed at the bottom, but I've only heard one person call Mercy "Little Miss Mercy." I turn it over, trying to find anything else, but there's nothing. I slide my fingertip under the fold of the lined paper, holding on to the playbill and other letter with my other hand. But just as I'm starting to open it, footsteps outside startle me.

"Greta?"

Oh no. I whip around, hitting the locker door with my shoulder as I do, the sharp sting zipping up my arm. Ignoring the pain, I stuff the playbill and notes into my thankfully oversize back pocket.

Across from me, the door cracks open, followed by Liam and his arched eyebrow.

"I was worried you got sick or something," he says, stepping into the room. "Since you ran out. The show's over, but the cast is doing meet and greets—they'll be back soon. I didn't see you outside, so I figured you might be here."

"I got lost," I stammer, knowing that I must be turning beet red. "And, um, you were right. I did feel sick. All the light effects, I think. So I found the closest bathroom. But I wasn't actually sick. False alarm."

There's no way he buys it, but I put on my best smile and take a big step away from the locker to try to salvage this. I don't think he saw me holding the papers, but they feel heavy in my pocket anyway.

"Well, the performers should be wrapping up soon, so we should probably head back," Liam says, looking from me to the locker. "If you're feeling okay, of course."

Is he mocking me? I can't tell. But either way, he turns around and steps outside. As he does, I slide my hand into my pocket, pushing the papers farther down so they don't peek out over the top. Then I follow him out into the sunshine, matching his steps as we walk back toward the theater.

And only just in time, too.

The performers come around the corner, laughing, their faces sweaty and makeup slightly smudged. Lauren's at the front, her red-panda head cradled under one arm, black rings around her sharp eyes.

Eyes that lock on me.

The notes seem to burn through the fabric of my shorts as I fight to keep my breathing normal. I look down, avoiding her gaze as she slips past me into the greenroom. I don't breathe until she's disappeared inside.

What did you do, Lauren?

CHAPTER ELEVEN

MONDAY, JUNE 16
1:23 P.M.

AS WE MAKE our way back to the theater, Neil calls us to let us know that it looks like Rocket will be down through the end of the day. He gives us his blessing to stay at Jungle and even goes so far as to bring our stuff over for us, which Ivy says was just his excuse to look through her latest romance novel.

Still, I'm grateful. Working at Jungle is infinitely better than working at Rocket, mostly because we actually have relatively huge stretches of time in between each show. It's not like at Rocket where one show ends and another pretty much begins, save for at lunch. Here, we have roughly an hour between the end of one show and the beginning of the next show's preshow.

Initially, I thought this might give me time to give the notes and playbill another look, but there's nowhere to really hide with them since ushers and technicians take their breaks in the theater itself. So I tuck the papers and playbill into my bag and try to put them out of my mind, then pull out my phone to try to find anything I can on Mercy to satiate my burgeoning obsession.

Unfortunately, Mercy Goodwin is a ghost.

A few websites pop up that list Mercy Goodwin's theater résumé, along with her headshots. There are also a handful of newspaper articles about local theater productions that she was a part of. At first, excitement thrums through me as I scan the different titles, looking for *A Streetcar Named Desire*, but it's not on her list. But why else would she have the playbill, unless maybe it was her favorite play or part of her personal collection? I put the thought aside and keep searching, eventually finding an obituary for her mother, Miriam "Mimi" Melrose, in which Mercy is listed as her only surviving relative. Here there are pictures of Mercy's mom, a pretty woman with waves just like Mercy's. In one photo, she's beaming as she points to signs above that say Broadway and West 34th Street, which reminds me of what the news spot said about Mercy being bound for Broadway. Seeing this reminds me of Hailey, who was also supposed to be bound for Broadway. That's what Silvia said, after all.

A chill zips through me, and not just from Adventure's highly effective air-conditioning. More and more, I'm starting to worry that Mercy met the same fate as Hailey. Especially with that note.

And if you cross me again, I swear to God I'll break your pretty little neck.

I close out of my search on Mercy and bring up a new one on Hailey. There're obviously way more results for Hailey. I find childhood pictures of her at dance recitals and talent shows and see that before Hyper Kid she was in local theater. But somehow, every article finds a way to bring it back to her death.

It's not surprising, I guess. What made Hailey's life unique was how it ended. Maybe, if she'd had more time, there would've been more to write about. But she didn't.

I finally end up on the same article that Neil was reading earlier. It was written five years ago on the fifteenth anniversary of her death and mostly focuses on what I already know, though near the end I'm surprised to see a few new details.

> That night, Portman spent most of her time dancing and socializing with other performers in the Entertainment department. During rehearsals, Portman is said to have become close with several other talented actresses in the show. We caught up with them to see how life changed that night because of this grisly tragedy.
>
> "You just never think it will happen to you," says Rebecca Kerrigan, now 36. "We were just hanging out that night, talking about boys we liked and boys we didn't like. Hailey left us to go pick up stuff from her locker, and she just never came back. How does that even happen?"
>
> Another performer, Krystal McCartney, now 39, agrees.
>
> "I'm telling you, you don't know how many times I replay that night in my head," she laments. "Why didn't we insist on going with her? Why didn't we make her stay with us? I know the answer. We didn't imagine something like this could happen. But part of me thinks that I knew something was going to happen. I can't explain it. I just had a bad feeling. And I wish every single day that I had listened to it."

I stop reading. It feels like the wind's been knocked out of me. Because that is exactly how I feel about Mercy right now. Like I *know* something's happened, even if I can't put my finger exactly on what.

By the time we're on our last break before the last show, my mind feels like a full-on hive of bees. I need to do something to distract myself.

I would bother Ivy, but she's asleep, *He Called Her Name* splayed across her face to block out the lights. And Liam's on the stage now, using the extra time to work on the trapdoor, which Lauren complained was "still sticking" during the last show, whatever that means. I consider the fact that Liam seems to know Mercy, at least a little, from working at Jungle with her. And, even though he's a questionable source, given his nefarious activity, I can't ignore that he's an option for information.

I glance at where Liam's fluff of hair sticks up from beneath the stage, then make my decision.

I walk up the small set of stairs on the side of the stage, and from this angle I can see his face and his hands as they jostle some kind of tool into the mechanism beneath the stage.

"Hey," I say, quietly to not wake Ivy.

"Hey," he says, matching my volume.

"Can I help?" I ask, pointing at what he's currently battling with a wrench. At least, I think it's a wrench.

He glances at me, then nods. "Sure. Can you hold this piece still?"

He taps one of the boards that snaps in place for the trapdoor. It looks like, at one point, it fit smoothly, but now it's bent slightly, so the bolt keeps popping out. I sit down next to him and hold it as straight as I can, watching Liam's hands. His phone buzzes on the stage next to him, and he peeks at it without stopping his work. But whoever is texting him, he ignores.

For a moment, we sit in silence, me holding the piece while he works on it with his various tools. As he does, I think about the different ways I could try to start this conversation, and I wish I had time to research the right way to handle it. But that would look weird, if I stopped now and pulled out my phone. So I decide to ask the most obvious question I can think of.

"What's wrong with it?" I ask, nodding down at the trapdoor. "Lauren said it was sticking?"

He twists the wrench. "It's been broken since yesterday morning. I don't actually know what happened. It was fine when I left on Saturday."

I nod, biting the inside of my cheek. How can I steer the conversation to Mercy? I need a strong transition, a way to effortlessly guide the conversation so he thinks I'm just talking casually about a mutual coworker. I consider the words, but nothing sounds right. I need to speak soon or this silence will eat us both alive. Need to say something. Need—

"How well do you know Mercy?" I ask, the words falling out of my mouth before I can stop them.

He blinks, looking up at me before wiping his forehead with his free hand.

"I mean, not really well, I guess?" Liam says. "Just, like I said before, I think she's really talented. Why?"

"I just . . . it really doesn't seem like her," I say. "To not show up for work. Not that I know her or anything. But just, you know, from what you guys have said about her . . ."

Liam nods. "She definitely takes this job seriously. But everybody has emergencies."

"Yeah," I say, because that is true. "It's just . . . I dunno. Was she, um . . . was she okay? At work?"

I can tell by the way that Liam's eyebrows arch up that he's totally confused about why I'm asking this. Why I'm prying into Mercy Goodwin's life. I could tell him about the conversation I had with her, but that seems . . . invasive. That was a private moment between me and her, and I shouldn't be just throwing that into random conversation. And I definitely can't mention what I found in her locker. He'll for sure decide I'm a weirdo and not give me anything at all.

For a moment, Liam just sort of watches me. Then, with a small sigh, he speaks.

"I don't know that she really gets along with the other performers," he says. "On a personal level."

This makes me sit up. "Really?"

He shrugs. "She just kind of does her own thing. She's really focused on her future, on the next level. And they're . . . well, this is just kind of a job to them, you know?"

I wince. I know that feeling. That feeling where you take everything seriously and no one else does. It basically describes every group project I've ever been a part of. An endless list of tags on Google Docs and presentations with my name on them because "Greta should do it since she cares so fucking much."

I realize I haven't answered Liam's question. That he's watching me, waiting for me to tell him why I'm bringing it up in the first place. And maybe I can tell him something without telling him everything. So I don't look crazy. So he knows why I care.

"I know this sounds super weird," I admit. "But you know the party? You were there, right? Well, I talked to her there, and she seemed sort of . . . anxious. Freaked out, even. She kept looking around like she was expecting someone to pop in."

I glance up at Liam's eyes, knowing that I'm rambling, which is exactly why I shouldn't have started this. But now that I have, I find that I can't stop.

"And also, Lauren was really pissed that the TV thing focused on Mercy. She said she wanted to find her and . . . well, I don't know what, but she sounded pissed. And what you just said, about Mercy not getting along with everyone . . . well, it's just . . . what if they did something?"

Liam arches an eyebrow. "Did something? Like what?"

"I'm not going full *Dateline* panic or anything here," I say quickly, even as my brain screams that yes, I am going full *Dateline* panic. "But there's more. I overheard Lauren and Allie arguing about Mercy 'deserving' something, and they talked about blood and, well, Allie straight-up admitted to hiding something when I was listening to her mic—"

"You heard them talking about Mercy?" Liam cuts in, pausing his fight with the trapdoor to look at me directly.

"I know I shouldn't have been listening," I say, bristling. "But you were the one who gave me the headphones, and I—"

"No," Liam says, cutting me off, but not in a harsh way. In fact, he has the nerve to wince after he does it, glancing back at where Ivy's still passed out.

"Sorry," he says. "I just meant . . . I wasn't saying you were wrong to listen. They're not supposed to say anything private on those things. They know I can hear. I just meant . . ."

He's fumbling for words, and he looks down as he runs a hand through his hair. A nervous habit, I realize. But why is he nervous?

"I know this sounds weird," I say, drawing his gaze back to me. "I know *I* sound completely unhinged. But you know Mercy and everyone else, right? So please, just tell me Mercy's totally fine and I'm making a big deal out of nothing. Tell me so I can stop thinking about this."

He doesn't answer. The room is completely silent. So silent that I can't help but turn around to see Ivy, still passed out on the bench, her book splayed across her face. But when I look back, Liam's watching me almost as carefully as he was watching that trapdoor while he tried to fix it with his wrench.

His eyes also wander to Ivy, then back to me. His voice drops even lower this time when he speaks.

"I don't think you're unhinged, Greta," he says in a voice that sounds almost . . . rumpled. Can a voice sound rumpled? Liam's does. "Really. I don't," he adds.

It's the tiniest affirmation, the slightest vote of confidence, and it undoes me completely. Because now, I'm not just rambling. I'm steamrolling any semblance of leaving this conversation sounding slightly sane.

"She was terrified at that party, Liam," I say. "And what if they're who she was terrified of? What if they did something to her? I know Allie said she called in sick, but what if something's happened that made her do that? Or what if it's a lie? She had told me she wanted to tell me something, but then she didn't show up to work and she's not answering my texts. And I know I don't know her that well, but it's just . . . well, you said it yourself. That's not like her."

His eyes widen, then drop, then lift up to mine again. It's like he's weighing something, and then he glances over at Ivy. I follow his gaze. She's still asleep, book on her face.

"At the bigger theme parks, the director's usually at all the shows, or almost all the shows," Liam explains, choosing each word with care. "For quality control and to see how audiences are reacting. But since James is a supervisor *and* a director—and because, well, Hyper Kid's sort of cheap—he can't be at all the shows. And when he wasn't here . . . well, the other performers did things to Mercy."

"Like what?" I ask, heart racing.

"Nothing that extreme," Liam says. "Like moving her presets before shows, swapping her shoes with a pair that was too small."

I deflate a little. None of those things sound intense enough to match what I read in the note.

"Why would they do that?" I ask, then remember Lauren at the party. "Was it just jealousy?"

Liam chews his lip.

"I mean, Mercy didn't exactly make herself popular," he says. "Giving notes to other performers is never a good idea. That's the director's job. And—"

"So she deserved it?" I say, puffing up immediately.

"No, definitely not," he says quickly. "I'm just saying. She was a little intense, that's all. And they obviously took it too far."

I glare at him. "It sounds like you're taking their side."

He sighs and pinches the bridge of his nose before looking back at me.

"Greta, I'm trying to say that it's possible they did something," he says. "It might not be as bad as you're thinking, but they were always the worst when James wasn't around, and now that he's on his retreat . . . I dunno. It's possible; that's all I'm saying."

"I know something's wrong," I say, the sudden and fervent need to prove myself to him pulsing through me. "If only I could . . . I don't know, find out more about her. Talk to more people."

"Because you need to make sure she's okay?" Liam asks, voice soft in a way that makes me blush at his question.

"Of course," I say, voice shaking slightly. "Once I know she's fine, I won't have to worry about this anymore."

For a moment, Liam doesn't say anything. He snaps something together on the trapdoor, then sits back, the work apparently completed. Then he turns his gaze to me and smiles.

"Well, it's not listening on a hot mic, but you could always ask around tonight," Liam says.

"Tonight? What's tonight?"

He tilts his head. "Ivy didn't tell you?"

I stare at him, opening my mouth to respond, when someone answers behind me.

"Ivy didn't tell her what?"

I spin, and Ivy's standing on the stage, one hand on her hip, the other checking her nails. My heart turns to stone. How long has she been here? What did she hear?

"About bowling tonight," Liam says, grabbing a can of WD-40 before walking over to spray it on the right wall's hinges. "Did you not tell her?"

"Shit," she says, gently smacking herself in the forehead with the heel of her hand. "I mean, technically, this is also Gene's fault. He's been your official trainer, so he was supposed to tell you. But still."

"A staff event?" I ask, heart starting to beat even faster.

"Please tell me you're free," Ivy continues, reaching out to grab my hands like she's guiding me in prayer. "Neil will kill me if I fucked this up by forgetting to tell you. It's my job to give you the 'official calendar,' but I forgot with Gene and his five-hundred-page training manual. It's a twentieth-anniversary thing. We're going bowling."

"Of course," I say, feeling more frazzled by the second. "But . . . it's tonight? After work?"

Ivy nods, dropping our hands. "Yeah, right down the road. The shitty bowling alley in Del Cruz, or, I guess, *one* of the shitty bowling alleys in Del Cruz. It's 2000s-themed since, you know. Twenty years. People are dressing up, but you don't have to. It's whatever as long as you're there."

Something inside me lights up. Dressing up. Meaning, I'll have another chance to make Grey see me as more than an usher, to wear something that isn't my polo. To talk to him. To charm him. Maybe even to ask him about what it is that Allie's been up to, or get a better read on what he thinks happened to Mercy.

"Absolutely," I say. "I will absolutely be there."

Ivy laughs, typing something out into her phone. "Don't get too excited. It's still a staff party. Can one of you drive us?"

She's turned back to where Liam is standing, finished with the wall, his face looking slightly drawn as he watches me. Our conversation buzzes in my mind, just as, in my pocket, my phone actually buzzes. I pull it out and find Ivy's address, sent to me via text. I'm panicking, realizing I'm going to have to tell her that I'm not legally allowed to drive passengers.

But then Liam says, "Sure, I'll drive," saving me from the embarrassment.

"Great," Ivy says. "It's settled, then. Text Liam your address."

Something in my heart thumps. Liam. Driving me to bowling. Well, not just driving me. Driving Ivy and me.

"Right," I say, then, realizing that sounds too eager, I add, "It's cool."

I am so failing at being effortless, but thankfully, Ivy just grins before turning around to jump down off the stage. Which leaves me with Liam, who's watching me with his brown eyes sparking in the theater light.

I'm already regretting telling him as much as I did, for rambling. But at this point, I don't have a choice. I have to trust him a little bit, even with everything I know about him.

Even if there's a voice inside—a voice that sounds a lot like Caroline—telling me that this is a huge mistake.

CHAPTER TWELVE

MONDAY, JUNE 16
6:54 P.M.

THE MORE I think about it, the more I'm convinced that this is my destiny.

I'm the one who's supposed to find Mercy, the one who's supposed to pull her out of the clutches of whatever metaphorical ocean has seized her. It's up to me to look into this because clearly, I'm the only one sufficiently concerned. I texted her again before clocking out, but as expected, I haven't heard anything back. But that's okay. I'll keep trying. And in the meantime, I've decided to treat tonight like an actual investigation. One that will hopefully lead to answers that I can make sense of.

Answers that lead me to Mercy so that I can save her.

Although, I can't completely banish the thought that something... irreversible might have happened to her. But I do my best to bury said thoughts, telling myself I'm getting ahead of myself and being overly dramatic, something a true investigator would never do.

When I looked up first investigation steps online, one of the most frequently referenced steps was to check the places that the missing person would normally occupy, which means I need to find out where Mercy lives. I did a Google search to find Mercy's home address and found one listed in Del Cruz as occupied by both Mercy Goodwin and Rachel Goodwin. I couldn't figure out who Rachel Goodwin is, but I assume she's a relative. If Mercy's not home, hopefully Rachel will at least be able to give me more information.

Do I have time to do this? Probably not, given that Liam and Ivy are picking me up soon. But I can't help it. I have to check. It's like an itch on my heart that needs to be scratched, and I have no choice but to give in to it.

As I drive to Del Cruz, I put on a playlist meant to support me in transitioning into an investigative state. I figured it's like the calming playlist Mom uses when she's trying not to stress out about an event she's planning . . . but for me, it'll help me solve crimes. I found it on Spotify, and yes, I mostly just repeated the *Criminal Minds* theme song, but I do think it got me into the necessary headspace. By the time I'm pulling into the cul-de-sac that Mercy lives on, I'm buzzing with possibility.

Mercy's address leads to a small duplex tucked away in the corner. There's a well-manicured yard and a few rosebushes in the front, and it ultimately reminds me of the calendars that Mom likes to buy with pictures of cookie-cutter houses and cookie-cutter animals. In other words, very little personality, unless that personality is old and floral.

I gather my courage, walk up to the door, and knock, steeling myself for this conversation. But even after waiting for what feels like minutes, there's no answer. Not even the telltale footsteps of someone coming to check who is there through their peephole. I ring the doorbell, too, listening as it echoes in the house.

Nothing.

Dread pools in my stomach, but I tell myself it's not a crisis that no one's home. It doesn't mean anything. It just means that, for now, this house is a dead end. I need to focus on my other clues, the ones I already have in my possession.

I started leafing through the playbill in my car before I left, but then I looked up and saw Grey walking past. I couldn't risk letting him—or anyone else—see what I had in case he recognized it as Mercy's and realized I stole it from her locker. So I forced myself to wait. Even here, I spot nosy neighbors walking by, looking at me in my idling car. I need to get home and look through these where no one can stop me or judge me. Luckily, I still have a little bit of time before bowling.

I leave Mercy's house and drive home, then sprint in past a confused Mom in the kitchen, shouting at her that I have to get ready for a work event.

And I *do* actually need to get ready for a work event. In fact, my outfit should be the pinnacle of my concern. But that can wait. That *must* wait until I've taken a closer look at everything I brought home from Mercy's locker.

I let Jasper into my room, lock the door, and sit on the floor. He curls up nearby to observe the proceedings, then yawns and promptly falls asleep. As he snores, I gingerly extract the papers from my bag, turning each one over in my hand like a precious artifact before spreading them out on the rug in front of me.

I examine the playbill first, opening it to look inside. It looks pretty standard: list of cast and crew, biographies, a few advertisements. I flip back to the beginning, scanning the cast again in case Mercy's name just wasn't listed online. And as I do, my breath catches in my throat.

Because Mercy's name isn't there. But *Hailey Portman's* is.

Hailey Portman? As in *the* Hailey Portman? I flip through to the biographies, looking for Hailey's picture.

And there it is. Her dark eyes are settled on me, watching me through the camera all those years ago. Almost like she was waiting for me to find her.

This is a playbill to Hailey's show. But why would Mercy have it? I turn it over, finding the back's been torn. For a moment, I worry that I did that, but then I see how soft the edges of the paper are, like they've been handled like this for a long time. I remember the plaque in the greenroom, the one of Hailey, and consider that maybe this is a keepsake that goes with the plaque. Maybe it's something all the cast members hold on to for luck? I don't know. I've heard theater people have traditions like that, but I'm not sure.

I set the playbill down and turn to the notes. I reread the one from earlier—the one I'm almost positive Lauren wrote—but don't find anything new or revelatory, even with the *Criminal Minds* theme echoing in my head. So I finally unfold the note on lined paper, finding the handwriting to be tight and cramped on the page. I read slowly, taking in every letter the way a true investigator would.

> To the light of my heart,
>
> I know you're torn now. You don't want to admit to me what you feel, but I see it. You think you have to leave me behind, but you don't understand. I'm going to go with you. You'll never be alone now. I will follow

you every step of the way, and we'll shine together. We're meant to be: two stars in the same beautiful sky.

Let your heart tell you what to do. Let it lead you directly into my arms.

"Greta!" Mom's voice singsongs up the stairs. "Do you need any help getting ready? Do you want me to curl your hair?"

Her voice startles Jasper awake, and he barks as if there's some unseen threat and rushes over to the door at Mom's voice, walking all over the playbill and the other note. I manage to snatch them before he completely ruins them with his stomping, cursing as I do.

"Hon?" Mom calls again. "Did you say yes?"

"I'm fine!" I shout back, hysterical as I let a whining Jasper out of my room. "I'm totally fine!"

But I'm not fine. My whole body's shaking as I hold on to the playbill and the papers. One letter of hate and one of love. Why was Mercy keeping these things? And who was writing to her and calling her the "light" of their heart? I try to think back to her at the party. This letter suggests the person was giving Mercy the choice to be with them. Did she reject them? And if she did, what did they do as a result?

I check the time on my phone. Liam's going to be here in fifteen minutes. I really do need to get ready. But I can't. Not yet.

In a moment of complete lost sanity, I pull up Mercy's thread. This time, I don't text her. I call her, holding my breath as it rings.

But I don't have to wait long, because, after just one ring, it goes to voicemail. Mercy's voice fills my ears, soft and quiet.

"Hi there, this is Mercy Goodwin," she says. "I can't come to the phone right now, but please leave me a message. Thank you."

And then, a harsher, more robotic voice jumps in.

"The mailbox of the person you are trying to dial is full. Goodbye."

It clicks off, and I stare at my phone. I contemplate checking Mercy's social media. It's the next logical step, after all the research I did earlier, but that would mean reactivating my own accounts. I've deleted all the apps, and I'm not sure I'm ready to reopen them. Still . . . isn't it the easiest way to get what I'm looking for? I look down at my phone, suddenly regarding it like a potentially poisonous plant.

Later, maybe. For now, I need to get ready. I don't have time to think of anything on theme, so I haphazardly choose black denim shorts and a faded gray tank top that I think looks semi-vintage. I twist my messy hair absently into a claw clip and ignore the eyeliner that I should touch up, swiping on some gloss that I dig out of my purse. I'm ninety-nine percent sure it's expired, but I don't have time to find anything else.

My phone buzzes, and I launch myself to catch it as it vibrates toward the edge of my dresser, then sit back as I open up the notification. A text from Ivy.

> sooooo sorry i think whatever made you sick earlier has gotten me. i feel like shit.

I panic. Just me and Liam? No, no, no . . . that's bound to go the absolute wrong way.

Me: But isn't it mandatory?? What about Neil???

It's too many question marks—Caroline used to hate when I wrote texts like that—but I send it anyway. Ivy's response comes back quickly.

i'll handle neil. just go have fun. 😌

Then, after another second passes, there's another text.

actually could you do me a huge favor?? i'm supposed to change the showtimes tomorrow and i think i really need to sleep in. can you do it?

I stare at the texts. I've never changed the showtimes before. I'm pretty sure it involves keys and magnets, but that's all I know. Yet at the same time, Ivy's asking me for a favor. My fingers are hovering over my phone when she texts again.

liam knows how to do it... i'm sure he'd show you if you asked 😌

Which I don't understand. Is she insinuating something? I decide to ignore it.

Me: Of course. I'll ask him tonight.

If there even is a tonight. In fact, maybe I should cancel. Maybe—
"Hon, your date's here!"
It's Mom's voice, carrying up the stairs of our house so loudly that I want to scream. Because she did not just say "date," did she? And did Liam hear her? Oh, god.
I sprint down the stairs, mortified to find Liam already standing in the doorway, chatting away with my mom as Jasper circles him. Mom's laughing at something he just said, and then she sees me and smiles.

"There she is!" Mom declares. "Greta, I was just telling him about how you tried out for gymnastics—"

"Running late," I say, nearly falling down the stairs to cut her off. Because yeah, okay, I tried out for gymnastics. But I did not *make* gymnastics. In fact, I had such a horrible attempt at tumbling that I had to be escorted out by the coach, who spent roughly thirty minutes assuring my mom that he'd "never seen anyone try to bend that way" and he didn't think this would be the sport for me.

"Of course," Mom says, trying to tug Jasper away from Liam. He's doing his best to climb up Liam's leg to get more ear scratches. But rather than letting Mom tug Jasper away, Liam bends down and gives Jasper his full attention.

It's this moment that almost breaks me completely. Because looking at Liam as Jasper nuzzles against his hand does something . . . disconcerting to me. It's a trick, an unfair one, and it's dangerous if I don't see through it.

"Aw, Jasper loves you, Liam!" Mom says, grinning at me. "Let me get my phone for some pictures. This is just too sweet."

"Time to go!" I declare, practically sprinting to the door, the moment effectively broken. "Jasper, let him go. Love you, Mom!"

Liam waves at my mom as I determinedly shove him out the door. I can see she's trying to get her phone out of her pocket, and I know photos won't end with Liam and Jasper. If she gets that phone out while we're still in the house, she'll have us posing on the stairs like it's prom. There's no coming back from that.

"I like your mom," Liam says as I shut the door firmly behind us. "She's nice."

I glare at him, trying to recover some of my dignity. Ivy mentioned the possibility of costumes, but Liam's not wearing one. Instead, he's wearing a vintage Killers shirt, a gray jacket, and white

Vans. It's weird to see him out of the button-down. I wish he were in his button-down. It'd make it easier to deal with him, to remind myself that he's a red flag hidden under a green one.

Liam follows me to the passenger side of a ridiculously ancient Honda Civic—complete with peeling black paint and a dinged bumper—and opens the door. For a minute, I panic, thinking he's going to make me drive, but then I realize he's just . . . holding open the door for me. He's so close that I can see the line of lighter skin on his neck where his tech shirt usually hides him from the sun. His hair's still a tiny bit damp from an earlier shower, the fluff momentarily contained by some kind of product that he must not normally wear, something with a hint of coconut in it.

"After you," he says, and I pointedly avoid his eyes as I duck into the seat.

I settle into Liam's front seat, taking exaggerated breaths through my nose to try to calm myself down. Based on my GPS, in a matter of twenty-six minutes, we'll be at the bowling alley.

"So," Liam says, sinking into the front seat. "Ivy bailed. That's unfortunate."

I nod. "Unfortunate" is a good word for it because now I have to sit here next to Liam in his too-small car with the information I've been reading swirling like dust in my head. Dust that I now need to decide if I share with Liam.

"You sure you're feeling better?" Liam asks, one hand on the steering wheel as he glances over at me. "I know Ivy said it's mandatory, but I doubt it's actually a big deal if you aren't up to it."

"Oh no," I say. "I have to go. I . . . well, it's like you said. I want to ask more people about Mercy."

Liam nods. "All right. Just wanted to make sure."

For a moment, Liam stays silent, running his free hand through his hair. This action must stir up the coconut scent because it suddenly floats between us.

"I know we don't know each other very well," I say, filling the silence to avoid spiraling. "And I said a lot of things earlier that probably freaked you out. But . . . I promise I'm a good person."

No matter what you've heard or seen.

He smiles a little, looking sideways at me. He seems to relax, putting both hands on the wheel.

"I know you're a good person, Greta," he says. "I knew that as soon as we met."

Now I blush, remembering how I slammed my hand onto his because of what I thought he was looking at.

"I just want to make sure I understand what you're looking for," he says. "So I can help you."

I blink at him. "You want to help me?"

"Well, no offense, but you seem like you might be in need of some support," he says. I open my mouth to argue, but he cuts me off. "I'm assuming that's what you were doing in the greenroom today? Looking around for clues about what happened to Mercy?"

Immediately, I panic. I was so obvious, and now he's probably just waiting to tell me to get the hell out of his car. I stare at the floor, not knowing what to say in my defense.

"It's okay, Greta," he says suddenly, drawing my eyes up to his. "Like I said, I think you might need some help with this, but I get why you're doing it."

I brighten. "You do?"

"Well, sort of," he says with a laugh. "I think you're someone who cares a lot, and hey, maybe there is something a little weird going on."

"Really?"

He nods. "I mean, Mercy took her job more seriously than anyone I knew. Like, some might say *too* seriously for a theme-park job. If anything, I'm curious. So . . . did you find anything in the locker?"

I'm so caught off guard by his offer to help that I almost forget that I need to be wary of Liam. However, there's no denying that having someone to talk to about this makes me feel better. And besides, we have a prime opportunity tonight. Maybe I can use Liam to my advantage while also keeping him at arm's length. I can tell him about some things without telling him *everything*.

"I found an old playbill and some weird notes," I admit.

I describe them to him, telling him about how the playbill was actually from a show Hailey was in and about the stark differences between the two notes. He thinks through each detail, considering it before responding.

"Jesus," he says. "Who would write something like that?"

"Lauren," I say without hesitation. "I heard her call Mercy 'Little Miss Mercy,' and I already told you about how she said Mercy 'deserved' whatever's happened to her."

"Still," Liam says. "That's harsh."

"And then Allie's definitely hiding something, even if she didn't write the note," I say. "She told Neil that Mercy texted Grey, but like I told you, Mercy hasn't answered me at all. So I also want to try to figure out how she's involved."

Liam nods. "Fair enough. So what do we do next?"

"We?" I repeated, startled.

"Didn't we just agree to work together?" Liam asks with a grin. "Tell me what the plan is."

Do I trust him? No, not completely. But I want to. This is it, after all. Diving in. Going into the riptide on purpose rather than stumbling toward it. I take a breath to steady myself at the thought.

"I want to figure out the last place Mercy was seen," I say. "All my research says that establishing a last known location is essential."

Liam thinks about this. "That would be the party, right? At least, as far as I know, it was the party."

I nod. "Yes, but I want to narrow it down. I saw her in a bedroom, but then she left. Did she go home right away or go somewhere else first?"

"Are we supposed to ask people that?" Liam asks.

"No," I say. "That would be too obvious."

Liam pulls out his phone, opening up to his photos. He swipes until I spot some pictures from the party.

"I've got this one," he says, texting me the photo so that it pops up on my phone. "But it's from pretty early. Definitely before it sounds like you talked to her."

I lean over his shoulder to look at it. It's Mercy at the party, standing near the front door, eyes on something out of frame. And Liam's right. The time stamp is definitely before Mercy and I spoke in the bedroom.

I consider this. "I think we can just eavesdrop a little more, see what people say. All of Entertainment will be here tonight, right? So just be on the, um, lookout for anything useful and then report back."

Liam gives me a smile. "Excellent. Official partners in crime."

"No," I clarify, even as something warm rushes through me. "We're just . . . casually investigating independently before conferring as a pair."

"Whatever you say, Sherlock," he says, giving me a faux salute. "Still sounds like partners to me."

I roll my eyes, then glance at my house. "We should get going. My mom's probably watching us through the window."

He nods, putting the key into the ignition. But then, suddenly, I throw my hand out onto his arm, fear replacing the buzz inside me.

"We have to be careful, though," I say. "We can't be, you know, weird or anything. Because I need people here to, um. Well, you know."

I blink, not knowing how to finish the sentence in a way that doesn't sound pathetic. I need people to like me? I need people to accept me?

But Liam just puts his hand over mine and smiles.

"It's cool, Greta," he says. "Don't worry about it. I've got you."

And then his touch is gone, his hand back on the steering wheel.

I've got you.

For a moment, it's tempting to fall into the trap of safety. But I see it for what it is. I have to. Liam might look like what would happen if a blueberry muffin and a corgi morphed into a human being, but I've been misled before.

Still. Tonight, at least, I'll allow it. I'll let someone else help me.

Beside me, Liam starts the ignition, and we back out into the night.

Bowl This Way is one of those bowling alleys that clearly got a facelift to keep up with the times, which doesn't make a ton of sense to me. It feels like the point of a bowling alley is that the whole activity feels out of time, but Bowl This Way is doing the most to look hip and cool. The problem is that it can't quite decide on an aesthetic. There's neon everywhere, from the glowing deer-head skeletons mounted by the lanes to the letters that spell out "LOVE" on the other wall. There's also a heavy dose of red chevron on the carpet, plus some Padres memorabilia decorating the back. Like in all bowling alleys, there's an arcade, which also, unsurprisingly, glows. The frenzy of bowling-lane sound effects battles the techno remix of an old Britney Spears song, and the screens above each lane are showing different 2000s music videos.

That part, at least, makes sense, since this event is supposed to be 2000s-themed, after all. Ivy's right that not everyone followed the dress code, but there're plenty of butterfly clips, shimmery silver eye shadow looks, newsboy caps, and fake belly rings to go around. We spy Keenan and Jackie near one of the lanes after we grab our shoes. Keenan's wearing a mesh shirt and has spiked his hair up, while Jackie might be dressed for the theme or just . . . dressed. Her hair's pulled back into the kind of intentionally messy braid-bun thing that I'm always trying to do but have never mastered, and her dress actually works with her bowling shoes.

"Jacks, you're not listening to me," Keenan's saying as we walk up. "I swear to God, I'm going to get discovered. I'm totally the next Conner Coffin—"

"We're not here together," Jackie says to Liam and me. "I just want you guys to know that."

We leave Jackie and Keenan alone and make our way through the crowds, Liam taking pictures on his phone as we go. He tells me that he took a photography class last summer and got really into it, and he posts some pictures on his social media. Then he asks for my username so he can follow me, which means I need to find a subject change—and fast.

"I looked up investigating tactics earlier," I say. "One of the websites I read said it's important to remain open to all potential possibilities. 'Keep an open mind and an open ear,' it said."

"You googled how to investigate?" Liam asks, smiling down at me, making me blush.

"Forget I said anything," I say. "But you know, a real Watson wouldn't make fun of his Sherlock."

Liam laughs, eyes tracking a crowd of Grimsons standing together at a lane, all of them varying degrees of tall and lanky, along with several technicians who I don't have time to register the names of.

"Fine, fine," he says. "Why don't we find the performers and try to see what we can overhear? Looks like . . . ah, there they are."

He nods behind me, and I turn to follow his gaze. A group of performers has settled near the air-hockey table and pinball machines. I recognize Lauren and Kara. Lauren's wearing a tight sundress while Kara's in a light pink crop top and a frayed denim skirt, both of them looking unfairly beautiful. And beside them, Allie holds court, outshining them both in a glittery tube top and low-rise flare jeans that are straight out of a 2000s music video. The crochet-knit bag I saw in her locker earlier swings from her shoulder, only slightly out of place with the rest of the look.

"Okay," I say to Liam. "There's an empty table behind them. I'll go sit there while you stand in line for food. I'll see what I can hear."

Liam nods. "Fair plan. But one question. What do you want me to get?"

I blink at him. "What do you mean?"

"Food-wise," he clarifies. "Weirdly delicious nachos? Pizza with a burnt crust? Questionable corn dogs?"

It tugs a smile out of me. "Nachos, obviously."

He grins. "You got it."

I'm still smiling as he turns away to get in the long line to order, but I remind myself of the task at hand and the smile drops off my face.

I move as inconspicuously as I can to the table behind them and sit down, keeping myself angled slightly away from the group, though with a view if I turn my head just so and pretend to look at my phone. Which I do. Immediately.

Is it slightly creepy to eavesdrop on these people? Maybe. But I swallow my pride and tell myself it's worth it if they say something that helps me figure out what happened to Mercy.

Allie pokes at her salad as she listens to Lauren and Kara go back and forth. Her long curtain of blond hair falls over her shoulders, pulled back from her face with a headband.

"Worst fears," Kara says, pointing at Lauren. "Go."

"Oh, god," Lauren says. "Definitely the ocean."

"The ocean?" Allie snorts. "Lauren, you literally live on the beach."

"I don't mind it being near me," Lauren says. "I just don't want it on me."

Kara laughs while Allie rolls her eyes.

"You don't want it 'on you'?" Allie says. "Good. I bet it doesn't want to be on you, either."

"Look, don't judge me just because you've been swimming since you were born or whatever," Lauren says. "Just because some of us prefer to look pretty on land rather than getting slammed into by waves—"

"But what is it?" Kara asks. "What in the ocean are you afraid of?"

Kara's tone is the same one my teachers have when someone gets a little too spicy during a class discussion, the kind that tries to stamp out any serious argument before it can get legs.

"It's nothing *in* it," Lauren says. "Or, I dunno. Maybe it is. I'm not afraid of, like, sharks or whatever. But have you ever really thought about what it would be like to drown? God, if I go in the pool and get water up my nose it burns. Imagine that in your lungs."

In spite of myself, I shiver. I don't like to think about drowning or death at all. The thoughts make me glance over at the line for food, where Liam's inching toward the front. He catches my eyes and raises his eyebrows in a silent question, but I don't have anything. Not yet. Only things that make me feel uncomfortable.

"So you're a little bitch basically," Allie says, and even though there's a slight upward lilt in her voice suggesting she's teasing, something dark also rings in it.

"At least I'm afraid of something really powerful," Lauren says. "What're you afraid of, Allie? Snakes? Serial killers? Dying like that girl in the gondola?"

At the word "gondola," Allie stabs her bowling-alley salad with a fork, her gaze down. The silence is the thick kind, the kind that sticks.

"Do you really need to bring that up?" Kara asks. "Seems a little brutal."

"What?" Lauren asks with a shrug. "Neil was talking to me about it this morning, so I guess it's been on my mind. Plus, don't you guys think it's creepy that they never took down the gondolas?"

Neil was talking to Lauren about the gondolas?

"Doesn't surprise me," Allie says. "You know Hyper Kid's cheap as shit."

It makes me feel like I should be doing something, writing something down, sorting through what they're saying. That's what a real investigator would do, right? I wish I had a notebook, even though it would look too obvious if I started taking notes right now. But—

"Why was Neil bringing it up, though?" Kara asks. "Seems a little creepy, as far as conversation starters go."

"You know Neil," Lauren says. "That guy is a certified creep. But no. He actually asked me if I'd heard anyone talking about it. Blamed the twentieth anniversary and said he wanted to make sure we all felt 'safe.' But it was just super awkward."

"Why wouldn't we feel safe?" Kara asks.

"I think he was just looking for a way to talk to me," Lauren says. "He was trying to look down my shirt the whole time."

"You think every guy's hitting on you," Allie says. "Narcissist much?"

"Oh, please," Lauren says. "We're all narcissists. We're performers."

She laughs at her own joke, the sound high and piercing. No one else joins in. Instead, Allie just takes another bite of her salad, her gaze never rising from the iceberg lettuce in front of her.

"Mercy's the worst, though," Lauren continues when no one answers. "By far."

Instantly, I'm sitting straight up. I nearly drop my phone and have to steady my hand to keep it from falling. I open up my Notes app, holding my breath as they continue to talk.

"God, she would spend hours in front of that mirror in the greenroom saying her lines over and over," Lauren continues. "So pathetic."

There's another stretch of silence, and I watch Allie carefully. Was Kara involved in all of this?

"I think we gave Mercy enough shit," Kara says, answering my unspoken question. "Maybe we can lay off now."

"I agree," Allie says. "Especially since *some* of us could do with some more line practicing, *Lauren*."

"Oh, bite me," Lauren says, tapping her cherry-painted nails on the table. "Like I told you before, *Allie*, I don't know why you ever defend her. Especially when I told you the kind of home-wrecking shit I saw her getting up to."

Home-wrecking shit? What does that mean?

"Careful, Lauren," Allie says, voice as crisp as her salad. "Your jealousy is showing."

The tension isn't just palpable now. Whatever was masquerading as jokes and sarcasm has now been smoothed and sharpened into open disdain. I wait for Lauren or Allie to crack, but Kara gets there first.

"Whatever," Kara says. "I'm just saying, I don't blame Mercy for taking some time away. In fact, I wouldn't even be mad if she bounced and actually *is* going to Broadway like she said she was going to. Or maybe she booked a cruise. My sorority sister did that."

"No way," Allie says, a laugh suddenly bubbling up out of her. "Mercy wouldn't do that. If we're beneath her, she's definitely not doing a *cruise*."

Lauren smirks, clearly encouraged by Allie's reentry into the conversation. "I dunno. I'd love to book a cruise. You'd never see me again."

"I thought you said you were scared of the ocean," Allie says. "Now you're booking a cruise?"

Lauren's nails do another rolling tap on the table. She purses her lips, smearing her plum lipstick. When she smiles next, in the flickering blue light of the pinball game to her left, it looks like a drop of blood against the whiteness of her teeth.

"You're right," she says. "No cruise for me. But maybe, if we're lucky, Mercy will drown on hers. If she's not dead already."

There's a sharp intake of breath from either Kara or Allie or both. Or maybe it's me.

"Jesus fucking Christ, Lauren," Kara says. "Why the hell would you say that?"

"What?" Lauren snaps. "God, you guys are so serious. It was just a joke, okay? Besides, it's her fault for being so fucking difficult. Plus, I'm better anyway, so who cares?"

I'm not sure I'm breathing anymore. I stare at my Notes app, the lines empty because I don't even know how to write down what I'm hearing.

"No," Allie says softly.

"No what?" Lauren asks, annoyance in her tone . . . annoyance laced with something else. Fear, maybe?

"No, you're not better than Mercy," Allie says cleanly. "No matter what happens, that fact won't have changed."

Lauren's mouth tightens, but she doesn't disagree. They stay silent, all while I fight to make sense of everything they've just said. Because it's not lost on me that—even though Allie did just defend Mercy's station as the best Perky—she also didn't disagree with Lauren about Mercy being "difficult." More than ever, I think that Lauren did something to Mercy—and Allie's helping her cover it up, albeit somewhat regrettably.

Kara's the one who breaks the silence. "You don't really think she booked a cruise, do you?"

Allie starts to answer, but she's interrupted by a flurry of movement. I lift my head to see Jackie, Silvia, Keenan, and Liam coming toward me with trays of bowling-alley food. Liam's eyes widen a little at me as he walks over, giving me clear "This just happened" energy.

"I'm just saying, what's wrong with calling her Mexican?" Keenan's asking loudly as they sit down at my table. "How am I supposed to know that Ivy's Colombian?"

"Oh, I don't know, Keenan, maybe don't assume every brown person is Mexican? Maybe just pay attention?" Jackie snaps at him, grabbing a nacho and pointing it at him like a sword.

"Sorry, Greta," Silvia says, tilting her chin up. "These two are having a bit of a . . . lovers' spat."

"No," Jackie clarifies. "Keenan's being a jackass about Ivy."

"I made a tiny mistake," he says. "I said she was Mexican. What's the big deal?"

"I can't even deal with you right now," Jackie says, holding up her hand before turning her eyes to me and my empty Notes app. "Hey, Greta. What's up?"

"Oh, Liam was getting us snacks," I say, immediately flushing. "I wasn't trying to do anything, um. Weird."

Jackie arches an eyebrow at me, and then looks at Liam. A small smile creeps onto her face. She looks like she's about to say something when a shrieking laugh sounds behind us, and I glance over my shoulder to see Lauren's head tilted back as she shakes with laughter. The other performers watch her with muted faces. I blink at her. It doesn't make sense why she's laughing. At least, not this hard. Did they change the topic? Did—

And then I see him.

I don't know how Grey snuck up so effortlessly, how I didn't even notice him appear. But he's standing there now, behind Allie, haloed by the neon light of an arcade sign behind him. He's casual in an unbuttoned Hawaiian shirt and white tank, balancing a blue backpack that he settles on an empty seat at their table before taking a seat close to Allie. His hair is tousled, a carefree smile on his face as he watches Lauren, who is still laughing like she's watching a stand-up-comedy routine. My stomach tightens. I don't like seeing Grey with them, even though I know, technically, that he belongs with them.

"God," Jackie says, whispering next to me. "I didn't think it was possible, but Lauren's laugh sounds even worse than her high note."

I snort in spite of myself, even though it's not a very nice thing to say. Then I remember that Lauren's the one who said all those terrible things about Mercy.

"So," Grey says, running a hand through his hair. "You ladies seem like you're having a good time."

"We are now that you're here," Lauren says, the copper space buns on top of her head bobbling as she leans toward him.

"Jesus, Lauren," Kara mumbles, rubbing her temples. "What's wrong with you? Are you drunk or something?"

"No," she whines, before giggling and batting her eyelashes at Grey.

Grey, to his credit, ignores her brazenness. He pulls his phone out of his pocket and begins to text or scroll, the universal sign for freedom from an awkward encounter.

"Seriously!" Lauren asks. "I'm not. I'm just excited. Aren't you guys excited? I just think—"

"Should we bowl?" Allie asks, her voice high and clipped, wielded like a pair of scissors that effectively cuts Lauren off. She stands up next to Grey, glaring at the others.

"Don't worry," Grey says, winking at the group. "I'll give you ladies a fighting chance."

There's giggling from Lauren, and I watch as she also stands and tries to position herself by Grey—only to be stopped as Allie marches firmly in lockstep with him toward the lanes. They leave their trays of picked-at food on the table, sashaying away from us. And as they go, Grey snakes his hand around Allie's shoulder, pulling her close.

And that's when I put it together.

Allie's boyfriend.

Allie and Grey are together.

Pieces fly together: Lauren saying she saw Allie's boyfriend—Grey—with Mercy. Allie accusing Grey of hiding something from her. Even Lauren calling Mercy a "whore" at the party. Is this why?

But it doesn't make sense. From everything Liam told me, Mercy kept to herself and didn't get along with the other performers. And Grey . . . Grey would never cheat on his girlfriend. He's not that type of person, that type of *man*.

But then a tiny voice reminds me that he flirted with me, even though he's supposedly with Allie. Unless I misjudged him. Unless . . . is Lauren overstating Allie and Grey's relationship? Is it one of those on-again, off-again relationships? Then I remember the letter I found in Mercy's locker, the one that addressed her as "To the light of my heart." Did Grey write that? But no. That's impossible. And yet . . .

"Even here, they need to make sure everyone notices them," Jackie says, drawing me back to their conversation. Keenan's eyes track the performers as they walk away, and I would guess that their short skirts and shorts are a big part of the reason. But I realize that Jackie's right. It's not just their looks. They do whatever it takes to get you to watch them perform, even when there isn't a stage. It's in how Allie leans into Grey, tossing her hair. She wants us to see that she has him. She wants everyone to know. Including me.

I shake my head as the understanding settles, telling myself I can't afford to get distracted by this tragic realization. If anything, this is even more reason for me to pursue my investigation—it's now more important than ever. Because I knew Lauren was jealous of Mercy for her own reasons, but did Allie have her own motive for hurting Mercy?

Further, I realize Jackie's change in subject has given me an opportunity. One too precious to lose. I glance at Liam, and he raises an eyebrow in question. Hopefully, he'll follow my lead now.

"Yeah," I say, hoping I sound casual as I keep my voice low. "They're a little, um, loud. You know . . . they were talking about Mercy."

"That poor girl," Silvia clucks, shaking her head.

"Dude," Keenan says. "Poor girl? She didn't have to work at a shitty theme park today. She's living better than the rest of us."

Silvia purses her lips like she wants to say something, but doesn't. I don't know how to prompt her, either. I don't know how to process what I've heard or how to get more information. I start to formulate a new question, something about Mercy and drowning and—

"Let's bowl," Silvia says neatly, standing up and cutting off my question. "We don't want all the good lanes to fill up."

No. No, no, no. How did my window close so quickly? But it doesn't matter now, because everyone's already starting to clean up their stuff.

"Right," Liam says, meeting my gaze. "We'll grab the food and bring it over there."

Jackie and Keenan don't need much of an invitation. They

head for the lanes with Silvia close behind, Liam and I lagging and bringing up the rear with the trays of food. Next to me, Liam walks closer, inclining his head and keeping his voice low.

"What'd they say?" he asks. "You look like you've seen a ghost or something."

"They were saying all kinds of things," I say, heart beating fast as I try to figure out where to start. "And there's definitely beef between Lauren and Allie about Mercy. It was . . . it's hard to describe. But Allie definitely knows more than she said. I'm going to try to stick close to her. And maybe you can keep an ear out for Lauren. God, she was so mean."

"Right," Liam says. "How mean—"

"No, Keenan, I will *not* be putting that as your name."

We've reached the lane where Silvia, Keenan, and Jackie have settled in. Silvia is at the keyboard, looking murderous, while Keenan holds his hands in front of her like he's praying.

"I mean cats, obviously," he tells her. "I swear on my life. It means I'm a *cat* magnet—"

"Ay chamaco, no sé por qué tengo que trabajar contigo."

She puts his name in as "Mentiroso" instead, which makes him groan. Liam turns to me, clearly wanting to continue our conversation, but before he can, Silvia's waved him over to help her with something on the keyboard. He gives me an apologetic look, but I nod at him that it's fine. Because I still need to get my thoughts together, anyway.

"Silvia, why didn't you dress up?" Jackie asks when it's time for Silvia to add her name, nodding at Silvia's plain jeans and black button-down shirt. "I thought we'd see you in some cool retro look."

Silvia rolls her eyes. "You kids. Most of you look like you're from the '90s anyway. But I did dress up. See?"

She taps something on her shirt I didn't notice before, a shiny gold badge. It looks like the plastic ones we wear at Hyper Kid, except that it's made of thick metal and looks more "vintage" than anything anyone else here is wearing. She takes it off and holds it up so that we can get a better look. When it's passed to me, I examine it. Across the top, it says HYPER KID MAGIC LAND ENTERTAINMENT, while on the bottom, it reads: OPENING DAY TEAM.

"It's very rare," Silvia says, a touch of pride in every word. "They only gave them out to those of us who opened the department. Usually, I keep it at home, but tonight felt special."

I nod, turning it over in my hand. On the back, Silvia's name has been engraved. I hand it back to her, and she smiles. I want to ask her more about it, but I'm distracted by a squeal from the next lane, where the performers have already started their game.

I glance over, seeing that Lauren's just hurled her ball down the lane as the other performers laugh and groan. The ball rolls almost immediately into the gutter. I've already tried eavesdropping tonight. Is there a way I can ask one of the performers a direct question? Maybe my move is to get closer and try to initiate a conversation with one of them, particularly Grey. He'll tell me the truth about Allie. I know he will. He'll have a thoughtful explanation, and we'll laugh about the misunderstanding. Or maybe I can even get the information from Allie. She was coy with her answers to Lauren, possibly on purpose. Maybe I can—

But then I stop myself. I said I wasn't getting distracted. I said I was looking into what's happened to Mercy. Whatever I ask, it needs to tie back to that. A real investigator wouldn't lose focus, would they? I'll only ask about it in order to figure out Allie's possible motive. I'll separate myself and my own feelings because I must. A girl's life might be at stake, after all.

I scan past Lauren to where Kara's sipping from a plastic cup while Grey eats a slice of pizza near the front of the lane. Their names are on their bright red scoreboard, all of them accounted for except Allie. I head back toward the seats near the line of bowling balls to choose from so that I can pretend to retie my bowling shoes, which have already come undone. Only there's nowhere to really sit, as most of the seats are taken up by the performers' stuff. I even recognize Allie's crochet bag, heart racing.

Kara materializes next to me, catching me off guard as she snatches her own bag and begins to dig. She pulls out a packet of pills and pops one, then looks at me when she sees I'm watching her.

"Birth control," she explains. "You okay?"

I've never talked to Kara before, but like with the other performers, I find her presence effectively freezes me in place. Perhaps a flaw in my plan.

"Yeah," I say, voice too high. "Just looking for a place to sit. Um . . . do you think Allie would mind if I moved her bag?"

She shrugs. "Probably, but who cares? She's outside taking a call."

Kara replaces the packet of pills in her purse, then flits away as quickly as she arrived. I look from where she was just standing to Allie's bag. I'm not completely unhinged to the point I would consider going through it right now, in the bowling alley, in front of other people. But maybe I could angle it slightly as I move it to get just a quick peek inside. Which is ridiculous, obviously. What am I expecting to see? A hunting knife? A ransom letter?

I shake the thought from my mind and quickly push Allie's bag to the side. Unfortunately, I'm a little too eager with my push, and the slight movement sends the top contents of the bag spilling out onto the plastic chair. This includes Allie's wallet, her phone, and a pink flashlight that nearly goes flying off the seat.

"Shit!" I murmur, darting forward to grab it before it can fall. I glance over my shoulder and to my right, seeing if anyone saw, but thankfully, everyone's still involved in the game. I snatch the wallet and flashlight, tossing them both back into the bag, which is lined in a slippery, satiny fabric that clearly made it so easy for the things to slide out. I then reach for her phone and go to stuff it into the bag—

But then, I stop. I remember Allie's phone from earlier. It had a thick pink case. This phone has a slim case, one that's clear and covered in stars. And didn't Kara just say that Allie was outside taking a call? If that's true, then whose phone is this? I turn it over in my hand, and it lights up with the home screen.

Behind me, I hear whoops of excitement. Silvia's added all our names to the screen, and the game appears over a bright green backdrop. Liam's there, helping Jackie pick a ball. Everyone's distracted. No one is watching me.

I look back at the phone. It's a picture that looks strangely familiar, and I stare at it, trying to make sense of what I'm seeing. And then, it clicks.

This is the picture of Mercy's mom, the same one from her obituary.

Suddenly, the phone vibrates in my hand, lighting up with a call. A name replaces the picture of Mercy's mom, and I stare at it like it's a bomb.

Neil.

For a moment, I forget I'm holding someone else's phone, and I imagine that Neil's seen my sneaking around and my handling of other people's property. That he's calling me because he's going to fire me. I drop the phone and it clatters to the floor, then hurriedly snatch it back and throw it into Allie's bag before darting away from the chair, breathing hard.

I do it just in the nick of time, too, because before I know it, Allie's walking back from outside. I glance at her, spotting the pink phone from her locker clutched in her hand. She pockets it, then moves to throw her arms around Grey. I can almost hear her purring into his ear, and I have to turn away.

Liam's watching me when I look up. He's standing next to Silvia, waiting to pick up a bowling ball, but his gaze is inviting. A question. Did I find something?

But I don't know yet. Because it doesn't make sense, Allie having a phone with Mercy's mom as the background. Unless it *is* Mercy's phone.

Unless, when Allie told Neil this morning that Mercy texted Grey saying she was sick, it wasn't Mercy texting. It was Allie.

Because this is just as bad as I thought. In fact, this might be worse. Because Mercy would need her phone. There's no way she'd go days without it, without reporting it. Which means . . .

Something so terrible has happened that the phone is the least of her concerns, if she's even able to *have* concerns at all. An image of her gagged and bound surfaces in my mind, and this time, there's no way to banish it.

It's image after image, each one worse than the next.

Mercy beaten. Mercy drowned. Mercy's blood on the stage. Mercy's blood in a gondola, dripping down.

What if I'm too late?

CHAPTER THIRTEEN

TUESDAY, JUNE 17
7:12 A.M.

"**I'M TELLING YOU,** they are hiding something huge. Why else would Allie have Mercy's phone and be using it to call her in sick?"

The park has a rosy glow this early in the morning, the barest slivers of sunlight slipping over the painted statues of Hyper Kid and Dingle and Ranger that line the path we're currently on. Liam's sitting behind me in the driver's seat of one of the park carts while I change out the showtimes on the huge boards that dot the park, just like I promised Ivy I would.

Being here this early in the morning is actually perfect, since it gives me ample time to talk to Liam about everything that happened yesterday. After I found Allie's second phone—*Mercy's* phone—I was immediately whisked into proper bowling, so there wasn't time to talk to Liam alone. And then Jackie got too drunk on bowling-alley beer, so we had to drop her off on the way to my place. By the time I got home, I was too exhausted to think about my next steps, but that's probably for the best. Processing time is essential to an investigation, after all.

Once I woke up, though, I was completely reinvigorated and ready to recommit to figuring this out. I dug around in Mom's old office supplies to find an empty notebook, which I used this morning to write down my theories and thoughts up this point. Just like a real investigator would. I think it will help me sort through everything to identify what's important and what's just a distraction. To figure out what happened and save Mercy—if she can even be saved.

Because, even if I can't seem to say the "d" word to Liam right now, I can't control the growing terror inside me telling me that Mercy's lying lifeless somewhere. The only thing that's getting me through is that maybe she isn't gone yet. Maybe there's still time. But I can't say those things to Liam. Not entirely. I've made him think I'm worried that Mercy's in grave danger, but dead? That, I can't quite say yet. Maybe because I'm worried that, if I do, I'll be speaking it into existence, and I refuse.

Instead, I'm running Liam through every moment from last night. It helps that we can do this together while he drives me around in the cart, cutting our time down and making it so I'm not out of breath from walking all over the park.

"And why was Neil calling Mercy?" I ask for the fortieth time as we whiz through the park on the cart. "They don't have any reason to talk, do they? I mean, performers call in to Grey—not Neil. And it was after hours. It couldn't have been a work-related call, could it?"

"Probably not," Liam says, parking the cart in front of our fifth sign. "Though he might've stayed after to work with Mike on the

Rocket issue. I was wondering why he wasn't at bowling, anyway. They must've stayed to get it fixed, right? Otherwise, they would've called you and told you to stay home."

I chew this over as I hop out of the passenger seat and walk toward the sign. You'd think that they'd have figured out a digital system by now, but no. Instead, we have to peel off the old showtimes—a magnetic strip—and replace them with today's showtimes, storing the old ones in a hidden compartment near the bottom of the sign. The magnets are cool to the touch, a June gloom settling in this morning. There's dew on the exterior of the sign that flecks off onto my skin as I shut it and lock it with my key, and all around me there's the ever-present mist creeping in from the ocean. Normally, with the park packed with guests and employees, you don't feel or notice it, but now, with just Liam and me alone in this sleepy part of the park, it's hard not to.

"I guess so," I say at last. "But didn't you say it was weird that Neil was getting involved at all?"

Liam shrugs. "Neil's always been kind of a weirdo, though. Sort of needs to have his hand in everything, you know? And—oh, that magnet's a little off."

He leans forward and squints toward the board. I follow his gaze and notice that he's right. It's tilting. I push it up with my fingertip, making sure it's properly aligned with the edge of the sign itself.

"That's true," I say, thinking about Neil's reaction with the maps on my second day working Rocket. He does seem to want to control every little detail, much to Gene's dismay.

"But why would he be calling Mercy?" I ask again, the dew on my fingertip making me shiver.

"If he *was* calling her," Liam reasons. "We don't know for sure that was Mercy's phone. You didn't test-call it, did you?"

"What do you mean?"

"Like, did you call Mercy's number from your own phone to make sure it was hers?"

Shit. No. I didn't. The idea didn't even cross my mind. Liam must read this on my face because he nods along.

"So our first step would be confirmation," he says. "But even then, we'd also need to figure out why Allie has it. Maybe she just grabbed it by accident because Mercy left it at work."

I snort. "There's no way this was an accident. Allie's up to something."

"Right," Liam says. "But didn't you say Lauren was the one who wrote the note? And Grey—"

"Allie's the key," I say, definitively. Because Liam wouldn't understand. He doesn't know Grey the way I know Grey. He doesn't know about the awful rumors about Grey and Mercy—rumors that I've decided must be false but nonetheless may have swayed Allie to horrendous action. I wait for Liam to push me on this as I hop back into the cart, but he doesn't. Instead, he just sort of sighs and runs his hand through his hair.

"Was this the last one?" Liam asks. The leather seat's chilly, and the edge is peeling off the side. I worry one of the torn bits with my fingers, grateful to have something other than my cuticles to shred.

"One more," I say. "Castle Land."

Liam nods, stepping on the gas so that we instantly zoom forward in the cart. Now I have to wrap my arms around myself because the cold smacks my bare skin as we whiz down the empty walkway. It's so early that we don't see another employee in all of Mega Town, though once we hit Castle Land, I spot a few red shirts sweeping near Knights Challenge, the busiest restaurant in the park. Liam comes to a stop in front of the last sign, and I hop out with my last magnet in hand.

"You're right, though," I say as I unlock the board. "About Neil. He does have a weird vibe. And yesterday, he was . . . sort of twitchy. Remember?"

"Well, yeah," Liam says, his last syllable tilting up slightly as he bursts into a yawn. He recovers before continuing. "He's always twitchy. Especially around girls. *Especially* pretty girls."

My cheeks heat up as soon as he says it, making my face the same color as the fire-engine-red sign in front of me. I glance over my shoulder to see Liam grinning, loving every second of my discomfort.

"It wasn't like that," I say. "He wanted us out. And it wasn't the first time he was sneaking around. What if he and Allie are in cahoots?"

I swap out the magnet and turn the key, relocking the sign into place. I tilt my head, double-checking that everything's straight.

"Cahoots?" Liam asks. "Pretty sure no one's used that word since maybe 1850."

I toss a glare at him over my shoulder, deciding the magnet's not quite straight. I reopen it and adjust.

"Besides," Liam says. "This is Neil we're talking about. A rule follower, through and through."

I look back and raise my eyebrows at him. "There's nothing wrong with being a rule follower."

He laughs, holding up his hands in mock surrender. "I didn't say there was. Just saying it doesn't surprise me."

"Hm," I say, not sure what to think. Liam might be right, that Neil was just being Neil. But something in my gut tells me there's more to it.

"Hey," Liam says. "How're we doing on time?"

I check my phone. "We burned through that, thanks to the cart. Why?"

"Well, remember when I told you about the castle turret?" Liam asks, pointing at something behind me. I turn around to where the titular castle of Castle Land stands tall and proud, towering over the outdoor stage beneath it. There's an open doorway at the center where the cast clearly enters and exits, plus a small balcony up top.

"I don't remember that," I say, avoiding eye contact.

"Sure you do. I told you about it back when you were suspicious of me," Liam says, grinning. "And I was just trying to show you something cool."

My cheeks heat up immediately. "I'm still suspicious of you, you know."

"Aw, no way," Liam says. "I'm your Watson, remember?"

I stick out my tongue, then look back up at the turret.

"Is this where . . . well, is that where you sell from?" I ask, tentatively. The turret does look cool, and I don't want to scare him away.

"Where I sell what?" Liam asks.

"Your, well. You know," I say, lowering my voice. "Your drugs. Since you're a dealer."

For a second, he's quiet, still staring at me with those wide, shocked brown eyes. Kind of like a baby deer, only with more hair.

"Oh my god," he says, and then, without warning, he's thrown back his head, laughing. Laughing, I realize with a sinking feeling, at me.

"It's not funny," I tell Liam, cheeks burning.

"Yeah," he says, back to grinning. "It is. Because I don't deal drugs, Greta."

"But Ivy calls you Dealer all the time," I say. "I thought..."

The thought runs out. What else do people deal except drugs?

Now he looks embarrassed. His runs his hand through his hair again, reigniting the fluff.

"I, uh, sell the password at school," he says. "The Wi-Fi password. They keep changing it, but I always figure it out. You can only get a few sales in before word gets around, but people get desperate when they're stuck in stats. And I've got a workaround for the Zscaler they use, so the other kids pay me to get them past the blocks. Ivy went to my high school, and she was one of my best customers before she graduated."

"You're kidding me," I say, though to my surprise, I'm smiling now.

A dealer of Wi-Fi passwords and Wi-Fi hacks. I would've never thought it was a thing, but I bet they had that at Coastal Canyon, too. How else were kids constantly playing *Tetris* and Coolmath Games on their school computers?

Liam shakes his head. "Hey, it's a good way to make some extra cash. I'm saving for Comic-Con."

I blink at him, and he coughs.

"So yeah," he says. "The turret's not my 'spot.' Just a sort of makeshift storage space for Entertainment stuff. Old scripts, props, things like that."

"And we could just go up?" I ask, feeling much more excited now that I know Liam's just a total nerd.

Liam nods. "Of course we can. They never lock it, and even if they did, you're with the guy with the keys."

I roll my eyes as he jingles his keys in my direction.

"Let's go," I say. "But for the record, my suspicions remain."

Liam laughs, then parks the cart and steps out. We set out to the castle together, a sliver of blue sky finally creeping through the clouds as we go.

Once we climb the stairs on the side of the stage, I follow Liam through the open doorway that leads backstage, glancing at the A-frame sign on it that reads ARRR, MATEYS! COME SEE US IN OCTOBER WHEN WE SAIL BACK FOR MORE ADVENTURES.

"We do a pirate show for Halloween," Liam explains. "It's actually pretty cool. You have to queue up the sounds for the sword fight at just the right time. The swords are foam, so, you know, it's up to the technicians to really sell the magic."

He puffs up his chest importantly, and I laugh.

"They're probably up in the turret, actually," he says, leading me around through the stage's back door. The stage itself is just a basic shell holding up the fancy exterior that's exposed to the park, so the back is a bit of a letdown. Liam points to the stairs that snake along and up the back, directing me to follow him up them.

"I promise, the turret itself is sweet," Liam says, reading the disappointment on my face. "Very mysterious. Exclusive. Only the coolest people are allowed in."

I roll my eyes, even though I'm grinning at his obvious overselling.

"You said it was always unlocked," I say.

"But for the sake of being dramatic," he says, pulling out his keys once we get to the top of the stairs and dangling them in front of me. "Let's pretend that today it wasn't and you had to depend on me."

"You're being ridiculous." I laugh as he slides the key into the comically large lock on the door. I'm suddenly aware of how high up we are. The wind seems to whistle all around me, and the mist from earlier seems closer to a fog. Or maybe Liam's flair for drama is rubbing off on me.

"Here," he stage-whispers, "all the secrets of the park will be revealed."

He flings open the door, and he's right; all the secrets of the park are packed wall to wall: giant skulls, rubber swords, stacks of paper, binders, smoke machines, and, at the center of it, a throne. We walk in farther, moving into the dusty space, and I take in everything as I turn to the side, a scream dragged out of my throat before I can even puzzle out what I'm looking at.

Neil, his face purpled and his eyes bulging, hangs from the ceiling, his glasses askew and broken on his nose.

CHAPTER FOURTEEN

TUESDAY, JUNE 17
8:51 A.M.

I KNOW BEFORE I open my eyes that it's too quiet.

I'm not in my room. I'm sitting up, and whatever surface I'm on is hard, unrelenting. My fingers tap against it, feeling the cold smoothness. Actually, everything about wherever I am is cold. The air on my cheeks sends a shiver up my spine. It carries the metallic tinge of blood.

"Hello, Greta."

My eyes fly open. A girl sits across from me, one I've only ever seen in news articles and on social media. Hailey Portman's dark brown hair falls in loose waves around her slender face, eyes flashing. It's hard to make out much more, given how dark it is, even though she's sitting so close to me that our knees almost touch.

I realize that we're rocking, high up in the air. The gondola. Back, forth, back, forth, the movements lazy and slow. But with each rock, Hailey's eyes seem to sharpen, and the moon finds its way in through a small crack in the ceiling.

Then I see her skin.

The cuts don't follow any kind of order or pattern. She's slashed from temple to lip, then forehead to cheek, then straight across her neck. She's wearing a blue dress that hugs her curves, and I can see that the cuts continue down her arms. Her blood seeps through her dress at her stomach, her hips. She catches me looking and grins, and her smile bubbles over with red.

"Have you figured it out yet, Greta?" Hailey purrs. Her voice is low and breathy. She leans closer to me, reaching out for my knee with her hand. "Have you figured out where they killed me?"

I try to answer her, but nothing comes out. Hailey spits blood onto the floor.

"Was it here, Greta?" Hailey asks, her voice higher-pitched now, affected and mocking. "Was it here in the gondola? Or is this just where they dumped me? Come on, Greta. You should know this by now."

I edge away from her, but her hand comes around my wrist. She squeezes, tight, and I start to scream.

"That won't work," Hailey says. "They can't hear you. No one's coming, Greta. They left me here all night because no one can hear you. Don't you understand?"

But I scream anyway, scream until I'm hoarse, as Hailey's eyes flash under the moon. I yank away from her, turning so fast that my hand slides through hers, slick as it is with blood. But when I look next to me, I'm no longer alone.

"Greta?" Mercy asks, blinking at me.

She's in the outfit she wore to the party, the white jacket, her hair curled exactly the same way. Except she, too, is covered in red, covered in slashes, bleeding from her cuts and her mouth.

Her hands come up, and at first, I think she's going to hug me. But then I feel her fingers on my throat, see the sad fury in her eyes.

"Why didn't you save me, Greta?" she asks, and now there are tears sliding down her cheeks, cutting tracks in the blood. "Why didn't you save us?"

A knock on the gondola window rips my attention from Mercy, and even through the haze, I can see someone outside. Hovering in the air, suspended, neck swollen, eyes blackened, beating on the window.

Neil.

His eyes are wide and unseeing from behind his broken glasses.

"There's glass in my eyes," he shouts. "Don't you see? There's glass!"

He brings his hand down, hard, splintering the gondola window with his fist, just as Mercy's hands tighten on my throat. Just as Hailey's hands cover my eyes, smearing them with blood.

"You should've saved us, Greta," they say. "You should've saved us all."

The scream starts in my stomach and ricochets through my throat, just as they block out my vision. It reverberates in my ear, pushing me down, down, down—

"Greta! Greta, can you hear me? I need you to stop screaming."

My eyes fly open, my breath catching as I sit straight up. I look around, expecting the windows of the gondola, but I'm not in the air anymore. I'm on the cold tile floor of a room that looks a lot like the Jungle greenroom, though there are slight differences. There're fewer lockers, and the headshots sprinkled across the top belong to different faces. I move my hand and find a couch cushion on the ground behind me. When I look back at the couch, there's a spot where it's been pulled from, making it look like a kid with a lost front tooth. The exposed part of the couch is dusty and stained. The stain stretches from the back and disappears under the other cushions, almost black.

When in doubt, you must assume that the fluid in front of you is blood.

"Easy, Greta," someone says, and I flinch at the voice. It's a girl, maybe five years older than me, maybe more, with hair the color of cherry soda. She's pushing a bottle of water toward me, and I take it with shaking hands. I sip greedily, finding that my throat's raw.

Because I've been screaming, I realize.

"No sudden movements, okay? We need to figure out if you have a concussion."

"A concussion," I say, the words gummy in my mouth. Everything's still slippery. Everything's still shiny. But why would I have a concussion? Why would—

And then I remember.

Neil.

Dangling.

His broken glasses dangling over his nose, over his pimples.

"Drink, Greta," the girl says again. She's in a light blue polo, the kind the Medical team wears. I try to focus on her badge, to figure out her name, but my vision's blurry. A tear runs down my cheek, and the girl hands me a tissue.

"Drink," she repeats, grabbing a flashlight and shining it into my eyes.

"Where am I?" I mumble, blinking at the light, fisting my hand around the tissue. And then, I remember something else. Something more important.

"Where's Liam?"

The girl drops the flashlight and pulls something else out of her bag. A blood-pressure monitor. She fixes it around my upper arm as she talks.

"You're in the Castle greenroom," she says. "There aren't any shows running out of here, so you can take all the time you need to recover."

"Where's Liam?" I repeat.

She smiles as the wrap she put on my arm begins to constrict.

"He's okay," she says. "Very worried about you, of course. We think he caught you before you hit the ground, but we need to make sure."

"He . . . he caught me?"

She nods, guiding me so that I'm lying back down on the couch cushion. "Deep breaths, Greta. It's going to be okay, but we need to keep you on the ground in case you faint again."

"But where is he now?" I ask, panic rising in my chest.

The girl looks down at the monitor as the wrap around my arm releases.

"Liam? Oh, I think he's giving his statement. The police want to talk to you, too, once you're up for it. Luckily, doesn't look like a concussion, but you'll be woozy from fainting."

"The police?" I ask, heart thudding in my chest.

"Just regular procedure," she says. "It's just a statement because you technically found the body."

The body.

Neil's body.

And I have to give a statement.

"But . . . ," I mumble, not sure how to say what I want to say.

That I don't want to talk to the police, because they terrify me. What if they bring up what they know about me? What if they tell everyone I work with that I'm a criminal?

"You don't understand," I say, pushing on the cushion so I can stand. I get up onto my knees, then hobble onto each foot. I'm nearly snapped back by the girl's blood-pressure thing, which I rip off with my free hand.

"Greta, you should stay seated," the girl says. "No quick movements."

But I'm already moving. The room is swimming, but I'm moving.

"I need air," I say. "I need—"

I stumble toward the door, reaching for the knob. I must've stood up too fast because the world seems to dip and I have to grab for the wall. I scramble toward the knob again, reaching with my fingers. . . .

Before I can close the knob in my grip, though, the door swings open, nearly knocking me back. Two figures appear, and one of them rushes toward me before I can fully comprehend who they are.

"Mija!"

"Silvia?" I choke as she pulls me into a tight hug, the entire room filled with her floral perfume.

"I was so worried," she says, pulling back so she's an arm's length away from me. Her hat is slightly off-center, and her eyeliner is smudged behind her glasses. She's been crying, I realize. Because of course she has. Neil's dead.

"Oh, pobrecita," she says, clutching the cross necklace hanging over her polo before pulling me into another hug. "You poor, poor thing."

"Silvia, you need to let her breathe," another voice says, a deep voice that dips into a chuckle at the end.

I look over Silvia's shoulder at the source of this voice. It's a man I've never seen before—no, wait. I have. But I don't know where. He's tall and lanky, wearing a paisley-printed pink shirt and light blue slacks. His skin is smooth, and his light brown hair is parted cleanly to the side. He smiles, showing white teeth that seem to sparkle along with his green eyes.

"Greta," he says, stepping forward and holding out a hand. "I'm so sorry for what you've been through this morning. I'm James."

I take his hand and shake it, using it as a temporary anchor as I steady myself after Silvia's hugs. She's hovering next to me, looking from me to the girl to James.

"James is our supervisor," Silvia explains. "For performers and ushers."

I blink. James. James K. Murphy. That's who I'm meeting. The man from the news broadcast and my research about the park. My boss's boss.

My dead boss's boss.

"I'm sorry we're meeting this way," James says. "But I came as soon as I could. I was at a retreat this week, but I left immediately to see to all of this."

"Thank god," Silvia says. "Everything's chaos."

James smiles tiredly. "We're taking care of it. Everyone from Entertainment's heading home, and we're calling anyone who's not already in."

"They want me to talk to the police," I croak, finally finding my voice. I was worried I'd lost it to the rawness in my throat.

James shakes his head. "I know. I tried to hold them off, told them you were recuperating. But they won't budge."

"But she's clearly still recovering!" Silvia cries, wringing her hands in the direction of the girl from Medical. "Isn't she?"

The girl looks from me to James. She sighs.

"No concussion, though she might be a little unsteady after passing out," she says. "But they'll want it before she leaves. Shouldn't take too long."

James considers this, then looks at me. "Up to you, Greta. I can try to hold them off until your mom gets here, but she said there's traffic coming from downtown."

"You called my mom? Was she mad?"

James gives me a sad smile. "Of course not. Greta, you haven't done anything wrong."

But he doesn't know that. He doesn't know that I actually have done a lot wrong, and the police know every detail.

"She should just rest," Silvia says. "Wait for her mother."

James nods. "Like I said, your call, Greta. But whatever you decide, I'll be there with you."

"You will?" I ask, wishing I wasn't trembling in front of this man. He turns to the girl, who is now packing up her blood-pressure monitor, and whispers something to her. She responds, nodding in my direction, and I'm pretty sure I hear her say "Get her to drink water" under her breath. Then she's meeting my gaze once before she slips out of the room.

"Of course," James says. "It's normal to feel a little nervous talking to the police, even though you have nothing to worry about."

"And it's just a statement?" I ask.

James nods.

"It'll be over before you know it," he promises. "Just a quick statement about where you found Neil. And if they do anything to make you uncomfortable, I'll put a stop to it right then and there. But again . . . only if *you* want to."

I nod, even though the slippery feeling is starting to ebb in place of the pure electricity of fear. But I'd rather do this now and get it over with, especially if they've already made Mom leave her job early. I want to get away from everything and find Liam, talk to him about . . . all of this.

"I want to talk to them now," I say. "I'm ready."

"You're sure?" James asks.

I nod. "Yes. And can someone call my mom and tell her not to worry? I don't want her to panic."

"Of course," James says. "I'll do that and get the officers. I think they're just about done with Liam."

I nod again because, apparently, that's the only thing I have the energy to do. James leaves, and it's just Silvia and me in the greenroom. She's not wearing her fancy badge anymore. Back to the regular plastic one. I almost laugh, thinking of how she told me only yesterday that ushers aren't allowed in greenrooms. Since then, I broke into one and ended up receiving medical attention in another. It might be an usher record.

Silvia doesn't say anything about this, though. She picks up the couch cushion from the ground, fitting it back into place and brushing off the dust from the floor. She then pats the seat, and I walk over and lower myself down. She sits beside me and takes my hand. Tears well back up in my eyes.

"You don't need to worry about talking to them," Silvia says. "James knows them. He's had to work with them a lot over the years. Security issues, you know. People at shows acting weird. Fights. He's used to them. You'll be safe as long as he's there."

I nod, feeling a little better.

"But I wish you didn't have to do this at all," Silvia mutters. "This place is cursed. Ay Dios mío."

I swallow. I don't know what to say to that. I don't feel as dizzy as before, but instead, everything feels like soup sloshing around in my brain. Parts that seemed so important from right before I passed out are fighting to get to the surface, but nothing can quite stick.

"This stays with you, unfortunately," Silvia says. "I wish I could tell you it doesn't, but it does. Always. Gene has never been the same. Finding someone after they've passed. It haunts you."

In my mind, it's like someone bumps into the soup bowl, like everything shifts just a little. Silvia's words don't make sense, but words rise to the surface that I latch on to.

"What do you mean . . . Gene?" I ask, and her grip tightens over my hand.

"Oh," Silvia says, shaking her head. "Oh, it was so horrible. He used to work in Sanitation back then. They only moved him to Entertainment after the first year to cut down on the walking with his bad knee."

"Wait," I say, realization dawning as I turn to look into Silvia's misty brown eyes. "You aren't saying . . . was Gene the one who . . . with Hailey? The one who—"

"He doesn't like to talk about it," Silvia says, dabbing at her eyes. "After that first drop, when Gene looked up . . . and then they brought her body down, of course, and he saw what that monster did to her."

When in doubt, you must assume that the fluid in front of you is blood.

"I thought you knew," Silvia murmurs, her voice quiet. She lets my hand drop so she can wipe away her tears. "I thought I told you, but it must've been someone else."

My hand hangs there, cold without the warmth of Silvia's. Pieces are clicking together now. Things are solidifying. And I'm remembering.

"It's a curse," Silvia says. "All of it, happening again. I warned him."

Warned him?

"Wait," I say. "Who else was asking about this?"

Silvia makes a clucking nose in her throat. Outside, I hear the sound of a cart zipping up the road, a parking brake being latched. Feet hitting the gravel road.

"Neil," Silvia says, barely above a whisper as she sniffles. "I told him to leave the past alone. But he wanted to rehash it."

Neil. The article on the computer. Asking Lauren about the killing and if she felt safe. And finally, talking to Gene, the very person who apparently found Hailey's body.

Right before I found Neil's body in the turret.

It's cold in the greenroom, but it seems to get even colder still.

"Well, and Mercy," Silvia adds suddenly. "I told her, too, but that was different."

The floor drops out from under me. I whip toward Silvia, feeling the sting of pain that comes with the rush of movement.

"Mercy?" I ask. "But why—"

The door opens, and James reappears before me.

"Greta? The police are ready to speak to you."

CHAPTER FIFTEEN

TUESDAY, JUNE 17
9:26 A.M.

THE TIME BETWEEN the moment when James tells me the police are here to the moment when the officer appears from behind him takes seconds. It's a flash, really, only enough time for James to step aside and the officer to walk into the room.

And yet, in that instant, everything drops out from under me. I look up as James steps aside, as the officer materializes in front of me. In that moment, everything's wiped away, even Silvia's confession just now that she talked to Mercy about Hailey. That I'll have to sort through after I survive this.

Because I recognize this officer.

"Hello, Greta," Detective Kupferle says, striding forward.

Panic zips through me, hot and sharp and all over. I don't even have time to worry that it might be him. It's the kind of fear that seems so impossible that thinking about it doesn't even make sense.

His eyes are narrowed in the same way they were last time we spoke. He's chewing on something, a toothpick, the sharp edge flashing out from between his teeth.

I'm in Assistant Principal Taggert's office, the sound of his Keurig burbling in the background. I shift in an unforgiving plastic chair so that I'm sitting on my hands to keep from tearing off my nails. My mom's on one side of me, and my dad's on the other. The air-conditioning is blasting. My mouth is dry. I can still smell smoke because it must be caught in my hair.

And Detective Kupferle is standing to the left of Taggert, his back straight and his eyes fixed unrelentingly on me.

"I brought Detective Kupferle here today to make something clear to you, Greta," Taggert says, sighing at the end of the sentence. "Detective Kupferle sees what happens when cases get dire. When there's no turning back. You don't want to have to see him again, do you?"

His question is barbed, and it sticks in me. There's no way to respond that will satisfy anyone in the room.

"Your parents have agreed to pay for the damage," Taggert continues. "Which is incredibly gracious. And, due to your father's long-standing relationship with the school, we've agreed not to press charges."

My tears burn down my cheeks. I can't look up. I just want to leave this office. If I don't, I'm going to scream.

"But you're on a path to destruction," Taggert continues. "And we know how it starts. Grades slip. Friendships splinter. But then, someone gets hurt. Maybe not today—thank god—but someday, unless you change."

"Is this really necessary?" Mom interrupts, breaking Taggert's monologue. He narrows his eyes at her, but she presses on.

"Terry—Mr. Taggert—I understand that you want to stress the

severity of this to my daughter," Mom continues. "But Greta knows she made a mistake. And if you'd put a stop to the bullying she's been enduring—"

"Let's not make excuses," Dad says, cutting through Mom's words. "What Greta did was terrible. We take full responsibility."

"I understand," Mom says, shifting her glare from Dad to Taggert. "But bringing in your homicide-detective friend to make a point? Don't you think that's a bit extreme?"

In the corner, Detective Kupferle shifts slightly, and I'm forced to look at him. His sleeves are rolled up. His dark brown hair is receding on his forehead. His eyes are sharp and gray.

"Your daughter could've killed someone today, Mrs. Green," he says. "I think my presence is extremely appropriate."

I shiver, both in my memory and now, on the greenroom couch, avoiding his eyes.

You don't want to have to see him again, do you?

"I heard you passed out," he says. "Are you feeling better?"

No, I want to say. No, I'm not feeling better at all, because seeing you makes me feel nauseated and like I could throw up all over your boots. But I don't say that. Instead, I feel Silvia's hand patting me on my knee as she stands up.

"Chin up, mija," she says in a voice low enough just for me. "This will all be over soon."

She then nods to both James and Detective Kupferle before leaving the room. Without her, I feel even more like I'm drowning.

"Greta?" James asks, taking the other seat on the couch. He keeps his distance, not quite as close as Silvia was, but close enough that I know he's there for me.

"I'm all right," I say, looking at James rather than Detective Kupferle. "I'm ready to give my statement."

Detective Kupferle chews on his toothpick, then pulls a paper pad out of his pocket. He also takes out a recorder, which he sets next to him on a stool by the lockers. Then he grabs a folding chair from next to the lockers and pops it open before taking a seat. His eyes—just as gray and cruel as I remember—settle on me.

"I'm going to record you, Greta," he says. "As you give your statement."

I nod, and he presses a button on the recorder.

"Please state your name."

I do, feeling that the room has gone from too cold to too hot. Once I finish saying my name, the silence stretches on, and I look at James for help. He nods, mouthing the words "It's okay" in my direction.

"Have you known Neil a long time?" Detective Kupferle asks.

I shake my head. "No. Just since I started working here."

"Did he get along with people?" Detective Kupferle asks. "Friendly?"

I think about this. Was Neil friendly? He was nervous more than anything. And when he hired me, I felt so grateful that he wanted me at all that I thought he was nice just for giving me a job. But that's not really nice, now that I think about it. I gave a good interview, was a good prospect. Hiring me wasn't nice. It was smart.

"Neil prioritized work," I say simply. "He was a good boss."

"And was he happy?"

"Excuse me," James cuts in. "It was my understanding that you were just here to take Greta's statement. This feels more like an interrogation."

Detective Kupferle's lips settle into a thin line, which is impressive given how thin they already are. I can tell he doesn't like that

James is here to interject, but he doesn't say so. He just scribbles something on his pad before continuing.

"I'm just trying to get a full picture," he says. "Was he upset about something yesterday?"

I stare at him, not understanding the question. And suddenly, something cold twists in my gut. Does he know about my questioning Neil? Does he think my questioning had something to do with Neil hanging himself?

"And how would the poor girl know that?" James asks, voice cold. "She barely met him a week ago, and he is—was—her boss. Detective, if I didn't know better, I'd think you might be badgering Greta."

My whole body warms. I remember what Silvia said, that I'm safe with James. And I do feel safe. Even now, he's glaring at Detective Kupferle like he has absolutely zero fear. Like he's protecting me. And I'm so grateful, so unbelievably grateful, but then I see that Detective Kupferle's glaring right back. My hands sweat as a new worry hits me. Is James going to push him too hard and he'll reveal what he knows about me? Oh, god. Oh, god.

"I can tell you what happened," I say quickly. "Liam wanted to show me the turret because I'm really into Hyper Kid stuff. He said there were old props and set pieces. So we went up there after changing the showtimes. We opened the door, and . . ."

I swallow. Even though I've brought it up, I don't actually want to remember what I saw. I just want to get through it so I can never think of it again. I'm sure my face has gone pale, and I wonder if he will tell me to take my time or offer me a glass of water, because I've watched TV shows where officers did these things. But Detective Kupferle doesn't. He just waits, looking at me the way my dad used to look at cars that were taking too long to park at Trader Joe's.

"I looked inside," I say, voice shaking. "There was so much stuff. It was like it was spilling over. And then, in the middle... was Neil."

Detective Kupferle nods, writing more. "Go on. Describe the rest of the scene."

I think of Neil, of his usual blue polo shirt and his pasty white skin and his angry pimples. Of his eyes, always darting around, his hands always nervous and shaky, but especially yesterday. And I think of his glasses, always sliding down his nose—

His glasses.

I force myself to be back at the door of the turret, looking in, seeing his body hanging from the rafters, his swollen neck and face. His glasses. His *broken* glasses. The part I can't erase from my mind no matter how hard I try. But why would his glasses be broken if he hanged himself?

"I think you have enough photos of the event to say what he looked like," James cuts in. "There's no need to traumatize her."

"We just want—"

"He was hanging," I say, blinking away the blood and the memories. "That's what I saw, and then I passed out."

Detective Kupferle doesn't start writing again immediately. He stares at me, as if he's sifting through me and my answers. I wonder, as his gaze pierces through me, if I should tell him about Neil and what he was looking into before he died. And what about what I've been looking into? Should I tell him what I've found out about Mercy? I should, shouldn't I? What if it's relevant? What if it helps—

"You'll forgive me, Mr. Murphy," Detective Kupferle says slowly, "if I don't just accept Greta's words without question. We know one another. And I know that she can . . . well, she can err on the dramatic side. To her own detriment, and to the detriment of others. It's gotten her into trouble before."

It's those words that make my entire body seize up, that startles me into silence. Shame and anger burn through me, and my eyes find the ground.

He's going to ruin me. He's going to ruin everything. I could never trust him.

"Are you calling her a liar?" James snaps. "After the morning she's had, you have the audacity to insult her?"

"No one's insulting—"

"Enough," James says, rising from the couch. "You've got her statement. If you need anything else, you can talk to me or to her parent. But you've tortured this poor girl enough."

That same warmth from before blooms inside me again. James's face is red and furious, his eyes narrowed. But his rage isn't directed at me. It's at Detective Kupferle, who, for his part, looks murderous.

"There's no need to get emotional," Detective Kupferle says, then cuts his flashing eyes to me. "Greta, that will do for today. But—"

"That means you can go, Greta," James says, still glowering at Detective Kupferle before turning to me. Instantly, his eyes soften as he waves me out of the greenroom. Once we're outside and the door is shut behind us, the sun beats down on me fully, almost immediately turning my cheeks red from the heat. All the earlier June gloom has burned off, making what happened only a few hours before feel like a lifetime ago. Beside me, James takes a deep breath and shakes his head.

"Don't worry about him. I'll handle it," he says, meeting my gaze. "Now, where's your stuff? At Rocket, I assume?"

I nod, mouth dry. I don't know if I have any words left.

James looks over my shoulder, down the access road to where the break area behind the castle is. I don't want to turn around and look at it, because I don't know what I'll see. They must have it taped off, right? Like in the movies? Neil's body isn't still there, right? I'm holding my breath trying not to shake as James waves to someone behind me.

"Lauren! Lauren, can you help me with something, dear?"

All the shock of the morning is still coursing through me, making it so that his words don't immediately compute. By the time they do, there're footsteps behind me and the smell of strong floral perfume appears at my side.

"Sure, boss," Lauren says sweetly, flipping her red hair over her shoulder to glance at me. "I was just telling all the performers not to talk to any of the newspeople on their way out. And then I heard you were here and wanted to come check on you. You must be going through so much. I want to do whatever I can to help."

I stare at her, freckles shimmering in the sunlight. I've never heard this level of sugary sweetness in her voice before, except maybe when she was talking to Grey last night. She's got a tote bag slung over her shoulder, and she's wearing sweatpants and a tight tank top with a dark green bra sticking out the top. Her eyes flicker from me and back to James, as if she's annoyed that I'm still standing here.

"That's lovely, Lauren," James says kindly. "And thank you for your concern. But it's Greta here who I need you to help."

Lauren's smile falters ever so slightly as she looks back at me, but it's pasted back on quickly enough as James continues.

"Can you walk Greta to get her stuff from Rocket?" James asks her, still smiling down at her. "She's had an unbelievably tough morning, and I'd rather she not be alone."

"Oh, that won't be necessary," I say, the words coming out sandpapery and rough, forced out of my teeth through sheer panic. "I can just go. It's okay—"

"Greta," James says, turning to me as he puts a hand on my shoulder. "It's okay to need help. Just let Lauren walk you over, all right?"

I don't know what to say. I don't want to tell him that I can trust Lauren about as far as I can throw her, and considering my abysmal PE grade, that's saying something. But now isn't the time for that, especially not with Lauren's eyes narrowed in my direction. The second James turns back to her, they of course soften, but I know the truth. She hates being asked to do this, and she's only doing it because James is the one making the request.

"Of course," Lauren says, shouldering her bag again and waving me forward. "Let's go, Greta."

Without another choice, I follow Lauren down the access road and leave James behind. I barely have time to remember I'm not trying to look over at the area behind the castle, but it doesn't matter. Large white tarps have been put up to keep anyone from seeing into the area. I keep up with Lauren's clipped steps as we walk. The farther and farther we get from the castle, the more I see other employees milling around, some of them whispering, some laughing. Two girls who are standing off to the side of the access road look at me and then look back at each other, eyes wide.

"That's her," one of them says, not bothering to lower her voice. "The one who—"

"Don't you two have work to do?" Lauren snaps, cutting them off with a slice of her voice. "What the fuck's wrong with you?"

My cheeks burn, and not just from the sun now. The girls are flabbergasted, mouths hanging open as if unable to believe the words that Lauren just shouted at them. Lauren, however, looks completely unbothered as she marches forward, lifting one hand in the air to examine a broken nail.

"God, people suck," she says, running her thumb over the place where the nail must've snapped off. "Can we hurry? I just made a nail appointment and don't want to be late."

I nod, still in semi-shock. She's moving faster now, and I have to practically jog to keep up with her. She looks down at me as I do and raises an eyebrow.

"Why're you walking like that?"

I pant. "Well, you're sort of walking fast."

"Oh, sorry," she says, thankfully slowing down. "I just have really long legs, you know, so it's hard for me to remember what it's like for shorter people."

She tosses her hair. "Anyway, don't you want to get home faster? God, I can't imagine what you had to deal with. Finding him. That must've been horrible. I have a really sensitive stomach, so that would've completely ruined my day."

I stare at her. I don't know what to say. And honestly, it doesn't seem like she really expects a response. She's back to checking her nail again as we approach the end of the access road and turn past the offices.

"And god, can you believe it's Neil? Like, I was literally just talking to him yesterday. And now he's *dead*. Over. Just like that. Which is terrible. And you know, I wonder if I should've seen it coming. He was so freaked out about that girl."

I blink. That girl. And then I remember, through the fog of everything, Lauren telling the other performers about Neil asking her about Hailey.

"And then this whole Mercy thing," she continues. "That wasn't making his life easier, either."

I trip over a rock in the road, body flung forward so that Lauren has to grab my arm to stop me. When she does, I feel that sharp edge of her broken nail digging into my skin.

"What the hell?" she asks. "Are you okay?"

I nod, struggling to stand up. "Did you . . . did you say Mercy wasn't making his life easier?"

Lauren rolls her eyes, releasing me from her grip. "Obviously. James left him and Grey in charge, right? And then he's got shit breaking all over the place and Mercy calling in. And Grey's useless, okay. If it weren't for me saving the day, literally every show would've gone down. And Neil told me he was worried she wouldn't come back at all. Wanted to make sure I was prepared to go on. Needed *someone* to count on."

"W-why? Why did he think she wouldn't come back?" I stammer. We're standing a little ways from Rocket, and I'm dusting my legs off, trying to prolong this moment. Because what is Lauren saying exactly?

"Oh, just because she couldn't wait to leave us," Lauren says. "Everyone always wants to act like she's the second coming, but she doesn't give a shit about this place. I told her that at the party, too. When I found her outside, I told her."

"You what?"

But Lauren's started moving again, apparently done waiting for me. I scramble after her as she continues to throw words out.

"I was supposed to be in that TV spot," Lauren says. "But Little Miss Mercy had to steal the spotlight as always. Do you know what it's like to kill yourself for something and have someone else take every little crumb away from you—even the crumbs they don't even really want?"

She flings open the door to the back of Rocket, hitting us both with a wave of the brutally cold air. She steps inside, and I follow. I go to the lockers, pretending like I don't know where my bag is as Lauren checks her makeup in the camera app on her phone. I have to keep her talking. This is an opportunity I won't get again, and I need to get every bit of information that I can. But how? One of the articles I read earlier talked about investigators using personal empathy as a strategy. It's worth a try.

"No," I say carefully. "I don't know exactly. But my best friend... well, my ex-best friend just seemed to have an easier time with life. She was always asking me why I couldn't get it right. And I didn't know what to tell her, whether it was class or social stuff or... or guys."

Lauren's eyes blink from her phone to me, unsettling me with her perfectly curled lashes.

"I just know it hurt," I continue, thinking fast. "When people held me to her standard. I was trying, but they didn't see that. They only saw her."

This is a mistake, I think, regretting everything I just said. Lauren doesn't care. If anything, she's another Caroline, and this will only make her stop talking.

But then she sighs, digging into her bag for a peachy lip gloss that she applies with trained swoops of her hand while she talks.

"You can't understand how people's minds work," she says. "Some people are just fucked up. Like Mercy. She was always carrying around this little journal, and I was sure she was writing about the rest of us. Little critiques that she could run off to James with. But I wasn't going to let her ruin anything more for me, so I took it to see what she was writing about us."

It's like the floor underneath me drops out. Liam told me that the other performers and Mercy didn't get along, that they messed with her stuff. But what Lauren's describing sounds like a diary. And if she took Mercy's diary . . .

"It didn't have anything interesting," Lauren says, pursing her lips into the camera. "It was *so* boring. Just these weird notes about performances. Absolutely worthless. But then, at the party, when I confronted her about stealing the TV spot, all she wanted to know was if I took her precious journal. I told her to get over herself, and she started crying and ran off into the woods. And then the next day no-shows. So it just goes to show that we have no idea what other people are thinking. Some people are just weird."

She pops the lip gloss back into her bag, turning to look at me before waving her hand at the lockers. "Did you get your bag? I do need to get to my appointment, you know."

But I can't breathe. So many of Lauren's words are ricocheting in my brain, choking the air out of my lungs.

"God, why're you looking at me like that?" Lauren says, eyes narrowing even more. "It's not like I was going to keep it. I was going to give it back to her the next day, but *she's* the one who didn't show up."

I shake my head, trying to wipe off my expression. I desperately need a better poker face.

"Oh, I wasn't, um," I start to say. "I just—"

"Seriously, it's nothing," she says, reaching into her bag and pulling out a composition notebook. "Look for yourself. I was going to give it to James anyway."

She shoves it into my hands before stepping back and folding her arms. I nearly drop it but manage to hold on to it.

"I know you're judging me," she says, eyes still narrowed. "Everyone's always judging me. But tell me, what would've happened if I no-showed? You think Mercy would've saved the day? I don't think so."

I realize there're tears in her eyes, shining under the fluorescent light. I open my mouth to speak, but she turns away before I can.

"Can we go now?" she asks. "I'm going to be fucking late."

I start to tell her that of course we can, but she's thrown open the door before I can say anything. I grab my bag, still balancing the notebook, and follow her outside. She doesn't say another word until we're at the Wardrobe lobby, clocking out.

"Give that to James, okay?" she says, turning to glance at me before she wipes away some smudged mascara under her eye. "It's not my problem anymore."

And then she's gone, red hair swishing behind her, leaving the too-sweet smell of her perfume hanging in her wake.

CHAPTER SIXTEEN

TUESDAY, JUNE 17
3:16 P.M.

MOM WAS WAITING for me when I finally got to the parking lot. As soon as I saw her, all the adrenaline that had been running through me with Lauren evaporated. I tried not to cry too much because I didn't want her to worry. And also, crying would hurt. Crying would make it real. And I was too tired. As much as I wanted to go through the journal, I couldn't do anything while she was hovering over me, forcing me to eat something and then putting me straight to bed. And I don't honestly even know if I would've had the energy even if I had been alone.

When I wake up, it's to Jasper barking and then running over to lick my hand that's hanging over the side of the bed. There's a cup of water on my nightstand that Mom must've placed there while I was asleep, and I drink it greedily. I check my phone for the time, not fully understanding why I'm just now waking up in the afternoon.

Until everything comes screaming back to me, including the throbbing ache in my head.

"Hon!" Mom calls up the stairs. "You awake?"

"Yeah," I manage. Jasper's still barking and bolts from my room and down the stairs, the sound echoing as he goes.

Mom's head appears in the doorway. "You've got a visitor."

I sit up. A visitor?

"Your friend from last night," Mom says with a smile. "Are you feeling up to seeing him?"

For a moment, I don't understand who she's talking about. And then I put it together.

Liam.

I jump out of bed and, just like Jasper did, bolt down the stairs and then out the front door. I keep going until I find Liam parked in our driveway, standing next to his car, back to me. His hair is fluffier than ever, as if he's been running his hand through it nonstop. I let out the tiniest choked sob at the sight of him, at the fact that he's here. At my house. The sound makes Liam turn around, his gaze finding mine immediately.

For once, I don't think about what I'm doing. I stumble forward and throw myself into him. His arms come around me without hesitation as he hugs me tight against his chest. And I let out a sob. I cry harder than I have all day, against him, burying my face in the starchy fabric of his button-down, shaking in the safe encircling of his arms.

"It's okay," Liam says, one of his hands moving. "I've got you."

I tense, thinking he's about to push me away, but instead, his hand comes to my head, resting there, stroking my hair with the gentlest touch imaginable. It makes me cry even harder.

We stay there for a moment, me clinging to him in the driveway. But eventually, he pulls back just a little so I can see his face looking down at me. There're dark moons under his eyes that weren't there earlier, redness taking over the white. He's more than tired, and I know because I am, too. But when he looks at me, the only thing I see is relief.

"I'm so sorry, Greta," he says. "I had no idea."

It takes me a moment to understand what he's apologizing for, and then I realize it's for taking me to the turret. But it never even crossed my mind that he had done that on purpose. I wanted to go up there as much as he wanted to take me.

"I know you didn't," I say, stepping back slightly to make more space between us. "I'm just sorry for Neil."

Liam's hands drop from my shoulders, but they don't leave me completely. He holds on to my elbows.

"I wasn't sure if I should just come over," Liam says. "But I couldn't stop worrying about you."

I manage a smile. "I'm glad you're here."

And I am. So unbelievably glad to not have to face the weirdness of today alone. Because as nice as Mom's trying to be, she doesn't get it. Not like Liam.

"You want to come inside?" I ask. "My mom might fuss a little, but I would really appreciate the company."

Liam smiles. "I'm not going anywhere, Sherlock. Not until you tell me to."

I feel the blossom of something warm in my chest. We head inside, with Liam pausing to greet Jasper, just like last night. I tell Mom Liam's going to keep me company, and she tells me to let her know if I need anything while she works in her office.

My room feels small with Liam in it. My bed's messy since I

was just napping, plus my investigation notebooks are flung all over my desk. I catch sight of my hair in my mirror and nearly pass out again, hurriedly fighting it into a claw clip before turning to Liam. He's sitting on the floor with Jasper happily flopped over with his head on Liam's leg, so I grab my bag and sit next to them.

"It just doesn't make any sense," he says. "I just can't believe he killed himself."

I nod, not knowing what to say. I don't want to think about it, and yet, it's all I can think about.

"I mean, I know the guy was a little weird, but it sucks he felt like this was the only way out," Liam continues. "Like he didn't have anyone to talk to or whatever."

The words jolt me, sticking inside.

"Lauren said he was talking to her about Hailey Portman," I say. "And he was also talking to Mercy. She said he was freaked out."

Liam tilts his head. "Why?"

I shrug. "I don't know. But then . . . you remember last night at bowling, right? He was calling Mercy."

"Do you think he was trying to tell someone what he was going to do?" Liam asks. "Like . . . he wanted someone to talk him out of it? Because god. I just never thought Neil would do something like that."

I shiver as the memory of my nightmare resurfaces, Neil pounding on the gondola and screaming.

There's glass in my eyes. Don't you see?

Glass. Because of his broken glasses. Because—

"Wait," I say, thoughts freezing as I stand up straight. "Oh my god."

"What?" Liam asks.

Because now that I'm remembering, it doesn't make any sense.

Why would his glasses be broken if he hanged himself? I think of Detective Kupferle grilling me about finding him. I think—

"*Detective* Kupferle," I say, realization clicking. "He's a homicide detective. They don't think Neil hanged himself. They think someone killed him and made it look like a suicide."

"What?" Liam asks, shaking his head. "No. No way."

I nod. "Think about it. His glasses were broken. Are we supposed to believe he got into a fight and then decided to hang himself?"

It's almost laughable, now that I'm thinking about it. Whoever killed Neil, they made a huge mistake. But why?

He wanted to talk to Mercy. He didn't come to bowling. Somewhere in between making that phone call and this morning, someone killed Neil.

He wanted to talk to *Mercy*.

I think of the journal Lauren gave me. I know she said it didn't have anything interesting in it, but what if? What if Mercy's disappearance is connected to Neil's murder?

"Greta," Liam says. "You're looking a little . . . well, let's just say this. Do you have something to share?"

"Maybe," I say. "Possibly. Definitely."

I pull out the notebook that Lauren gave me and pass it to Liam.

Liam arches an eyebrow. "Um, have you been sneaking into greenrooms again without telling me?"

I shake my head. "Lauren gave this to me."

As he examines the cover, I tell him about Lauren stealing the journal from Mercy, yelling at her about it at the party, how the journal's full of Mercy's notes on her performances. But I also tell him about the theories now spinning around in my head connecting Neil's death to Mercy.

"I haven't looked through it yet," I say. "Mom was sort of hovering, and I was tired."

I feel guilty saying that. Investigators shouldn't get tired, right? The investigation can't wait. But Liam only nods.

"Of course you were," he says. "So you think this might have something telling us what's happened to Mercy?"

He passes it back to me, and I stare at it in my lap. It's a plain composition book, its corners slightly bent. The cover's softer than the new ones I usually get for school, and the spine's been cracked a thousand times over. When I flip through it, I see that nearly every page is full of careful, loopy handwriting in every pen color under the sun. There are Post-it notes stuck to several pages, though I don't pause to read any of them.

"We won't know unless we look," I say.

Liam nods as Jasper lets out a loud yawn. "I guess Lauren already looked through it and said there's nothing. So what could be the harm?"

I nod, taking a breath as I settle back down next to him. There's no name anywhere on the journal, not on the front or the first page. I position the notebook between me and Liam, balancing it on our legs so we can both read at the same time.

Performance Notes: May 3
Need to get a better handle on the high note
   in verse 2
Do breathwork homework
Coming off stilted in opening mono—rework tone

I keep flipping, finding that most of the pages seem to follow this format: a title, a date, and some bulleted notes. A few pages have scattered Post-it notes stuck to them, some blank, some with a handful of words.

I pause on another entry.

Performance Notes: June 2
Transition needs smoothing
Sharper movements in dance
K watched again

I pause on the last three words. Liam notices them as well, putting his hand out to trace a line underneath them with his finger.

"Who's K?" he asks.

I shake my head. "I don't know."

I keep turning pages. On several of the entries, we see the same words: "K watched again." I look at Liam, confused.

"Who would be watching them all the time like this?" I ask. "Isn't James the only director?"

Liam nods. "Maybe she had a code or something?"

It's weird, but I don't have any answers for him. So I keep flipping until I pause on a page near the back, one that's filled from the top to the bottom with the same line, over and over and over again.

Funerals are quiet, but deaths—not always.

My heart seems to calcify in my chest. I've heard that before. *Mercy* said that to me the night of the party. Something hums in my brain. I turn back to the front of the journal, trying to see if one of the earlier entries gives me a clue.

"What are these Post-its?" Liam asks, stopping me from turning another page.

On the May 6 entry, there's a Post-it that says: *Get opening-day schedule*

On May 9: *Ask Neil for map*

On May 15: *Cross-check with opening-day schedule*

On May 28: *Streetcar cast list?*

I consider each of them, trying to make sense of them.

"Seems like things Mercy needs to do," I say. "Like tasks. And this last one . . . hang on."

I get up and find the playbill and the two other notes, handing them all over to Liam so he can look at them. As he examines them, I pace my room, trying to piece together everything spinning in my mind.

"Mercy's Post-it talks about *Streetcar*," I say. "And that playbill is for *A Streetcar Named Desire* when Hailey was in it. But why would Mercy have that playbill?"

"Maybe she's a fan?" Liam wonders, turning over the playbill to touch the ripped edge. "Some sort of true crime–theater fan combination?"

I purse my lips. It doesn't sound like Mercy to me. And that line. Why did she say that to me at the party?

"Wait a minute," Liam says, holding up the notebook. "Greta, look at this. The handwriting on the Post-its . . . it's not the same as the journal."

I nearly fall over trying to get close enough to him to see what he's pointing out. And when I do, my mouth falls open.

Because he's right. The Post-its don't have the same loopy handwriting as the journal entries. This handwriting is prim and precise, almost like a font you could literally type on a computer.

"Whoever wrote these Post-its definitely didn't write these entries," Liam says, turning the notebook over. "And honestly, now that I'm looking at it, this thing looks old. Really old."

And oh my god.

Oh my god.

It all comes together.

Lauren saying Mercy always had the notebook with her. Silvia telling me that Neil talked to Mercy about Hailey. Neil calling Mercy the night he died.

Funerals are quiet, but deaths—not always.

Mercy saying that line because she wanted to know why it was written over and over again in this journal.

Because it's not her journal.

"She was trying to figure it out," I say, eyes widening. "She was investigating, too."

"What?" Liam asks, clearly confused. "What're you talking about?"

"This isn't Mercy's journal," I say, stunned as the words come out. "Mercy found Hailey's notebook. She and Neil were using it to figure out who killed Hailey Portman twenty years ago."

"But if that's true," he says, "are you saying someone killed Neil because he was looking into this?"

I don't know that, but I'm starting to think it must be true. And Mercy . . . I keep thinking about our conversation, her wide, frightened eyes. Is that why—

I gasp.

"The notebook," I say. "Mercy was going to show me the notebook!"

CHAPTER SEVENTEEN

WEDNESDAY, JUNE 18
9:09 A.M.

MERCY GOODWIN WAS trying to solve Hailey Portman's murder.

It's something people have been trying for years, each person picking up the different pieces and trying to put them together. Her older boyfriend. The conversations she had at the park. Her family history. Even the gossip that you only get if you dig really, really deep about how Hailey wasn't always the nicest person.

But Mercy found something that no one else had: Hailey's own words.

Now the question is . . . what happened to her because of what she was doing? Her riptide finally has a name, but still no explanation. It certainly doesn't tell me why Allie would be calling in sick for her.

It's a puzzle I'm determined to pick up and solve for her now that I'm the one with the notebook. Now it's up to me to try to figure out what, exactly, it all means. Mom didn't let Liam stay much longer yesterday—insisted I needed "rest"—but she's letting me meet him this morning. Which is good, because I desperately need to talk all this out. It also helped that, last night, we got an email that all Entertainment shifts have been canceled, which meant we both have the day free. I texted him and suggested doughnuts, and now he's waiting for me in the driveway. Before I go, Mom gives me a long hug, followed by the extra cash in her purse that I can use for doughnuts.

"Sugar fixes everything," she tells me, just before kissing me on the cheek. "And remember, I'm doing the Gillfillan birthday, so I'll be home late. Text me if you need me."

I nod, tell her and Jasper goodbye, then head outside. From here, I can see that Liam's head is down, his hair is even more unwieldy than usual, poking up on one side. It makes me wonder if he slept as badly as I did. I had the same nightmare as before with Neil, Hailey, and Mercy on the gondola. But then he lifts his head and notices me, and a bright smile bursts onto his face.

I hold up the cash. "By-the-Sea Doughnuts?"

"Careful," he says. "Saying something like that might just make me fall in love with you."

My cheeks flush, and he keeps smiling as I get into the car. It's just a joke, obviously. It does nothing to me. And when I tuck my hair behind my ear, I'm not doing it so that he can see more of my face. I'm doing it because I'm nervous, but again, only because of everything that's happened during the past twenty-four hours. Liam is . . . Liam is just my investigating partner. Nothing more.

Still, I'm getting used to Liam's car, the feel of how low it is to the ground. Here, everything feels closer, including Liam. Liam and his fluffy hair and dark jeans that have little creases near his thighs. It's not exactly comfortable, but it's definitely not uncomfortable, either.

"So," he says, pulling out of the driveway. "Did you stay up all night reading?"

"Obviously," I say, holding up my notebook. Not *the* notebook. I don't feel safe taking that out of my room. I've stored that safely in my nightstand drawer.

"I've made several flowcharts and tables in here for us to review," I say. "I've also taken pictures of the key pages and notes for us to review together."

"All right," Liam says. "So I know you said in your text that you wanted to talk things out—"

"Mercy was trying to figure out who the Gondola Killer is," I say, words tumbling out of me. "I think she was suspicious of whoever this 'K' person was who kept watching. There were several Post-its with question marks next to that name. And then there's figuring out how the notes tie in, since they were in the locker."

Liam nods, bobbing his head to the song that's playing softly underneath our conversation.

"So you want *us* to solve Hailey's murder," he muses, "in order to figure out what happened to Mercy."

"Precisely," I say, flipping through my notes. But before I can continue, Liam's already parking at the doughnut shop. By-the-Sea Doughnuts is my favorite doughnut shop by far. There's a bright mural painted on the side, and the front is covered with at least a thousand different stickers. We order and then take a seat at one of the spare tables outside. Liam takes thoughtful bites of a chocolate glazed while I devour my maple bar.

"I still think we should go to the police," he says. "Like, immediately. Clearly, Neil died because of this."

I bite the inside of my cheek. "We don't know that for sure yet. I mean, we have our theories, but we don't have any real evidence.

205

And we don't know how the performers and everything tie in to this. Like, why does Allie have Mercy's phone? Until we have a complete picture, we need to figure this out on our own."

Secretly, the idea of having to talk to Detective Kupferle or anyone else about Mercy makes my skin crawl. I don't trust them. Maybe, I think, we can talk to James about it if it comes down to it. He can help us.

"I think we should follow Mercy's plan," I say, pointing at the picture with the remains of my maple bar. "Figure out what happened, find something concrete, and *then* go to the police."

"Yeah, sure, but I feel like I should maybe point out the obvious here," Liam says, finishing his doughnut. "Mercy's plan led to her going *missing* at best. And we still don't even know if she's, you know. Alive."

It's the first time either of us has said it out loud, and it makes my stomach flip with the doughnut inside. But I refuse to be dissuaded.

"All we know is that she needs help," I say. "We can't give up on her. I think we need to build a timeline, figure out the last places she was seen. I've done a lot of research on the investigative process, and they all say that's where to start."

Liam snorts. "Who says, exactly? *Law and Order*? Reddit?"

"That's not important," I say, dusting sugar off my palm. I don't want to tell him that he's right.

"What about going to Mercy's house?" Liam says. "We could knock on the door. She could answer, tell us she really is sick, and then we can talk to her about what happened."

"Oh," I say, semi-awkwardly. "I did that. I tried, but no one was home."

"Well," Liam says. "Maybe we try again. It can't hurt, right? With everything we've found out?"

I sigh. He's right. I did only try once, and it does feel like a step we shouldn't ignore.

"Let's go," I say. "It's only a few minutes away."

We throw away the paper bags our doughnuts came in and head in the direction of the address. Within minutes, Liam is pulling up in front of Mercy's duplex.

"Okay, so we go to the door, and we say we are friends of Mercy's and we just wanted to check in because we haven't seen her at work," I say as Liam parks the car. "Right?"

Liam nods. "Sounds fair to me. Let's hope she's home."

I doubt it, I think, and then regret the thought immediately. I *should* be hoping Mercy's home. That would mean she's alive and well, just avoiding work.

We follow the path up through the pristine yard, careful not to step on any of the flowers that line the walkway. This time, Liam's the one to knock and ring the doorbell, and I hold my breath, waiting for the same silence from when I came by myself.

Only this time, there isn't silence. This time, there's the yapping of a small dog, followed by someone shushing it and heavy footsteps before the door opens in front of us, revealing a severe-looking woman with high, overly rounded eyebrows and long silver hair that's twisted into a bun on her head. She's wearing gardening gloves that have fresh dirt on them, the smell of earth competing with some kind of lemon scent from the house.

"I'm not interested in solar panels," she says to us. "I told you last week to put it down on your form so I wouldn't be harassed again."

Both Liam and I blink, but thankfully, he recovers before I do.

"Oh, we're not here with solar panels," he says. "We were wondering if, um, Mercy Goodwin lives here? We're her coworkers at Hyper Kid. Are you Rachel Goodwin?"

The woman's already thin lips purse. "I might be, but Mercy doesn't live here anymore. She moved out weeks ago."

"Oh," Liam says, exchanging a look with me. "Do you maybe have a new address? Or—"

"Mercy hasn't bothered to leave me one for mail forwarding, so no, I don't have one," Rachel says. "And even if I did, I wouldn't give it out to two random strangers who showed up on my doorstep. Now, I have my begonias to get back to."

She starts to shut the door, but I throw myself forward before she can.

"Please, ma'am," I say. "We're coworkers, but we're also Mercy's friends. And we're worried about her. Do you think we could maybe talk to you about some things? Get your insight?"

The woman's eyes narrow. Behind her, the dog that was barking starts up again, and I glance over her shoulder to see a small white terrier that looks like it might be down to one tooth. After considering us, she shushes the dog, then waves us inside.

"Follow me to the backyard and we can talk while I garden," she says. "But I don't have all day. I don't want to spend hours out here melting in this heat."

Liam and I don't argue. We follow her through the small hallway, which is meticulously clean. We move quickly because Rachel moves quickly, the little dog jumping at our heels as we go. We're in the backyard before we know it, a small gated area with an array of different plants, both potted and in the ground. Rachel leans over a plot, a bag of soil next to her, and stabs at the ground with a trowel. The *chuck-chuck-chuck* sound is the only thing among us for a moment, until she cuts her eyes to us.

"Well?" she says. "I thought you had questions for me?"

"Right," Liam says. "We, um . . ."

He looks at me and makes a face, as if to say, "What now?"

"Mercy hasn't been showing up to work," I say. "We've tried to call and text her, but she doesn't respond. And—"

"Hmph," Rachel interrupts. "No surprise there. My niece has never had any thought for anyone but herself. Always talking about her dreams and what she wants to do. Has no patience for reality."

"She's your niece?" Liam asks, to which Rachel nods.

"By blood, yes. Her father—my brother—and Miriam split up a few years ago, and he didn't maintain a relationship with them. When Miriam died, I took her in until she finished high school, at my brother's request. But we never got along. How could we when all she ever wanted to do was go on this audition and that? I tried to tell her that her dream would only lead to the same heartbreak it led her mother to. But she never listened. Too stubborn."

The words swirl among us, undercut only by the continued sound of the trowel striking the earth. Rachel wipes her forehead and shakes her head.

"You say she's stopped showing up to work, stopped responding," she continues. "That's what she does. She never wanted to be in this house. She was always out on auditions or running on those damn trails up there in San Joaquin Hills. Never mind that I could've used her help with chores. You could tell she didn't want to spend a second here that she didn't have to."

The disdain in her voice is laced with disappointment, and it stings. Because I know that tone. It's the same one my dad used when discussing me with Assistant Principal Taggert. Critical. Ashamed. It makes my eyes burn, and I have to look at the ground.

"My point is," Rachel says, putting a plant into the freshly dug soil, "you shouldn't be worried about this. She's probably gone off to New York like she was always threatening, and she'll come crawling back at some point. Hell, she was supposed to come pick up a box of stuff from me, but did she? No. Because she's only focused on herself, like I said. Expects me to take care of it."

I perk up. "She left a box of stuff?"

I exchanged another look with Liam, trying to keep my breathing steady.

"I mean, we could always take that off your hands," Liam offers. "If it's an inconvenience. We could give it to her when she comes back to work."

Rachel waves a hand, sending dirt flying at the little dog.

"It was going on the curb anyway," she says, standing up. "Come on. Take it and leave."

She walks us back inside and grabs a small box off the counter, the name *Mercy* written across the top in Sharpie. She thrusts it into Liam's arms without ceremony, then gestures at us to move.

"There," she says. "Now get. Before this heat turns nasty."

We don't need to be told twice. We head outside, thanking her as we go, listening to her dog bark as the door swings shut.

We walk to Liam's car, settling back into the seats. The quiet of the neighborhood around us makes every noise feel louder, like the birds in the trees are screaming rather than singing.

We both look at the box in Liam's lap like a bomb about to go off. He looks at me, then at my nodding gingerly takes the top of the box off, and we both peer inside at the mismatched belongings: several T-shirts from various theater companies or productions, a pair of battered running shoes, an iPhone charger, a bag of old makeup, and a Polaroid headshot of Mercy. In the picture, she stares out at us, her eyes as piercing in the photo as I remember them being in real life.

"There's nothing," Liam says. "Nothing important, anyway. Well, at least we got to talk to the aunt—"

"Wait," I say, reaching over the edge of the box to grab a lined piece of paper that's stuck under one of the shirts. I turn it over and examine it, reading it quickly.

> *You blocked me, which shouldn't be a surprise. You always thought you deserved the last word. Maybe you won't even read this. But I have to write it anyway.*
>
> *I thought we were mature enough to handle this. I tried to be. I get it. You don't love me the way I love you. And that's fine. I swear to God, Mercy. That's fine.*
>
> *I never said I didn't want you to go to New York because of me. I just don't want you to go if you're just living your mom's dream. If it really is your dream, then go. Like I said, I don't care.*
>
> *But don't go because you think you have to.*
>
> *I'm not making any sense. Whatever. Don't talk to me again, okay? We're done.*

"Well," Liam says, reading over my shoulder. "That brings us to two weirdly threatening letters."

I think about this. "But this one's old. The aunt said she hadn't lived here for a while. I don't know what to make of all of this."

Especially since the aunt's harshness toward Mercy has me even more confused. How could someone be dismissive of their own niece? Unless . . . unless Mercy is really like she said. But I can't believe that. I remember the things people said about me, the lies they spread. Even my dad bought into them. Rachel's just another person who doesn't understand Mercy. Like Lauren and her rumors about Grey and Mercy. They don't see the real Mercy.

Not like I do.

I reach into the box and grab the running shoes, turning them over.

"Do you remember what Rachel said? Mercy was always going running in the San Joaquin Hills."

Liam nods. "Yeah? So?"

"Well, Lauren told me that Mercy ran into the woods after their argument," I say. "And now we know that Mercy knew those trails pretty well. It's also her last known location, based on what Lauren said."

"So you want to go to the woods?"

I shrug. "I think that, after yesterday, some fresh air sounds nice. Maybe it'll help us think. Get into Mercy's headspace, you know?"

Liam considers this, then grins.

"Ready when you are, Sherlock."

Liam makes quick time driving to the San Joaquin Hills. It's way less creepy here during the daytime, and when Liam parks his car I take in the houses that line the street. They're larger and spread farther apart than the cookie-cutter houses we passed on the way in, with sprawling front yards. Liam and I walk up to the house from the night of the party, and then I follow him onto the trail that snakes along its side.

As we walk farther into the trees, I'm suddenly aware of just how alone we are, I mean, minus the occasional joggers and stuff. And how he's just here with me, even though he doesn't need to be.

I try to imagine asking Caroline to do something like this with me. Caroline would've wanted an itemized list of every activity I was planning and why. She would've poked holes in my theories about Mercy and everything that's happened and would've found every reason not to go with me to investigate. We wouldn't have even made it to the car, and that was before everything in our friendship fell apart.

"So," Liam asks, cutting through my thoughts, "how do you know Detective Kupferle?"

I jolt, panic zipping up my spine. I've made it this long without Liam finding out my secrets, but I didn't think this through. If he finds out, will he decide he doesn't want to hang out with me anymore? What if he casts me aside?

"I mean, the guy seemed like an asshole," Liam says before I can answer, kicking a rock near his shoe so that it bounces in front of us. "I knew I hadn't done anything wrong, but five minutes with that guy, and I sure as hell felt like I did."

A laugh streaks out of me, unbidden. Because Detective Kupferle definitely has that effect on people. Looking back, I'm sure that's why Taggert brought him in. He wanted me filled with nothing but guilt and shame—as if I wasn't already overflowing with both.

I glance over at Liam, knowing that I'm probably blushing because it's impossible for me to hide anything with my face. I don't know whether it's Mom or Dad I can blame for the fact that I turn instantly red when I'm feeling embarrassed, but I do.

"If it's a bad memory or something, you don't have to tell me," Liam says. "I just, I want you to know that you *can* tell me this stuff. If you want to."

"It's not that," I say, shaking my head. "It just . . . it doesn't matter. It's not important."

I hate that my eyes are misting over with tears. We turn down another path, this one heading deeper into the woods. I try to keep ahead of Liam so that he can't see my eyes.

But then he puts his hand out and takes mine, gently, so that I could pull away at any time. He's stopped, and the touch makes me stop, too. I risk looking at him, right at his brown eyes. They stay steady on me, like the quicksand that every cartoon ever warned me about. I'm never going to be able to move with him looking at me like that.

"Greta," he says. "I just want to make sure you're okay. Because if you need someone to talk to . . . I'm here. And I'm not going anywhere."

I let out a half-hearted laugh. "You don't know that. What if I murdered somebody?"

He arches an eyebrow.

"Okay, bad joke," I say, wincing. "I just mean that you say that, but you can't know."

Because Caroline and I literally had necklaces that said "Best Friends Forever," and it didn't matter.

He keeps watching me, and now I'm struggling in the quicksand. I need to look away from those eyes.

"Okay," he says. "So yeah, if you murdered somebody, I might have to, you know, rethink this. But something tells me that's not what happened. So . . . if you want to tell me, I'm here."

His lips quirk into that infuriatingly adorable half smile, and he kicks a little at the ground between us. "After all, you didn't shun me when you thought I was a drug dealer."

It surprises a laugh out of me, and I shift slightly on my feet.

I have to tell Liam *something*. Maybe I can tell him about what led up to my meeting Detective Kupferle without telling him the very last piece of the story, the one that would make him never want to speak to me again.

And then I realize something that surprises me.

I *want* to tell him. At least, I want to tell him about the beginning part.

There's a cluster of medium-sized rocks just a little bit off the path, and I nod toward them. We walk over and sit, and I fold my hands in my lap and take a breath. For this part, I know that I can't look at Liam, I have to look at the dried leaves on the ground. But he doesn't push me. He sits on his rock and lets his knees touch mine, not in the way that pushes or presses, just in the way that reminds me that he's here.

"I liked this guy," I say. "His name was Brad, and I thought he liked me back."

I tell him about how Brad would ask me for help in precalculus, how he started DMing me for help on homework, and how, eventually, he asked for my number. I tell him about Caroline, too, how I didn't tell her, because she said we shouldn't be dating at all because we had to focus on our classes. I tell him about how, one night, when I was home alone, Brad texted me and asked me to send him a naked picture.

I wait for Liam to move his knee, but he doesn't.

"I thought he liked me," I say, and my voice is thick, even if the tears haven't started falling yet. "So I took some. And . . . I sent one to him, of me. I was topless. I know it was wrong. I know—"

Liam takes my hand, and I grip it, hard. Because now I am crying. Now the tears are every bit of shame leaving me.

"It doesn't matter," I say. "I did it, and the next day, when I got to school . . . I really thought he was going to ask me out or something."

My voice is hysterical now. Because Caroline's voice is taunting me in the back of my mind, and I push her away as I keep going.

"He showed the whole lacrosse team," I say. "Every one of them. And I didn't know until I was called into the assistant principal's office."

"What an asshole," Liam says, and his voice is darker than I've ever heard it before. "Who the fuck does that?"

I shrug. "Guys, I guess."

"No," Liam says, squeezing my hand again. "No, that's bullshit. He's—"

I can tell he wants to keep going, but his eyes find mine, and he stops. Maybe because he knows that I'm not done, or maybe because he realizes that it doesn't matter what he thinks right now.

"They told me that my picture had been 'circulating,'" I say. "The assistant principal . . . he told me that it was illegal to produce child pornography, and did I know that I could be arrested?"

Liam drops my hand. "What the fuck?"

I nod. "I didn't know, obviously. I just knew that . . . I mean, I'd seen other kids send nudes and stuff. But I was sent home. It was horrible."

"Jesus," Liam says, shaking his head. "So that's why Detective Kupferle was there?"

I avoid his eyes. I'm not lying, I tell myself. I'm just skipping through part of the story.

"Yes," I say.

"Wait," Liam says. "What happened to Brad?"

I blink at him. "What do you mean?"

"What happened to him for sharing your picture?" Liam asks, anger in his voice.

"Oh," I say. "He got detention, I think. And he had to turn his phone in to the front office every day during school for the rest of the year. And he promised to delete the photo, which he said he did but obviously didn't."

I say obviously because whatever they made him do didn't stop him from printing out pictures. Which didn't stop me from going down to the locker room and—

But I'm not telling Liam that part, especially since right now he looks straight-up . . . well, murderous. He shakes his head. "But that doesn't make any sense."

I look at the ground. I remember, when it first happened, that this was my instinct, too. That it was Brad's fault. I wanted to tell Assistant Principal Taggert that; I remember the question bubbling up from inside me. . . .

But then the shame. The shame drowned me.

"School wasn't the same after that," I tell Liam quickly, before he realizes I'm holding back. "I . . . things were just uncomfortable, so I did my work from home for the rest of the school year, about a month."

Another not-quite-lie, and I cover it by swiping at my cheek. The tears aren't coming out anymore, but my face is wet and puffy.

"But even though I wasn't at school, my life still sort of fell apart. Caroline didn't want to talk to me anymore," I say. "My reputation after that . . . well, she said I wasn't the person she thought

I was. I deleted all my social media. I couldn't handle the messages. Maybe they would've stopped, but I couldn't handle it if they didn't."

Now Liam's voice is cold. "So *then* what happened to Brad? If he said he'd deleted the photo but lied?"

I shrug. "Taggert said it was my fault because I created the photo in the first place. He told me in our last meeting . . . 'The internet is forever. This is what I was trying to tell you, Greta, about why this is so dangerous.' He said he was trying to help me."

Liam doesn't have words for that. It's funny. I've been so upset with myself that I realize that I haven't saved a lot of anger for Brad. Because thinking of Brad has filled me with so much anxiety for so long that I haven't had room for other emotions. Seeing Liam like this . . . angry for me . . . I don't know what to do with that. But of course, he doesn't know the whole story. And it has to stay that way.

"Anyway," I say. "I figured that I needed a fresh start. A rebrand. And so, I decided to get a job. I hoped that I could . . . that I could find people who didn't know. Who would give me a chance as me without all of that. And . . . and people did. The other ushers. Ivy. You."

I meet his eyes and smile. He takes my hand and rubs his thumb over it.

"But I guess it still doesn't make sense," he says. "Your school had a homicide detective come to . . . what, scare you straight or something?"

I tense. Does he realize I'm leaving something out?

"Yeah, something like that. They're friends," I say. "Taggert and him. It was a favor, basically. My mom was really mad about it."

"Jesus," Liam says. "Well, your mom and I can start a club. Seems like an abuse of power if you ask me."

I laugh. "I'll join, too."

He leans toward me, letting our foreheads touch. It's not a full hug, but somehow, it's better. It says he really is staying here with me. That he's not abandoning me.

"I can see why Mercy likes being out here," I say, realizing just how red my face must be. "It's really peaceful."

Liam nods, helping me stand up from the rocks. "Yeah. It's nice. I'm not much of a nature guy, but even I like this."

We continue walking, following the jogging trail. We're still nearish to the houses, but we're getting farther. We come upon a small clearing that has a small ditch by the trees where there are piles of leaves and twigs, some sort of den made by animals, probably. Liam takes pictures of different parts of the trail as we walk, saying things about how perfect the sunlight is right now. As he does, I try to imagine Mercy out here. It's nice now, but I remember it was raining the night of the party. What did she do when she was out here? Did she just cry? Call someone for help? Or—

Something in the dirt glints at me, a spark of sunlight catching on metal. There, covered in dried leaves and dried mud, is the edge of something gold.

I bend down, digging through the earth with my hands. I grimace at the feeling of dirt underneath my fingernails. But I keep going until I can shimmy whatever I've found out of the packed mud. As I do, the sharp metal corner slices my palm, and I yank my hand back with a hiss.

"Be careful," Liam says, moving closer to take my hand. "Shit, Greta, you're bleeding."

But I brush him off. Because it doesn't matter. I've seen that gold before. I've seen it recently.

I use my nonbleeding hand now to dig, more carefully than before, until I finally can pick up what I've found.

"Is that . . . is that Silvia's gold badge? From bowling?" Liam asks, confused. "But why would that be out here?"

I brush off the dirt, taking in the familiar lettering. I hold my breath as I turn it over, as I see the smear of red on the back that's crusted over the engraved words.

Because it's not Silvia's name on the back. In fact, it's not her badge at all.

It's Hailey's.

CHAPTER EIGHTEEN

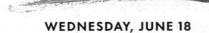

WEDNESDAY, JUNE 18
10:51 A.M.

I STARE AT the piece of gold still glinting in my hand. I wipe the dirt off with my thumb, turning it side to side so that it catches the sun. Hailey's name is written in the same looping, engraved cursive that Silvia's is.

"It's Hailey's badge," I say, looking up at Liam. "Silvia said they were given these at the opening-night party, right?"

"But why would it be out here?" Liam asks, looking it over. "Why is it here at all?" I consider his question, staring at the gold. I run through all the possibilities in my mind, just as I keep swiping my thumb over the metal.

"Mercy could've found it," I say, feeling my body thrum. "She brought it to the party. It might even be what she wanted to show me."

"But then why not show you right then?" Liam asks. "If she really did have it on her."

I bite my lip. I don't know the answer to that.

"Maybe the notebook is what she wanted to show me," I say. "Maybe that was the test. If I passed, then I'd get to see this."

I turn it over again in my hand. I bring my other hand to wipe the sweat that's starting to bead on my forehead, but Liam grabs my wrist.

"You're still bleeding," he says, holding my hand out. And he's right. It's not a terribly deep cut, but it is still a cut.

"We need to get this cleaned off before it gets infected with all this dirt," Liam says. "And you probably shouldn't keep touching the badge. Since it's, you know. Probably part of a crime scene."

"Shit," I say. "You're right. And now . . . now we really should call the cops, right?"

"Probably for the best," Liam says.

My heart sinks, even though I should be happy to pass this job off, especially now that it's clear that the stakes are much, much higher than we could've realized. Mercy found this, this item that probably has DNA and who knows what else on it.

"What if there's other stuff out here?" I say. "I should keep looking. Or . . . or mark the spot or something, before we leave."

"One thing at a time," Liam says. "I'm going to go get you some wipes and some gauze for your hand—"

"What are you, a doctor?" I ask, snorting a little.

"My mom's a nurse," he says. "She makes us keep a first aid kit in the trunk."

"Oh," I say, feeling more than a little ridiculous.

"I also have some plastic bags," he says. "I'll put the badge in there. While I do that, you can look around a little, but don't go too far."

"Okay," I say, passing the badge to Liam. Ever since he said "infected," it's like I can feel the pulse in my hand. I know, logically, that it doesn't happen like that . . . or does it?

"I'll be right back," Liam says.

And then he's gone, holding the badge out to the side like it's a snake about to bite him.

It leaves me free to do what I said I would. Liam won't be long, so I just sort of poke around with my nonbleeding hand in the same area. But I don't find anything. Not like the badge. It's quieter without Liam. I can hear the birds chirping and squirrels skittering through the trees. I can hear the snap of a twig—

I whip around at the sound.

It sounded like a footstep, but the clearing is empty except for me.

"Liam?" I call out, even though he can't possibly be back that quickly.

Now I really do feel my blood pulsing through my hand. The pace quickens along with my heartbeat.

Someone attacked Mercy for that badge, I think. Someone found out Mercy was looking into the Gondola Killer and wanted to stop her from figuring everything out. Someone knew she had it, and they came for it. The Gondola Killer? Or someone working with him?

And what will he—they—do to me and Liam once they know we have it?

I don't think. I leave the clearing, hurrying after Liam, but I've always had a terrible sense of direction. Panic doesn't help. I'm barreling through the brush, trying to find the path we were on originally, and I can't stop imagining that more twigs are snapping.

There! To the left. And over there. And—

"Greta?"

I whirl around, hands up in front of my face, eyes wide. It takes me a moment to process who's in front of me, but when I do, my breathing immediately steadies.

"Ivy?"

She's in all black, the material slick against her brown skin. A tattoo of a scorpion's stinger peeks out of her sports bra, and I can finally see the sun and stars inked on her wrist, the one she normally hides under the sweatband at work. Her curls are pulled into a messy ponytail, her cheeks flushed.

"Shit, Greta, I didn't know you ran out here," Ivy says, face cracking into a grin. "Why didn't you tell me? These are my favorite trails to hit after work."

I look down at my clothes. I'm in sweats and an old T-shirt. I guess I can pass this off as running attire. But just as I think that, I see my dirty hands, one still bleeding, and Ivy's gaze dips to them as well.

"Um, summer homework," I say quickly. "For my . . . science class. We have to collect soil samples. There was a rock where I was digging."

"That sucks," Ivy says, uncorking her water bottle as she steps closer. "You should rinse that off."

Before I can say anything, she's pouring the cold water over my hand, washing away the bigger chunks of dirt and blood. It's not clean, but it's better than it was, though the blood almost immediately beads up again to the surface.

"Liam's here, too," I say. "He went to get me bandages."

Ivy smirks. "Of course he did. Come on. Let's go wait over there for him."

She waves me over to a long, flat rock where we can both sit down. I don't know what to say to her. Does she know I'm lying? She must know I am, and I hate that this is becoming a pattern. I should tell her the truth. I can trust her, after all. This is Ivy, my savior at Hyper Kid. I take a breath.

"You doing okay with all the Neil stuff?" Ivy asks, breaking in before I can ask.

I blink. Oh. Yes. Neil. I've been so caught up with Mercy and Hailey that I nearly forgot about him. Except for my nightmare, I guess.

"Grief's weird," Ivy says. "I know you only just met him, but it'll probably still hit you hard. Be gentle with yourself."

I nod. "Are . . . are you okay?"

She shrugs, rolling her head to crack her neck, making the joints pop.

"Honestly? Not really," she says. "We had a . . . complicated relationship."

I blink, waiting for her to continue. She glances at me, sips her water, then continues.

"We didn't get along," she says. "He was such a fucking try-hard and a general pain in my ass. And yet, well. Maybe I shouldn't say."

I nudge her with my shoulder. "You can tell me. My mom told me it's good to talk about this stuff."

Ivy laughs. "Well, she's right. Sounds like Neidy—my sister—only less annoying. She's always telling me to 'open up,' but that's easy for my perfect sister to say. But yeah. I guess I should talk about it."

She takes another sip, measuring out the words before speaking again.

"We hooked up a couple times," she says. "Neil and me. Don't look so surprised. I make all kinds of terrible choices."

225

She follows this up with a laugh, probably based on the shock on my face.

"It was a few months ago," she says. "I was going through a hard time. The girl I was in love with had just told me she didn't love me back. It wasn't her fault, love sucks, but I was pissed. And Neil was there, and shit. I just went for it because I knew he'd never say no. He wouldn't reject me. And I know that's a fucked-up reason to be with someone, but whatever."

I watch her as she says this. To me, Ivy's always looked like someone who could never be rocked, who never, ever had a low moment. The kind of person brave enough to protect me from the lacrosse boys. To stand up for me. I don't quite know what to do with this Ivy, vulnerable and quiet.

"Liam sort of mentioned that you had a, um—" I search for the word. "An affinity for assholes."

That gets a snort out of her. "Pinche chismoso. Not that he's wrong. Hell, he doesn't even know about all of them. But still."

I smile. "He was saying it as a compliment, I swear. He thought you deserved better."

Her eyes flash, and she grins at me. "Did he now? And when did he say this? On your date?"

Now I blush, almost as red as Ivy's water bottle.

"We're not on a date," I say, even though my heart thunders at the admission. "We're just hanging out."

Ivy waves her hand in the air. "Oh, come on, Greta. Just admit it. You like him. And I'm proud of you. For a second there I was worried you were going to follow in my path and only crush on assholes."

"W-what do you mean?"

She gives me a look that says I'm the most pathetic, ignorant person on the planet.

"Don't give me that. You know I'm talking about you slobbering over Grey," she says. "An actual douchebag. A literal stain on the human race."

It's like she's slapped me. "Grey's not a douchebag. He's upstanding. He's—"

"Look, I know you're not going to believe me, but I'm going to try anyway because I'm talking from experience here," she says, pinning me with her brown eyes. "Stop making people a priority when they make you an option. Stop liking boys who don't give a damn about you, and start paying attention to the boy who thinks you walk on water. Okay?"

It's all I can do to stare back at her, fumbling over a response. What do I say to that? And does she know just how deep those words are cutting me?

But I don't get to respond, because Liam's suddenly running up to the rock, out of breath and holding a pack of wipes and some gauze. His eyes land on me, then on Ivy, as he tilts his head in confusion, looking like Jasper when we bust out the laser pointer.

"I ran into Greta on my run," Ivy says happily, standing up. "Good to see you, Dealer."

"Ivy," Liam says, out of breath. "You're . . . are you okay?"

"Not yet, but I will be," Ivy says. "I'll let you guys get back to it. Are you working tomorrow?"

Liam nods. "Unless they cancel."

"Cool," she says. "See you then."

And then, she's grinning at me before taking off in the other direction. I turn back to Liam and shrug. He walks over, taking out one of the wipes and running it over my hand. I shiver at the touch but tell myself it's just because of the cold sting of the cloth.

"I can do that," I say, trying to take it from him.

227

"It's cool," he says, finishing it before I can and moving on to the gauze. "I've got you, remember?"

Another shiver, and this time, I can't blame it on the wipe. I need a change of subject.

"Right," I say. "So I was thinking. Even if we do call the police, I still think we need to figure out how the other performers are involved in this. Like Allie calling in for Mercy. Do they know about Mercy investigating Hailey's death? And if they do, why do they care? How are these things related? That's not something I want to tell the cops unless we have evidence, you know?"

Because the last thing I need is to lie to the police, even accidentally. Not with everything I'm still hiding from Liam. And also, I can't help feeling this is a thread I need to tie together. Is Lauren secretly the daughter of the Gondola Killer? Did one of Allie's famous relatives have a tie to the park twenty years ago? Theories that would've sounded unhinged before, but now I'm wondering if they're closer than I think.

"That makes sense," Liam says, gesturing for me to walk back to the car. "So what do we do next?"

"I think I need to confront them," I say. "Or, at least, Allie. She's the one with Mercy's phone, after all."

Liam raises both eyebrows. "Confront her? Like, fight her?"

I roll my eyes. "Definitely not. I just mean ask her questions. Like I did with Lauren, I guess, only this time on purpose."

"But what if she's dangerous?" Liam asks. "You know, since you sort of suspect her of possible . . . well, murder."

I wave my hand. "I'd be safe about it. I'd do it somewhere public. But not at work. She's always surrounded by her performer posse."

"Well, you could always catch her in the morning," Liam says. "At the beach."

I scoff. "The beach?"

Liam nods, pulling out his phone. He scrolls through social media as we finish our walk back to his car, then clicks on a profile that instantly populates with approximately one thousand bikini pictures of Allie. My cheeks burn as Liam flips through them until, finally, he stops.

"She's always posting about her morning surf sessions," he says. "At Grandview. You could always talk to her there. Pretty sure none of the other performers surf."

I stare at the picture of Allie that Liam's showing me. Of course Allie surfs at Grandview. She couldn't surf at D Street or Swami's instead. It had to be this beach, the one that's a potential land mine for my own insecurities and fears.

In Rancho Paloma, which beach you go to is essential. There are different beaches for different purposes, for different people. Moonlight is the tourist beach that's also good for a casual day or a night spent around its bonfires, the one you go to if you're in Junior Lifeguards or being dragged there by your parents. Stonesteps is for casual beach days, and Swami's and D Street are great for surfing.

But Grandview is the beach that everyone from our school likes to go to. It's the beach Brad went to after lacrosse practice with the rest of the team, flinging themselves into the water, chasing and tackling each other in the surf. I know because he would post about it, and back then—before I deleted everything—I would welcome every beach update with hungry eyes. Eventually, Caroline and I started going there ourselves, and while she read a book, I would wait for Brad and the others to appear on the sand. Once he did, I would drink in his athleticism, his ease, his charm. I would hope that one day I would join him at Grandview in the sand, entwining our hands, possibly entwining even more. Now I wish the entire thing would cave into the ocean, never to exist again.

Except it can't cave into the ocean, because I need to go there tomorrow to talk to Allie, apparently.

"Greta?" Liam asks.

I tell myself not to panic. Allie surfs early, which cuts down the chance of any run-ins with people from my past life.

"It's a great idea," I tell Liam. "I'll talk to her first thing tomorrow."

"Do you want me to go with you?" Liam asks. "Just in case?"

I shake my head. "That would look too suspicious. You need to be at work."

"I guess," Liam says as we near the street, approaching his car. He opens my door, then crosses to the driver's side. But before he sits down, he freezes, face going pale.

"What is it?" I ask.

He looks around his center console, on the floor, in the door compartment. He even glances over to my side.

"It's impossible," he says. "We were gone for five seconds. Where did it go?"

Ice drops into my veins. "What's gone?"

He brings his eyes up to mine, panic laced in every feature.

"The badge," he says. "Greta, someone took the badge."

I jump out of the car, looking on the street in case it fell out. I run along the road, looking for the glint of gold, but there's nothing but concrete. At the sound of a car driving past, my head whips up, eyes focused on the driver. A driver I'd recognize anywhere.

"Allie followed us," I say, breath quickening. "Allie took the badge."

CHAPTER NINETEEN

THURSDAY, JUNE 19
6:12 A.M.

I'M NOT MAD at Liam. Really. I'm not mad, because this tells me we're on to something; we're getting close. Liam refuses to see this positive because he thinks this means we're in more danger than ever before, but I think he's just being pessimistic. He also really doesn't want me to go confront Allie alone this morning after she just stole the badge yesterday, but I don't have a choice, because we need the badge to go to the police. Without it, we don't have anything concrete tying Mercy's disappearance to her investigation of Hailey. That badge was everything, and now, it's up to me to get it from Allie.

Because this is my destiny. *This* is my path. And I'll do whatever it takes to find Mercy.

I park in a neighborhood near the Grandview steps. As I slink through the street, I pass several tanned, lithe bodies pulling on or peeling off their wet suits, revealing the kind of muscle I can only dream of.

But it doesn't matter. I'm not here to surf. I'm here to study. To research. To interview, hopefully, if Liam's right and Allie is here. To put the slippery pieces of this investigation together.

To save someone's life, or at least, to get some answers.

I walk down the Grandview steps with my heart in my throat, clinging to the rail that guides me down the sand-slippery wood. The sky is bright and clear, the water dotted with tiny figures. I sweep the waves with my eyes, searching for Allie, but I'm too far away to make out anyone clearly. I brush past a wet suit–clad man with sun-bleached hair, the brief contact with the sopping-wet cold of the neoprene leaving me shivering through my sweatshirt.

What am I going to say to Allie if I get the chance? I've been practicing since Liam and I talked it through last night, and I woke up early to write down the ideal questions in my notebook. But all of it sounds practiced, rehearsed, and I know I won't get anything out of her if it feels like I'm prying. I need to be like the detectives I've read about and watched on TV, the ones who slip in a knife disguised as a question to unearth what they're really looking for.

Why did you have Mercy's phone, Allie? No, that's too direct.

Where'd you find Mercy's phone? When did you find the phone? Are you just a petty thief, or is this something worse?

Do you know why Neil was calling Mercy right before he died?

Why is the badge important, and how did you know to steal it?

I've reached the sand. The figures farther in the water are still fairly faint, but I can make out a few of them who are closest to shore. A guy with long dark hair. A woman with a short bob. No Allie, so I'll have to wait.

I set out my beach towel on the sand and get out my notebook and pen. I go through my questions, eliminating options one by one. I still don't feel like I have the right rhythm. So I flip back through the chart I made last night about everything we know up to this point. I follow the lines I've drawn, connecting details about Allie, Lauren, Neil, and, of course, Mercy and Hailey. I make another list of people who are connected but not necessarily suspects: Kara, Gene, Silvia. All of it spins, none of it linking together the way I need it to. I hesitate, adding Grey's name at the last moment. Not because I actually suspect him—how could I?—but because he is technically part of this, since Mercy is calling in sick to him. Or she was. With everything canceled yesterday, I don't know what happened with her. Another question for Allie.

And, of course, Lauren's gossip about Grey and Mercy together. Not that I believe it. But I need to know if Allie does, if that's her motive.

Then I get out my phone, checking online. I avoid social media, as always, keeping to local news and blogs. It appears that the local media has agreed with me and Liam and decided that Neil's death *wasn't* a suicide, the details of his bruised throat and signs of head trauma written about over and over and over again.

I swallow the bile building in my throat as the memory of Neil's body resurfaces, followed almost immediately by my nightmare of him beating on the window of the gondola. The way his eyes were nearly swollen shut, the way his voice choked on the blood gurgling in his mouth.

I shake my head, forcing the image away, forcing myself to look back at the article on my phone. I scroll past all mention of Neil, looking for anything else that might be relevant. One article speculates that Neil's death might even be connected to the Gondola Killer, given the twentieth anniversary coming up. Maybe, they posit, the killer's been called back to wreak more havoc. I keep reading, eyes sticking on a part near the bottom.

Of course, all Rancho Paloma locals will remember the tragedy that first befell Hyper Kid Magic Land during one of its opening celebrations. The murder of a young performer has never been solved, giving rise to the infamy of the mysterious Gondola Killer. The original victim's family refused to answer too many questions when asked for their thoughts about the connection between that murder and this one, saying only this:

"Hailey Portman was a beloved daughter, sister, and actress. She deserves peace after all this time. If her killer truly has reemerged, we pray they will finally be brought to justice."

My stomach turns at the words. No matter how many articles I've now read about Hailey Portman, there's something about reading this one and the words of her family that makes me feel truly sick. Maybe because I'd never thought about how Hailey's family is still alive. They're not frozen in time like she is. They're still here, having to deal with this all over again. And Neil's family, too, will forever have to relive this tragedy along with them. And Mercy—

"So you're following me now?"

I drop my notebook in the sand at the sound of her voice. Allie. I look up, and she's blotting out the tiny sliver of sun, covering me in her shadow.

Her hair's wet, clinging to her neck and cheeks, her eyes and face are devoid of their usual smear of stage makeup. It's infuriating because she looks better like this; the blue of her eyes stands out against the freckles she normally covers up. Her skin shines from the water, her wetsuit clinging to every curve of her body. I think of Liam finding the pictures of her in her bikini, the way his eyes seemed to linger. Something hot burns in my chest, and I grab my notebook from out of the sand.

"Are you the only one who's allowed to go to the beach?" I say, wishing my voice didn't squeak on every syllable.

Allie smirks. "Get real, Greta. We both know you're more of an indoor cat. Now cut the bullshit and tell me why you're here."

I don't know what it is that makes something inside me snap. Maybe it's the smug expression on Allie's face, one that says not only am I an "indoor cat," but I'm an ugly indoor cat who's missing whiskers and might have a slightly electrocuted look to my fur. Or maybe it's the memory of her snapping at Neil or the way she hung on Grey or the way she looked so ungodly beautiful in her pictures that Liam scrolls through every day, apparently. Not that it matters, or, at least, not that that last part matters. Or it shouldn't matter.

But whatever it is, I do snap. Completely. I push myself to standing so that we're almost face to face, and I'm practically spitting when I snarl at her.

"Fine, Allie. You want me to cut the bullshit? I'll cut the bullshit. I saw you take the badge. I know you've been calling in for Mercy on her phone. So you better start explaining everything to me now and give me that badge back, or you can go ahead and be a suspect when they don't find her at home."

It's satisfying, actually, the way the smile drops off Allie's face in one fell swoop. Her normally suntanned skin pales ever so slightly, and her blue eyes flash as they widen. All of it happens instantly, though it only lasts a second. Then Allie's back to narrowing her eyes, trying to pretend that nothing happened.

Too bad she's not that good of an actress.

"What?" I ask. "I thought we were cutting the bullshit. Because I can keep going. What about the blood you cleaned up? I know all about that, too."

Water drips from Allie's suit and hair onto the sand. The anger in her eyes is a burning, heavy thing, and her chest rises and falls with her rage. When she speaks next, it's through gritted teeth.

"You wanna lower your voice?" Allie says. "Because I don't think the entire beach wants to hear about your pathetic theories."

I laugh. Because now, I know she's scared. She avoided every single one of my questions. I've got her.

"Just tell me the truth," I tell her, and I do lower my voice just a little bit to keep her from bolting.

"We didn't do anything," Allie says, but her eyes don't meet mine. "So what, we moved her shit occasionally. And Lauren might've went a little too hard on a stage push. But we didn't do anything wrong, all right?"

I glare at her. "I heard you talking about the blood Lauren cleaned up—"

"Oh, come on," Allie says. "That was just a little accident with the trapdoor. Grey just messed with her a little right before her cue, and she toppled over and sliced up her arm. These things happen, all right?"

The trapdoor. Of course. They broke it. Is that where they hurt Mercy? But no . . . that was before the party. A dead end, but not the entire story.

"What about you and Grey and Mercy?" I demand. "Lauren's rumors about the two of them. Were you furious? Did that make you—"

She snorts. "Oh, now it's 'rumors'? Everything else you believe immediately, but when it comes to Mercy and Grey, it's a rumor?"

I freeze. "Well, I . . . it just didn't seem like his character."

Allie laughs again, low and cold. "Oh, it's his character to be a fuckboy, all right. Lauren told me she saw the two of them at that party together. But I wasn't surprised. Men in theater. But he's making it up to me. Don't worry."

I stare at her, not understanding. That doesn't sound like Grey. And if it is like him, why would she stay with him? None of it makes sense. How can she act so casual about all of this? Still, there's something in her eyes that tells me I've hit a nerve. An important nerve, but one I shouldn't push too hard on immediately.

"Tell me why you have the phone, then," I say. "If these things aren't a big deal. And tell me why you took the badge from Liam's car at the trails yesterday. Better yet, give me the badge."

At that, Allie's face changes. It's hard to read her expression. Her eyes widen, then narrow, and then her lips purse. Because I've caught her?

After a beat, she looks around, checking to see that no one else is listening. And they're not. Right now, it's just the surfers in the water and clear sand to the right and left.

"I don't know what you're talking about with a badge. But the phone . . . it isn't what you think, all right?" Allie says. "Yeah, I've got it, but I can explain."

Vindication courses through me, faster than any extra-strength Tylenol that Mom's ever given me for a headache. It's like lightning striking from the sky, potent and electric.

"I knew it," I say. "I knew you were doing this, that you were hiding this. And now—"

"Oh, let's not get ahead of ourselves," Allie says, gaze darkening. "Because we both know you're not going to do anything. Not since I know your secret."

237

The world around me seems to splinter and crack as her words sink in.

Because no. It's not possible. She's bluffing. She doesn't know—

"Did you really think no one was going to recognize you?" Allie taunts. "God, Greta, everyone at Del Cruz High knows about your little scandal. My brother's on the lacrosse team, so I've heard all about you. And if you're not careful, everyone else will hear about you, too."

"It's not . . . ," I murmur, thinking about Liam in the woods. "It wasn't my fault. Those boys—"

"Oh, those assholes sharing your nude might not have been your fault," Allie says. "I'll give you that, even if you made a fucking rookie-ass mistake. But we both know that's not where it ended, don't we?"

I swallow. My hands are shaking at my sides, and I can't tell whether it's terror or fury making them that way.

"My brother said the whole Coastal Canyon team holds you personally responsible for their losses at the end of last year," Allie says. "That because of your little stunt, they were never quite able to recover. That the real reason you had to leave school is because you were a goddamn pariah, a psycho who lit the locker room on fire."

I am immobile. No, actually. I am back in the locker room, standing on the concrete, watching flames lick up the wooden beams in the room.

"What would people at work say, Greta?" Allie asks, eyes narrowing down at me as she smiles. "What would they do if they knew you were behind that?"

She tosses her sea-soaked hair over her shoulder, then walks a few feet to where she set her surfboard in the sand. She snatches it, then turns back to me.

"I'm sure you'll keep this all in mind," Allie says. "See you later, Greta."

CHAPTER TWENTY

THURSDAY, JUNE 19
7:35 A.M.

AFTER GRANDVIEW THERE'S nowhere to go but home. I still have another hour before I need to be at work, and, frankly, I need a place to melt down where no one else will see me.

Allie knows my secret. Allie knows the worst part of me. She knows and is threatening to tell everyone if I don't keep quiet about the phone. And the badge . . . maybe I was wrong about the badge. Am I wrong about everything?

I burst in through my front door, finding Jasper wiggling in front of me, excitement at someone being home overwhelming him. I drop to the ground, gathering him up into my lap and letting him lick my cheek while I attempt to process all the emotions circulating through me.

I obviously can't let this affect my investigation. After all, a real investigator would put the case first, right? They wouldn't let anything detract from it, especially not something like this. Then again, a real investigator probably wouldn't have a skeleton like this hiding in their closet.

Do I tell Liam the whole story? Let him know everything so that we can truly be in this together? But just the thought of Liam potentially recoiling makes my skin feel itchy, especially when I remember Allie's disgusted expression. No. I can't tell him.

It figures that Allie would do something like this, would be this kind of cruel. I was right about her from the beginning. Because yes, Lauren was brash and rude and bordering on belligerent, but at least she was open about it. Allie operates like a snake, hiding under the surface, hoarding her secrets until it's safe to strike.

But I'm not going to let her get away with it. I refuse. I just need to regroup, maybe go to the police after all. If only we still had the badge—

Jasper growls low, the sound like a tiny motor starting on my legs.

"What is it?" I ask him, scratching him behind the ears. "Hear something?"

His growl deepens as his ears tuck back. He even pulls his lips away from his teeth, revealing the sharp points of his canines.

It's not like Jasper to growl like this. Usually, he can be counted on to make immediate friends with whoever walks through the door. So I pause my scratching to listen, trying to decipher what it is that has him on edge.

Mom's gone at another event for work, which means everything in the house is silent, save for Jasper. Outside, there's the faint sound of birds chirping, but nothing else. Just a regular morning. Except—

Suddenly, I hear it. Footsteps, shuffling footsteps, and something like clanking. It's not coming from inside the house, but rather from just outside.

The garage.

Gingerly, I pick Jasper up off my lap and set him down next to me on the ground. He continues to growl as I stand up and move, padding as quietly as I can through the hallway toward the kitchen, which attaches to the garage. I keep listening, trying to make out the sounds.

More footsteps. More clanking.

Almost like someone's . . .

Trying to get in.

I swallow the fear bubbling up inside me. A real investigator wouldn't be afraid. They would be thrilled at the possibility of a clue, right? This intruder can't be a coincidence. This has to mean I'm getting closer.

As I move through the kitchen, I pull a knife off the counter. I hoist it in front of me like a sword, stepping as quietly as I can toward the door. I reach out, twisting the knob, easing the door open.

And then, I throw it wide, stepping into the dark—

"Jesus fucking Christ."

I blink, knife still held high, as the garage comes into view. It actually isn't dark, since someone's already turned on the light, and immediately, I see who must have been making all the noise.

"Dad?"

He's standing in front of me, holding an old dark green golf bag, one I've seen stuffed to the side in the garage and covered in an array of cobwebs. I heard Mom complaining about it on the phone once before when she was talking to my aunt, telling her about how Dad can't just "store his crap here" anymore. She said he lost that privilege when he left his family.

Now Dad looks guilty to be holding it. He's in the fancy kind of "athleisure" clothes that the worst kind of guests at Hyper Kid tend to wear, the ones who always like to complain about things that I can't control, like how hard the benches are or the weather being "too" sunny. I wonder when he started dressing that way. I wonder who he's dressing like that for.

"Hey, kid," Dad says, straightening up slightly as he sets the golf bag down next to him. "I didn't know you were home."

I stare at him. The last time I saw my dad, he and Mom were arguing about how to "deal" with me and my transgression at school. He was telling her he couldn't spend thousands of dollars just for me to throw my life away. He told her she was raising me to be a "slut" and a "criminal," and Mom shut the door in his face.

"I thought I'd just swing by and grab these," he says. "One of my golf buddies, well, his son's going to join us next week. We were talking about how expensive clubs are, and I remembered this old set, so I thought I'd pick them up. Plus, you know, lots of memories here. I like to keep a little trophy from every club I go to. Balls, tees, just something. And I know how your mom hates these clubs, anyway. It'd be killing two birds, so . . ."

He trails off, looking around and massaging the short beard on his chin. It makes him look even more like a jerk.

"Are you still working at that theme park? Because I thought—"

"I'm about to leave, actually," I say. The words are thicker than I want them to be. I want them to be hard. I want them to be angry and cutting. But instead, they sound like I'm recovering from a cold or like I swallowed a bucket of dust before trying to talk. They betray me, just like he did.

"Right," he says, and he finally looks at me. He claps his hands together and tries to smile, like this is normal, like nothing's wrong.

"I'm proud of you for getting that job, you know," he says. "After everything. It's what I told your mom I thought you needed. Something to help you, you know, refocus."

I hate that that's what I thought, too. Hate that he's right about anything related to me. But I can't say that. I can't say anything because I'll cry, and if I cry, he might think he's why I'm crying, and I'd never forgive myself for that.

"You can go back to school there, you know," he says. "I've been talking to Terry, and he'll let you. I made a case for you, kid. Said this social-media garbage has taught you all the wrong lessons. And you know that Terry and I go way back, and he appreciates how much I've donated over the years. He listens to me. Helps me out. You remember how he smoothed things over with the police. He used those connections for us. Plus, you've realized you made a mistake, so—"

"I'm never going back there," I say, and shit, shit, shit. It's impossible not to hear the tears in my voice, in my throat.

"Greta," Dad starts, and he begins to walk toward me. "Kid, it's okay. We'll fix it."

"You won't fix anything!" I scream at him. "Don't you get it? All you do is break things. Why the hell are you even here? Why didn't you just let your friend buy his own fucking clubs?"

Dad's eyes widen. Jasper barks. But I don't care. I glare at my dad as tears stream down my cheeks, and my whole body shakes.

"Leave us alone," I force out. "Please. Get out of here. This isn't your house anymore."

And then I run, back through the garage and into the living room. I give Jasper the quickest kiss, hoping he stays far, far away from Dad and the garage. I race to my car, getting in before Dad can chase me down.

Not that he would. If I've learned anything from my dad, it's that he's never cared about me. Only how I affect his reputation.

But I *will* prove him wrong.

Because it's my destiny to solve this, to figure this out, to save Mercy—if it's not too late.

And I'm not running away now that I'm this close to doing so.

When I walk up to the Hyper Kid security station, it's instantly clear that the news of Neil's death really has spread like wildfire.

For one, there are multiple police officers in the parking lot and just past security. They loiter near one another, talking in hushed voices, pausing only to glare at the employees who walk by.

When I stop to swipe in, I notice the guard who usually sits in his chair, idly watching the cameras, is gone. In his place is someone I don't recognize speaking to an officer as he gestures to the screens that observe the park. He points at one specifically, and even though his voice is low, I catch snippets of it as I walk through the turnstile.

"—camera there is the one that should've caught them," he says. "Not sure why the footage is so damn blurry."

"And there's not another camera?" the officer asks, eyes narrowed. "Another view? Maybe James could help us, if he's available."

I want to pause and keep listening, but at that moment, the officer's gaze lifts to me. I throw my own eyes down to the sidewalk and keep walking, not wanting to draw any attention.

Wardrobe is also buzzing. Instead of the usual lone, sleepy

worker swapping out uniform polos that have seen better days for new ones, three employees are clustered together. As I clock in, their buzzy conversation drifts through the air. Each person speaks over the other so that it's less a conversation and more a smattering of opinions bubbling up over one another.

"They tried to make it look like he killed himself, but really, he was dead before they hung him up."

"Have they pulled you in for an interview about him yet? Heavy stuff."

"Never trusted him. He must've been into something that made him a target."

"My mom says he was a drug addict."

"*My* mom watched the news, and they said it was the Gondola Killer for sure."

"But that was twenty years ago."

"So? No one knows how old the killer was then. They could still be young for all we know."

"Or maybe it's their kid, taking up the family profession. Didn't they do that in the new *Scream* movies?"

I push away, through the doors, heading for the Entertainment office, but it's closed off. An officer outside tells me to head straight to my "designated workstation" for the day. I take that to mean Rocket and head over there, not anxious to disagree. But as I'm going, I look back.

Is the office part of the crime scene? Are they going through the files, trying to find clues about Neil?

"Weird shit, right?"

I jolt, not expecting Ivy, who has materialized from the shadows of the hedges that line the back of Rocket. She's got a new book tucked under her arm—*The Secrets We Keep*—and looks relatively okay, given what we talked about yesterday. Still, when she smiles, I know there's plenty she's hiding.

She falls into step with me as she speaks. "What a shit show. Did you get the all-staff email about how they're 'here for us' and the therapists they've got on site? And oh, by the way, remember we're not allowed to talk to the media 'for our own safety'? Great stuff. Better than some of my books."

I smile. I did read the email, even though I know I won't be talking to anyone at Hyper Kid. Not now with everything I'm hiding. I'm relieved that Ivy and I are scheduled together, even if her advice from yesterday still burns in my mind. Hopefully, she won't bring it up again, especially given the chaos around us.

"You're right that the email wasn't very helpful," I say. "Are we adjusting the shows?"

"Nope," she says. "Business as usual otherwise. They did make me 'temporary usher lead,' which just means I get to deal with the bullshit as it comes through."

I stare at her. "You're the lead?"

She nods, giving me a tired smile. "Silvia and Gene turned it down. They just want to work and not have to worry about anything else. Shit, I don't really want the responsibility, if I'm honest. But it's an extra two dollars an hour, so I said sure for now."

"That's great," I say, then wince at the implication. "I mean, not great, seeing as, um, Neil . . ."

"I get it," she says. "Don't stress, Greta."

I let out a breath as we head into the back of Rocket. It's weird to be in here, seeing everything so remarkably unchanged. And of course nothing's changed since Neil died. Neil didn't die *here*. But after something so horrible happens, it feels like things *should* be different. And I guess, outside, with all the cops, things have changed. But in here? It's still the same.

"Well, another day, I guess," Ivy says, bending backward so that her back cracks. "I'll get the glasses. Can you test the show?"

I nod. She sets her bag into one of the lockers, then heads out, leaving me alone.

I head out to the theater and run a quick test show, feeling jittery every step of the way. When it's over, I head backstage and get out my phone to check for messages from Liam. The last thing we said was that we were going to meet later to recap what I learned from Allie, but there's nothing new. Now I don't even know what I'll say. And I can only hope I don't run into Allie after earlier.

"God, I hope we don't have big crowds today," Ivy says, returning with a partially full glasses cart. "Wardrobe's apparently too busy gossiping to do their job."

I laugh a little, even though my heart isn't in it. The whole room feels strange and devoid, more than I even expected.

"You okay?" Ivy asks, laying a hand on my shoulder.

I shrug. "I heard them talking on my way in. Do you . . . do you think it's true what people are saying about the Gondola Killer? That they're back?"

Ivy keeps her hand on my shoulder for a moment, squeezing it, then she pulls a claw clip out of her pocket and uses it to put her hair up.

"Oh, I dunno," she says finally. "I believe in the existence of shitty men. And I believe that shitty men can never hide their shittiness forever. It always comes out in the end."

I nod, even though I'm not sure if I believe that. After all, the Gondola Killer's gotten away with his crime for twenty years.

"I'll sweep the left side if you take the right," Ivy says. "Try not to think about this too much, okay? You'll get lost in it if you do."

She squeezes my shoulder once more before leaving. I grab one of the brooms and head out to the right side. It's summer, so the jacaranda trees are dumping their sticky purple flowers on a nearly constant basis. I ready myself to attack them, swinging the door open, when I hear a grunt on the other side of the door.

Shit! Was there a guest hiding on the other side of the door? We get those sometimes, especially with people trying to find a place to smoke. But as I'm stammering apologies, readying myself for an angry guest, I realize I haven't accidentally smacked a door into a guest at all.

I've smacked a door into Gene.

"Oh my god!" I say, dropping my broom as I race forward to where Gene is rubbing his shoulder. He's wincing a little, but he waves me off with his other spindly hand.

"Just a bump," he says. "My own fault. I didn't knock four times to let you know I was out here."

He straightens up, thankfully, assuaging my fear that I had permanently brutalized the old man. Then he grabs the broom that he must've dropped and gets to work on the concrete walkway, swish-swishing against the downpour of jacaranda blossoms that I was right to expect.

"Um, Gene?" I ask, as nicely as I can. "I don't think you're scheduled here."

He looks over his shoulder and smiles at me. "I got here early. Couldn't be at home. I didn't want to watch the news this morning."

He drops his head, moving the broom as he continues his assault on the blossoms. And I realize exactly why Gene didn't want to stay home, exactly what news he's trying to avoid.

Neil. Neil and the Gondola Killer and Hailey Portman and everything else.

"Isn't it harder to be here?" I ask, even though it might be rude. In fact, I know it's rude, and I wait for Gene to scold me. He pauses his sweeping, turning to rest an elbow on the handle of his broom.

"We all failed that girl," Gene says. "We should've been more accountable that night. More alert. And after she died . . . we shouldn't have stopped until we solved what happened to her. I kept looking, you know. I watched every special, looked up every article. But it wasn't enough. And now this? This is our punishment. *My* punishment."

"But you were just an employee," I say. "A really unlucky employee."

"Just an employee?" Gene asks, laughing. "I thought I taught you better, Greta. It's our job to follow protocols, our job to keep things safe. Someone didn't keep those gondolas safe, I'll tell you that. And I'll tell you what else. Now that Neil's died, more things are bound to come out. Ugly things. And I don't think any of us are ready for them."

Gene's eyes are always watery, but now, tears slide down the heavy tracks in his cheeks. He shakes them off quickly, avoiding looking at me, but the whole thing makes me want to sob just the same.

"Do you think he's really back?" I ask, shivering even though it's already warm.

Gene shakes his head. "Know your enemy, Greta. Like these crows I'm always battling. I know them better than I know myself at this point. I know their hideouts. I know their tricks. And when it comes to that murderer, I know this isn't the same. Whoever killed Hailey . . . that was intentional. They knew her. They were proud of that crime and weren't hiding it. Her death was their victory."

The words wash over me, pieces sticking like froth from a wave. Gene's use of "victory," especially, makes me pause. Like the killer would see her death as a win. As something to be celebrated.

"What makes you say that?" I ask, heart beating so fast I feel it in my skull. "That the killer saw it as a victory?"

"It's just one of the theories," Gene says. "From way back. They . . . they recorded everything they found on Hailey. Every item in her purse. But there was one thing missing. Her badge. The one we all got. Because that . . . that *demon* took it. Whoever they were, they wanted everyone to know they'd done it on purpose and were keeping that badge as a memento. Sick, I know, but that's how these guys work."

At once, Dad's voice from earlier floats back to me.

I like to keep a little trophy from every club I go to. Balls, tees, just something.

Instantly, it's like I'm in the ocean, fighting to get to the surface after a wave's rolled over me. Because I realize what, exactly, Mercy found with that badge.

The trophy. The Gondola Killer's trophy. The evidence she knew would tie him to the crime.

The evidence Liam and I had before someone stole it right out from under us.

CHAPTER TWENTY-ONE

THURSDAY, JUNE 19
5:47 P.M.

BY THE END of the day, my whole body is sore. I don't know if it's just all the Rocket shows catching up with me after a day off or what, but everything aches. By the time I have to take the glasses back to Wardrobe, I just want to collapse.

Ivy's been hovering near me all day. I think I scared her earlier with my questions, so she's been checking on me constantly. It's giving young-Silvia vibes, and although I'm grateful, I think part of my exhaustion has come from her keeping tabs on me for the past eight hours. The other part's been waiting to tell Liam what I learned from Gene.

Everyone must be on edge, I think. James even stopped by earlier while I was passing out glasses to check on us.

"Take it easy," James said. "No need to push yourself."

And maybe I did push myself a little too hard, but it doesn't matter now. Soon, I'll be able to go home and reread the notebook for the thousandth time and make more charts and figure this out without interference. Well, except Liam. I wouldn't mind interference from him.

I push the glasses cart up the hill, past the employee smoking area where a handful of officers are chatting. There're fewer of them around than earlier, and I didn't actually see any in the park. I wonder if the Hyper Kid overlords have insisted on them keeping as behind the scenes as possible, so as not to freak out the guests.

One thing's for sure, though. Neil's death definitely led to an increase in true-crime-junkie attendance today. When Ivy and I walked to the Caf for lunch, I saw a line at the gondolas for pictures. I guess those articles I was reading this morning are getting significant traction.

"Insensitive assholes," Ivy said, not bothering to keep her voice down.

I wonder if there was also a line at the turret. Do people know that's where he died? I bet, even if Hyper Kid tried to keep it under wraps, there'd been no stopping it. I shiver at the thought as I approach the reopened Entertainment office. The door swings open just as I'm about to pass it, so I have to stop with my cart for whoever it is to exit.

That's when I see him. It's only been a couple of days since I last laid eyes on him, and Grey still seems to sparkle when he steps out of the door. And yet . . . something's dimmed for me. Is it the fact that he's with Allie, or what she said about him? Or Ivy's comments? Or just my general mood today?

Whatever it is, my white whale no longer seems as pressing as he did before.

"Greta!" Grey says, grinning when he sees me, which throws me off a bit, given the somberness of the day. He's wearing a hoodie and gym shorts, so he must be on his way to work out.

Maybe that's how he's dealing with grief and despair, I think. Nature's antidepressant: weight lifting.

"Hi, Grey," I say, unable to move the glasses cart because he's standing in the way.

"Hell of a day," he says, attempting to run a hand through his long hair. He must hit a snag because he's forced to pull his hand out before he gets all the way to the ends.

"Yeah," I say. "It's been really sad."

"Right," Grey says, again not seeming really bothered at all. "You know, I was hoping to see you at Jungle. I thought you said you were getting trained there."

"Oh, right," I say. "Well, um, Neil would've been the one making the schedule next, and obviously he . . . I, um. I don't think he got around to it."

"It's a real shame," Grey says, reaching down to the edge of his hoodie so that he can pull it over his head. As he does, he pulls up the tank top underneath, revealing the hard planes of his abs. I inhale sharply at the sight, seeing the usual tattoos that curve and bend along his body. I realize for the first time that all his tattoos together look sort of like a child's sketchbook, specifically, a child who is experimenting at drawing . . . and isn't actually very good.

"You know, Lauren missed her lines again, and I had to sort of lay down the law as the lead," he says. "But it's important, as a leader, to do this kind of thing thoughtfully. I can't just tell her 'You suck,' you know? You have to feel out this sort of critique. So I sat her down, and I talked her through it all. I told her to just watch me and do what I was doing. I think it really helped."

As he blabbers on, it hits me that I'm . . . annoyed at him. I'm annoyed that he's a *lead*, that this is what he thinks of as helpful. But when Mercy gave feedback, she was "difficult." Sure, Mercy didn't have a position of power. But I have to imagine whatever advice she gave was better than "do what I do." The thought makes me bold.

"Grey," I say, trying for gentle even though I'm irritated. "I've noticed that, um, Mercy Goodwin hasn't been coming to work. And with everything happening with Neil, I'm just a little nervous and wondering if you know anything about her. Like if she's okay. Or maybe she's told you what's going on?"

He blinks, and it's hard to tell if he's surprised by what I'm asking or by the fact that I ignored his monologue about Lauren.

"I just know everyone's been worried about how sick she must be," I say. "To still not be here, you know. Did you do . . . did you do a house call or something? To check on her?"

Something flashes in Grey's eyes, and his entire expression hardens. The sight is so off-putting, so changed, that I step back, dragging the glasses cart with me.

"Mercy won't be coming back," Grey says, his voice a cold knife in the evening air. "She quit."

"She . . . she quit?" I ask, completely taken aback. "Just like that? Did she call in? Or is that what she told you at the party?"

"What do you mean, at the party?" Grey asks, eyes narrowing.

"Oh, I just know you two were, um, together—"

"Why are you asking me this?" Grey asks, stepping closer. "Did Allie say something to you?"

I blink, confused. "What? No. I just—"

"I think you're poking your nose into places it doesn't belong," Grey says, folding his arms over his chest. "And I'd be careful about that, if I were you."

"I was just asking—"

"Greta?"

I turn at the sound of Ivy's voice. She's striding up, her hair down now, wild curls flying around her shoulders. Behind her, I spot Liam, who's glaring at Grey like he might try to punch him in the face.

"Looks like Greta's trying to get by you, pretty boy," Ivy says, fixing her glare on Grey.

She passes me one of the bags she's carrying, which I realize is mine.

"Excuse me?" Grey snaps. "How dare you talk to me like that."

"Why, because you're a performer? We're trying to clock out, and you're blocking her way."

"I'm a lead—"

"Yeah, well, so am I now," Ivy says. "Move it."

Grey's eyes narrow to blue slits. I can tell he wants to say more, but in the end, he just steps back so that we can pass. I push the cart down to the Wardrobe door, Ivy and Liam following behind me.

"Jesus, what a prick," Ivy says as we duck into Wardrobe and hand them the cart. "I told you. Performers are the worst."

"Maybe just that performer," Liam says, his voice close to a growl.

I want to defend Grey. It was my fault, wasn't it, for asking too many questions? He was just protecting Mercy's privacy, wasn't he?

But even as I have that thought, I remember that he was just being an asshole. And guys being assholes is not my fault.

"I feel like I just need to go to bed," I say, massaging my temples. "Today was intense."

"Oh no, you don't," Ivy says, linking her arm through mine as she frog-marches me out of Wardrobe. "Nope. No way. Because Dealer and I were just talking about how we're going to do debut practice tonight."

"You're doing what?" I ask Liam over Ivy's shoulder.

"Ivy, I said I couldn't tonight—"

"Nope," she says. "No bailing this time. We all need this."

"I'm confused," I say as we walk outside together. "What's happening?"

"We're all going to Liam's," Ivy says. "Before my summer school class. He has practice, and he can't keep putting it off."

Liam gives me a terrified look. "Ivy—"

"I already grabbed your bag," Ivy says, tossing it to me. "And we're getting out of this hellhole now. I'm going to stop by my place real quick, and then I'll be over to meet you both. No excuses."

I meet Liam's eyes. Yes, we have a lot to do. But also, I don't know how to get out of this without saying what's going on. And as much as I love Ivy, I'm not ready to talk about this with anyone except Liam.

"We could use a break," I say quietly.

He can't argue with that, so he just sighs.

"Fine," he says. "But I promise you, you're going to regret this."

CHAPTER TWENTY-TWO

THURSDAY, JUNE 19
6:33 P.M.

LIAM'S BEDROOM HAS a slightly musty boy smell, which isn't exactly bad. It's like deodorant and mildly dirty socks. It's relatively clean except for a pair of track pants on the floor. His bed is made, if somewhat sloppily. The navy-blue comforter has been pulled up but bunches in the corners, and his pillows are just stacked one on top of the other. One thing, though, is that Liam strongly favors knickknacks, particularly of the music and comic variety. Figurines are lined up on the small desk he's sitting in front of in a crooked office chair, and he's watching me as I pace his room.

"So," Liam says. "You're clearly great at taking a break."

I glare at him. I've filled him in on my trophy theory, which he agrees makes sense. What he doesn't know is what we do with this information now that we've lost the badge.

"We'll take a break as soon as Ivy gets here," I say. "Until then... I just want to talk things out. See if we're missing something."

"Right," Liam says. "Well, I'm still firmly on Team Call the Police.

We might not have the badge, but we still have the notebook. And your theories make a lot of sense."

I chew my lip. "Just . . . give me one more day. I feel like I'm so close. Just one more day, and then we go to them with everything we have."

Liam rubs his hand on his chin before returning to the whiteboard that we've set up on his desk, the one erased to clean perfection so that we can write all the details we know so far. I was surprised that Liam had a whiteboard until he told me that he invested in it last year for sessions with his AP Chemistry study group. It tracks with everything I know about him that he would be nerdy enough to have held on to it.

We organized the board into columns—*What We Know* and *What We Don't Know*—and summarized the notes. Now Liam turns back to the board and, under *What We Don't Know*, writes: *Is the Gondola Killer back, or do they have an accomplice? How are the performers connected to the Gondola Killer stuff?*

A low bark booms from the corner of the room, and Liam ignores it. Snuggled up in a tattered old dog bed is Hector, Liam's squat, long houndlike dog. Hector's fur has a slightly desaturated quality with little white furs spread among the brown patches. One ear has a big scar on the side, and his eyes are cloudy. But he is one hundred percent adorable and obsessed with Liam. He's also keeping me sane right now as I try to think clearly.

"Allie's still the most guilty to me because of the phone," I say. "I think she's working with the Gondola Killer."

"Why would she work with a literal killer, though?" Liam asks.

He's right. It doesn't make sense. I stare at the notes, both on the whiteboard and in my notebook. The pieces are there. Why don't they fit?

I glance at Liam, who's now tapping his lips with the Expo marker. The movement shakes me, shifting my thoughts from killer theories to . . . his mouth. I know, with everything going on, boys should be the last thing on my mind. Even boys like Liam. But I can't help it. He's distracting.

It doesn't help that he's changed. Not spiritually. Literally. He's not in what he was wearing earlier. As soon as we got to his place, he went to his bathroom and changed into what he will be practicing in. The shirt is so thin that I can see the outline of his chest muscles, which are muscles I wasn't aware existed and which take significant time for me to process. The shirt also is not quite long enough, either, or maybe the basketball shorts that he's wearing are too big on him because there's a gap between shirt and shorts and I can see the edges of his hip bones. They're the same pieces of anatomy I saw on Grey earlier, and yet the effect is completely different.

The doorbell rings, blaring through the house, which makes Hector bark and howl. It also stuns me back into remembering that I'm here because someone might be dead, and I need to get my head on straight.

"Ivy's here," Liam says, mercifully getting up. "We can get back to it later."

I nod as he heads to open the front door. Hector gets up from the corner and follows, and I bring up the rear.

"Finally!" Ivy's saying with a laugh when I pop my head into the hall. "Debut practice time. I've been waiting for this."

She's standing with Liam in the entry, Hector bouncing up and down at her legs. She drops her heavy duffel bag onto the floor to pet him, cooing the whole time.

"So are you finally going to tell me what's going on?" I ask.

"It's not a big deal," Liam says. "I mean, it's kind of embarrassing...."

"Déjate de vainas," Ivy says. "This is awesome."

"I'm in a debut," Liam explains, pronouncing it day-boo. "For my cousin."

"It's sort of like a quince or a sweet sixteen," Ivy explains. "It's a Filipino coming-of-age party."

"It's horrible," Liam groans. "I have to do a waltz. And Tiya Ani wants me to send her a video so she knows I'm practicing."

"Who's Tiya Ani?" I ask.

"My aunt," he says. "My cousin Alliya's mom. She's married to my mom's brother, and she's the worst."

"You're acting like you have to go to fucking war," Ivy says, rolling her eyes. "It's just a dance."

"You say that because you're good at dancing," Liam says, "and you don't have twenty cousins saying you dance like your white dad whenever you go to birthdays or weddings or anything."

Ivy scrunches her nose. "Then just be good. It's not hard."

Liam glares at her. "Thanks for the help."

"Look, stop worrying," Ivy says. "I'm here, so let's waltz. Greta can take notes and film."

I nod. "I can do that."

"I guess I'll get the laptop," Liam says, sounding like a man resigned to his doom.

Ivy and I head out to the garage while Liam gets his laptop from his room. His parents are still at work, so the garage is currently car-free and the perfect place to practice, especially with the door open so that a breeze filters in. The space is relatively organized, at least as garages go. You could still park two cars in it—something you definitely can't do at my house—and the edges hold various totes full of decorations and kids' stuff. I see one box marked *Vincent* and point to it.

"What's that?" I ask.

"Vincent's Liam's older brother," Ivy says. "He goes to ASU. He's not a total asshole like Neidy is, but he's close."

"Neidy's your older sister, right?" I ask.

"Yep, and she also just graduated college," Ivy says, rubbing her temple. "All summer she gets to run off to Europe with our parents to celebrate her 'achievement,' and I get to sort through the mountains of graduation gifts coming in the mail."

"Sorry," I say. "I didn't mean—"

"It's fine," Ivy says. "You're an only child, right?"

I nod.

"Lucky," Ivy says. Then she digs through her duffel bag, full of towels, socks, at least two water bottles, jeans, more clothes, and sneakers, and plucks out a small speaker.

On cue, Liam appears in the doorway, laptop in hand.

"All right," he grumbles. "Let the torture begin."

Liam sets up the laptop and then grabs me a chair from the kitchen to sit next to it. I get out my notebook so that I can take down notes during the practice for Liam to review later.

"So the waltz," Ivy says, dragging Liam out to the center of the garage. "Have you been practicing at all?"

"Yes," Liam says. "I mean, kind of. Hard to do solo."

Ivy rolls her eyes. "Let's see the video again before we start."

Liam shows Ivy a video on his phone that his cousin sent with the dance. They watch it a few times together, and then I queue up the song that they'll be dancing to. When I press Play, the song fills the garage from Ivy's speaker, all tinkling piano keys and violins.

Ivy stands behind Liam to start, and he reaches up over his

shoulder to hold her hand. He shakes a little, and I catch him counting out the music. Then, as the piano notes continue to flutter through the air, she steps forward, and he twirls her. It's a slightly awkward twirl because Ivy is taller than Liam, but she doesn't stop him.

"Keep going," Ivy tells him. "Just keep counting."

I realize that Liam's eyes stare at the floor, at his feet, as his lips mouth the number of beats. They continue the waltz, cutting across the floor, until the music rises to a flurry. Almost as soon as it ends, Liam puts his hands on his face.

"I'm terrible," he says. "Alliya's going to be so pissed."

"Alliya asked you to be in this because she wants you to be in it," I say from my corner, even though I have no idea if that's true.

"No," Liam says. "She had to. There's a hip-hop dance, too, but she said she didn't want me to 'hurt myself by attempting it.'"

Ivy snorts. "Let's go again."

They dance across the room, replaying move after move until Ivy stops us.

"You're doing something weird with your feet," Ivy says. "But I can't figure out what. Here, Greta, you come dance."

At the same time, Liam and I both say, "What?"

"I need to watch you dance to figure out what's wrong," Ivy says. "Greta, come on. It'll be easy since Liam's leading."

I look from Liam to Ivy, my ponytail whipping back and forth across my neck. Do I want to dance with Liam, his hand on mine, basically closer than I've ever been? Yes. Obviously. But Ivy's here. And I'm not exactly the best dancer. But also . . .

The sooner Liam figures this dancing thing out, the sooner we can get back to sleuthing.

"I'll do it," I say, standing up so abruptly that my notebook and pen crash to the floor.

"No, Greta," Liam says, holding up his hands. "You can't learn it that fast. It's okay."

"Excuse me, yes, I can," I say, tossing my ponytail over my shoulder. "Besides, my mom always said that we learn faster by teaching."

"Plus," Ivy says, "we'll be able to record you and send it to your aunt."

Once again, Liam looks between us and then sighs. Ivy takes this as a yes and waves me over. She holds out her phone and shows me the video. On the screen is a pretty girl with short black hair who must be Alliya and a boy who looks both proud and annoyed to be there.

"All right," Alliya says in the video, her voice high and prim and patronizing. "Now watch carefully."

The music starts up, but now, instead of focusing on the song, I watch how the girl and the boy move. Eventually, Ivy puts the video down and shows me herself. I follow her footwork—the most important part, she says—and then, when she thinks I'm good enough, she calls Liam over.

"Okay," she says. "Now try it for real with Dealer."

Ivy takes my spot in the corner with her phone ready to record, and Liam steps up in front of me. He pushes his hair back, his eyes on the floor, as we both wait for the music to start. I hate how nervous he looks, hate it even more when I stop to overthink that he looks that way because he's about to dance with me.

"Hey," I say quietly to him. "It's just me."

His eyes rise to meet mine, and they are wide and brown, and there are little flecks of even darker brown just there near the pupil.

"That's the problem," he says, almost too low for me to hear. "It's you."

His hand takes mine, and the touch sets off a spark and a shiver from the place where our skin touches. His other hand finds my waist, just as the music swells, and I can't breathe. Liam's body is too close, and his shirt is too thin, and I can see every single muscle in his arms as he twirls me.

And then I don't know what we're doing, only that he's pushing and pulling me across the floor, as if there's a current of water guiding us. I don't know if we're doing any of the moves right, only that with each touch of his skin on my skin, my heart threatens to fall right out of my chest, a static ball of energy that zips up and down my body.

I must be shaking because his hand squeezes mine. I look up at him and his eyes are wide and soft, his eyelashes too long to be allowed, his face so close to mine that I hold my breath.

The song peters out, soft and quiet, leaving us standing there, still touching as silence fills the garage.

"Well," Ivy says, bringing us back to reality and making us jump apart. "That was good. Didn't follow the choreography exactly, but at least you loosened up."

I glance over at Liam, who is staring at the floor and fluffing his hair again.

"I, well," he says. "I forgot what to do in the middle."

"Uh-huh," Ivy says, and I see that she's got a half smile going as she starts to pull her hair up into a ponytail. "It was around the kick-ball-change."

"Yeah, right," Liam says. "I can, um, work on that. I—"

Ivy yelps, interrupting Liam. The hair tie that Ivy was trying to use to corral her curls snapped, flying across the room.

"Shit," she says, searching around for it. "I think I have a clip in my bag. Greta, can you check? I need to find that hair tie. I don't want Hector to choke on it."

"Of course," I say, bending over to look through the duffel bag.

And the gym stuff I saw earlier was just the tipping point of what's inside. I dig through the contents: three different romance novels, plus a battered old Kindle, and more workout clothes. Finally, I feel something plastic near the bottom.

"I think I found it," I say. "Gimme a sec—"

I unearth a large black claw clip, but it's caught on a button. I pull it harder and unearth what it's hooked on—some piece of clothing that's buried at the bottom of the bag. It's stuck to a silver button, and as I pop open the clip I see what the silver button is attached to.

A denim jacket.

A white denim jacket.

A white denim jacket with patches and . . .

And dark brown stains on the sleeve.

"Toss it over, Greta," Ivy calls. "I found the hair tie."

I stand up so fast I nearly fall backward as I move away from the bag, covering up the jacket with the workout clothes. Ivy's on the other side of the garage, the broken hair tie in hand. She's holding her hair up, waiting for the claw clip, and I run it over to her as quickly as I can.

"Thanks," she says, twisting it up in her hair. "You're a lifesaver."

"I think I'm going to go take a shower," Liam says, jerking me back to reality. "That's all I can do for today."

"That's fine," Ivy says, crossing the garage to grab her speaker. "Perfect timing, actually. I've got to head to class."

As Liam leaves, I watch as Ivy tosses the speaker into the duffel without a second glance. She grabs a towel that she'd pulled out during the dancing and tosses that in there, too, and then she's zipping up the bag.

It'll be gone soon. The jacket. Do I stop her? Do I—

"You're good for him," Ivy says suddenly, and I realize that I've been staring. But she's smiling at me, in that Ivy way that I've learned to crave at Hyper Kid. That smile meant I was doing something right. It meant *I* was right.

"Oh," I say, and my voice is shaky. "I don't know."

"You're good for all of us, Greta," she says, shouldering the bag as she steps closer. "I hope you stick around, even with all this weird shit."

She grins, and I force a grin back.

"See you later, Greta," she says, and then she's walking away, out of the garage and to her car, the bag in hand.

The second she's gone, I smack the garage door closed and race inside to Liam's bedroom. I pull my phone out of my pocket and swipe until I find the picture Liam sent me of the party.

"Oh my god," I say, my voice hoarse. Because I can't breathe.

Mercy Goodwin stands by the door wearing a white denim jacket. There are tiny patches on the side, sewn-in additions to an otherwise blank slate.

There's only one reason why Ivy would have Mercy's jacket—the one she was wearing the night she disappeared.

Only one reason.

And it isn't a good one.

CHAPTER TWENTY-THREE

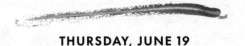

THURSDAY, JUNE 19
7:12 P.M.

"IT CAN'T BE Ivy. It's impossible."

Back in Liam's room it feels entirely different since I told Liam about the jacket. Now he's the one pacing, moving like he's trying to burn holes into the floor, and I could swear his hair's drying at warp speed after his shower because of the laps that he's doing.

"Ivy and Mercy never even talked at work," Liam argues. "Why would Ivy even care about Mercy? She hates performers."

"Exactly," I say. "What if she hated them so much that she snapped?"

"Ivy would never do anything to hurt someone," he says. "And she has no connection to the Gondola Killer. It just doesn't make sense."

"But it does," I say. "She was on the trail at the same time we were. She left before we did. Clearly, she was looking for the badge. Maybe she even took it from your car."

"I thought you were sure Allie took the badge," he says, shaking his head. "And Ivy would've had to run really fast to beat us back to the car."

"She also had a connection to Neil," I say. "They hooked up and argued—"

"You're kidding me," Liam says. "Now you think she killed Neil *and* Mercy? That's just not who Ivy is. I'm telling you."

I know he doesn't want to believe it. And I get it. Because it's Ivy. Ivy, who's always looked out for everyone, especially him. Especially me. But the facts don't lie, and for the first time, things are adding up.

"You really think it's her," he says. "You know that people have made more than one white jacket, right?"

"Liam, there were the same patches. And there were stains," I say. "*Blood*stains."

"But you don't know that," he says, pausing his pacing. "You're assuming."

When in doubt, you must assume that the fluid in front of you is blood.

"What happened to Allie and the phone?" Liam asks. "What about everything Lauren said? What about Grey being an asshole? Mercy was supposedly hooking up with him, right? Or do you not want to look into him because you like him?"

It's like he's slapped me. "Of course not. And I can question him next, if we need to. But Ivy has the jacket, Liam. I can't ignore that. It all adds up. Ivy must have some connection to the Gondola Killer, and she found out Mercy was looking into it. She probably saw her with the pin or the notebook. So she found her and . . ."

"And what, Greta?" Liam demands. "What exactly do you think she did?"

Silence falls in the wake of his question.

I wish Liam could see just how much I hate this, too. This is Ivy we're talking about. The person who took me under her wing immediately. Who made working with Gene livable. Who got me trained at Jungle.

I don't want to lose her. I don't want to lose any of them.

"We should go talk to her," I say. "Go to her house. See—"

"She's got class tonight," Liam interrupts. "And besides, do you realize what she'll say if you accuse her of this?"

"Fine!" I say, throwing my hands up. "But we have to do something. Maybe we finally go to the police, like you've been saying—"

"*Now* you want to go to the police?" Liam says, cutting me off, voice rising. "What happened to needing something concrete?"

"We *have* something concrete," I say. "The notebook and the jacket—"

"So we potentially ruin Ivy's life over nothing?" Liam snaps back. "Did we not talk to the same douchebag cop, Greta? The one who was horrible to you? Because that's not someone I trust to handle this the right way if we're wrong."

"Then we can ask James to help us," I say. "He'll make sure he isn't a jerk—"

"He wasn't just a jerk," Liam says with a harsh, hollow laugh. "He kept trying to get me to tell him things, like why we were there so early and did I have any problems with Neil. Bullshit that had nothing to do with a regular old witness statement."

"He did that to me, too," I say. "And I know that isn't okay. But this is Mercy's life."

Liam's eyes fix on me, steady and warm and endless.

"He wanted me to blame you, Greta," he says. "Detective Kupferle wanted me to blame *you* for what happened to Neil."

Suddenly, my entire body is frozen. I don't know why I brought up the police in the first place, other than that my head is spinning. Because I know this isn't something to write off. I know that this is connected to Mercy, and I know that I'm the one who's supposed to pull her out of this riptide. And Liam has to see that. He just has to.

But now . . . what did Detective Kupferle say to him?

"That's impossible," I say, voice shaking over the syllables. "I was with you."

"Obviously," Liam says, shaking his head. "But he kept saying things to me. 'That girl gets in over her head sometimes.' 'She's not someone you can trust.' 'She'll do anything to get even with someone.'"

I look down, trying to not let the sting of his words show on my face because I still don't know everything that Detective Kupferle told him. I don't know if I'm doomed. But if Liam knew the truth . . . why would he have stayed with me all day? Why would I be here at all?

I can tell he knows he's hurt me because he steps closer until he's standing in front of me.

"Greta," he says. And there it is again. My name. My name and how he says it. Everyone else, they say my name like two throwaway syllables. Cheap, easy syllables. But not him.

"But why do you need to prove this, Greta?" Liam asks. "I know why you *want* to. I know you think you're supposed to. But is this still about helping Mercy, or is this about proving that you can do this?"

"Of course this is about Mercy!" I say. "I'm the one who wants to solve this. I'm the one who cares—"

"And I'm glad you care," he says. "But we can't just jump to accusations like this. Ivy's life isn't a game."

I bristle. "I know that. And I won't go to the police, okay? But I need to at least talk to her and find out the truth. For Mercy."

"Fine," Liam says, the hurt in his tone matching mine. "Do what you want. But if you're going after Ivy . . . I can't do that. Because I know she wouldn't hurt Mercy. I just know."

I hate that the tears choose this moment to escape down my cheeks. I hate that we've come so far and he won't trust me. I hate that, even as I hate all of this, I just want to run into his arms and hold on to him and never let go.

But that won't bring Mercy Goodwin back.

"I'm sorry," I say. "But I have to look into this."

He nods. It's a slow, sad kind of nod.

"I'll take you home," he says.

I rub my sleeve on my cheek, mopping up the tears there. We leave his house, walking past Hector and his sad little bark, and I get into the car, knowing everything's changed. I try not to cry as much, but it doesn't work. The tears slip down, silent betrayals as the car rumbles beneath us. Neither Liam nor I say anything, not until he pulls into my driveway.

"Maybe it's best that we step away," he says. "Maybe we were in over our heads."

It's his final appeal for me to stop, but it doesn't work. My mind's made up. He must see it on my face because he sighs and looks down at the steering wheel.

"I guess I'll see you at work," he says, voice stiff.

"I guess so."

I get out of the car. I don't slam the door intentionally, but the sound feels loud anyway. I head straight inside, and thankfully, Mom isn't home. Jasper is, though, and he follows me all the way to my room, snuggling up to me when I crash onto my bed.

It's his wet nose I feel on my hand as the tears pour out without any sign of stopping.

I let myself cry. It's the kind of cry I haven't done since maybe early June, a new record for me. But then, slowly, reality seeps in, and I remember why I'm crying.

I remember there's still a girl in a riptide, and I need to save her.

It's Jasper who shakes me out of my trance. He licks my hand—no doubt smelling Hector—and peers up at me with his big eyes. Concerned for me, maybe, but also it's late and he needs a walk. More than that, I realize, *I* need a walk. According to my research from earlier, walks help people process things and recenter themselves.

Struggling to solve a case? Go for a walk! You'll be surprised what getting the blood pumping can do for putting clues together.

I leash up Jasper and head outside, letting the thoughts churn inside me. And I think the advice might be working, though it did not address two important factors: the Rancho Paloma heat and my fresh heartbreak. Both weigh on me now as I urge Jasper forward in our neighborhood, but I know I have to push both of them aside.

I roll the details over in my head as Jasper pants beside me. When he pauses next to a bench in a shaded green area by the community pool, I let him take a break and pull my notebook out and start writing, willing the pieces to make sense on their own.

Suspect: Ivy
Dislikes all performers
Also hates Neil
White denim jacket in bag—Mercy's??—with bloodstains

I stare at the last line. Is it possible it's a coincidence? The white jacket could be Ivy's own jacket, and maybe those brown spots were . . . I don't know, barbecue sauce or something.

But somehow, I just don't think that's true.

And yes, I still don't know how Ivy's connected to the Gondola Killer. But I won't figure that out unless I do something.

Near my feet, Jasper makes a little annoyed groan. It's getting dark but still at least ninety degrees out, so I can't really blame him. I persuade him to make the walk back to the house, and once we're inside, he rushes to his water bowl and slurps.

There must be a way to figure out if Ivy knew Mercy, if she had any reason to dislike her. I stare at Jasper, and then suddenly, it hits me.

I don't know if Mercy has social media, but I'd bet anything Ivy does. And if I can use her social media to eliminate her as a suspect, possibly see if she's taken a picture in her own white jacket . . . then I won't have to take this further. I won't have to lose Liam or Ivy. And even though that means opening my accounts and seeing those messages again, I'm willing to do it for them.

I grab my phone, redownload one of the apps I deleted before, and tap it open. I log in, clicking the button that asks me, "Do you wish to reactivate your account?"

I'm not scared anymore. I click Yes, and the app flares to life after several excruciating moments. I ignore the envelope icon, the one that tells me I have 132 unread messages, all preserved and unopened from the day I deactivated in May. I go straight to the search bar and I type *Mercy Goodwin*. I'm not surprised when nothing pops up, though. She didn't seem like the social media type. And besides, that was just my first search. The next one might be more important.

When I type in *Ivy Villanueva*, she's at the top of the list, her picture a close-up of her face: her pouting lips, her thick eyeliner, her middle finger held high. I click it, thanking every star in the universe that it's public. And then, I begin to scroll.

At first it's mainly just monthly photo dumps, selfies on the trails where she runs, artistic shots, quotes she likes. But as I go further back, there are photos of Ivy in high school. She's wearing her graduation robes and cap, and the caption says, *See you never, fuckers.* A few posts earlier, she's in a slinky dark red prom dress. She's in a classroom with the teacher standing behind her while she makes a face. She's—

She's at Moonlight Beach, and she's sitting on a towel, a book in her lap, a girl in star-shaped sunglasses and a polka-dot one-piece bathing suit sitting beside her.

Mercy.

I check the date. This picture is almost five years old, from what would have been Ivy's freshman year of high school. And underneath it, there's a comment from someone—not Mercy, but someone else.

whos_neidy: looking good vee! 🔥 tell mercy to remember us when she's a star.

I stare at the picture. This means that Ivy *does* know Mercy. And she doesn't just know her. Based on this picture, they were friends. Something she never told us. And then something else: I hear Ivy's voice from the trail floating back to me.

The girl I was in love with had just told me she didn't love me back.

Is it possible? Were they more than friends? At least, in Ivy's eyes? I'm grabbing for something else, the note from the box of Mercy's things. I find it and read it over and over, settling on a line in the middle.

You don't love me the way I love you.

Oh my god.

Ivy was in love with Mercy. The motive that Liam thinks she could never have had . . . it's all right there, spelled out in the note.

I'm out the door before I can think or breathe. I tell Jasper that I love him and to be a good boy as I lock it, and then I drive to Ivy's house.

To break in.

CHAPTER TWENTY-FOUR

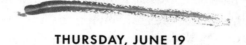

THURSDAY, JUNE 19
8:52 P.M.

I PARK DOWN the street, far enough away that it's a bit of a trek to her actual house. I'm eternally glad that she sent her address before the party that night, especially since I'm still having enough trouble convincing myself that this is the right thing to do. The last thing I need is to break into a stranger's house. At least I know Ivy's should be empty right now. The rest of her family is still in Europe for her sister's graduation trip, and Ivy's in class.

As I walk up the street, I try not to think about the fact that Ivy's my friend or what Liam will say when he finds out what I'm doing. I pack all those feelings up and focus because tonight, I'm an investigator looking for Mercy. If anything, I'm looking for something that might say that Ivy most certainly did not hurt Mercy. I'm looking to be wrong. Even if I don't feel that I am.

Ivy's house is clean on the outside with a cozy, lived-in quality. Little hand-painted signs hang in a vegetable garden in the front lawn, and though it's dark, I can see one that says Tomate and another that says Albahaca. The picket fence was once white but now has chips of wood showing through. There's grass, but it's faded in patches. The porch light's not on, leaving the front yard cast in darkness. The curtains are drawn, too, though there's a small car parked in the driveway. It must belong to her parents or Neidy because it's not the truck that I've seen Ivy take to work.

I let myself through the gate, checking for neighbors as I go, but I seem to be alone. No one's outside, and the cul-de-sac is quiet.

I knock at the door and wait, but no one answers. The house sounds deserted, and I peer inside through the stained-glass window in the center of the door and can't see anyone. I try the handle and, to my surprise, it turns.

Unlocked.

Because I'm meant to go into this house. I'm meant to find Mercy Goodwin. It really is destiny.

I step inside to the sound of a creaking floorboard underfoot, and I freeze. Still, no one appears, so I quietly pull the door shut behind me. Pictures cover the walls, glamour shots of Ivy's mom, whose curls Ivy and her sister have both inherited. There are high school pictures of Ivy and Neidy. Neidy looks like she might be softer and taller than Ivy, especially when they're photographed together. Ivy's smile looks mischievous, sometimes forced, but her sister always looks as if she was just told that she won the lottery.

I don't dare flip on a light, so I pull out my phone and tap the flashlight to navigate. The house opens to a small hall that leads to the living room on the left and a kitchen on the right. The kitchen is working with a yellow, rooster-accented theme. Bowls are stacked in the sink and takeout bags are lined up on the side.

I cross through the living room to get to the hall that leads to three doors. Quietly I peek into the first, which is the main bedroom and must belong to Ivy's parents. I move on to the second and peer inside a tidy bedroom, which my gut tells me is Neidy's. That only leaves the last one, the corner one. The one with the closed door.

I push it open.

Ivy's room has the same messy-but-put-together vibe that Ivy does. Her current romance novel is tossed onto her nightstand, while the rest of her collection is lined up on shelves. Several lipsticks and eyeliners crowd the dresser. Her bed isn't completely made, but the sheets are pulled up and her pillows are stacked.

I check her desk, not sure what I'm looking for. My chest tightens. Maybe Liam was right and coming here was a mistake.

Then I hear it. The creak of another floorboard, but I didn't make it.

I listen to the silence of the house, waiting for Ivy to enter her bedroom and find me lurking, but nothing happens. No more creaking. But something else.

It's quiet, so quiet that I might not have heard it if I wasn't listening. It's like . . . music, but muffled. Voices speaking, maybe, but almost like they're underwater.

I leave the bedroom. I go back to the hall, walking on tiptoes, listening for the sound, wondering if whatever it is hears me, too.

I follow the sound to the back of the house, muffled again, but definitely there. And that's when I realize that this part of the house has a distinct error. Partially hidden under a long runner is a floorboard that doesn't totally match the rest. Its lines are just slightly off, and there in the corner, nearly hidden by a particularly leafy potted plant, are hinges.

Without thinking, I pull the rug aside, and that's when I see the small leather loop. It's barely noticeable, but now that I've seen it, I recognize it for what it is: a handle.

Because this? This is a hatch.

Leading to some kind of basement.

Leading, maybe, to Mercy.

I pull the leather loop as quietly as I can, but it creaks as the floorboard comes up, and light blooms out from below, illuminating a flight of stairs. But if there's one thing I know it's that nothing good happens in a basement. Movies and TV shows have made that perfectly clear, and as I look down, I can't help but imagine manacles, torture devices, and maybe a coffin.

Still, I didn't come this far to be derailed by my own hysteria. Whatever is down there must be faced, and I must be the one to face it. I turn off my flashlight, take a steadying breath, and pocket my phone. Then I remember something I read during my initial research on sleuthing. How you need allies, but more than that, you need to keep your allies in the loop.

Just in case, I pull my phone out again and send my live location to Liam. I fully expect him to ignore it, but at least he has it. In case I'm added to the coffin tonight. Then I slip my phone back into my pocket and take another deep breath. I take the first step. Then the second.

Then the third.

On the fourth step, I hear someone move.

On the fifth step, I scream.

Because they've grabbed me by the arm.

CHAPTER TWENTY-FIVE

THURSDAY, JUNE 19
9:04 P.M.

THE HAND COMES out of the dark next to the stairs, and my scream echoes off the concrete walls. I'm kicking myself for not looking up self-defense skills, but I refuse to die here because of lack of research. I struggle backward, trying to scramble up the stairs. But the hand tugs me forward, even as I try to wrench away.

"Jesus Christ, what's going on?"

I whip around to see a figure at the top of the stairs, cast in shadow. They're haloed by the light from above, but I'd recognize those curls anywhere. Curls that fill me with relief and then, when I realize where I am, terror.

"Please don't scream again," a soft voice next to me says. "It's really loud down here."

I'm still staring at Ivy, thinking this is it, I'm done, and why didn't I hug Mom one last time? And then . . . and then I process what I've just heard. What I've just seen.

I turn, and my eyes go from the small hand with chipped red nails to the wispy blond hair falling in front of bright hazel eyes.

Mercy's eyes.

"Mercy!" I gasp. "You're alive."

And she looks . . . okay.

She smiles, still holding on to me. "Yes, I'm fine."

"Good work on finding her, though," Ivy says, stomping down the stairs, and I try to back away.

"You have to let her go, Ivy," I say, dredging up my confidence. "This—"

"Calm down," Ivy says, passing me. She walks to the wall and flicks a switch, and the light goes on, illuminating the room. It's small but oddly cozy: there's an older television resting on a dresser, a violet sofa, a beanbag chair, some storage bins along the back wall, a duffel bag on the floor that's spilling out clothes.

Beside me, Mercy tugs on my wrist again, leading me down the stairs.

"It's okay," she says. "I promise. I was just watching *Vertigo*, but I turned it off when I heard you upstairs."

"How did you know it was me?"

She laughs. "I didn't, but I knew you weren't Ivy. She stomps."

"I also warned her you might be coming," Ivy says. "After I saw your face when you were looking in my duffel bag. I totally forgot I left that jacket in there."

I stare at her, horrified. She knew? She knew that I saw?

"Have a seat, Greta," Ivy says, and she sounds the way she does at work, calm and cool and slightly annoyed.

When I don't move, she sighs. "Listen, I promise I'll tell you everything if you just sit down. Is Liam up there wandering around in my parents' bedroom? Should I get him, too?"

I flush. "He's not here."

Ivy smirks. "Just us girls, then."

"Did you bring any food?" Mercy asks suddenly.

Ivy rolls her eyes. "You need food for this? Really?"

"Well, it's a very long story," Mercy says. "And to tell it properly, we might want to have snacks."

Another roll of Ivy's eyes. "Can I order some later?" she asks. "Once we've proved to Greta that I'm not planning to chop you up into little pieces?"

"Wait, so no one was, uh, killed? Or hurt?" I say, and immediately realize how ridiculous I sound. Obviously, at least one person has died.

I look at Mercy, and she looks even paler than she was moments ago.

"I think you better start, Merce," Ivy says quietly. "From the beginning."

Mercy sighs. "Yes, well, all right. But I still think we should have food."

She tucks her hair back behind her ears, leveling me with a bright gaze.

"It's not a nice story, see," she says. "No, it's not a nice story at all."

CHAPTER TWENTY-SIX

THURSDAY, JUNE 19
9:26 P.M.

IT'S A BIT like picking a scab, listening to Mercy walk me through what happened. At first, it takes a tiny bit of digging at the corners, and then, before you know it, you're pulling on the edge, letting blood trickle out over your skin.

Some of it, I already know, like about how she and the performers didn't get along from the beginning. How she took the job seriously—"Too seriously for someone playing a literal panda," Ivy suggests—and how she started leaving the greenroom to get away from the noise. She'd move around the park to find quiet spaces, including the one where she told me to meet her.

But the turret ended up being her sanctuary, especially once she found the notebook.

"I didn't know what it was when I found it," she says. "I just started reading it. It was stuffed in a corner with a few other things . . . a playbill and a letter."

"Hailey's show," I say. "*A Streetcar Named Desire.*"

Mercy nods, then pulls something out of her pocket. It's a corner of the playbill that's been ripped off, written on in black Sharpie.

Funerals are quiet, but deaths—not always. Love, Hailey Portman

"She'd signed it," Mercy says. "But it was stuck under some huge crate and ripped when I pulled it out. I kept this portion with me, though, once I started looking into everything. And then, of course, there was K's letter."

I blink at her. "Letter?"

"If you found the playbill," she says, "then you also found K's letter to Hailey. He was her stalker. It took me forever to figure out who he was, but eventually, I realized I didn't need to look far. He was right there on the playbill. *Kenneth,* a crew member on her show.

"He also worked at Hyper Kid," she explains. "He followed her from there to here. I think he was something in Attractions. But when I looked online and in the records, I couldn't find any Kenneth who worked in rides at Hyper Kid. I ended up asking Neil, since he was such a Hyper Kid fanatic. I told him I was just interested in the story from a historical perspective, and I didn't tell him I had the notebook."

Mercy sighs, adjusting on the chair.

"He said he'd look into it," she continues. "At the same time, my issues with the other performers were getting worse. Lauren pushed me during one show, which I reported to James immediately. She lost the opportunity to play Ranger—which she'd been gunning for—and was furious. And then, obviously, her scene at the party."

She takes another breath. "Meanwhile, Neil was looking into things. He'd found some photos of Hailey from that opening night, and he showed them to me, plus walked me through some facts he'd unearthed. He had all these theories from these true-crime blogs and Reddit pages . . . things about how killers behave, what to look for. He took it further than I thought he would, honestly, but I was thrilled. I felt like we were really on the edge of something, and he promised to keep looking.

"And then, the day of the party, all our performances were off," Mercy continues. "I asked Grey, Allie, and Lauren if they could stay to help me work through it. Lauren was . . . well, she didn't like me 'bossing her around,' but they stayed. I thought everything was fine until I tried to make my entrance through the trapdoor and . . . and Grey grabbed me from behind."

"Fucking asshole," Ivy says, looking angrier than I've ever seen her. "Fucking *ass*hole."

"He was trying to mess with me, I think," Mercy says, avoiding Ivy's eyes. "He'd been hitting on me for weeks. I knew he wanted something physical, something I had no interest in. He crossed a line. I struggled, and then he let me go when I kicked him in the shin. It made me fall forward, and my costume got slashed on the metal part that lifts up the trapdoor. I got blood everywhere. Ruined the costume, too."

I suck in a breath, remembering the slashed panda costume I saw in Wardrobe. Allie had called Grey a fuckboy. But this? This is . . . this is horrible. My stomach twists as Mercy continues.

"Allie and Lauren insisted we keep it to ourselves," Mercy continues. "Clean up the blood, turn in the costume, whatever. I think they were worried I'd tell on them. And I'll be honest. I planned to. Not on them, but on Grey. As soon as James got back from his retreat, I would let him know.

"I stayed longer in the theater after they left, just so I could regroup. When I got to the offices, everything was dark. No one was at their desks. I decided I'd write James a note requesting a meeting as soon as he got back. I didn't want to email him or text him, seeing as I didn't want to bother him on the retreat. But as I grabbed a Post-it to write the note, I noticed something on his desk."

Here, Mercy swallows. She closes her eyes. And then, she opens them.

"He has all this stuff," she says. "Pictures. Posters. News clippings. And badges. He didn't have as many as Neil, but he had a few. And one of them . . . was gold."

Mercy walks over to the coffee table and opens a drawer, pulling out a small Ziploc bag with a gold badge in it. The same one Liam and I found on the trail. She walks back and holds it out for me to see.

"But how . . . how did you . . ."

I glance back at Ivy, who's smirking.

"I'm faster than I look," she says. "And you and Liam have about zero subtlety talking about this shit."

I stare at it now, the pieces snapping together. James had the badge. Hailey's badge. Which means . . .

"James killed Hailey?" I ask, jaw hanging open. "But . . . but you said Kenneth . . ."

"He is *Kenneth*, Greta," Ivy says, jumping in. "James *K*. Murphy. He went by Kenneth as a kid. James K. Murphy is a stage name. It flips his actual name: Kenneth James Murphy. Neil found it in the records when he was looking. Plus, Mercy recognized his handwriting from the love letter—if you can call it that—he wrote to Hailey."

"And there's *Streetcar*," Mercy says, elbowing Ivy. "Show them the picture, Vee."

Ivy grabs her phone, scrolling through her photos until she finds the cast photo of Hailey that's hung up in the greenroom. The one of when she was in *A Streetcar Named Desire*.

And there, off to the side, is a twenty-years-younger but undeniable James K. Murphy.

Oh.

Oh.

"But the badge," I say. "You saw it on his cubicle wall and took it? He just had it out there?"

"I think James got a kick out of keeping that badge out in the open," Mercy says, shaking her head. "His way of showing Hailey he'd won. He got to be at Hyper Kid."

"That's sick," I say, shaking my head. "But you brought it to the party?"

"Neil had told me about the badges," Mercy says. "They were wearing them in the pictures he showed me. I . . . I feel terrible that he must have kept looking into this after I disappeared, that maybe his death was my fault."

"It wasn't your fault," Ivy says. "It was that asshole's—"

"But wait," I say. "Why not go to the police at that point? Once you had the badge and knew it was James?"

"I meant to," Mercy says. "That was my plan. I was keeping the badge on me for safekeeping."

"Which I told her was a terrible idea," Ivy interjects. "The police part, at least. Considering how shitty the police in this town generally are."

"Well, yes. Ivy and I disagreed," Mercy says. "She believed the cops listen to James and James alone."

"What?" I say. "But when they interviewed me . . ."

But I stop, thinking back on how James protected me when

Detective Kupferle interviewed me for my statement. Or I'd *thought* it was protection. Was he actually keeping me from spilling too much information?

"Never mind," I mumble.

"Either way," Mercy continues, "I wanted to try going to the police after I got everything together. And I would've, but then the journal disappeared."

"Lauren," I say, realizing. "She took it."

Mercy nods. "I figured one of them had, so I went to the party to find out who. James was supposed to be gone for a week anyway, completely unplugged. I had time. Or so I thought."

Chills ripple through me as I hold my arms tighter to my chest.

"While everyone else was watching the TV spot," Mercy says, "Grey found me alone. He said that James had called him right before he got to the party and asked where I was and had I shown him anything. He hadn't *told* Grey what I'd taken, but I knew right away that James had figured out what I'd done. He must still have been at the office. Maybe he was in the bathroom. But the point is . . . after I talked to Grey, I knew James was coming to find me. I went outside to call for a Lyft there. But then Lauren confronted me outside, eating up time. I knew the trails well enough to know that one of them lets you out in another part of the neighborhood, so I decided to take that and call the Lyft away from the party. I thought I'd be safer there. I was wrong.

"He saw me from the road when I entered the trail," she says. "He'd parked along the side. He never even went into the party, just followed me into the woods. I ran, tried calling the police while I was running, but he knocked my phone out of my hand and sent it flying. He wanted the badge back, obviously. He told me he knew I had it. That I wanted a piece of Hailey as much as... as much as he did."

She chokes up a little here, shame crossing over her features before continuing.

She describes the way he snuck up on her, the low snarl of his voice in the woods. The way he covered her mouth after she screamed. How she thought she was going to be murdered, just like Hailey, only instead of a gondola, they'd find her body in the woods.

"He was choking me," she says. "Everything was so dark, and my head was pounding. And then, Ivy was there, and she was covered in dirt."

I blink, looking to Ivy. I knew Ivy had some role to play here, even if it wasn't the one I originally pictured.

"I don't understand," I say, looking from Ivy to Mercy. "James attacked you, and Ivy... you stopped him?"

Ivy's leaning against the wall, her arms crossed, the flickering basement light casting her face in partial shadow. She pops a chip into her mouth, chewing carefully and swallowing before speaking again.

"I hit him in the skull with a rock," Ivy says. "He was going to strangle her, and I stopped him. And I thought I'd killed the bastard. I *wish* I killed him."

I stare, processing this bloody turn. I shake my head as understanding continues to dawn.

"But why didn't you go to the police *then*?" I ask. "Why didn't you tell them James attacked you and possibly killed someone else—"

Above us, a crash sounds that seems to shake the entire house.

I whip toward the sound as Ivy stands up, pitching her head toward the upstairs.

"Probably a tree branch," Ivy says, though for once, she doesn't sound sure.

Above us, it's quiet, and then, unmistakably, we hear them—footsteps. Heavy, creaking footsteps. Whoever it is moves slowly through the halls, stopping in places above us. I can tell that Ivy and Mercy are straining to hear where the footsteps go, watching the ceiling above as if they can clearly imagine the trespasser's path.

"They're going into your room," Mercy whispers. "Just like Greta did."

Ivy looks at me. "You went in my room?"

My eyes hit the floor. "I was investigating."

Up above, the footsteps move again, and this time, I can imagine them going into the hall.

"Will they see the hatch?" Mercy asks.

"Let's hope they don't notice it," Ivy murmurs.

More creaking followed by flurries of movement. My breath catches. Were we followed? Is it James?

A soft thump above answers me.

"Well," Ivy says. "Guess they did notice."

I look from Ivy's grim determination to Mercy's sudden and complete terror. It grips her, holding her in place.

"What do we do?" I ask Ivy. "Where—"

But Ivy's ahead of me. She grabs me and Mercy and drags us over to the side of the stairs, hiding us from view. Then she rushes across the room and hits the lights, and we are once again awash in darkness.

"Ivy—" I whisper, but she holds up her hand.

"Stay quiet!" she hisses, and I hear her shuffling around with something on the other side of the stairs.

Above us, the footsteps continue, no doubt searching for the handle. Or deciding what to do. Or calling for backup. Or grabbing a weapon. There are lots of possibilities, none of them good for us.

The hatch lifts up, revealing boots in the dark. They take the steps one at a time. Beside me, Mercy sucks in a breath, and I clutch her hand, hard.

"Hello?" a voice calls down. "Greta, are you—"

Ivy leaps out of her corner, brandishing a baseball bat. There's a curse and footsteps, and then I hear a body rolling and bumping down the steps. Whoever it is lands in a heap on the concrete floor, groaning—

"Shit!" Ivy cries, throwing aside the bat. "Shit!"

She drops to the floor, next to the person. Mercy and I poke around the corner as soon as she does, and that's when I see who's in a heap on the floor.

"Liam," I breathe out.

CHAPTER TWENTY-SEVEN

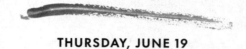

THURSDAY, JUNE 19
9:47 P.M.

HE'S HERE. HE'S actually here.

I can't breathe. In the darkness of Ivy's basement, it all feels impossible. Improbable. Not just Liam being here, but everything else. None of this was in my research, not on the blogs I read or the podcasts I listened to. And now . . . now I find out that yes, technically, I was right. Ivy did something unthinkable, but not for the reason I would've thought.

And besides, none of that matters quite as much as the fact that Liam's *here*.

"Are you okay?" Ivy asks him, shaking him by the shoulder. "Liam, talk to me."

He coughs, cracking one eye open. "Are you going to hit me with the bat if I say no?"

Ivy pushes him away with an eye roll. "No seas bobo," she mutters.

Mercy runs forward out of the shadows and bends down, offering him her hand. He goes to take it and then sees whose it is, which leads him to promptly scuttle backward on the ground.

"Holy shit! You're—you're—"

"Alive," Mercy says serenely. "Yes, thank you."

He looks between Mercy and Ivy, eyes wide and mouth gaping. The sight of him sets me on fire, totally and completely, breaking me into pieces that only he could tape back together. I want to run to him and throw myself on him, but I resist. I have to resist because maybe this is all a hallucination and I passed out just like Mercy did in the woods.

"What the hell are you doing here?" Ivy demands of Liam, wrenching him up so that he's standing.

He laughs, dusting himself off. "Um, I feel like maybe I should get to ask some questions first? Like why you attacked me with a baseball bat? Or . . . why you have a missing person in your basement?"

"Nah," Ivy says, shaking her head. "I want to know why you were sneaking around my house."

He looks between the two of them again, and then, his eyes light on me. Relief washes over him, positively drenching him, and his half smile is soft and inviting.

"I was looking for Greta," he says.

I was looking for Greta.

Five simple words, but they're beautiful and amazing and I'll cling to them forever. Because he didn't give up on me. He didn't write me off. He didn't abandon me.

Ivy follows his gaze to me and then throws her hands up. "Unbelievable."

"She sent me her live location," he says. "And, so, I was, um, watching it. And when she didn't move from the same place and didn't answer her phone—"

"So you broke into my house?" Ivy says. "How'd you get in?"

He glances at me, then back at Ivy. "It was unlocked?"

"Oh, for fuck's sake," she says.

I wish I could run to him. I wish I could hug him. But I'm frozen because I don't know what to do right now. I don't want to ruin anything, and seeing as I, apparently, always ruin things . . . I stay still.

"Greta?" Ivy asks, looking at me with raised eyebrows. "Want to confirm that you're fine before Liam has a full meltdown?"

"Okay," I say, hiding my newest blush by coughing. "Ivy and Mercy were just, uh, filling me in on what happened. We'd just left off at, um . . ."

"Mercy getting attacked by James," Ivy summarizes.

"Technically foiled by you hitting him in the head with a rock," I add, and then, at Liam's face, I continue, "because you were saving Mercy."

"Hopefully, I at least gave him a concussion," Ivy says.

Ivy and Mercy take turns filling Liam in with a much more CliffsNotes version of the story than I heard. He's a good listener and asks the right questions. When the story has been told for its second time and reached the attack-at-the party moment, Liam shakes his head.

"So wait," he says. "Why *didn't* you guys just go to the police after he attacked Mercy?"

"I needed the badge—which I must have dropped while I was running away from James—and the notebook. I still didn't know who had taken it," Mercy says. "Everything hinged on what Hailey wrote in there about 'K' watching her. I didn't trust that the police would take me seriously without it, seeing that they always defer to James."

"But why didn't you just come into work?" Liam asks. "Why not tell, I don't know . . . HR?"

Ivy snorts. "James has the police in his pocket. He definitely also has *HR*."

"Plus, my phone was gone," Mercy says. "And Ivy told me someone had started texting Grey telling him that I was sick. I assumed James was behind it, that it was some sick game of chicken. He was forcing my hand and waiting me out at the same time. He could paint me as this unreliable, irresponsible employee while he waited for my next move."

"But James doesn't have your phone," I say. "Allie does. I saw her with it, and she admitted to it."

"Allie?" Mercy asks, confused. "Why would Allie be working with James?"

"I don't know," I say. "She said she had a reason, but she wouldn't tell me what it was."

"And there's something else," Liam says. "Neil was calling you, Mercy. The night before he was found. Why?"

The room goes quiet.

"I can only assume he figured it out," Mercy says after a moment, her voice soft and frayed. "He might have even confronted James. I don't know for sure."

"So, what?" Liam asks. "James killed Neil because he was poking around?"

"That's my best guess," Ivy says. "But again, without that notebook, no one will buy that. James has so much fucking clout in this town, and the cops are his literal buddies."

"Plus, he's been hiding in plain sight for years," Mercy says. "I think he came back to Hyper Kid as a statement, that he owns this place. He's daring us to question him because he thinks there's no way we'll be believed. And, I guess, he's got a bit of a point. He's one of the best actors for a reason."

I feel sick.

"But now," Mercy says, smiling, "we can actually put an end to this. Tomorrow. You have the notebook, Greta?"

I nod. "Yes. At home."

"Then we go to the police together," she says. "They can't deny all of us, everything we've seen."

I agree. "That's great. Whatever you need."

"Perfect," Mercy says. "Until tomorrow, then."

Liam and I walk out of Ivy's house together with the information spinning between us. It stopped raining, but the air still feels damp. Part of my brain is fighting for me to run home, to get to work on the parts of the case that I still need to solve. I also want to look up self-defense and how it relates to murder laws—are those a thing?—but mostly, everything feels like a steady stream of electricity buzzing through me. Just energy, or adrenaline, or something, because I'm practically bouncing on my heels as I walk to my car. Liam's there next to me, his sneakers soft and quiet on the pavement next to my bouncing. Everything about him is steady and calm and even and together. But me?

I feel like I'm about to explode. At first, it feels like the good kind of explosion, the victorious kind, because I was right, wasn't I? Ivy *did* have something to do with Mercy's disappearance. Mercy didn't just stop showing up to work, and there was someone at Hyper Kid who drove her away.

I was right. I mean, yes, none of it was exactly what I thought, but...

Suddenly, the explosion doesn't feel like victory. It feels like I've been yanked underwater, like I'm the one in the riptide now, like little pieces of me are being tugged on in a billion different directions as I try to swim for the surface.

I walk faster, electricity zipping down my legs. Liam's behind me, though I can tell he's trying to keep up. I don't know what I'm doing, only that we're almost to my car, and somehow, I just need to get to it, need to have somewhere to escape to. The first tear sneaks out and streaks back into my hair, and I wipe it away before he can see. But as I do, his hand touches my shoulder, and I stop. More tears, and I know soon I'll be shaking.

I should run. I know what's coming, don't I? I know. He's going to tell me how ridiculous I was, how we've done enough, how he only followed me because he didn't want me to get hurt but that this doesn't change anything from before.

And I can't. I can't hear all of that. In there, for a moment, we were a team again. I need to live in that for a little longer.

"Hey," he says, and his hand moves from my shoulder to my chin, gently guiding me to look back at him. And even though it's dark and the only light is a flickering streetlamp, I know he sees the tears because of how his eyes widen.

"Greta," he begins, and there's concern etched in his voice. "What's wrong?"

How do I explain? Liam doesn't know what it feels like to be drowning, to get swept away from your entire life before you even know what's happening. Because Liam's an anchor, immovable and strong.

He shifts a little on his feet as he wipes my tears with his thumb, but it's pointless because they just keep slipping out. I hiccup, turning away from him and his touch as I look down the empty street.

He's quiet for a moment before he speaks again.

"Did . . . did all of that sort of freak you out?"

No. No, that was all fine. I'm fine. Because I asked for this, didn't I? I wanted to investigate this. I went searching for it.

"Because it freaked me out," he says, and his voice isn't steady anymore. I look over, and he's watching me with those warm brown eyes.

"It did?" I squeak.

"Of course it did," he says, shaking his head as he runs his hand through his hair. "There's literally a killer on the loose. And Mercy . . . I can't believe she had to deal with all of that."

He blows out a breath, and my eyes fall on his hands at his sides. They're shaking, just like mine.

"But we're going to solve this because of you," he says, and now his gaze meets mine. "Families are going to have answers because you wouldn't let up on this."

His words are like someone pressing on a bruise that you don't know you have until they touch it. More tears slide out, but it's different than before. These tears are almost shocked out of me. Because there's reverence in Liam's voice now. There's awe.

For me.

"You were so fucking brave, Greta," he says. "You knew something was wrong, and you didn't wait around like I did. Like the rest of us did."

I bite my lip. It's hard to look at him when he's looking at me like that. Like he doesn't want to look at anyone else ever again.

"Ivy was brave," I say, looking at the gravel on the road. "She did things. Literally, she saved Mercy. I just found stuff out."

"Yeah, Ivy was brave," he says, stepping closer to me. "But don't you see? Ivy can't do this by herself. She needed help, and you were there without any questions. I've never met anyone like you. You're perfect."

But suddenly, I'm aware of just how *not* perfect I am. Of how much Liam doesn't know. And how, if I don't tell him now, I might never tell him again.

"I'm not perfect," I say, tears stinging my eyes. "I'm actually a criminal. I should've told you before, but I'm telling you now, okay? I burned down the boys' locker room. I was trying to burn the pictures they had of me—they printed them out since admin took their phones—but it got out of control. I burned everything. All their equipment. They thought I'd . . . they told everyone I'd gone insane."

Liam doesn't move. He just stares at me, still holding my hand, even though I wish he would stop. It will only make it worse when he throws it away in disgust.

"It was all the Axe body spray," I say, tears sliding down my cheeks. "It just . . . I've never used a lighter before. I didn't realize how fast it would happen. I didn't mean for so many things to catch on fire, all their bags and sticks and stuff, and the sprinklers . . . they weren't working properly, but I didn't know that. And then . . ."

I stop because Liam pulls his hand away to cover his mouth. I imagine he's shocked and dip my head, preparing to walk away. I start to explain, but then I stop again because . . .

He's laughing.

Actually laughing.

"This isn't funny," I say, swiping at my tears. "I was unofficially expelled, you know that? They lost their playoff game because of me—"

Liam's laughter only seems to surge in response, his whole face red. I glare at him until, at last, he pulls his hands away from his face, wiping tears in the process.

"Oh my god, Greta," he says. "That's so metal. You're such a badass."

I blink. What did he just say?

"Did you not hear me? They lost their playoff game. The rest of their season—"

"Because they suck," Liam says. "Not because some of their equipment was damaged. Jesus, I put that together the first time I heard."

"What do you mean, 'the first time I heard'?" I demand, confused.

"That detective guy told me all about this," he says with a shrug. "And I'll repeat what I said to him to you now: sounds like the assholes got what they deserved."

I stare at him. This entire time, I've held this secret close to me like a barb. But Liam . . . not only does he not care, but he's actually impressed?

It's like the undercurrent thrumming through me stills, and everything, even the night sounds, go quiet. I wipe the last tears from my cheeks as I stare down at my Chucks. I grabbed them at the last minute right before I left because they were black and I wanted to be discreet. The last time I wore them . . . was it that night I went to Caroline's? I remember looking at them then, seeing the tiny blue stars I let her draw on the right toe. I'd meant to throw them away, but then I couldn't, and Mom must've put them back in my closet. I look up, away from them, and turn to Liam.

And I know I probably look puffy and red and my hair's definitely come loose from the claw clip I slipped it into haphazardly on my way over, but you'd never know it from Liam's expression. He looks at me like I've just told him that it's a three-day weekend and we don't have school on Monday. Or like he's just found a pen that glides perfectly across the page. Or—

"You're incredible, Greta," he says. "You know that, right? Locker-room fires and everything."

I don't think. I don't evaluate the situation or the possibility of what will happen next. All I know is that the undercurrent inside me crackles and splits open. I let it lead me, throwing me forward until Liam is against me, his chest against my chest, his lips on my lips. He reacts with his own electricity, his hands feverishly wrapping around me as his mouth responds to mine.

It's like the stars surround us, and I swear I can see the light popping all around as he leans me against the car, as I angle my hips against him. And I'm tumbling into nothingness as I lose myself in him and his frenzied hands and the way his words thrum through me.

You're incredible.

In my fantasies, I dreamed that someone would say that. That someone would see me and tell me I was all the things. But it is so much better now that it's real. That it's him.

We pull away eventually, both of us coming up for air. But even as he stops all the kissing, he keeps his forehead against mine, his eyes open just there above my own. And he smiles, sheepish and sweet.

"Is it bad that our first kiss was right after you were crying?"

"Oh my god," I say, pushing slightly away from him. "No. It was great. I mean, you're great. Better than great. And—"

But he doesn't let me finish rambling because he pulls me into him again, melting in the darkness of the street, his fingers tracing circles down my back until he reaches my hips.

"You're not going anywhere?" I ask him, wanting to add all the other words rolling in my mind but not knowing how.

He presses his lips to my ear as he whispers, "I'm right here, Greta. And I'm not leaving until you tell me to."

It's the last thing he says before I shut him up completely with my mouth.

Eventually, though, we're forced to stop. Liam asks if I'll be okay driving home, and I tell him of course. I give him one final kiss, promising to text him when I'm home. I get into my car, completely unable to wipe the smile off my face. I catch sight of Liam walking home in the rearview mirror and smile even bigger when he turns around and waves, just before disappearing around the corner.

My first kiss. My first kiss *ever*. And it was perfect.

I'm momentarily immobilized by giddiness. Even with everything still up in the air, I'm not alone. Liam's by my side.

I'm still smiling when someone bangs on my window.

When the passenger door's ripped open and an arm shoots in, wrapping around my face so that a hand is pressed over my mouth.

The strong smell of cologne threatens to suffocate me as the arm tightens.

"Hello, Greta," Grey says, face swimming next to mine as I feel the press of something sharp at my side. "Fancy going for a little drive?"

CHAPTER TWENTY-EIGHT

THURSDAY, JUNE 19
11:16 P.M.

I'VE NEVER SEEN this look in Grey's eyes.

Earlier, he looked annoyed. Irritated. Even angry. But now? Now Grey's blue eyes flash with a sort of wild energy, like a wolf who's caught his prey.

After all, it looks like he has. I don't know what Grey wants with me, but it's clear he's in full control. After he shut the passenger door, he barked at me to turn the car on and drive straight to Hyper Kid. He kept one hand on my mouth as he dug the tip of his knife into the skin just above my hip, warning me that, if I screamed, he would bury the knife in my gut.

I didn't question him. The knife itself is huge, bigger than a chef's knife, and clearly sharp enough to pierce through my sweater. He keeps it there now as I drive, eyes on the road, hands unmoving while tears slip down my cheeks.

"Why are we—"

"Haven't you been asking enough questions, Greta?" Grey

snaps at me. "All week, poking around the park, asking questions. Listening in. Haven't you ever heard of privacy? You're just like Neil. Couldn't keep his nose out of someone else's business, and look what happened to him."

Outside, trees and flowers fly past the window. Grey's made me take the long way down El Camino Real, avoiding the freeway. It's dark, darker than it feels like it should be, even for almost midnight. But somehow, the streetlights just feel dimmer tonight, especially as we close in on the employee parking lot.

"Why are we here?" I ask, even as the knife bites into my side again. Grey's not being careful with it. It moves when his hand moves, and I force myself not to cry out as it digs in again.

"I told you to stop asking questions," Grey growls. "In fact, you can just shut up entirely. We're going to walk up to security, and I'm going to tell them we're meeting James for a late-night rehearsal. You're just going to nod and smile. Got it?"

"We're meeting J-James?" I stammer, eyes finally leaving the road to look at Grey. His face is cast in the light of the passing streetlamps, giving him heavy shadows under his eyes that turn his face into a skull—just like the tattoo on his arm.

"Scared, Greta?" Grey says, smirking as he twists the blade. "Think your boss might be a little disappointed in you?"

Does he know I know who James really is? He must. I see it in the evil wink of his eye.

"Finally putting it all together?" Grey asks. "I thought you were close earlier with that whole 'calling in' thing. Did you figure out it was me calling in for Mercy?"

"You . . . you were calling in?" I ask, shivering, trying to keep him talking even though it's terrifying. "But I found the phone in Allie's bag."

"Because that bitch tried to take it from me," Grey says, fist punching the glove box. "I found it in the woods after Mercy took off, and then Allie tried to accuse me of cheating on her with Mercy when she found it in my stuff. 'Why else would you have it?' She also couldn't put two and two together. But I got it back. And honestly, at that point, I didn't need it anymore. I had enough evidence of her calling in, just like James wanted. Because James is always right. I take it you at least figured out *that* part?"

He unleashes a cruel, barking laugh as he waves me through a yellow light.

"You and Neil have the same problem," Grey says. "You figured it out, but you didn't *do* anything about it. Well, I guess Neil did something. Asked me to meet him up in the turret after work, didn't he? Said he had something important to tell me."

Grey laughs again. "He really picked the wrong one?"

All the color must drop out of my cheeks because my body freezes.

"You killed him?"

"See, you were a few pieces shorter than I expected," Grey says. "Honestly, I expected more from you, Greta."

"But why?" I ask, because even though he's told me not to ask questions, I have to. It doesn't make any sense.

"Because James can get you anything in this town, or didn't you know that?" Grey practically cackles. "He's going to get me parts I could only dream of, Greta. My ticket to the big time. Producers. Theater, sure, but TV, too. You saw me on *Rancho Paloma Morning News*, right? I'll be everywhere thanks to him now. And yeah, okay. I wasn't supposed to kill Neil. Just see what he knew. I got a little carried away. But James understands. He understands me, and I understand him."

I don't say anything as terror seizes me. As Grey monologues gleefully, brandishing that knife.

I need to get out of the car.

"You're not going anywhere," Grey says, reading my mind. "And I'd be careful if I were you. Neil didn't think I'd hit him until I did. Like I said, I got caught up in the moment. Just didn't know my own strength."

He lets out another low, barking laugh as I turn in to the parking lot. I glance down at the knife, wondering if they can see it on the cameras. But of course not. Even through the windows, it'd be nearly impossible to see.

"Park right there," Grey directs. "And remember—nothing but smiling and nodding. If you say a word, I'll slice your throat before you can even get the first syllable out."

He punches the button to turn off the ignition, then grabs my keys from my cup holder and puts them into his pocket.

"Open your door," he commands, and I do as he says.

I try to force myself to breathe as Grey gets out of the car, pushing the knife up his sleeve so that just the tiniest sliver of the blade peeks out, glinting in the moonlight. I watch as he comes around to the driver's side, and for a moment, I consider trying to restart the car to get away from him, seeing as the keys are still close enough for it to start. But before I can take action, Grey's there at my open door, knife-free hand held out.

"Let's go," he says. "No dawdling. And don't make any eye contact. You look fucking terrified."

He flashes a grin of triumph. I try to do as he says as he wraps an arm over my shoulder, keeping me close as we walk up to the security booth. I hate that I ever wanted this kind of closeness with him. Because now it makes me want to scream.

The security team has to notice, right? They have to see that this isn't normal? Besides, it must be close to midnight by now—

"Evening, Pete," Grey says to the security guard.

"Burning the late-night oil, Grey?" Pete asks with a chuckle. "James let me know you might be in."

"Gotta get everything perfect," Grey says with a smile. "We've got some more TV spots coming up."

"I understand," Pete says, eyes shifting to me. "You got your ID?"

I stare at him, trying to signal with my eyes that this is very, very not okay. That he needs to call 911 right now. But then I feel Grey's arm tighten over my shoulder and remember I'm supposed to be looking at the floor.

"I . . ."

"She left her ID at Jungle," Grey cuts in. "I can vouch for her until we leave. I'll make sure she shows it on the way out."

No! I want to scream. Tell this asshole no. Tell him no! I am clearly in distress!

"Of course," Pete says, waving us through. "Have a good night, Grey. Greta."

I can't help it. I glare at the security guard as I walk through the turnstile. If I get killed tonight, I know who the hell I'm haunting afterward.

"This way, Greta," Grey says, leading me back into the dark.

I knew Hyper Kid would be way creepier after dark, but it's even worse than expected. Part of it's Grey and his knife, but part of it's the park itself. The whole thing's full of sounds that, during the daytime, must blend with the usual theme-park noise. Now each sound effect swooshes up out of nowhere to jolt me as I walk past, my footsteps punctuated by the hiss of a sword slicing through the air or the clatter of something metal hitting the ground. Grey's dragging me past the lake in the middle of the park when I hear a rustle to my right that makes me jump, and I stop, eyes fixating on where the sound came from, trying to place it.

Two glowing eyes look out at me from a bush. A rabbit, I think, its ears flattened on its head, peering out at me with terror. I'm not supposed to be here. This is supposed to be its final moment of freedom, and we've ruined that.

"Keep moving," Grey says.

A smashing sound effect makes me jump, and Grey's grip tightens dangerously. I try to breathe, to calm down, as we move toward Adventure Theater.

There's a creaking noise above, and I glance up at the gondolas ahead. We're near the entrance, and my throat tightens as we move underneath them. I pray that one of them will suddenly snap free and give me a chance to run, but of course, that doesn't happen. They just swing in the breeze, which is picking up for a summer night.

"Inside," Grey says, pushing me slightly so that I stumble into the doors at Adventure Theater. They're unlocked, which I think is strange, until I hear another voice from inside.

"Good evening, Greta," James's voice calls out. The theater light is warm compared with outside, the faint scent of cotton candy and popcorn lingering from the day.

I step farther in, Grey's hold on me loosening now that we're inside. I spot James standing ahead, eyes on the stage briefly before they swing to mine.

"Please, have a seat," he says, gesturing at the benches.

Grey holds up the knife. I do as I'm told.

"You'll have to forgive Grey," James says. "He's woefully ill-mannered. I've tried to teach him, but it's been tough."

Grey laughs at the joke, but James frowns. This shuts Grey up.

"We have a favor to ask, Greta," James says. "You see, it's come to my attention that you've found an important item from my past, and I'd like to have it back."

"I don't know what you're talking about," I lie, shakily, hoping he'll put it down to nerves.

"Oh, Greta," he says. "Let's not do that. Let's not lie. Grey told me you've been poking around, asking about a mutual friend of ours."

What does he think I have? The badge or the notebook? Or both?

"Should I jog your memory?" James asks. "Neil seemed to think I'd find it in Mercy's locker, but it wasn't there. Did you take it?"

I swallow. "Ushers aren't allowed in the greenroom."

James smiles. "Of course not. But Grey told me that you've been asking about Mercy. And you were the one who found Neil's body. And, well, I had my friends at the security station pull some access-road footage that shows you entering the greenroom a couple days ago. So . . . forgive me, but something tells me you've been snooping."

I try not to react to this, but I know I'm turning red, that my skin's betraying me.

"Maybe I should have someone pay a visit to your mom," James offers, his tone remaining cool and unchanging. "She's alone, isn't she?"

I shiver at the threat, fighting the urge to sob. I have to do something.

"Is it . . . is it a notebook? Is that what you're looking for?"

"That's the one," James says, clapping his hands together. "Lauren told me about it, though of course, she didn't realize what she had. But she said you were supposed to turn it in to me. Pity you didn't follow her instruction."

"It's in Rocket," I say, doing whatever it takes to keep him far, far away from my house. "I locked it in there today when I was working."

Rocket puts me back closer to security. Rocket gives me a chance to get away.

"That's a lie," James says, sounding almost disappointed. "I checked there already. Every locker, in fact."

Shit, I think. Shit, shit, shit, shit. I need to act and act fast. I need to figure out a way to break them up. To get Grey and his knife away from here.

"Fine," I admit, hoping I sound like I'm giving up. "I was trying to . . . to figure out something that it said in the notebook earlier. I was trying to piece it all together. So I, um . . . I went to the gondolas, and I was looking around. I wanted to see if the rumors were true. If there's still really blood stained on the inside."

James is looking at the ground when I say that, but at the last word, his lips curve into a smile. He shakes his head, meeting my eyes.

"And?"

The coldness of the question, the simplicity, the *hunger* of it, all make my blood burn. I lift my head.

"I didn't see," I say. "Some kids ran by to take pictures, so I hid the notebook in a gondola but didn't go in myself."

James raises an eyebrow. "You hid it in a gondola?"

I nod. "The one closest to the line. I figured it was a safe place."

"Hmm," James says, rubbing his chin. "I can tell most of him doesn't believe me. But that's okay. I just need a smidgen of doubt. A little, tiny, almost insignificant sliver—

"An interesting choice," James says before snapping his fingers in the air at Grey. "Grey, go check."

"What?" Grey asks, indignation puffing out his chest.

"You heard me," James says coolly. "I'm sure she's lying, but we'll call her bluff. Go check the gondola. We'll be right behind you."

Grey narrows his eyes at me, stabbing the air with the knife.

"You sure you can handle her?" Grey asks.

James smiles, pulling back his jacket to reveal his own knife in his belt. "Oh, I think I can. It's not my first time, you know."

At those chilling words, Grey leaves us, the door swinging shut behind him. And now, it's just me and James.

"So it really was you," I say. "You're the Gondola Killer."

James chuckles. "Oh, yes. Though I've never liked that name. Not quite theatrical enough for me."

I glare at him, hating this man. I wonder if I could run, if I'd make it. But something tells me Grey didn't actually take the bait. If I had to guess, he's waiting just outside to grab me if I try to leave.

"You know, I've always felt a special tie to this theater," he says. "The room where it happened, if you will."

I tense. "What?"

"She came back here that night," he says. "Hailey. She wanted to practice singing alone since they'd just finished putting the stage and everything else together. I followed her, of course. I was always following her, whenever I could. I was in love. Not that she appreciated it."

He paces in front of me, examining the knife.

"This would've been easier," he says. "I had to make do with a box cutter. Thankfully, they'd just soundproofed the place, and there was plastic all over the floor from the sets and walls that they were painting. I barely had to clean, just rolled her onto one of the pieces. No one was over this way, you know. I just carried her out and put her in the gondola myself."

He talks about it like he's describing a grocery trip. My stomach churns, and I taste bile in my throat.

"It was lucky that the cameras were down," he says. "Or maybe not lucky at all. In fact, if you ask me, it seems like fate."

I shiver, hating the way he grins at the memory, the way someone might when talking about graduation or a wedding or something. Something special that's stuck with them, even after all these years.

"You really are a monster," I spit out, even if I know it will anger him.

But instead, he just laughs again.

"Am I?" James asks. "I've wondered myself. But really, the more I've sat with it—and I've sat with it for twenty years—the more I'm convinced that I did the world a favor. Because I was nothing but kind to Hailey. I tried to dote on her. I tried to admire her. I would've given her everything, but to her, I was just a boy she could toy with. She didn't take me seriously. I wasn't an actor back then. Just a stagehand. And then, even here, they wouldn't hire me to be in the show. Not at first. I was a mere ride operator."

He clears his throat and pushes back his hair from his eyes, fixing me with a glinting stare.

"Neil figured that part out," James says. "There's a picture of me on the first map, the happy employee operating our very first roller coaster. I guess you have to at least give them credit for noticing how photogenic I am."

He laughs at his own joke. I think I might pass out again.

"It was Mercy who really dug too deep, though, isn't it?" James asks with a sigh. "And she stole my badge, too. But don't worry. I'll deal with her later."

"You're not getting away with this again," I say. "You—"

Another cold laugh. "Oh, Greta. I've gotten away with this for twenty years. Do you know how long I've had that badge displayed for? And no one batted an eye, until Mercy's meddling. But not to worry. Once she's taken care of, I'll get away with it again. And haven't you figured out why? I'm merely pulling the strings this time. I've got other people now to handle the ... messier details."

I wince. Grey. He'll make Grey kill me, then Mercy. He won't have to lift a finger this time.

"His perfect role, honestly," James says with another wicked grin. "Almost like he was born for it."

"You're a coward," I say. "A coward and a—"

"Oh, let's not say that," James says. "You're sounding a bit too much like Hailey, I'm afraid. She used me for attention and then discarded me when she was done. Said I'd never amount to anything because I was a 'loser' who hid in the shadows. But she was wrong, wasn't she? I'm famous now—for more than one reason. And let's be honest. I'm far more famous now than Hailey ever will be ... more so than she would've been even if she hadn't died. If she hadn't been so damn difficult."

He laughs again. I hate him. But more than I hate his words and his smirks, I hate that he's right. Not enough people know Hailey's name, and if they do know her, they know her because of how she died. Hailey never got a chance to be more. Because James stole that from her.

"You're right," I say, choking out the words. "You are more famous—for now. But after tonight, I'm going to make sure everyone knows Hailey's story. And Mercy's. And even Neil's. Because we should care about people for their lives, not for their deaths. And once I'm through, you'll be just a footnote in their stories. Some washed-up, creepy-ass actor no one actually gave a shit about."

His eyes narrow, and I know I've struck the right chord. So I don't wait. I bolt from the seat before he can get closer, straight for the doors. I run so hard that, when the door opens and Grey *is* standing there, just like I thought, it hits him straight in his nose, sending him flying onto his back.

"Fucking hell!" Grey calls as he hits the ground.

"Get up, get up!" I hear James scream at him. "She's getting away!"

And I *am* getting away. I need to move before James or Grey catches up to me. I'm not fast, and I have no idea if James or Grey is. So I turn to the left, fleeing into the only place that will give me height rather than distance.

The gondolas.

I have never been trained on the rides, but I did pay attention during my tour. I know that they make the controls as easy to operate as possible, understanding that it will be mostly teenagers running them. I race for the front of the line, where the control panel box sits off to the side. There're several different buttons and knobs that say things like Auto Dispatch and Function Enable and Power and—

There!

A green button, one that has a very old piece of electrical tape underneath that says Ride Start.

I slam some of the other buttons, including Power, then the Auto Dispatch, and then, at last, Ride Start. There's a groaning sound as the gondolas spring to life for the very first time in twenty years.

Then they start to move.

They're slow enough for people to get on continuously, and they begin to cycle through. Red, yellow, green, blue, purple—all of them lifting up into the sky. I watch them, catching my breath. I'm not sure I really thought this through. Do I just jump onto a gondola?

"You bitch! Get back here!"

I whip my head back, seeing Grey barreling toward me through the line, knife raised. James is behind him as well, and there's no denying the absolute murder in his eyes.

There must be cameras back here now, right? Someone has to be seeing this? Or at least noticed the gondolas running?

But something tells me Grey doesn't care about that. Not now. Something has snapped inside him, and the only thing he cares about is catching me.

I race toward the gondolas, jumping into the first one I see. It's purple, and there's a faint tinkling sound crackling through the speaker that's trying to come to life. I barely have time to notice it, though, when Grey, knife raised, bursts into the gondola just as it's starting to lift up from the ground.

"Wrong move, Greta," he grinds out, arm ready to swing.

But I'm ready for him. I duck under his arm as it swooshes

above me, then leap from the gondola to the ground, hitting the concrete hard as I land. Grey realizes too late what I've done and tries to scramble after me, but the gondola's already climbing.

One down, I think, only to turn and see James coming for me through the line.

I'm just going to have to hope he's slow, I think, then race in the other direction.

I streak through the park, away from him, toward Mega Town. All around me, pops and whizzes and bangs sound out, along with the ever-present voice of Hyper Kid urging, "Come on, kids! It's time for an adventure!" Still, I force myself to move faster.

Because unfortunately, James is not slow. Not even a little bit. As I run past a display of flowers twisted into the shape of Dingle the Dalmatian, James gains on me by several feet. When I duck into the shrubs, trying to find a shortcut, my feet slip on the uneven terrain, and I fall hard, landing on my elbows in the dirt.

Behind me, James's hand closes on my foot.

"I warned you," James grinds out. "I told you it wasn't my first time. I told you, but you underestimated me, just like she did."

I scream, and he yanks me hard, pulling me so that he's above me, glaring down at me with rage burning in his eyes. His hand closes over my throat, just as the glint of his knife appears gripped above me.

"I had time to cut her up," James says. "I won't have that with you. But I'll tell them I tried to stop Grey. I'll tell them—"

Crack.

For a moment, James's eyes widen in disbelief, and his knife-wielding hand stills before his grip loosens and the knife falls into the dirt.

Then he crumples, and I roll away from him, heart hammering in my chest.

Above me, Mercy stands, a Hyper Kid collectible paperweight in hand. I spy the tag still attached to the bottom, covered in blood.

"Hi, Greta," Mercy says. "Sorry it took us so long."

I stare at her, breathing hard, still not understanding what I'm seeing. In the moonlight, her skin and eyes seem to glow, making her look as otherworldly as the characters in Space Land.

"Us?" I ask, breathless, head whipping around.

And then, I see them.

Security guards and police officers running toward us. They grab James and pull his hands behind his back. I hear them saying something about his rights, but I don't even think he's conscious. They pull him up, whisking him away to a cart that's been parked up the way.

"Greta!" Liam shouts, appearing from Mercy's side. There's Ivy, too, I see, just behind him, but she's quickly hidden as Liam pulls me into a hug.

"Don't ever do that again," he says, holding on to me tighter than Jasper holds on to his toys. *"Ever."*

"I didn't have a choice," I say, gasping so that Liam backs off a bit on the intensity of the hug. "Grey—"

At that moment, there's shouting, followed by a scream. I cling to Liam, my eyes darting around, then see that the security officers are pointing up.

At where someone's hanging from the outside of a gondola, screaming bloody murder.

"Is that . . . is that *Grey*?" Ivy asks. "Jesus—"

"I thought that ride wasn't operational," one of the guards says. "Somebody get that boy down!"

But right when he says it, Grey falls, shrieking as he tumbles through the air.

"Oh my god!"

"Hurry, get the medics—"

The crowd of security and police officers rushes forward to where Grey fell into a cluster of bushes. I watch them, horrified, as Mercy and Ivy help me stand up.

"Aw, did he die?"

All four of us whip around at the sound of the new voice, turning to look at the figure now walking toward us. In the dim light, it's hard to recognize her at first, but then, her blond hair catches and shimmers under the stars.

"Allie?" I ask, mouth dropping open. "What're you—"

"Someone had to call the police," Allie says, rolling her eyes as she steps forward. "You certainly weren't going to, were you?"

"What?" I mumble, confused. And then, I see what she's holding up in her hand.

Hailey's notebook.

"I told the cops I had a huge break in the case," she continues. "Called them after I grabbed this from your house this afternoon. I was hoping to find the badge, but this turned out to be pretty useful on its own. By the way, your dog is *terrible* security, and you really should tell your mom to start locking your doors."

I look at Ivy, Liam, and Mercy, eyes wide, but they seem just as confused as I am.

"Look," Allie says, turning to face Mercy. "I'm sorry for what I did, all right? I thought you were sleeping with Grey, especially after I found your phone in his bedroom. But then when 'you' started calling in sick, I realized what Grey was doing. And that's when I started looking into things right under his nose and saw he was a full-on creep and James's personal killer lapdog."

I stare at her.

"But you . . . ," I start to say. "You threatened me."

"Look, I didn't know who to trust, okay?" Allie says, throwing her hands up. "My boyfriend turned out to be a murderous asshole. I had to keep a close circle. Especially since I was going up against James."

Ivy snorts. "Guess I can't blame you."

Behind us, there's a flurry of activity, and several officers rush past carrying Grey's body. As he goes, he moans, and I think I see a trickle of blood down his forehead. Then we watch them load him onto the same cart as James while someone shouts for them to call an ambulance.

"Don't worry," says the security guard who stops by us. "We're going to take care of everything from here. We've got an ambulance on the way."

And even though I don't totally know if I believe him, I find that I feel nothing but relief in the moments that come before I pass out for a second time this week.

CHAPTER TWENTY-NINE

FRIDAY, AUGUST 15
10:54 A.M.

"GRETA, WHY DO you feel you would be a good fit for this job?"

The air in the Jungle Jam theater is cool, not yet full of bodies moving through its maze of blue benches. There's no popcorn to be swept from its floor, and its stage is empty for now. In the back halls, I can hear Allie pacing as she walks Dustin, our newly-promoted-to-main-cast Hyper Kid, through the lines he messed up yesterday. She catches me watching and waves, but then her eyes narrow at Dustin as he fumbles another line.

"Dude, get it together," she snaps at him. "This is a real show, okay? Take it seriously. People actually give a shit about what we're doing."

I smile at her, shaking my head. She's right, though. Ever since our visit before, Jungle Jam's been getting actual attention. Possibly for sensational reasons, but attention is attention.

"Greta?"

Liam taps me on the shoulder, drawing me back to him and

this moment. We're sitting side by side in the tech booth, him with a notepad in his hands as he reads my practice questions to me.

"Right," I say. "Well, something that is key to a strong leader is an ability to realize the potential of your employees, and I am always on the hunt for potential. I'm also good at finding strengths. Really, it comes down to the ability to assess—"

"You sound like a robot," Ivy says, popping her head up from where she lies on a nearby bench. "Try to sound like a human, okay?"

I steady myself. "Right. Well, Liam, I try to see the good in people. I listen to people."

"Good so far," Liam says.

"I really hone in on what they can bring to the table," I continue. "And—"

"Did you really just say 'hone in'?" Ivy laughs. "Are you leading a group of theme-park ushers, or are you bringing them back to your home planet?"

I throw a paper clip at her. Ivy has officially stepped down from her de facto usher lead duties. She said the work was too much a distraction from her new passion, writing her own romance novels.

I remind her of this, asking, "Don't you have a novel to revise?"

"Don't you have a debut to practice for?" Ivy says, sticking her tongue out.

"We're all practiced and ready for next week, thanks," Liam says.

"Yeah, whatever," Ivy says. "Besides, as far as my novel goes, you have to let it sit in the metaphorical drawer. It's part of the process."

"Well, if you ask me—"

"Come on," Liam says, gently drawing me back to him. "Try again."

"This is ridiculous," I say. "My track record clearly indicates that I am an excellent interviewee."

"Wasn't that your first interview ever?" Ivy asks.

I don't dignify her with a response.

"Right," Liam says. "How about a new question . . . here we go. How are you at getting along with other people?"

Ivy snorts, but I straighten up.

"I don't get along with everyone," I say, "but with the right people, I think I get along just fine."

Liam smiles. "Good answer."

Then he drops his voice. "I wish I could kiss you, but we're at work."

I glance over at Ivy. She makes a gagging noise, but I ignore her.

"I don't need to follow all the rules, you know," I say back to him, leaning forward. "I mean, not all the time. In an extreme circumstance—"

"Excuse me," Ivy says, throwing a paper clip that hits me in the head. "Can we be professional, please?"

But she's grinning, and the three of us laugh. It's the kind that fills the theater to its brim, echoing off the walls and rushing back to us. It's the kind that I never want to end.

"Hey," Ivy says, her laughter cut off by the buzz of her phone. "Look who it is."

She answers the call, and we don't need to see the name on the screen to know who's on the other end. Mercy.

"Hey," Ivy says. "How's the city?"

There's a pause, an "uh-huh, uh-huh," and then a scream as Ivy jumps up from the bench.

"She got it!" Ivy yells. "She got the audition!"

And then we're all on our feet, and Allie comes running over, and I swear I can hear Mercy's laugh from the phone as we all scream. Dustin looks terrified on the stage, but we ignore him.

"It's just an audition," Mercy's voice crackles through the phone. "It's just—"

But we scream again, drowning her out, because we know that nothing is "just an audition" after what we've been through. Because in this moment, there's no stopping Mercy, and there's no stopping us.

"It's time," Liam says, phone alarm ringing. "You all ready?"

We look at each other and nod. The others peel off, but I stay a little longer, letting Liam's hand linger on mine.

I glance down at my badge. Now it displays my full name, slightly squished, but every letter clear and bright among the stars.

Yes. I'm ready.

I'm ready for anything.

I'm ready for it all.

ACKNOWLEDGMENTS

In true Greta fashion, I have overthought, overanalyzed, and overgoogled what should go into one's acknowledgments. I have stressed and agonized over what to say and who to thank while knowing that I will probably still accidentally forget someone. I want to say all of the words exactly right, but we might just have to collectively decide to accept a tiny bit of flailing. After all, this dream has not come true overnight. It's been a long road, and so many people have helped me along the way.

To Michelle Wolfson, the person who has been in my corner all these years, I can't begin to thank you for how you have changed my life. You never gave up on me. You listened to my every idea with an open mind, and then you went out and championed those ideas into the world. You kept fighting for my stories until we got this, the dream opportunity. And you've continued to be there every step of the way. Thank you for everything.

To Krista Marino, who saw Greta and this story so clearly and fiercely, you made this book better than I could have ever imagined. Working with you has been a dream come true, and I am forever grateful for the care and attention you have given this story—and me. You believed in Greta and loved her in a way that even I couldn't believe at first, and the book is so much better for it. Thank you for seeing these difficult girls and helping me guide their story to new heights.

To Lydia Gregovic, for being another powerful voice and champion for this book, my gratitude knows no bounds. Thank you for sticking with this project even when your own list began to take off, and thank you for setting up every five a.m. call along the way. And to Emma Leynse, thank you for joining the team and keeping everything organized. I so appreciate you both.

To the rest of my incredible publishing team at Random House Children's Books, I am forever indebted to you all. Barbara Marcus and Judith Haut, thank you for supporting *Difficult Girls*. Sarah Chasse and Adaobi Obi Tulton and Colleen Fellingham, thank you for going through every sentence with a sharp eye and a considerate hand. I'm so grateful for your careful attention to detail so this book could shine. To Kelly McGauley and the entire marketing team, thank you for making sure readers can find *Difficult Girls*. And to Cassie Malmo, for finding ways from the very beginning to introduce *Difficult Girls* to the world and for making dreams I didn't even dare to dream come true, you have my boundless gratitude. To Priyanka Godbole, thank you for championing this story and always going out of your way to find creative opportunities to showcase this book. And to everyone else, from the school and library team to the social media team, thank you for everything you did to bring *Difficult Girls* into the world. Books don't find audiences without the amazing work you do.

Thank you to Liz Dresner and Angela Carlino for the cover of my dreams. I could have never imagined such a brilliant representation of this story, and I'm so eternally grateful for your creativity and talent in designing something so stunning.

Next, to every person who listened to me ramble about early versions of Greta's story, who critiqued scenes or even entire drafts, who taught me to fall back in love with it, who answered my inquiries about whether body spray really could lead to a locker room fire (it can!) and all the other questions that would have gotten me on a watch list if I'd googled them . . . thank you. Thank you especially to Desme Hewson, Sam Lacy, Olivia Kerrigan, Brittany Sims, Ili Lacy, Tara Gillfillan, Jaysen Waller, Luis Reyes, Diane Fresco, Erika Thormahlen, Claudia Garzel, Joel Jennings, Maggie Light, Kaitlyn Beck, Christine Musgrove, Amanda Kirby, Tommy Kirby, Gabi Hamill, Conor Hamill, Jane Papageorge, CJ Eldred, Claire Long, Caitlin Addonizio, Angie Ohman, Jerry Bridges, Isabela Ortiz, Molly Ketcheson, and Brady Carlos.

Thank you to every author in this community who has made me feel welcome and answered my numerous questions. Special thanks to Ayana Gray, Karuna Riazi, Dahlia Adler, Rebecca Danzenbaker, I. V. Marie, Clare Edge, Megan Davidhizar, Megan Jauregui Eccles, and Channelle Desamours. In addition, I send a heartfelt thanks to every author who read and blurbed this book. I am still in awe that you read my words, and I'll always be grateful that you took the time to write such lovely things about *Difficult Girls*.

To my teachers—high school, college, and beyond—who taught me to love writing and how to build my craft, I am forever indebted to you for encouraging this dream of mine. You often had to answer an endless barrage of questions from me, and you did so with kindness, thoughtfulness, and grace. I want to especially thank Jill Lax, Erika Wanczuk, Lauren Monahan, Lauren Strasnick, Ryan Gattis, Amber Benson, and Taffy Brodesser-Akner for shaping my writing at a foundational level. I would not be here without you.

On the other side of the coin, to my students, both current and former, where would I be without you? You inspire me every single day, and I feel eternally lucky to have had the opportunity to be your teacher. If you've been in my classroom, you know that I am always pushing you to fight for your dreams. Thank you for cheering me on as I fought for mine.

To every theme park worker, whether you sang on a stage or cleaned up a protein spill, I hope you saw yourself in the pages of this book. I certainly thought of you every time I sat down to write about our shared experience. I also thought of summers spent sitting on a plastic throne wearing a princess dress and how that was arguably an easier job than writing a book, but I digress.

To the teachers, librarians, fellow authors, and readers fighting for literacy and the freedom to read, thank you for your important and essential work.

To my family, especially my mom and dad, thank you for telling a little girl who spent her days daydreaming and thinking up stories that she was on the right path. And to my in-laws, who have become part of my family, thank you for always supporting me in whatever I wanted to do. Thank you all for being there for me through the rejections and for encouraging me to keep going—no matter what. And of course, thank you for listening when I repeated the same story over and over again. I was honing my skills, I swear.

Lastly, Brendan. My best friend. My partner in life and storytelling. Thank you for reading the same scenes over and over again as I tweaked and changed and adjusted. Thank you for listening to me read scenes out loud—so annoying, I know—and offering your candid perspective on every moment. You never held back, and the book needed that. Thank you for holding my hand through the worst moments of both writing and life, through the grief, through the loss, through the fear, through the uncertainty, and for never wavering in your belief of me. We both chose to pursue our creative passions, and I will forever be in awe of your talent for storytelling . . . and forever grateful to benefit from your expertise when I'm writing. But seriously, I am so lucky to be on this journey with you. Love you always.

ABOUT THE AUTHOR

Veronica Bane spent her formative teen years working at a popular theme park. Following days spent as a princess and an usher, she graduated from Chapman University with a BFA in creative writing. Since then, she has worked as a high school English teacher in Lincoln Heights, California. When she's not writing, she's exploring Los Angeles with her husband and their beloved dog, Bodhi.

veronicabane.com